Acclaim for Kelly Irvin

"I do love a quick-paced, entertaining novel, and *The Heart's Bidding* is just that. I was immediately drawn into Toby's and Rachelle's stories and found myself rooting for them page after page. Kelly Irvin's latest belongs on everyone's keeper shelf."

—SHELLEY SHEPARD GRAY, *NEW YORK TIMES* AND
USA TODAY BESTSELLING AUTHOR

"Strangers at first, Maisy Glick and Joshua Lapp find solace in their unhappy circumstances in Kelly Irvin's *Every Good Gift*. Joshua, full of sorrow and doubt. Maisy, full of regret. Together, they forge a path forward in ways that will surprise readers. Irvin's knowledge of the Plain people shines in this endearing tale of love and redemption."

—SUZANNE WOODS FISHER, BESTSELLING
AUTHOR OF *A SEASON ON THE WIND*

"A beautifully crafted story of mistakes, redemption, healing, and grace. Kelly Irvin's *Every Good Gift* will captivate readers and tug on the heart-strings as characters brimming with real human frailty try to work through the consequences of their lives and choices with love and faith."

—KRISTEN MCKANAGH, AUTHOR OF *THE GIFT OF HOPE*

"The second entry in Irvin's Amish Blessings series (after *Love's Dwelling*) delivers an elegant portrait of a young Amish woman caught between two worlds . . . Irvin skillfully conveys Abigail's internal conflict ('How could Abigail put into words the longing that thrummed in her chest? The sense of loss, of missing out, of missing it all,' she reminisces about Amish life). Fans of Amish romance will want to check this out."

—PUBLISHERS WEEKLY ON *THE WARMTH OF SUNSHINE*

"Just like the title, *Warmth of Sunshine* is a lovely and cozy story that will keep you reading until the very last page."

—KATHLEEN FULLER, *USA TODAY* BESTSELLING AUTHOR
OF THE MAIL-ORDER AMISH BRIDES SERIES

"This is a sweet story of romance and family that will tug at heartstrings. It is another great story and great characters from Irvin."

—*THE PARKERSBURG NEWS AND SENTINEL* ON *LOVE'S DWELLING*

"*Peace in the Valley* is a beautiful and heart-wrenching exploration of faith, loyalty, and the ties that bind a family and a community together. Kelly Irvin's masterful storytelling pulled me breathlessly into Nora's world, her deep desire to do good, and her struggle to be true to herself and to the man she loves. Full of both sweet and stark details of Amish life, *Peace in the Valley* is realistic and poignant, profound and heartfelt. I highly recommend it!"

—JENNIFER BECKSTRAND, AUTHOR OF *ANDREW*

"With a lovely setting, this is a story of hope in the face of trouble and has an endearing heroine and other relatable characters that readers will empathize with."

—*THE PARKERSBURG NEWS AND SENTINEL* ON *MOUNTAINS OF GRACE*

"Irvin (*Beneath the Summer Sun*) puts a new spin on the age-old problem of bad things happening to good people in this excellent Amish inspirational . . . Fans of both Amish and inspirational Christian fiction will enjoy this heart-pounding tale of the pain of loss and the joys of love."

—*PUBLISHERS WEEKLY* ON *MOUNTAINS OF GRACE*

"Kelly Irvin's *Mountains of Grace* offers a beautiful and emotional journey into the Amish community. Readers will be captivated by a heartwarming tale of forgiveness and finding a renewed faith in God. The story will capture the hearts of those who love the Plain culture and an endearing romance. Once you open this book, you'll be hooked until the last page."

—AMY CLIPSTON, BESTSELLING AUTHOR OF THE AMISH LEGACY SERIES

"Irvin's fun story is simple (like Mary Katherine, who finds 'every day is a blessing and an adventure') but very satisfying."

—PUBLISHERS WEEKLY ON THROUGH THE AUTUMN AIR

"This second entry (after *Upon a Spring Breeze*) in Irvin's seasonal series diverges from the typical Amish coming-of-age tale with its focus on more mature protagonists who acutely feel their sense of loss. Fans of the genre seeking a broader variety of stories may find this new offering from [Irvin] more relatable than the usual fare."

—LIBRARY JOURNAL ON BENEATH THE SUMMER SUN

"A moving and compelling tale about the power of grace and forgiveness that reminds us how we become strongest in our most broken moments."

—LIBRARY JOURNAL ON UPON A SPRING BREEZE

"Irvin's novel is an engaging story about despair, postnatal depression, God's grace, and second chances."

—CBA CHRISTIAN MARKET ON UPON A SPRING BREEZE

"Once I started reading *The Bishop's Son*, it was difficult for me to put it down! This story of struggle, faith, and hope will draw you in to the final page . . . I have read countless stories of Amish men or women doubting their faith. I have never read a storyline quite like this one though. It was narrated with such heart. I was fully invested in Jesse's struggle. No doubt, what Jesse felt is often what modern-day Amish men and women must feel when they are at a crossroads in their faith. The story was brilliantly told and the struggle felt very real."

—DESTINATION AMISH

"Something new and delightful in the Amish fiction genre, this story is set in the barren, dusty landscape of Bee County, TX . . . Irvin writes with great insight into the range and depth of human emotion. Her characters are believable and well developed, and her storytelling skills are superb. Recommend to readers who are looking for something a little different in Amish fiction."

—CBA RETAILERS + RESOURCES ON THE BEEKEEPER'S SON

"*The Beekeeper's Son* is so well crafted. Each character is richly layered. I found myself deeply invested in the lives of both the King and Lantz families. I struggled as they struggled, laughed as they laughed—and even cried as they cried . . . This is one of the best novels I have read in the last six months. It's a refreshing read and worth every penny. *The Beekeeper's Son* is a keeper for your bookshelf!"

—DESTINATION AMISH

"*The Beekeeper's Son* is a perfect depiction of how God makes all things beautiful in His way. Rich with vivid descriptions and characters you can immediately relate to, Kelly Irvin's book is a must-read for Amish fans."

—RUTH REID, BESTSELLING AUTHOR OF A MIRACLE OF HOPE

"Kelly Irvin writes a moving tale that is sure to delight all fans of Amish fiction. Highly recommended."

—KATHLEEN FULLER, AUTHOR OF THE MAIL-ORDER AMISH BRIDES SERIES, ON THE BEEKEEPER'S SON

THE HEART'S
Bidding

Also by Kelly Irvin

THE HEART'S
Bidding

AMISH CALLING

KELLY IRVIN

ZONDERVAN®

ZONDERVAN

The Heart's Bidding

Copyright © 2023 by Kelly Irvin

This title is also available as a Zondervan e-book.

Requests for information should be addressed to:

Zondervan, *3900 Sparks Dr. SE, Grand Rapids, Michigan 49546*

Library of Congress Cataloging-in-Publication

Names: Irvin, Kelly, author.
Title: The heart's bidding / Kelly Irvin.
Description: Grand Rapids, Michigan : Zondervan, [2023] | Series: Amish calling novel | Summary:
    "Amish auctioneer Toby Miller and special education teacher Rachelle Lapp love their jobs
    so much, they're in danger of missing out on marriage and children of their own—until
    circumstances force them to face uncertain futures."--Provided by publisher.
Identifiers: LCCN 2023002664 (print) | LCCN 2023002665 (ebook) | ISBN 9780840709233
    (paperback) | ISBN 9780840709240 (epub) | ISBN 9780840709325
Subjects: LCSH: Amish--Fiction. | BISAC: FICTION / Amish & Mennonite | FICTION / Small
    Town & Rural | LCGFT: Christian fiction. | Romance fiction. | Novels.
Classification: LCC PS3609.R82 H435 2023 (print) | LCC PS3609.R82 (ebook) | DDC
    813/.6--dc23/eng/20230130
LC record available at https://lccn.loc.gov/2023002664
LC ebook record available at https://lccn.loc.gov/2023002665

To Grandma Irene and Grandpa Roy Elliott, Uncle Duane Elliott, and Mom (Janice Elliott Lyne) for the lessons in empathy, kindness, and human nature. Whether you realized it or not, you were good teachers.

Whatever you do, work at it with all your heart, as working for the Lord, not for human masters, since you know that you will receive an inheritance from the Lord as a reward. It is the Lord Christ you are serving.

Colossians 3:23–24

For consider your calling, brothers: not many of you were wise according to worldly standards, not many were powerful, not many were of noble birth. But God chose what is foolish in the world to shame the wise; God chose what is weak in the world to shame the strong; God chose what is low and despised in the world, even things that are not, to bring to nothing things that are, so that no human being might boast in the presence of God.

1 Corinthians 1:26–29

Glossary of Deutsch*

aamen: amen
ach: oh
aenti: aunt
bewillkumm: welcome
botching: clapping game
bopli, boplin: baby, babies
bruder, brieder: brother, brothers
bu, buwe: boy, boys
bussi, bussis: cat, cats
daadi: grandpa
daed: father
danki: thank you
Das Loblied: Amish hymn of praise sung at all church services
dat: dad
dawdy haus: attached home for grandparents when they retire
dochder, dechder: daughter, daughters
dumm: dumb
eldre: parents
Englischer: English or non-Amish
enkel: grandson
eppies: cookies
Es dutt mer leed: I am sorry

Glossary

faeriwell: good-bye

fraa, fraas: wife, wives

Froh Neiyaahr: Happy New Year

gaul: horse

gern gschehme: you're welcome

Gmay: church district

Gott: God

groossdaadi: grandfather

groossmammi, groossmammis: grandmother, grandmothers

guder mariye: good morning

gut: good

gut nacht: good night

hallo: hello

hund, hunde: dog, dogs

jah: yes

kaffi: coffee

kapp: prayer cap or head covering worn by Amish women

kind, kinner: child, children

kinnskind, kinnskinner: grandchild, grandchildren

kossin: cousin

kuss, koss: kiss (singular/plural noun)

maedel, maed: girl, girls

mamm: mom

mammi: grandma

mann, menner: husband, husbands

meidung: shunning, excommunication from the Amish
    faith. Shunning is a practice in which church members
    isolate, ignore, or otherwise punish someone for breaking
    community rules.

Mennischt: Mennonite

mudder: mother

narrisch: foolish, silly

nee: no

onkel: uncle

Ordnung: written and unwritten rules in an Amish district

rumspringa: period of "running around" for Amish youth before
     they decide whether they want to be baptized into the Amish
     faith and seek a mate

schieler: scholar, scholars

schtarem: storm

schweschder, schwesdchdre: sister, sisters

seelich gebortsdaag: happy birthday

sei so gut: please (be so kind)

suh: son

tietschern, tietschere: teacher, teachers

weddermann: weatherman

wunderbarr: wonderful

*The German dialect commonly referred to as Pennsylvania Dutch
is not a written language and varies depending on the location and
origin of the Amish settlement. These spellings are approximations.
Most Amish children learn English after they start school. They
also learn High German, which is used in their Sunday services.

Featured Families

Lee's Gulch, Virginia

Karl and Cara Lapp (grandparents)

Adam and Leah Lapp

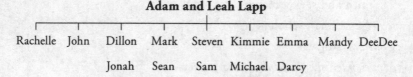

Rachelle   John   Dillon   Mark   Steven   Kimmie   Emma   Mandy   DeeDee

Jonah   Sean   Sam   Michael   Darcy

Silas and Joanna Miller (grandparents)

Charlie and Elizabeth Miller (parents)

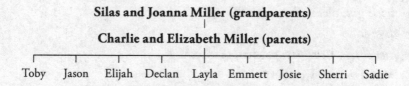

Toby   Jason   Elijah   Declan   Layla   Emmett   Josie   Sherri   Sadie

Jason (brother) and Caitlin Miller

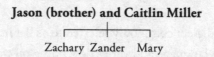

Zachary   Zander   Mary

Uriah and Samantha King (grandparents)

Aaron and Katherine King (parents)

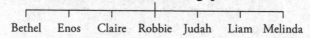

Bethel   Enos   Claire   Robbie   Judah   Liam   Melinda

Marilin and Jocelyn Yoder

Bonnie

Luke and Deanna Beachy

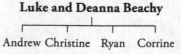

Andrew   Christine   Ryan   Corrine

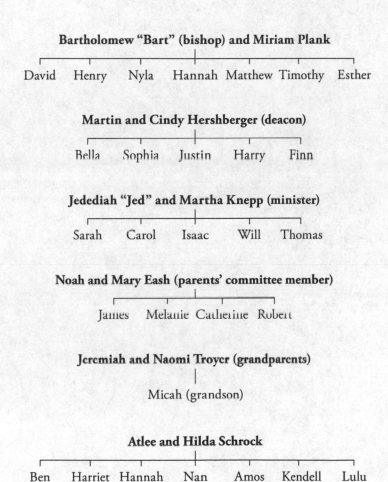

Bartholomew "Bart" (bishop) and Miriam Plank

David   Henry   Nyla   Hannah   Matthew   Timothy   Esther

Martin and Cindy Hershberger (deacon)

Bella   Sophia   Justin   Harry   Finn

Jedediah "Jed" and Martha Knepp (minister)

Sarah   Carol   Isaac   Will   Thomas

Noah and Mary Eash (parents' committee member)

James   Melanie   Catherine   Robert

Jeremiah and Naomi Troyer (grandparents)

Micah (grandson)

Atlee and Hilda Schrock

Ben   Harriet   Hannah   Nan   Amos   Kendell   Lulu

A Note from the Author

The Heart's Bidding explores both developmental and intellectual disabilities through the lens of its Amish characters and their corresponding worldview. Three non-Amish sensitivity readers, two of whom are parents of daughters with Down syndrome, read and provided feedback before the book was published. HarperCollins Christian Fiction Publishing House and I did this because we're keenly aware of the tender issues that may be raised by the disability community when encountering the Amish term *special* children and their view that these children are "gifts from God."

As a writer, I know better than most the power of words to hurt, demean, make one feel less than, and perpetuate stereotypes. First, know that I'm a Christian writer living with a disability. I came by my disability later in life. My struggle to accept this disability is ongoing. I don't see it as a gift from God. However, I respect and value the Amish perspective as Christlike and beautifully loving. Readers will see that the Amish believe all children are gifts from God. They employ the term *special* for these babies as a term of affection and love. Therefore I use it in the context of Toby and Rachelle's point of view. These are their views, not mine, as I walk a narrow path between what the "English" world finds acceptable and representing an authentic Amish voice.

I say all this to respectfully ask readers to honor the Amish view as loving, kind, and so much more Christlike than the worldly view of some would-be "English" parents who hold the belief that bringing a child into the world with disabilities is a choice that can be rejected. I have no doubt that Amish parents agonize, worry, and even shed tears over their "special children." But they choose an attitude of gratitude. I hope you will read and enjoy *The Heart's Bidding* in the spirit in which it is offered—to edify, provoke thought, and shed Christ's light in the world. God bless.

Chapter 1

*T*he single candle stuck in Toby Miller's oversized banana-
nut muffin spoke volumes, but it didn't say anything worth
hearing.

His brother Jason, a grin plastered across his bearded face,
struck a match and lit the candle. "*Seelich gebortsdaag, Bruder,*" he
sang off tune. "And many more, old man."

Twenty-nine wasn't old. Not by the world's standard. What
Jason really meant was old to be a Plain bachelor. He was right, but
he didn't need to know that. Jason already had a big head. "*Danki,*
but this isn't the time for this right now. You know *Mamm* will
have a birthday cake tonight." Toby blew out the candle and tossed
it in the wastebasket. He laid the muffin next to his lunch box on
the counter that ran below the back window of the Miller Family
Auctioneering Company's largest trailer, currently parked at the
Knowles County, Virginia, fairgrounds. "Did you double-check the
sound system?"

"I did. So did *Dat.*"

Toby glanced at the clock. Fifteen minutes until he had to be
on the platform ready to call the first piece of furniture. "And the
furniture's on the stage?"

"*Jah.* A six-piece, handcrafted, oak bedroom set." Grandpa Silas squeezed through the trailer door, bringing with him the mingled scents of nearby grills barbecuing chicken, sausage, brisket, hamburgers, hot dogs, and an assortment of other tasty meats. Like his grandsons, Grandpa's height stretched to only a few inches below the trailer's ceiling. He still stood ramrod straight despite his sixty-plus years and the painful osteoarthritis that attacked his joints. "Everything's ready. When did you become a worrywart?"

"He didn't. He's just trying to change the subject." Jason brushed crumbs from his blond, runaway beard and threw his muffin wrapper into the trash.

Toby didn't need a mirror to know what he looked like. His younger brother had the same slate-blue eyes, blond hair, broad shoulders, and height as Toby did. Except Jason's marital status had been rewarded with the beard. "He's twenty-nine and no closer to being married than he was a year ago. I don't care, but Mamm sure does."

Mom had a good heart and a streak of stubbornness when it came to her children's happiness. They'd better be content or she would know why. Maybe this would be the year Toby made her happy and gave her another daughter-in-law. How would he do that? Toby caught himself shaking his head. A man his age didn't go to singings, that was for sure. The words of his once-special friend echoed in his head: *"What woman would want to spend half the year raising children by herself while her husband plied his trade at auctions across five states?"*

His mother, grandmother, and Jason's wife all did it, but not Janey Hershberger. It took her two years of courting to figure out she couldn't see herself living that way. *"You may think it's normal, Toby, but no* fraa *wants to be at home alone half the year while you gallivant across the countryside."*

Toby shrugged on his jacket and settled his black hat farther back on his head. He was content with his life. Really, he was. Absolutely content. Really.

"Your mamm knows how important family is to a Plain man." A faint grimace etched on his grizzled face, Grandpa rubbed his swollen knuckles. "Family comes second only to faith."

Silas Miller started the auctioneering company in his midtwenties at a time when Plain communities frowned on the use of microphones and electricity for auctions. He overcame the objections and gained permission from the district to build a business that now supported three generations of Millers. A grandson didn't argue with a man of his experience. "Mamm also knows what it costs a fraa to have her *mann* traveling away from home half the year. It hasn't been easy for her."

"Nor for your *groossmammi* either." Grandpa tugged a prescription bottle from a knapsack on the counter. He winced as he turned the lid and dumped two pills into his calloused palm. "But I've never heard either one of them complain. Whatever you decide about courting is your business."

"Danki, *Daadi*." Toby rolled his eyes at his brother. Jason stuck out his tongue. He didn't always act like a married man with three kids and another on the way. Toby gave him another eye roll. "Grow up, Bruder."

"You first."

The trailer door swung open and stayed open, bringing with it a gust of cold air. Dad stood at the bottom of the steps. "Did you all fall asleep in there? It's time to get this show started."

"They were jawing me to death." Grandpa bolted for the steps faster than a man half his age. "You know how they are right before they get on the platform."

Antsy. That's how they got. Full of pee and vinegar, to quote Grandma Joanna.

Toby hopped over the steps and landed in the sparse, tender blades of grass just beginning to sprout this first week of March after a long, cold winter. Jason settled in beside him. Their brothers Declan and Elijah joined them with the two oldest Miller men in the lead. They were on the job.

At the platform they parted ways, ready to do their parts. Declan would handle the second auction of garden and farming equipment, while Jason had the third auction of livestock. Orville Katzman, who'd hired their company to handle the huge multi-family moving-slash-estate auction, met Toby at the bottom of the wooden steps. He handed Toby an updated list for the household goods auction. "How're you, Toby? Are you ready? I hear you're a bit older today."

"I'm ready, willing, and able."

To prove his point Toby snared the list and bounded up the steps. Taking his turn as auctioneer today served as the best birthday present ever. First up, get a feel for the crowd. He gazed out at the sea of farm equipment hats, baseball caps, straw hats, bonnets, black wool coats, and scarves that protected heads from a brisk, chilly March breeze. Some folks, coffee travel mugs in hand, lounged in their canvas camp chairs.

Others stood in clusters along the periphery or settled onto two sets of portable bleachers toward the back of the grassy field. They all talked at once, creating a swell of noise not unlike a flock of blue jays chattering. As casual as they might appear to the untrained eye, they were ready. They had their auction bid cards in their laps. They'd come to buy. And it was Toby's job to sell. Nothing could be better than the first auction of the spring season.

The usual bevy of young girls—sixteen, seventeen, eighteen years old—occupied the first row. It happened at every auction. They occasionally bid on small items but rarely bought anything.

Jason called them Toby's fan club. Emmett mostly glowered at them. Toby ignored them. They were harmless, but he was careful not to encourage them.

Adrenaline made his heart pump harder. His fingers tingled with anticipation. His whole body warmed. His cadence organized words in his head and prepared to slide toward the tip of his tongue. *Who'll give me ten dollars? Bid ten. Ten. Ten. Bid. Now fifteen.*

He strode to the auctioneer's table and picked up the microphone. His fingers held it lightly. Otherwise they would cramp before the end of the day. He took a swig from his water bottle and cleared his throat. The crowd quieted. He nodded at Elijah and Emmett. They would act as bid spotters, pointing out bidders he might miss. Elijah ducked his head and nodded. Emmett, who was younger but more outgoing, gave Toby a big thumbs-up. "Ready when you are, Bruder."

"Wait a minute." A smirk stretched across his face, Orville strolled over to Toby. He held out his hand. "Let me make a quick announcement."

What was he up to? A change in the consignments wouldn't give Orville an expression like a kid about to snatch a cookie from the cookie jar. Warily Toby handed over the mic.

"Folks, could I have your attention please? I want to take a quick moment to share two pieces of news with you." Orville had a high-pitched, whiny voice not suited for amplification. "Number one, today is our auctioneer's birthday. Can you folks give Toby Miller a nice, big happy birthday round of applause?"

Heat singed Toby's neck and face. He ducked his head. It was one thing to be the center of attention for the sake of his job, another for a birthday—everyone had them. No need to make a public spectacle about it. "Orville—"

A chorus of birthday wishes in both English and Pennsylvania

Dutch drowned out his protest. Several folks began to sing. Applause rang out. Toby shook his head. "Thank you, thank you."

"Announcement number two, folks." The crowd quieted. Orville moved to the platform's edge. He pointed at Toby's grandpa, who'd been busy making sure the furniture was properly lined up. "Many of you have been coming to these auctions for years. You know Silas Miller, founder of Miller Family Auctioneering Company. You know he started this business many moons ago, and his company has been our go-to company every year since. I thought you should know this will be his last auction here at the Knowles County Fairgrounds. He's retiring. Could you give him a hand, let him know how much you appreciate all his years of hard work?"

What? Something was wrong with Toby's hearing.

Grandpa never sat still. He loved to work. He loved auction-eering. He loved traveling. For a few seconds, no one reacted. Toby opened his mouth. He closed it.

Then the people were on their feet, clapping. Grandpa hardly seemed to notice. He kept right on working, the way he always had.

As if nothing had changed.

His absence would change everything. He wasn't just the boss, the administrator, the founder. He was a fixture in every good memory Toby had growing up—on and off the road. He was the level that kept the Miller men on an even keel mile after mile, year after year.

Such thoughts were selfish. Toby shoved them aside. If Grandpa felt the need to rest easy more permanently, he'd earned the right. Time for Toby to step up and take the load from his elder.

Dad couldn't do it, much as he might try. Grandpa handled the bookkeeping, record keeping, and bill paying. Dad had an aversion to anything that involved reading or writing. Nor was he a fan of the technology required to promote their business now that it covered an ever-growing region. Who would take over scheduling, maintenance of the trailers and equipment, and working with the folks who handled the company's website and computer work?

Toby sought out his father, who was moving an oak curio cabinet with Emmett. His expression grim, he shook his head and mouthed the words, *I'll explain later.*

Right now they had an auction to run.

Later, indeed.

Chapter 2

*E*nglish women had it easy. They didn't have to figure out how to use a porta potty while wearing long dresses. Rachelle Lapp smiled to herself as stepped from the squat structure that smelled of a mixture of cloying, fruity air freshener and other things she'd rather not think about. A small challenge among life's many. Plus it gave her three minutes of solitude.

She chuckled. Did a porta potty qualify as a good place to be alone? She wasn't that desperate. She loved her little brothers and sisters. Her siblings would be chomping at the bit to get back to the carnival packed into a small piece of Knowles County Fairground this first Saturday in March. She hated to disappoint them, but they were out of tickets.

Rachelle had saved enough money to buy them each a treat from one of the dozens of food booths that provided a buffer between the carnival and the adjacent auction. That would soften the sting. She had as much fun as they did going to the carnival and auction using what remained of her salary after she gave a portion to her parents to help support their big family. They loved auction days, and having a carnival plant itself on the fairgrounds at the same time was almost too good to be true. Rachelle didn't ride the rides, but she did live vicariously in their shining faces and laughter.

She let the door close behind her. The cold breeze blew away the porta potty's stink. Shivering, she buttoned her gray jacket. "All done. Who wants a funnel cake?"

"Me, me!" Sam's small frame came into dark focus against the sun behind him. "Me and Sean want funnel cakes."

"*Nee*, I don't either." Sam's twin brother shook his head so hard his straw hat shifted. "I want fried Oreo ice cream."

"Sean and I," Rachelle gently corrected. She encouraged the kids to speak English with her for practice. Most of the time they forgot or resorted to Pennsylvania Dutch when they became excited. When they did speak English, her teacher genes kicked in. "It's pretty chilly for ice cream, but it's your call. Why don't you get one of each and share?"

The twins sat cross-legged on the sparse sprigs of grass forcing themselves through the winter-hardened ground outside the row of porta potties. Where were the others? "Emma? DeeDee? Mandy?"

The girls sat on top of a picnic table several yards from the endless line of porta potties, *botching*. From the sounds of their breathless words, claps, and giggles, they were doing "Rockin' Robin." Mandy waved. "We voted. We decided on Frito pies and caramel apples, if there's enough money for two things. If not, we'll be happy with fried Twinkies."

All good choices. Rachelle did a mental head count. Three girls and two boys. She was missing two boys. Her heartbeat did a weird two-step. "Where's Michael? And Jonah?"

Sam cocked his head and wrinkled his upturned nose. He scanned the grounds as if his brothers would suddenly reappear. "They were here a minute ago."

"I know that. I was only in the bathroom for three minutes." Rachelle swung around for a full 360-degree review of the area. No chunky five-year-old missing a front tooth. No skinny eight-year-old wearing black-framed glasses with an elastic strip to keep them firmly in place. "Emma, where are Michael and Jonah?"

At eleven Emma was the oldest of the siblings on this outing. She should've been watching over them in Rachelle's brief absence. She popped off the picnic table and stuck her hands on her hips. "Michael wanted Jonah to win a teddy bear for him at the ring-toss booth. I told him nee because we don't have any more tickets."

"And then what happened?" Rachelle squeezed hand sanitizer from the bottle on a nearby stand. She rubbed her hands together harder than necessary. "Did he take nee for an answer?"

"You know Michael."

She did. The little boy had a stubborn streak longer than a country mile and a city block. Nothing Dad and Mom had done to guide him toward obedience seemed to work. "They can't be out there on their own, Emma. Michael's too young and Jonah's too sweet for this world."

A stranger could easily take advantage of them. Or take them away. It happened even in places like Lee's Gulch.

"I'm sorry, *Schweschder*. I was botching and I thought they were playing with Sam and Sean." Emma's face crumpled. Tears threatened. "I'll find them. I should've kept a better watch."

A small boy with no fear of strangers—no fear of anything in the world, really—and a boy with limited ability to understand all the ways the world could be dangerous were traipsing around together. Rachelle had been responsible for caring for her younger siblings for as long as she could remember. She was good at it. She changed her first diaper at five. Taught her little brothers and sisters to tie their shoes and say their prayers. Even as a grade school kid who herded her younger brothers and sisters like a gangly fair-headed shepherd. She reveled in it. Until just now.

"It's okay. I'll find them." She patted Emma's shoulder. "You need to stay here. Stay together, all of you. No one else runs off. I'll find them and bring them back."

"If we all search for them, we'll find them faster." Sam hopped to his feet and dusted off his hands. Sean did the same. They were so identical even Grandma and Grandpa had trouble telling them apart. "Me and Sean will go to the ring-toss booth. I reckon that's where they are."

And then Rachelle would be scouring the grounds for four boys instead of two. "Nee, someone else will get lost." Mom and Dad had entrusted her with the children. She was responsible for keeping them safe. "I'll be back as soon as I find them."

Sei so gut, Gott, *let no harm come to them. Sei so gut. Direct me to them, sei so gut.*

Following Sam's logic, she headed to the game booths first. The boys had no money, no tickets. How did they think they'd play? Did Jonah even understand he needed a ticket to play? Brushing the thought aside, Rachelle dodged a lady pushing a stroller over the uneven ground while eating a sausage on a stick with one hand. Then a man carrying a boy on his shoulders. The child was eating cotton candy. Some of it stuck to the man's hair. The crowd thickened as she approached the booths. Balloon pop, bean bag toss, milk-bottle knockdown, ring toss, spin the wheel. Any one of them would fascinate her boys.

Mom would chuckle if she could hear Rachelle's thoughts. They weren't her boys, they were her brothers, but somehow they were lodged in that place in her heart where there was so much love to give. Until she had her own, she poured it on these little guys along with her scholars at school. She had more than enough to go around. The more she gave, the more her supply grew.

Funny how that worked. God was love. Scripture said so. No wonder the supply never ended.

No boys in matching blue shirts, denim pants, suspenders, and matching jackets. No little boy whose dark hair stuck out from under his straw hat in scraggly tuffs because he needed a haircut and never wanted to sit still long enough for Mom to give him one. No short-for-his-age boy with that same hair and ocher eyes enlarged by thick lenses, who always wanted to please.

"Where are you?" Rachelle whispered. "Gott, where are they?"

She stopped at the ring-toss booth. The lady running it nodded at Rachelle's description of Michael and Jonah. "They were here about ten minutes ago. Two of the cutest little whippersnappers I've seen in days." She had the raspy voice of someone who smoked a lot. Her thin face creased in a jagged yellow-toothed smile at the memory. "I explained that they needed tickets to play. The littlest one was so disappointed I let him toss a few rings to perk him up."

"Then what happened?"

"Dang if he didn't get a ring on a bottle." The lady chortled. "Beginner's luck. So I gave them each one of the little penguins."

The stuffed animal would've fit in the palms of their hands. "Did you see where they went from here?"

"Honey, I had a crowd by then. All I know is they were thrilled with those little penguins. Kept thanking me over and over again." She stuck her hands with yellowed fingernails so long they curled into her smudged apron pockets and produced a crumpled pack of cigarettes. "Go to the fairgrounds office. They get lots of lost kids. They have a procedure for finding them."

Worry an ever-tightening iron ring around her heart, Rachelle squeezed past a cluster of high school boys crowding the booth.

Should she report them missing? Nausea rose in her throat. With every minute that ticked by, the more the possibility loomed that they could get into serious trouble.

Much longer and she'd have no choice.

Gott? Where are they?

Chapter 3

*A*n auctioneer focused solely on his job and nothing else from the time he picked up the mic until he called the last wringer-wash machine, quilt, or buggy. Toby took a deep breath and let it out. *Do the job. Focus.* He nodded at Elijah. His brother pulled the canvas drop cloth from the bedroom set.

"Next up we have a six-piece, handcrafted oak bed set with a mirror, king-size bed, end tables, dresser, and blanket chest. Number 33."

A ripple of "ahs" and "ohs" ran through the crowd. It was easy to tell who had scoped out this set beforehand. Those savvy bidders sat forward, bid cards grasped in their fisted hands, eyes squinting, expressions fierce.

Toby took another deep breath. *Here we go.* "Jump right in, folks. Who'll give me $1,000 . . . ?" The rapid-fire cadence was there, waiting for him. After ten years as a bid caller, the rhythm came as easily as breathing, even after a five-month hiatus. The beautiful bedroom set was an easy sell. The bids rose steadily until the price hit $3,300. Then he had to apply some pressure. "Come on, folks, this is a gorgeous bed set. Handmade. You won't find anything like this at a discount furniture store. It should've started at this price. Look at this handiwork. Let's go for a nice even number. Who'll give me $4,000?"

The white-haired English woman in the front row who'd been with him all the way held up her card. He pointed her out. "$4,000. Who'll give me $4,500? Bid $4,500. Now $4,500—"

"$4,200." A man wearing a black cowboy hat, who'd been neck and neck with the elderly woman from the first bid, thrust his card in the air. "I'll give you $4,200."

"You want to do this the slow way?" Laughing, Tobias dabbed at his sweaty forehead with a towel from the pile next to his water bottle. "Fine. $4,200. Who'll give me $4,300? Bid $4,300. $4,300. Now $4,300."

The elderly lady's card shot up.

"$4,300. Bid $4,500. Now $4,500. $4,500. Bid $4,500 . . ."

A few more scans of the crowd. Elijah shook his head. So did Emmett. Toby offered Black Cowboy Hat a thumbs-up followed by a thumbs-down. Frowning, Black Cowboy Hat shook his head.

"Sold to the lady down front for $4,300. Ma'am, what's your number?"

Next up was a treadle sewing machine on a beautifully hand-crafted stand. Then an oak table and eight chairs. A set of hickory rockers. The sun rose in the sky, warming the stage. Toby shed his jacket. Then he rolled up his sleeves.

The crowd was a good one. They'd brought their sense of humor with their wallets. They responded to Toby's jokes and stepped up their bids at his prodding. Now and then he switched to Pennsylvania Dutch to make the Plain families feel at home. On days like today, no better job existed.

Apparently two little boys standing near the platform's right side thought so too. Toby caught the younger boy mimicking his words and his every move. He chuckled. A mini-auctioneer in the making.

Another quick look told him the boys were Michael and Jonah Lapp, children of Adam and Leah Lapp, who lived down the road from the Millers. What were these two youngsters doing at the auction alone? Most Plain kids were able to take care of themselves at a younger age than their English counterparts, but Jonah was what English folks called *developmentally delayed*. Plain parents preferred *special*.

Michael probably thought he could take care of his brother. He was an independent soul. He had one arm wrapped around Jonah's waist. With his other hand, he mimicked Toby's efficient hand gestures aimed at the various bidders. His mouth moved as if he could follow Toby's every word.

Why not give him a chance? The crowd would love it. Keeping their attention and providing bits of entertainment were part of the gig. Toby squatted at the platform's edge. "Hey, Michael, do you want my job?"

Michael's grin stretched. His dimples deepened. He let go of Jonah and clapped. "Jah, jah!"

His expression confused, Jonah cocked his head. "Jah?"

"Jah! Don't you want Michael to be an auctioneer?" Toby swept his free arm out in a flourish. "Bring him on up here, Jonah. Come be my co-auctioneer, Michael."

Jonah ducked his head, but he trudged toward the wooden steps that led to the platform stage with Michael in tow.

"Let's give them an encouraging hand, folks!"

The crowd obliged. By the time Jonah's grin matched Michael's, the younger boy whooped and waved. Jonah mimicked his brother's moves. The more the English spectators clapped, the more the boys responded.

"Okay, my friend, here we go." Toby pointed to another bed set, this one solid oak, again handmade, with five pieces. "Where shall we start?"

Jonah let go of Michael's hand and scampered back to the platform's edge. Michael wrinkled his sun-freckled nose. "I think $1,000." The five-year-old had a lisp thanks to a missing front tooth. "Bid $1,000. Who'll give me $1,000?"

He tried to employ Toby's singsong cadence, but he immediately got stuck. Toby patted his shoulder. "That's okay. Here's how it goes. Bid $1,000. $1,000, $1,000. Bid $1,000. Now $1,500?" Toby slowed way down, letting each word hold sway. Michael pointed and waved like an old pro. "Bid $1,500, $1,500. Bid $1,500. You up front. $2,000? Who'll give me $2,000? Bid $2,000? Bid $2,500. $2,500. Who wants in? Now $3,000. $3,000. Bid $3,000—"

"Psst . . . psst . . . Michael . . . come down from there."

The stage whisper emanated from just beyond the platform. His concentration broken, Toby glanced down. Rachelle Lapp stood at his feet. Her hands were on her hips. Bright-red spots glowed on her cheeks. If looks could kill, Toby would be a deer hung on a hook ready to be dressed for its venison.

Rachelle shook her finger at him. "You too, Jonah."

"He's working with me." Toby moved closer to the platform's edge. Mic behind his back, he squatted and lowered his voice to match her whisper. "No harm done, really. I invited them up here."

"You should know better." Rachelle's steely expression matched the fire in her ocher eyes. She was a lit torch. "You may have permission to use an electric microphone and stand on a stage in front of a crowd. These *buwe* do not. They don't know any better, but you do."

"*Es dutt mer—*"

"Sorry or not, you're an adult. You shouldn't take advantage of Jonah." A tendril of dark, almost-black hair had escaped her prayer covering. The desire to brush it from her face came over Toby, as surprising as a cloudburst of rain in August. "Just send them down here, sei so gut."

He would never take advantage of Jonah. The Millers had a child with an intellectual disability. Sadie was nine and she had Down syndrome. She was Toby's favorite sibling—although he didn't spread that around.

He scrambled back from the edge—of the platform and from the realization that he'd known Rachelle Lapp, seven years his junior, all her life, but he'd never really seen her. Rachelle had grown up far too pretty for her own good—or maybe it was for his good.

Chapter 4

*T*he boys were safe. Nothing could be more important than that. Rachelle sucked in a breath and let it out. Her arms and legs quaked. Her heart hammered. The fact that Michael was on the platform, using a mic, the center of attention, wasn't the end of the world. He was five, after all. The stares pierced Rachelle like hot pokers. *Sorry, Gott.*

She straightened her shoulders and raised her chin. Women from her district likely were judging her—no matter how much Scripture said they shouldn't. The English folks probably wondered what the big deal was. Rachelle didn't care what either group thought—at least she tried not to care. But her parents worked hard to follow the *Ordnung.* Not only the rules themselves, but also the spirit of the law. After many years of tugging back and forth in Plain communities like Lee's Gulch, auctioneers had been given the right to use electric sound systems as a necessity for their jobs. They had to stand on stages and be the center of attention—their occupation required it.

On the other hand, people like Rachelle and the boys didn't use electricity. And they avoided the limelight. They were to keep themselves apart from the world. Not strut around on a stage. Toby

Miller knew that. The man stood above the crowd like a beardless Paul Bunyan with his height, wide shoulders, a shock of blond hair peeking from under his straw hat over eyes the color of slate—sometimes blue, sometimes gray—and a rich, deep baritone that carried even without a microphone.

Not that she'd been staring at him at the school picnic last year or the church lunch two weeks ago. Not much. Everyone knew Toby was a confirmed bachelor, married to his job. He was at least twenty-nine to Rachelle's twenty-two. Neither of those facts kept her breath from catching when he caught her gaze at a Sunday lunch or when their paths crossed at a frolic.

Get a grip, Rachelle. She ignored Toby's sweet smile. He couldn't get in her good graces with those dimples. "Come on, Jonah. You too, Michael. Let's go."

His shoulders drooping, Jonah plodded down the steps. Michael peeked out from behind Toby. The auctioneer straightened and gave the boy a nudge toward the stairs. "Danki for the help, little guy. Maybe someday I can give you lessons."

Michael's frown disappeared. He skipped across the platform as if he weren't in the least bit of trouble. It took a hardened soul to stay mad at such a happy-go-lucky child. In this case, Rachelle would harden her heart. He'd done something dangerous—for him and for his brother. Mom and Dad would see to his punishment.

"Danki for loaning him to me." Toby seemed to think this was funny. He beamed. "He's a *gut* helper."

She hadn't loaned Michael to anyone. This wasn't the time to make that point. Rachelle turned her back on Toby and prepared to wade through the crowd.

"Michael auctioneer." His forehead wrinkled in an effort to pronounce the last word, Jonah took her hand. His was cold, damp, and sticky. "Toby said."

Despite an obstinate streak, Jonah generally did as he was told by adults.

"I understand that. But you shouldn't have left the porta potties. I told you to stay put." Rachelle took Michael's hand. She wanted both of them close. Michael trotted along, offering a smile to everyone in their path. They smiled back even as they moved out of his way, such was his charm. "What if you and Michael had gotten lost? That would make Dat and Mamm very sad."

Jonah's chin trembled. His eyes filled with tears behind lenses smudged with his greasy fingerprints. "You too?"

"Me too." She squeezed his hand. "I found you, so it's okay now. Just don't do it again."

"Schweschder mad."

"I'm not mad."

"Gut. No like mad."

"Me neither."

Together they traipsed back through the fairgrounds, passing the carnival booths that had gotten them in trouble in the first place. Michael didn't seem to have learned much. He kept tugging at her arm, begging to stop. Just one game of darts. One game of bean bag toss. Keeping him on course was like trying to herd tadpoles. Finally Rachelle halted in an empty spot between the fishing booth and the spin-the-wheel booth. She knelt so she could look at him eye to eye. "Stop asking, Michael. You don't get a reward for acting badly. You went off on your own and took Jonah with you. I'll not reward your behavior. Do you understand?"

Michael ducked his head. He kicked at a rock with his dusty boot. "Are you going to tell Dat and Mamm?"

"I have to tell them."

His lower lip protruded. "I didn't mean no harm."

"You have to remember Jonah is special. He may be older in

years, but in other ways, he's younger than you. If you ask him to do something, he'll do it. He likes to make you happy. You have to help him make gut decisions."

Herein lay the challenge of being a teacher and caregiver for a child like Jonah. Her job was to guide him as he grew older, while keeping him safe. He deserved some independence. But he also needed to be kept safe. A balancing act that some days seemed like walking across a narrow bridge with no handrails and a deep river flowing under it. She didn't swim all that well.

His chin jutting out, Michael glared. "But he's big. He's bigger than me."

"Jonah's body is getting bigger, but his mind isn't getting older. It won't, not like yours will."

Michael studied Jonah, who'd squatted in the grass to pick up a rock. "I have to watch out for him?"

"Jah, we don't want anything to happen to him."

Michael's glare faded. He squeezed past Rachelle and held out his hand to Jonah. "Let's go home, Bruder."

Jonah glanced up. His smile, the sunniest in all of Virginia, broke across his face. "Jah, Bruder, home."

He took Michael's hand, and together the two led the way back to the spot where Rachelle had left the other kids. Emma saw them first. She jumped up from the picnic table and raced across the field. "There you are. Finally. Where did you find them? Michael, what were you thinking—?"

"That's enough. We've already had that talk." Rachelle stepped between the irate girl and her brothers. "Like Mamm loves to say, all's well that ends well. We're going home."

"No treats, I guess." Sam's exaggerated sigh was mournful. "I sure wanted a funnel cake."

"How about pie instead?" Rachelle patted the canvas bag that hung from her shoulder. "Mamm asked me to pick up three pies. She wants to support our school fundraiser. We'll go home, do our chores, have supper, and then eat pie for dessert."

Everyone seemed to agree that was a good plan. Thank goodness. Weariness invaded Rachelle's very soul. Every few feet she glanced back to make sure her charges were staying close. It took a full ten minutes to arrive at the pie booth. A line of customers signaled the booth's popularity. All the families wanted to support the school, even if they were from other districts. Plus everyone loved pie. Several more minutes passed before they made it to the counter.

"Rachelle, it's gut to see you!" Elizabeth Miller waved to the kids who trailed after Rachelle like ducklings parading behind a mama duck. "Sadie, Rachelle's here."

Sadie turned around. A smear of cherry pie decorated one fair cheek. Her face lit up, her dimples—so like her brother Toby's—deepened. With a squeal, she dropped the towel in her hand and sped across the booth. *"Tietschern, Tietschern."*

The Millers' sweet youngest child had graduated this past week to making change—a task that delighted her. She wanted to work in her family's combination store this summer. Teaching her was a gift. "Sadie, how are you?"

"Gut. I'm gut." Ignoring the booth counter between them, the girl threw her short arms around Rachelle's waist in an enthusiastic, sticky hug. When she stepped back and pushed her smudged, dark-rimmed glasses back up her flat nose, the pie stain had transferred to Rachelle's dress. "I happy to see you."

"I'm happy to see you too." Rachelle straightened the girl's prayer cap before it fell off. Her scholars' hugs were the best—right up there with the ones from her family. "Are you having a gut time selling pie?"

"I love pie. *Cherry pie. Apple pie. Chocolate cream pie. Lemon m-meringue pie."* Sadie sang the flavors. Setting words to music seemed to make it easier for her to pronounce them. Only meringue came out in a stutter. Trying to talk clearly was hard for Rachelle's scholars with Down syndrome. *"Banana cream, strawberry-rhubarb pie."*

"You're doing such a great job remembering all the flavors too." Rachelle loved offering praise where it was due. Sadie's short-term memory often failed her when trying to memorize English vocabulary, but anything involving food stuck with her. "I imagine you're a great cheerleader for pie sales. We'll have a nice sum of money to renovate the school building."

The district's school was showing its age. Funds raised would allow them to replace the roof, repaint the exterior, and buy a new chalkboard. Rachelle also needed to buy more supplies. She made many of her visuals needed for teaching children with developmental delays, whether they involved poor eyesight, hearing, or weak muscle control, but even then the supplies were expensive.

Maybe that was the topic of the specially called parents' committee meeting this evening. Her dad hadn't said. Just that she needed to be home in plenty of time for supper and then the meeting. But then why a meeting at their house? Meetings that included the teachers were usually conducted at the school. And never on a Saturday.

She tried to push the unsettling thought aside. No sense in wasting time worrying. As if a person could turn it off like a faucet.

"I like pie too." Michael grabbed the counter with both hands and stood on his tippy-toes to peer over it. "I want shoofly pie and chocolate cream pie."

"Us too." Sam and Sean chimed in. "And peach pie."

"Can we get four pies? It takes a lot of pie to feed sixteen people." Deedee and the girls didn't want to be left out. "Especially when the boys are such hogs."

"Whoa, whoa. Everybody hold your horses." Laughing, Rachelle shook her finger at the cluster of kids pressing against her from all sides. "Mamm decided already. Pecan, peach, and lemon meringue pies. Those are Dat's favorites. You all need to back up a bit. Wait for me out of the way so other folks can get to the front of the line."

They knew better than to argue—that might lead to no pie at all. Emma led them aside—but not so far away that Rachelle couldn't still see them.

"And you, my dochder, need to get back to work." Elizabeth patted Sadie's shoulder. "Go get me some more plates and clean the pie servers. We don't want to mix flavors."

Sadie did as she was told. Elizabeth cut an apple pie in generous slices and slid them deftly onto Styrofoam plates for individual sales. "I heard you had a bit of a talk with my oldest *suh* earlier."

The gossip grapevine had twisted its way across the fairgrounds in record time. Heat spiraled through Rachelle. "I'm sure he meant well, but the buwe shouldn't have been up onstage, let alone using the mic."

"Toby loves what he does so much he thinks everyone should do it, I reckon." Elizabeth waved the pie server with abandon, seemingly unaware of the apple filling that plopped on the counter. She leaned closer and lowered her voice. "Today's his birthday, you know. Twenty-nine. He's such a hard worker. A gut man."

Toby's good qualities were no secret. So why bring them to Rachelle's attention? "Tell him I said seelich gebortsdaag and no hard feelings."

"I will." Elizabeth looked pleased. "I wish—"

"Mamm! Don't be bending Rachelle's ear about Toby." Elizabeth's oldest daughter, Layla, slid two chocolate meringue pies onto the counter next to the apple pies. She shot Rachelle an

I'm-so-sorry look. "He has only himself to blame for his lack of a fraa. If he can't make room for courting in his life, he'll never have one. No Plain woman will run after him. What can we get you today?"

A horrified cry split the air in the back of the booth. "Mamm, I drop pie on floor." Sadie's voice held tears. "It all dirty."

"Well, let's get it cleaned up." Elizabeth shrugged. "The first casualty today. That's not bad. I'll be right back."

Tutting like she was the mother instead of Elizabeth, Layla took a washrag to her mother's spills. "Forgive my *mudder*. She's not above matchmaking when it comes to her *kinner*."

"It's like you said, though. Talking to the women does no gut." By now Rachelle's cheeks had to be hot pink. She and Layla were about the same age, but they'd never been close friends in school. Beyond talking about assignments or being on the same team for volleyball and baseball games, they'd never really chatted about anything personal. "We're not in charge when it comes to courting."

"That's for sure." Layla's laugh brought out her dimples. The family resemblance was strong in the Miller clan. "If they were, it would be a lot easier and more organized. Everyone would be paired up and married in no time."

Rachelle managed her own laugh. Courting was a painful subject, but laughing about it helped. The grapevine being what it was in Lee's Gulch—or anywhere in the world—Layla likely knew Rachelle had turned down two marriage proposals in the last three years. Neither felt right. Her feelings hadn't been strong enough to prompt her to give up teaching. Her boyfriends had moved too fast, been too anxious. Her scholars needed her. It wasn't that she didn't want to get married and have children of her own. She did. Some day. If the right man came along at the right time. If he didn't, then she would be content teaching. More than content. Happy.

The image of Toby's smiling face popped up. Rachelle squashed it back down. Toby was far too sure of himself. Not to mention, much older. He wasn't in any hurry to marry—that was obvious.

According to the grapevine, Layla and her beau, one of the Plank boys, had gone their separate ways after only six months. No one seemed to know whose idea it was. Either way, Rachelle could commiserate over the difficulties of courting in a tiny Plain district. "That sure would be nice. But too much to ask, I reckon."

"Maybe. Maybe not." The other woman's mischievous expression didn't give Rachelle any idea what that noncommittal response meant.

Layla ducked away from the counter and immediately returned with Rachelle's pies. Rachelle paid and thanked Layla and the other women for all their hard work on behalf of the school fundraiser. She beckoned to the girls to carry the pies. "We'd better get going. Bye, Sadie," Rachelle called out. "See you Monday. Don't be late."

"I never late." Sadie trotted back to the counter and waved. "I love school."

"Gut for you!"

Halfway down the dirt road toward the buggy parking lot, Rachelle glanced back. Layla stood at the booth counter, arm around Sadie, still staring.

Chapter 5

*D*id you see how pink Rachelle's cheeks turned this morning when I mentioned Toby?"

As usual Layla's mother saw what she wanted to see. Layla accepted a bowl of mashed potatoes and a second one of gravy from her. She took them to the mammoth pine table in the Miller kitchen. It was so like Mom to want to talk about Toby's lack of a wife instead of the surprising announcement earlier in the day that Grandpa had decided to retire. Mom never talked about the auctioneering business. She said it was best left to the men. Period. Layla didn't agree. What the men did affected the women and children. Especially in a business that involved so much traveling. Toby's love life, on the other hand, was his business alone. "You embarrassed Rachelle by talking about Toby's attributes like he was a horse for sale."

"I did not." Indignation filled Mom's snort. She plopped a basket of hot, fresh rolls on the table next to a platter of fried chicken. Corn on the cob, pickled beets, mashed potatoes, gravy, and coleslaw rounded out the menu. They were serving all Toby's favorite foods for his birthday. Mom had also made his favorite German chocolate cake for dessert. "I just wanted to show her his good points outweigh his actions at the auction. Not that what he did was such a terrible thing."

Mom was all about wiggle room when it came to making the rules fit certain situations—especially when they involved her children. Her mother's undying loyalty to them made her that much more lovable. Layla had been the recipient herself on more than one occasion. "Bishop Bartholomew might not see it that way."

"Bart understands the nature of auctioneering. He's been your *daed*'s best friend since they were knee-high to their daeds' britches."

That didn't mean he granted dispensations for violating the Ordnung. Layla didn't bother to argue with her mother. She was a faithful rule follower, who also wanted what was best for her children. Sometimes those two paths veered in slightly different directions.

The Ordnung had to come first. Faith. Family. Community. Layla had heard this tenet all her life. At least Mother's focus on Toby's life meant she had less time to poke around in Layla's. If she was aware of the disastrous nature of her oldest daughter's attempt to court, she hadn't let on. Layla and Rachelle had this experience in common. Did Rachelle know that?

"Deanna Beachy told me today that Ryan has decided to move to Lancaster County to work at his *onkel* Charles's buggy repair shop."

Whoops. Maybe Mom *was* paying attention. Best to feign no knowledge of Ryan's situation. Ryan Beachy with the sea-blue-green eyes and black heart. "Really? She'll miss him. The whole family will." So would Layla, but maybe her heart would heal more quickly if she didn't have to run into Ryan at church or in town. Or anywhere. Since he dumped her for a girl in another district, she seemed to cross paths with him everywhere. "They still have a lot of family in Bird-in-Hand and Paradise. I'm sure they'll visit back and forth."

Most of Lee's Gulch's Plain families had migrated to Virginia from Lancaster County. The ties were strong despite the distance separating them. By van it was a six-hour drive.

"You won't miss him?"

"Why would I miss him?"

"Deanna seemed to think you had something to do with his decision."

"Whatever would make her think that?" Must've been that new girl. Someone named Sylvia. Layla busied herself placing napkins next to each plate at the table. "Where is Sadie? And Sherri? They're supposed to set the table."

"Josie is supervising their cleanup. They were both sticky messes. I don't think either one will eat much supper, considering how much pie they ate. Stop changing the subject."

Better Mom should focus on Toby's love life. Even if that meant Layla had to throw him under the buggy, so to speak. "Maybe Toby has another woman in mind—someone you don't know about. After all, courting is supposed to be private."

Not that Mom let that stand in the way of her matchmaking. She used the district's extensive, well-nourished grapevine to her advantage at every frolic, picnic, barbecue, and fish fry.

"Still changing the subject? Fine. Be that way. I won't tell you about the new bachelor who moved onto the Troyer property last week. His name is Micah Troyer, he's twenty-three, and he hails from Bird-in-Hand." Mother sounded more like fourteen-year-old Josie than a fifty-something mother of nine. So much for not telling Layla about this newcomer. "Deanna says he's easy on the eyes. Someone entirely new to our district might be just the right medicine for what ails you."

"Nothing ails me." Layla set a pitcher of water on the table with more force than necessary. Liquid sloshed over the sides. "I don't need help with my love life any more than Toby does. I'm happy being in charge of our store. I enjoy keeping the books. I like working with numbers. I like keeping track of inventory. There's no rush."

"I don't mean to rush you. It was just a thought. Deanna says his family sent him here because he's a hard worker and has a gut head on his shoulders. That sounds like a gut recommendation."

"You haven't even met this Micah Troyer. For all you know we'd be a terrible match."

"I'm just saying keep an open mind."

"This is about my heart, Mamm, my heart, not my head."

"Jah, jah." Mom situated the bowl of gravy next to the potatoes. "No need to be so touchy. I just want what's best for my kinner."

"I know you do, but sometimes you don't think things through."

"Like what?"

Time once again to attempt to shift the subject away from her love life. "For instance, if Rachelle and Toby were to get married, Rachelle wouldn't teach school anymore. All the kinner adore her, especially Sadie. She would be heartbroken if Rachelle suddenly wasn't her tietschern anymore."

Mom went back to the sink and began dumping dirty pans into a tub of soapy water. "Rachelle would be part of the family then. Sadie would see her all the time. She would love having Rachelle as her schweschder by marriage. Rachelle could tutor her."

Mom always saw the future through rosy lenses. A quality to be admired, for sure. Layla leaned against the counter and contemplated having Rachelle as a sister-in-law. They'd never been close, but Rachelle's work with Sadie and the other students revealed only good things about her character. "Now if we can just get Toby on board."

"He's on board. He just doesn't want to admit it."

"I'll call the men. The food's getting cold."

"And we don't want it to get too late for Toby's big birthday." Mom giggled like a teenager at a singing. "He's going to be so surprised. He'll love it. And so will Rachelle . . . one day."

If Mom's focus on Toby's love life didn't keep her from obsessing with Layla's, Layla would almost feel sorry for Toby. Almost.

Chapter 6

*D*ad and Grandpa's joint refusal to discuss the bombshell retirement announcement on the ride home from the fairgrounds hadn't sat well with any of the brothers. Toby corralled his impatience and the urge to share his opinion as he strode into the kitchen to take his place at the supper table. The fragrant aroma of fried chicken mingled with cake and fresh-baked rolls soothed him. As the oldest, he had to set the example. Grandpa wanted to tell his news his own way and in his own time. Orville had stolen his right to do that. Dad didn't want Grandpa to have to repeat himself.

A family meeting was in order.

All that made sense. Besides, they would adjust. Grandpa wasn't leaving Lee's Gulch. He wasn't dying. He'd still be there when Toby and the others came home from the road. He'd still be the family's cornerstone for many years to come. If God so willed it.

Gott, let it be so, sei so gut.

Jason and his wife, Caitlin, arrived just in time with their three little ones. With everyone laughing and talking at once, they squeezed more chairs up to the table. Mom dragged out two more high chairs and finally the entire Miller family sat down to eat.

As soon as they finished praying, Grandpa plucked a

drumstick-thigh combo from the platter and stuck it on his plate. He picked up his fork, studied the chicken, then let his gaze take in his big family. "I'm leaving the business in gut hands. Your daed has worked with me since he was a little *bu*. You follow his lead, you can't go wrong."

Toby glanced down the table at his father. Dad shoveled a forkful of pickled beets into his mouth. If he had concerns, it didn't show. For a man who worked best with his brawn and his hands, he seemed at ease with his new role.

"Toby, you'll be second in charge. You're the oldest suh. You have the most experience. You know the business inside out."

Maybe Grandpa didn't want to undermine Dad's authority. But it wasn't like him to mince words or to worry about a man saving face. "Understood."

Paying bills, ordering equipment, making sure they were paid promptly for their services, booking auctions, taking care of travel arrangements, working with the English man who maintained their website—these were tasks that Dad would have to handle or hand off to Toby. A laundry list of tasks that had to be overseen meticulously to make sure the business ran smoothly. Englishers might think of Plain people as living simple, rural lives, but the truth was, many were good businessmen who thrived within the confines of their beliefs.

Despite his age—or because of it—Grandpa was a sage entrepreneur who carefully incorporated practices that allowed the auctioneering company to grow and expand without violating the district's Ordnung. His would be big shoes to fill.

Toby sipped his water and cleared his throat. "It just came as such a surprise when Orville announced it to the world like that."

"We planned to do it this week. I only told Orville because he was bugging me to schedule an auction in May. He had a right to know I wouldn't be in charge. Then he jumped the gun on us." Grandpa shrugged. "I don't have to do things on your timeline. I'll tell you when I'm good and ready."

The rebuke stung, but he was right. Grandpa was the elder. He didn't answer to his grandsons for anything.

"We'll be fine." Dad snagged a roll from the basket as Declan passed it to Emmett seated on Dad's other side. "It takes all of us to run the business. We each bring our strengths to the job. One person leaving won't bring the company down."

Toby's head knew all of this. His heart wasn't so easily convinced. "I know it's not my business, but can I ask why now?"

"My arthritis is getting worse." Grandpa dropped a chicken bone on his plate. He wiped his mouth and hands on a napkin. "All the hours on the road, sleeping in strange beds in motels, eating diner food—my old body can't take it anymore. My knees hurt, my back hurts, my shoulders hurt morning, noon, and night. It's time."

He'd never once complained.

"You deserve the rest, but I reckon you won't know what to do with yourself." Toby pumped the words full of understanding. His younger brothers would follow his lead. "You've done nothing but work your entire life."

"He's planning to sit in his hickory rocker on the porch next to me, drinking *kaffi,* eating *eppies,* and watching the world go by. When he gets tired of that, he'll do chores on the farm." Grandma Joanna never talked much, but when she did, folks tended to listen. "There's plenty of work to be done close to home."

"I'll keep busy." His tone gruff, Grandpa nudged Grandma with his elbow. His version of affection, no doubt. They would never show outright affection around others, but a person often had the sense they were holding hands like a young couple. "We're moving into the *dawdy haus* at Avery's."

The clamor came immediately. "Why not here?" Declan asked. "We want you here."

"Jah, why not with us?" Josie chimed in. "We like having you here."

"You've been in business with us all this time." Emmett sounded particularly peeved. "Onkel Avery never wanted anything to do with it."

Ignoring the hubbub, Grandpa dumped more mashed potatoes on his plate. Grandma added gravy and a piece of corn on the cob to his plate without asking. Grandpa had no problem with his appetite. When the noise died down, he continued. "We've spent most every day together for most of your kinner's life. It's Avery and his kinner's turn."

The decision was made. Rehashing it would do no one any good. "Dat could shadow you next week to make sure he knows everything about the administrative side of the business." Toby brushed away the wistful feeling that a season in their lives had ended and would now be the well from which they drew stories told around the fireplace at night or on the road to yet another auction. "Maybe I could tag along as the backup in case Dat is busy with other tasks. We don't want any bills falling through the cracks or have scheduling mix-ups. When will your last day be?"

"I've been working alongside your daadi my whole life." Dad threw his napkin on the table and sat back in his chair. "I don't need to shadow him, and I don't need you tagging along."

It sounded like hurt pride talking. That wasn't like Dad. Maybe this change was harder than he wanted to let on. Toby held up his hand, palm up. "Of course not, but I might need a briefing. I'm not as familiar as you are."

Toby knew more about the technology side of the business but not the bookkeeping and scheduling. It wasn't a lie.

"That's a gut idea. It never hurts to have backup." Grandpa's tone was brisk, his gaze sharp. "Your groossmammi and I are planning a trip to Bird-in-Hand to visit your great-onkels and *aentis* in two weeks. So two weeks."

Two weeks' notice. Just like in the real world. This *was* the real world.

"Now that we have all the business squared away, can we get down to celebrating?" Mom started the fried chicken platter around the table again. "Eat up. There's plenty more food. We'll celebrate your daadi's retirement when the time comes, but today is Toby's day."

"I'm too old for birthday celebrations, but danki, Mamm." Toby winked at her. She loved celebrating her children's special days more than any Plain person he'd ever met. The days her babies came into the world still gave her great joy. "Your cooking hit the spot, as always."

"I'm glad you like it, and you're never too old to celebrate a birthday." Mom's cheeks turned rosy. She wasn't one for compliments. "Leave room for German chocolate cake and chocolate ice cream."

Also his favorites. Toby patted his flat stomach. "I always have room for cake."

"And presents." Sadie, who'd been dropping bits of chicken on the floor for Matilda the cat when she thought no one would notice, piped up. "Me and Sherri make you present."

She dropped her fork, shoved back her chair, and darted across the kitchen to the prep table. A stack of presents wrapped in brown paper sat next to the cake.

"Hurry, hurry." Sherri, another blonde-haired, blue-eyed mini-Mom, raced to join her. Together they carried the presents to the table where they crowded Toby, one on each side. "We worked on ours together."

Beaming at their unbridled enthusiasm, Toby obliged. The package contained two towels. The girls—most likely Sherri—had embroidered AUCTION DAY SWEAT RAG on them. The letters staggered slightly. Some were bigger than others. The colors were bright-red and blue. "Very nice. Danki. These are too nice to use."

"I hemmed them." Sadie held up the towel to show off her long but even stitches. "You have to use them. You get stinky. Sweaty."

"I can attest to that." Holding his nose, Emmett grimaced. "Pee-ew."

Toby's other siblings hooted and hollered in agreement. Ignoring them, he side-arm hugged both girls at the same time. "This is a very useful gift. Danki, *maed*."

A new straw hat, a fresh, updated *Rand McNally Road Atlas*, a travel mug, an insulated lunch box, a new duffel bag—each practical gift intended to make his job a little easier.

"You all are too generous, but I sure appreciate how much thought went into these presents." Toby tried on the hat. It fit perfectly and put the old sweat-stained, soiled one to shame. "I'm set for another auction season."

"We've got one more present." Mom took a last bite of cake, patted her lips with a napkin, and laid it aside. "Everybody, get your coats on. We have to go outside to see it."

More laughing and talking. Everyone scooted back their chairs and went to get their jackets. Like they all knew what was going on.

"What are you all up to now?"

"Get up, Bruder, get up." Sadie grabbed his arm. Sherri grabbed the other. Giggling, they tugged hard. "You have to see."

"Jah, quickly before they burst." Shaking her head, Layla laughed. She'd fetched the girls' jackets as well as Toby's. She held it out. "Put this on and get moving. For those two maed to keep a secret this long is a small miracle."

Toby obliged. The girls held on tight to his hands as they skipped alongside him to keep up with his long stride.

"Close your eyes, close your eyes." The girls halted at the front door. "No peeking."

"I'm not sure I trust you to guide me down the steps." Toby pretended to dig in his heels. "What if I fall down?"

"I catch you." Sadie's round face grew serious. "You no get hurt, Bruder."

"Wunderbarr."

With a little trepidation, Toby allowed them to guide him out the door, across the porch, and down the steps.

Around him his brothers and sisters whispered and giggled. Mom shushed someone. Grandpa's guffaw was louder than the rest. Grandma shushed him too.

"Now, now." Sadie patted his arm. "Look now."

Toby opened his eyes. A new charcoal-gray-topped buggy was parked on the gravel driveway. Someone had hitched his horse Almond—so named for his color—to the buggy. "That's a very nice buggy. Whose is it?"

"Yours, silly!" Josie clapped. "Everyone chipped in—Grandpa, all the onkels and aentis, all us brieder and schwesdchdre—"

"He gets the idea." Dad put his hand on her shoulder. "You've been driving my old hand-me-down buggy since you were sixteen. We figured it was time for an upgrade."

Buggies were expensive. Not like an automobile, but still. Plain boys received used buggies and their own horses for courting when they turned sixteen. Toby had been fortunate. His dad took good care of his property. The buggy was coming up on forty years old. The brakes and lighting had been reworked. The upholstery replaced a few times. But it had held together well.

"It's too much." Toby smoothed his hand across Almond's

withers. The horse arched his long neck and whinnied. "See, even Almond is overwhelmed. My old buggy was fine."

"Emmett will get your buggy." Looking mighty pleased with himself, Dad crossed his arms over his thick chest. Emmett whooped and everyone laughed. "This one's a rebuilt, so it's not brand-new. But it's much newer than the one you've been driving."

"Take a gander at the inside." Her face glowing, Mom threw her arm out in an elaborate flourish. "You won't believe the nice evergreen upholstery and carpet. It has two cupholders. It has a nice space for carrying groceries and other goods. There's storage under the seat for lap blankets. There's a battery-operated heater and a small fan. It even has a speedometer." She nearly bowed in her excitement. "Every man needs a nice buggy. For courting and for his family. This one has plenty of room."

There it was. Mom had mounted this campaign, as surely as Toby was one year short of three decades on this earth. Dad wouldn't do anything he didn't really want to do, but Mom had a way of making him think ideas were his. She wanted Toby to find a good wife. Plain women weren't prone to being impressed by buggies, but from a practical perspective, they appreciated starting out married life with a solid ride. "I hear you loud and clear, Mamm."

"Do you?" A self-satisfied smirk on her face, she glanced around. Dad and the others were drifting toward the house for more cake and ice cream. She nudged Toby in the ribs with her elbow. "I heard you had a run-in with Rachelle Lapp this afternoon."

Toby rubbed his ribs. "How did you hear about that?"

"She stopped by the booth and bought pies. You should've seen her red cheeks when I mentioned your name."

"They were red because she was mad at me for calling her brieder up on the stage."

"She told Layla to tell you happy birthday and no hard feelings."

"You told her it was my birthday?" In all likelihood, Toby's face was a deeper shade of red.

"So take it for a spin, Suh." She elbowed Layla. "You go with him. Keep him company."

Layla's face lit up. "Are you sure? We still have the kitchen to clean up."

"The maed will do it. And then they'll take their baths and go to bed. Church tomorrow." Mom made shooing motions. "Go. It's a beautiful evening for a ride."

For a couple, not necessarily for a brother and a sister. Toby stifled a chuckle. "Let's go, Schweschder. She'll only be happy if she gets her way. We all know that."

The laughter spilled out to the yard and spread through the crisp evening air. A birthday to remember indeed.

Chapter 7

*A*fter the excitement at the fairgrounds earlier, Rachelle didn't
have much oomph left for the parents' committee meeting.
She washed her hands and face with cold water, then scrubbed
with a towel to wake up. The parents' committee meetings, which
included the teachers, were usually held at the schoolhouse in late
afternoon so the teachers still had time to get home for supper, do
lesson planning, and get a good night's sleep. Dad's unwillingness
to share the meeting's purpose and Mom's insistence that she skip
cleanup only added to Rachelle's misgivings.

The hair prickled on her arms. Noah Eash was a school director,
along with her father and two other fathers. They'd been appointed
to manage the school—including hiring teachers as well as making
policies, maintaining the school, and taking care of finances.

Had a parent taken a concern to them about Rachelle or her fellow teacher, Corrine's, teaching? Their students loved them. Sure,
some days they couldn't overcome their wiggle worms. Some days
one or two were overly rowdy or cranky. But all children had good
and bad days. Rachelle and Corrine never let them get out of control. Nor did they ever have to raise their voices. What could they
have done to prompt a Saturday-night meeting?

Patience. Self-Control. Gentleness. Kindness. Faithfulness. Love. Goodness. Peace. Joy. She silently recited the fruit of the Spirit that guided her days as a teacher. The first two were the hardest, so she always put them first. If she managed the first seven, the last two came all on their own.

Rachelle straightened her prayer cap, repinned it, squared her shoulders, and trudged down the stairs to the living room. Her feet weighed ten pounds apiece. As she approached, she swept the room with a glance to get the lay of the land. Dad sat in the easy chair closest to the dark fireplace. Years of tending to horses' feet had given him broad, powerful shoulders, enormous biceps, and calloused hands. Noah sat in the glider rocker for which Mom had made pillows in a dark green that matched the curtains.

The other two directors had taken straight-backed chairs, leaving the sofa for Corrine and Rachelle. Corrine shot Rachelle a bewildered look. Rachelle shot it right back. *I don't know. Your guess is as good as mine.* Sixteen years of friendship made telegraphing messages easy. *Hang in there.*

You too.

"Evening, Rachelle." Noah sat up straighter, his expression all business. "I was just telling Corrine we'll make this short."

Rachelle stole a peek at her father. He'd sat up straighter too, but he reached for an oversized mug of coffee on the end table. Whatever was on their minds, Dad wasn't letting on.

He waved at the couch. "Have a seat. We have some school business to discuss."

Rachelle eased onto the couch close enough to her fellow teacher to smell her scent of cinnamon and vanilla—apple pie or cookies for supper? Rachelle clasped her hands in her lap. Her fingers were icy.

"The committee has decided to make a change in the special

kinner's schooling." With a glance at the other fathers, Noah eased forward in the chair and planted his hands on his knees. His tone turned gentle. "We wanted you to hear about it before we announce it to the rest of the *Gmay* after church tomorrow. Word has already started to get around, as often happens when something so important has been discussed as much as this change has."

Rachelle nodded. So did Corrine. What else could they do? Why did Dad's dark eyes, so like her own, fill up with empathy? It wasn't like him. He did what needed to be done and expected his children to respect his wishes and follow his lead. No matter how old they were.

"We've been approached by the Knowles County Consolidated School District, asking if we would be interested in sending our kinner with developmental and intellectual disabilities—as they like to call them—to their two elementary schools on the northside of town. They're feeding their special kinner from the other two schools into them. They've invited the other two Gmays in this area to join as well. They say combining resources will allow everyone to offer better classroom instruction and support services for all the kinner, not just theirs. They've chosen their most experienced teachers to head the program."

A plume of nausea arose from the pit of Rachelle's stomach. It curled its way up into her throat. She swallowed hard and opened her mouth. Noah raised his hand as if to say, *Don't interrupt.* "We all know how hard you two have worked together for the last three years. We have no complaints. The kinner love you. But the fact is, KCCSD can offer them so much more while saving our Gmay a substantial sum of money."

"Because the public schools are tax supported, we won't have to pay tuition." Dad ran his hand through his thick hair, still black with only a few strands of silver. He looked pleased at the thought.

As well he should, given he had fourteen children to feed, clothe, and educate. "We've always paid school taxes, and now we'll get some services in return."

Less money and more services—who could argue with that? It couldn't be allowed to matter how much she loved teaching these children. It couldn't be allowed to matter that teaching filled her heart in a way that no other activity ever had—ever could. Rachelle wrangled her objections to the ground, along with a sudden swell of tears that put her to shame. "So the decision has been made?"

A strangled cough to her right said Corrine fought a similar battle. Rachelle slid her hand across the couch's worn upholstery until her fingers met Corrine's and curled around them.

"Jah, it has." The apology written across Dad's sun-aged face only made it harder to stifle tears. "The directors met twice about it. We prayed about it and met again. Then we spoke with Bart, Martin, and Jed about it. They were in agreement."

If the bishop, deacon, and minister agreed, no one else would raise a voice in opposition.

"We know this puts you in a hard position." Eli Hostetler spoke for the first time. His three children were among the school's regular scholars. "We'll have twenty-five students next year. If we send these hard-learners to the Englisch school, we won't need two tiet-schere. We can save an entire salary. You both know how tight money is."

"Even without the special kinner, having two teachers is important when you have the age range we'll have. We can divide up the subjects by age group." Despite her intention not to argue with a decision that made sense, Rachelle couldn't let this point go unmade. "It also helps if one of the tietschere can't be there because of sickness. And if there are discipline problems."

Neither happened often. But they could.

"At least two of the kinner will be old enough to work with the younger ones. We have fraas who taught before they married who can fill in when the teacher is absent." Dad's expression remained kind, but his tone was firm. "Think of how Jonah will benefit from the Englisch school's specialists. His speech. His reading. His writing. He's struggled with English from the get-go."

Learning a second language when they hadn't mastered the first one was a challenge for all of the children with developmental delays. The children with Down syndrome understood so much more than they could speak, but weak muscle tone made it hard for them to be understood sometimes. Jonah's difficulties were in learning and remembering the vocabulary. His Pennsylvania Dutch wasn't bad, but his command of English was much more limited.

That didn't even begin to address High German. His sleepy eyes during church services were a dead giveaway that he didn't understand the parts delivered in German.

"He won't understand what they're telling him. He's so shy. He'll be scared." Rachelle studied the braided rug on the floor at her feet. She might not fight the decision for her own selfish reasons, but she had to stand up for her little brother. Had Dad thought of this? Surely he had. "Jonah doesn't do well with strangers."

"They won't be strangers for long. It'll be gut for him to spend more time with outsiders. It'll give him more confidence." Dad sounded so sure of this. Maybe he wanted to believe it. Or needed to believe it. He didn't have a choice either. "I know how much you enjoy teaching, but we must consider the greater good for the whole community."

"How will you decide which one of us remains as the tiet-schern?" Corrine's usual boisterous tone had completely disappeared, replaced with barely a whisper. "Like you said, we've been team teaching for three years. We both have experience. We both love our jobs."

"That decision doesn't have to be made right away." Eli jumped in again. "School's out at the end of April, so there's no sense in uprooting the kinner now. The new consolidated program will open at Eisenhower and Reagan Elementaries in the fall. A lot can happen between now and then. Especially for young maed your age."

Rachelle locked gazes with Corrine. Her eyebrows raised, her friend shook her head slightly. Rachelle stifled the urge to groan and roll her eyes. The men were banking on Corrine or Rachelle marrying before the fall—or at least reaching that point in courting where they knew teaching would soon become a thing of the past. Men being the way they were, these fathers likely had no clue where Rachelle and Corrine stood on the long, wide courting road.

Corrine had a beau. They'd been together two years.

How could this be the best way to determine who taught the children? It wasn't.

Rachelle and Corrine were best friends. They would never let this situation come between them. If Corrine didn't marry before September, Rachelle would step aside.

She would have plenty of time to find another position. Not teaching wasn't an option. Not just because of the money— although her salary went a long way toward helping her parents feed and clothe her thirteen siblings—but because nothing gave her more pleasure or sense of purpose. The other nearby districts might have openings—again, if one of the teachers married or moved away. Or she might have to consider a post farther away—away from her family and friends.

If necessary. Teaching was necessary. Not doing it, unthinkable. Teaching was more than a job. It was a vocation. A calling. Was it grandiose or prideful to think of it this way? Maybe this development was a lesson to be learned.

Gott, Thy will be done. So easy to say, so hard to do.

Rachelle's throat tightened. She took a long breath and held it—willing the tears into submission.

"Maybe the Englischers will need another tietschern or assistant at their school." She searched for a ray of hope in their situations. "That's a lot of new students."

"I inquired about that." Noah's gaze ping-ponged between Rachelle and Corrine. "Their tietschere must have college degrees. Two of them have training in special education and something they call *inclusion*. The assistants have high school diplomas and a certain number of college credits in education."

"Don't worry. You'll find another position." Wincing, Dad pinched the bridge of his nose. When had those lines etched so deeply around his mouth and eyes? He took after Grandpa Karl more and more every day. "Or maybe Gott's plan involves something different down the road."

The note of forced jocularity said Dad knew how this change hurt his daughter, but he had other hopes for her future. Dad would like for his oldest daughter to marry, settle down, and have children. Every Plain father wanted that for his daughters. So did Rachelle. Eventually. But if the right man didn't come along, she would be content to teach—more than content.

She let out her breath and scraped up optimism for Dad's benefit. *Patience. Self-Control. Gentleness. Kindness. Faithfulness. Love. Goodness. Peace. Joy.* "His will be done."

She strove every day to bend to God's will. Did it get any easier? What would Dad say if she voiced that question aloud? The Plain faith required them to die to self, to be obedient and humble, and to always put faith, family, and community ahead of their own desires. In this case, the children's well-being trumped her love of teaching them.

A hard truth. A bitter taste on her tongue. *Thy will be done, Gott.*

Noah stood and stretched. He cocked his head toward the other fathers. "We'd better hightail it home. Church comes early in the morning. Corrine, you'd better come along. You can follow me as far as Route 31."

In other words, the turnoff to the one-lane paved road that would take her to the entrance to her parents' farm. Corrine sent a beseeching glance Rachelle's way. Rachelle responded with an encouraging nod. "We'll talk tomorrow after church."

Corrine gathered up her crocheted shawl and stood. "Tomorrow then."

"Tomorrow." Suddenly that word was filled with much more uncertainty than before.

Dad walked them to the door, said good night, and returned to pick up his mug from the end table. "I need more kaffi. I might need another piece of pie too."

With that he started toward the kitchen.

Rachelle stared at his receding figure. His hair and beard needed trimming. "Dat? When will we tell Jonah?"

He slowed, stopped, and turned. Tired circles darkened underneath his eyes. "No point in bringing it up until late summer. He won't really understand or even remember. There will be plenty of time in August."

Plenty of time to prepare him for change. Jonah liked the same peanut butter and honey sandwich, Cheetos, apple, and Mom's homemade oatmeal-raisin cookies in his lunch box each day. He sat in the same place at the supper table every night. He couldn't settle down to sleep at night until Rachelle read at least one story, preferably two, to him and the younger children. Getting him to wear a new pair of boots was almost impossible. Same with straw hats.

No, he wouldn't like it at all. Neither would Rachelle. But the parents' committee was right. The children came first. This was best for them. *Gott, whatever is best for the kinner is best for me.* "Jah, plenty of time."

Chapter 8

*J*onah wasn't the only one who embraced the security of routine. In the tail end of a long day, a story and bedtime prayers were just the medicine to ease the anxious ache where Rachelle's heart should be.

She trotted up the stairs and scurried down the hallway past the girls' bedroom to the boys' room. Giggles escaped through both open doors. The children might be in bed, but they weren't asleep. Kimmie handled bedtime stories for the four younger girls. Rachelle had the four boys.

In their room, Jonah sat up in his bunk bed, his back pressed against a pillow, Runt sprawled across his legs. Instead of occupying their own full bed, Sam and Sean shared the foot of the bunk. Michael lay on the floor, playing with his wooden farm animals. Rachelle did a hop, skip, and a jump to avoid stepping on a calf lying with its tiny wooden legs straight up.

"*Ach* you know better, Michael. Once the pajamas are on, the toys go in the bucket." Rachelle knelt and pushed the gray metal bucket in the five-year-old's direction. "If you want to hear a story, you'd better be quick about it. You need to get to bed. You don't want to fall asleep in church in the morning."

"The pigs are playing in the mud. They're squealing. They're keeping everyone awake." Despite this observation, Michael did as he was told. "I'll get them settled down. They want to hear the story too."

"Gut. And you know better too, Runt." Rachelle stood and pointed at the massive mixed-breed mutt, who wore his usual mischievous expression. It was like having another toddler to mind. "Mamm's permission for you to be in the house depends on your gut behavior. That doesn't include getting your ginormous dirty body on the bed."

One floppy ear turned out the wrong way to reveal its pink interior, Runt cocked his big head and let his hairy body roll over so his belly was exposed. Like *Pet me, pet me. You love me, you know you do.* Jonah pulled him into his lap. Both males showed no inclination to follow Rachelle's instructions—men being men. "Runt want hear story too."

"He can hear it from the rug."

"He old. Hearing no gut." Jonah patted the narrow space to his right. "Sit here. Story."

Runt whimpered, a woe-is-me sound so like a child's whining. He was about five years old—still young even by dog standards. He'd been born on an icy February morning in the Lapps' barn, the runt of a litter of six. Kimmie, who had been the one to find the puppies, had named him. Now his massive body was big enough for Darcy, who was two, to ride around the house like he was a miniature pony. "One story, then down he goes."

When Mom and Dad came by to make sure everyone was safely tucked in for the night, they would make sure Runt kept guard from the rug. Another piece of Jonah's beloved routine.

Rachelle went to the small shelf hung next to the clothes pegs and picked out one of the boys' favorite stories—the fictional retelling of Noah's adventure surviving the big flood. It had been read so many times, the pages were loose. It didn't matter. The children could recite it from memory and so could Rachelle.

She took her spot on the bed and opened to the first page. The illustrations hadn't lost their vibrant colors. "I just love Noah's tunic. Don't you? What color is it, Jonah?"

Her little brother rolled his eyes. "Blue, Tietschern."

Once a teacher, always a teacher. She dove in, assuming the voice of each animal that took turns telling the story. "'"What a silly man, that Noah," the giraffe opined in his high, squeaky voice.'"

"'"What was that? Speak up." The owl frowned behind wire-rimmed spectacles. He had a deep bass voice and hearing aids. "I can't hear you."'"

"'"Noah is crazy,"'" all four boys shouted the line. "'"A crazy, old man."'"

"'"Crazy like a fox." The fox spoke up from his vantage point on a high cliff overlooking the huge half-built boat. "It takes one to know one. The drought won't last forever."'"

"Fox is red." Jonah leaned his head against Rachelle's arm. Runt wiggled until his head lay on her lap. "Frog green."

"Right on both counts." Rachelle pointed at the lion. "What does the lion say?"

They all roared together. "'"Noah has a plan."'"

"'Who does the plan come from?'"

"'Gott!'"

"'Who else does Gott have a plan for?'"

The boys aimed their thumbs toward their chests. "'Us!'"

It took a long time to get through the story with all the voices and shouts, but Rachelle wouldn't have it any other way. They weren't listening to her read. They were reading with her, learning spiritual truths, learning their colors and their numbers, all in English. Everyday life was filled with teaching moments. She didn't even have to search for them. That wouldn't change come September. She might have different students. She might live in a different place. That kind of change was hard. Why couldn't she trust God's plan for her?

"Read." Jonah tugged on her sleeve. "Read, Schweschder."

"Sorry. 'How many animals did Noah take into the ark?'"

"'Two of each.'" Sean piped up. "'They came into the ark two by two.'"

"Gut job."

"Which animal is your favorite, Michael?"

No answer. Rachelle peered over the book. Michael had curled up on the rug, a cow and a pig still clutched in his hands. He was asleep. She put her index finger to her lips. The twins and Jonah did the same. She moved more quickly through the rest of the story, but by the time she'd finished, Sam and Sean were nodding off too.

Only Jonah remained wide-eyed. Rachelle closed the book. "Aren't you sleepy?"

"Story sad."

Rachelle slid her arm around his shoulders. "Why do you say that?"

"Only two. Others died."

"True. Do you know why Gott did that?"

"Naughty?"

"Jah, the people were naughty. Gott decided to start over."

Jonah pushed Runt from his legs. He rolled away from Rachelle, hopped from the bed, and went to one of the room's two large windows. Runt immediately followed. Rachelle closed the book and laid it in her lap. She stretched her arms over her head. "What are you doing?"

He lifted the dark-evergreen curtain and peered outside. "It no raining."

"Nee. Why?"

"Me and Michael, naughty."

"Ach, Jonah." Rachelle slipped from the bed, stepped over Michael, and joined Jonah and Runt at the window. "Not that kind of naughty. Anyway, don't you remember after the flood, Gott made a rainbow as the sign of a promise to Noah that he would never send a flood again?"

"How long never?"

"Very long. Forever."

Jonah opened the window. He stuck his head out and yelled, "Never. Forever."

Ignoring the icy air that whipped into the bedroom, Rachelle stuck her head out too. "What are you doing, little bruder?"

"Reminding Gott."

His expression was so serious, Rachelle buried the laugh that burbled up inside her. Jonah didn't hold back. He let God know what he wanted and needed. With the faith of a child.

Gott give me the faith of a child. Forgive my unbelief in Your plan and power. Guide me. Show me Your plan for me and for Jonah and the other kinner. Sei so gut. Aamen.

Knowing the plan was only half the battle. Being able to accept it would be harder. She didn't have to tell God that. He already knew.

Chapter 9

*S*he should go to bed. Church would come early in the morning. A dull ache at the base of Rachelle's skull said a headache threatened. Yet her mind continued to spin faster and faster, like a merry-go-round out of control. Any minute it would spin off its track and launch itself into outer space.

She closed the boys' door and stopped for a second outside the girls' room. No noise. Down for the night. As Rachelle should be. Instead she meandered down the stairs, grabbed her favorite heavy shawl, and went out the front door where she stood on the porch and inhaled the night-cooled air. Two dogwood trees' leaves rustled as if excited at her sudden arrival. How could her life change so suddenly? Happy and content one minute. Anxious and flailing the next.

"Why so antsy?"

Grandma Cara's voice—made gravelly by an accident that injured her throat as a young woman—wafted from the shadows. Rachelle turned and peered toward the porch swing. It dwarfed Grandma's tiny frame wrapped in a thick quilt. In her bare feet soaking wet, she might weigh a hundred pounds. At five-two she was shorter than most of her children and many of her grandchildren. Yet none would think of crossing her.

Rachelle padded over to the swing and sat. The chains squeaked under her weight. The swing began to move. "I'm sure Mamm already told you the news."

"She did."

"I feel like all the lights went out in the world and I'm trying to feel my way forward in total darkness."

Grandma pushed her child-size sneakers against the wooden slats of the porch floor. The swing swayed gently. "Some people would call that an adventure."

"Others would call it a panic attack." Rachelle forced a half-hearted chuckle. "I know I'm supposed to rely on my faith and Gott's plan for me. I just told the buwe the story of Noah and the ark. I understand the lesson. And I do trust Gott. I just—"

"You're just human." Grandma's chuckle had more oomph to it. "Gott doesn't expect us to be perfect. He knows us too well."

"I'm not just worried for me and my job—that would be selfish—but for my kinner and how they'll adjust to such an enormous change."

But she was worried for her job. Teaching was like breathing. Without it who would she be? Teaching filled a place in her heart so well, she often wondered if she would be content without it.

It seemed as if she was about to find out.

"Anyone who knows you knows you're not a selfish person." Grandma tugged her sweater tighter around her shoulders. "You're a nurturer, and nurturers want to take care of everyone."

"Is that so wrong?"

"Nee, of course not. Your kinner need you to stand up for them."

A matter of perspective, no doubt. "Dat says that's what the parents are doing."

"Did I ever tell you that I attended public school as a little girl?"

It was hard to imagine Grandma, with her wrinkles upon

wrinkles, age-spotted hands, and parchment paper–thin skin that revealed a plethora of blue veins in her arms, as a little girl. "Nee."

"It was before our Plain districts started their own schools." Her expression blank, she brushed strands of iron-gray hair from her forehead. "Me and my schwesdchdre had to get on a bus every day and ride into town back in Pennsylvania. It smelled like gas fumes, and a radio with tinny speakers played too loud. The kinner yelled and bickered."

"How long did it take to get to the school?"

"More than an hour. Sometimes the smells made me feel sick." Her knobby-knuckled fingers plucked at the loose stitches in her shawl. "Then the district decided to build its own school. Plain districts all across the country were doing it. Plain parents wanted more control over what their kinner were learning. They didn't like the science especially."

"I'm surprised they allowed it from the beginning." If Rachelle had taught Darwin's theory of evolution, she'd have been out of a job a long time ago. "Not to mention the biology of the birds and the bees."

"They didn't have a choice for a long time. It's not easy to start your own school. Each district had to figure out how to fund and run it. That's not so easy. No one wanted the kinner to be lacking in basic education, but we didn't agree with the Englisch on what that should be. The parents wanted Scripture and hymns to begin the day. They wanted German to be taught. They wanted limited science and no sex education."

Some women would've had trouble saying those last two words aloud—not Grandma Cara. She picked up an oversized mug from the chest that served as an outdoor table and took a sip of its steaming contents. Knowing Grandma, it was likely her drink of choice: apple-cinnamon-spice tea. "I was just a *maedel*. I don't understand any of that. But I was so happy when our school opened."

"How was it different for you and the other kinner?"

"Me and my schwesdchdre jumped in a pony cart and drove two miles to the school." A smile created wrinkles atop her wrinkles. "The air was fresh. The sun shone on us. We could smell the flowers and see the trees. Once we got to school, we were in a small classroom with our friends. It was gut."

"That's wunderbarr, but did you get the same quality of education? That seems to be what's weighing the most with the parents' committee." As much as they insisted Rachelle's teaching lacked for nothing, the decision still felt like an implied criticism. "They want to do right by our special kinner."

"We learned what we needed to know. Do you think you teach the kinner everything they need to know?"

Be honest. Be fair. "These kinner are different. It's harder for them to learn." Rachelle groped for words to explain her predicament. "What they get from me is more than book learning. It's what the Englisch would call social and life skills. What to do when they're mad or upset, how to wait their turn, and how to share, but the Englisch specialists can do so much more."

"In my day, we were mostly concerned with our kinner learning reading, writing, arithmetic, English, and German." Grandma set her mug aside. "Are you teaching Sadie and Jonah and the others these subjects?"

"Jah, as much as they are able."

"Is their English improving? How's their German?"

Her questions felt like a job interview. Which might be a good thing. Rachelle needed the practice. "Jah, as much as they are able."

"I reckon that's all they need. They'll learn trades after they're done with their book learning, just like the other kinner. They'll be able to contribute to the community, each in their own way. That's what we hold most important, isn't it?"

"So you think the parents' committee is wrong?"

"It's not my place to argue with the committee."

"Is it mine?"

"That's a question you'll have to answer, not me."

"It's prideful to suggest I can do better than the Englisch specialists." Rachelle had experience teaching these particular students. Jonah was her brother. She understood their Plain background and lives. She loved them and they loved her. That should count for something—for a lot. "As a tietschern, I can see the value of speech therapy, physical therapy, and occupational therapy for the kinner. I don't have these specialists' education or expertise."

"But you know these kinner in a way the Englisch specialists never will."

"I wish you could say all this to Dat and the others."

"You have to speak for yourself. Offer your opinion, listen to their opinions, be part of the discussion, and then accept the committee's decision."

To do what Grandma suggested involved getting the committee to treat her like an adult and not a young woman. It wouldn't be easy, especially with Dad on the committee. "I can't disagree with Dat in front of the others."

"He's your dat. You see him all the time. Have a talk with him outside, just the two of you."

Rachelle scooched closer to her grandmother and took her hand. Her fingers were cold. The buzzsaw of crickets and croaking of frogs at their nearby pond offered her a comforting lullaby. Grandma's silence soothed her. Some things didn't change, her being one of them. Grandma squeezed Rachelle's hand. Rachelle squeezed back.

Change was coming, but they still had tonight.

Chapter 10

*T*he birthday buggy ride was far too much fun for serious conversation. Layla gave herself time to enjoy the novelty. She flipped a switch on the sleek wooden console. "Look, Toby, the turn signal." She flipped another switch. "Brights. And here is the switch for the hazards. Isn't the warm air from the heater nice?"

A good heater was just the thing for a buggy ride on a cold March night.

"Jah, jah, Schweschder. It's all wunderbarr." Laughing, Toby maneuvered onto the winding road that took them up and down the rolling foothills of the Blue Ridge Mountains. "Mamm even thought of the air fresheners. Those little pine trees smell gut."

"And look, you even have a glove compartment." Layla popped up the small door. "You can keep breath mints in here next to the flashlight."

Not a particularly subtle segue into the real topic of the day. Mom intended this to be a courting buggy. Would Toby jump on the bandwagon, so to speak?

"It's nice that the wheels don't squeak like the old one."

So he insisted on being dense. Toby was such a guy. Another tactic was needed. Layla tugged the quilt from under the seat Mom had stored there and tucked it around her legs. The task gave her time to think.

She let the silence lengthen for a few miles. The night was beautiful. Perfect for courting. Chickadees, robins, and tanagers chattered from their perches on the crepe myrtle, silver bell, dark-burgundy Japanese maples, and southern live oak trees. In time the crepe myrtles' flowers would burst open and this drive would be even more beautiful. As dusk deepened into night, an earthy aroma of wet leaves and mud floated in the air. It smelled like her mother after an afternoon working in the garden—serene, comfortable, at peace.

A wave of longing swept over Layla. Riding with Toby was nice, but a jaunt with a boyfriend would be so much more special. *Focus on Toby. This is about Toby.*

"So aside from Daadi's decision to retire, how was your birthday?" *Lame, Layla, so lame.* "How did the auction go?"

"It was gut. People came with their wallets. Orville was happy."

"So nothing out of the ordinary happened?"

Toby shot her an amused look. He could roll his eyes with the best of his teenage siblings. "Whatever you want to know, spit it out, Schweschder."

"I heard you had company on the platform for a bit."

"Stop trying to look so innocent. I know you and Mamm talked about me to Rachelle." His face reddened. "Meddling where you shouldn't've been."

"Mamm means well."

"And so do you, I suppose."

"You're not getting any younger."

"Rachelle is a nice *young* woman." Toby put the emphasis on young as if it were a huge stumbling block. "In a way, we're kind of alike."

Maybe this conversation was heading in the right direction after all. Layla sat up straighter. "She is nice and she's a hard worker. She has tons of experience taking care of kinner—not just the special ones at school but all those younger ones at home."

"Jah, she loves her job. Like I do."

Layla's optimism tripped and fell. "What makes you say that? Most tietschere only work until they get married."

"I say that because I've seen how she acts at the school picnics and even after church. She's always talking to her kinner, laughing with them, and playing with them."

"You *say* that like it's a bad thing. She's a gut tietschern. Her kinner need lots of attention. And it's great practice for when she becomes a mudder."

"It's different. She doesn't pay attention to anyone else. It's like they're her world."

Like a man couldn't compete with her love for her job. Like Toby and his job. Layla dug her heels in against the buggy's fiberglass floor. "For now, jah, but all that would change in a heartbeat if the right man came along."

"Once again you sound like Mamm." Toby snorted and snapped the reins. Almond picked up his pace. The horse's whinny carried in the dusky night. "You don't even know Rachelle well enough to offer an opinion on the subject."

"All Plain women want to marry."

Like all Plain men. The unspoken words lingered in the air. The *clip-clop* of Almond's hooves kept time with the rustling branches that dipped and swayed from the trees that lined the dirt road.

"What about you?" Toby's chin jutted. He shot the question at Layla like a carefully aimed arrow. "Why all this talk about me? I'm past my prime. You're not. Why isn't Mamm after you to marry?"

"Ach, she is, believe me." Layla squirmed. She loosened the

quilt over her legs. Her face grew warm. Even her ears were hot. "She's been talking to Ryan's mudder."

"Ach."

One syllable encompassed a bushel basket of empathy. Toby had been friends with Ryan's older brother Andrew since grade school. When Toby heard about the way Ryan had treated his little sister, he hadn't been happy. Unlike in the English world, Plain big brothers weren't allowed to speak their minds (or worse) when a guy hurt their sisters' feelings. No doubt he'd offered his opinion to Andrew, but even Andrew couldn't say much to Ryan. Such was the Plain world of courting.

A lump grew in Layla's throat. No, no. She was past this. She would not cry over a man so obviously not worth her tears. "Jah, ach."

"Why should I be in a hurry to experience the pangs of love when it so obviously hurts?" Toby's voice turned gruff. He cleared his throat. "I'm sorry, Schweschder."

"Don't be. I'm better off." Layla forced a chuckle. If only Toby would open up to her. But then he'd have to admit he, too, had experienced a love that hurt. Layla couldn't say anything. If she did, he'd know she'd overheard his conversations with Jason all those years ago.

"Little pitchers have big ears," that's what Mom would say. "Mamm's already picked out someone else for me."

"You are so blessed. Welcome to the club." Toby snorted. Almond's ears perked up. He neighed. Toby laughed again. "Even Almond knows you can run but you can't hide from Mamm's best intentions. You'd think she'd be busy enough raising kinner, keeping house, and running the combination store."

"You'd think. The thing is, I haven't missed courting since the whole mess with Ryan. I enjoy running the store." Mom and the girls made the baked goods, the jams, and the jellies. They planted and picked the produce. Layla took care of the business end. Buying supplies, doing the bookkeeping, keeping inventory, making sure there was change in the cash register, depositing the cash. Manning the cash register on the days she worked in the store. She liked it. "The right man will come into my life when Gott sends him my way."

"You're the brains about the business. You're gut at it." Toby rubbed his forehead as if it hurt. He sighed. "You got that from Daadi."

"It's not the business part that's really worrying you, is it?"

"It's part of it."

"You just realized Daadi won't be around forever." The realization had struck Layla like a wild pitch at home plate too. "I've never thought of him as being old. I reckon you haven't either."

"He's in every memory I have of growing up." Toby's broad shoulders hunched. "I keep telling myself he's retiring, not dying, but it won't be the same, not seeing him every day. He didn't just teach me how to auctioneer. He showed me how to find the North Star in the sky outside every motel we ever stayed in. He taught me to eat Louisiana hot sauce on my hash browns.

"He taught all of us every folk song known to man when we were driving cross-country." His expression pensive, Toby ducked his head as if he didn't want her to see his emotion. There was no need to see it. His sadness was evident in every syllable he spoke. "He taught me to tie my shoes, whistle, and blow bubbles with my bubble gum."

"Kinner couldn't ask for a better daadi." Layla didn't remind Toby that she and the other girls didn't have those same memories of Grandpa. Still, she understood. The girls had Grandma to teach them to bake friendship bread, embroider hand towels, plant flowers, and can bread-and-butter pickles. Grandma Joanna also played botch with them, hopscotch, and jump rope. No one was better at checkers or Connect 4. "We're all blessed. But it's like you said, they're not dying. They'll be down the road at Onkel Avery's."

It wouldn't be the same. Instead of drawing closer, they were moving farther away.

Layla carefully laid aside the bouquet of sweet memories. A person shouldn't be sorry something so nice came to an end, but rather rejoice that it had happened. Time to look forward rather than back. "You seem worried about Dat handling the office duties."

"Worrying is a sin."

The pat answer everyone learned in church and in baptism lessons. Talking the talk. "Also human. What makes you think Dat will have problems being in charge?"

"I think Daadi and Mammi have always tried to ignore the fact that Dat has trouble reading."

"You think he can't read?" Layla picked through a different treasure chest of memories from over the years. Dad with his Bible in his lap, murmuring verses. Dad sitting in the rocking chair by the fireplace reading *The Budget* newspaper. Dad reading storybooks to them on frigid winter nights. "He reads all the time."

"He can read simple stuff, but it's painfully slow."

"He's very smart. Why would he have trouble reading?"

Toby shrugged. "Mamm says it's likely a reading disability they never admitted to."

"You talked to Mamm about it?"

"Jah, back when I wondered why he didn't take over some of those duties for Daadi as he got older." Toby winced. "I asked him why he didn't, and he flat out refused to talk about it. He said he didn't do bookwork. He told me to do my job and let Daadi do his."

"He was defensive."

"Very."

"I can see why. No grown man wants to admit to not being able to do something as basic as reading." Layla's heart hurt for her father. He was such a good man, fair, even-keeled, faithful, and kind. "To go through life struggling with it and not wanting folks to know must be so hard."

"Nowadays they have plenty of resources for reading disabilities. According to Mamm."

"But he won't consider it."

"Mamm has tried to talk to him about it. He won't even admit it, let alone consider it. He probably figures it's too late."

"It's not too late." A thought struck Layla like a fierce north wind. "And I know the perfect person to tutor him."

"Who?"

"Who teaches our special kinner with disabilities?" Mom would love it. She would see it as killing two birds with one stone—if she stooped to such a cockamamie saying. Mom loved birds. "Who is Plain, experienced, and has the true heart of a teacher?"

"Huh." Darkness obscured Toby's expression, but he colored that single syllable with a dawning understanding that saw the irony of her proposed double whammy. "Mamm certainly would think it's a gut idea. Dad might be more open to the idea if it's Rachelle. He's known her since she was an itty-bitty girl. He knows how much Sadie loves her. Maybe. It could work."

Layla let the idea ride to give him—and her—an opportunity to review all the scenarios in their heads. Dad angry because they'd shared his secret with someone outside the family. Dad thinking about it. Dad coming around to the idea. Dad reading to Rachelle in the light of a propane lamp.

"Huh." Toby strung out the single syllable as if trying it out on his tongue. "You'd have to ask her."

"What? Why me?" The idea was to bring Toby and Rachelle together. "You should ask her."

"I hardly know her." A curious note in Toby's voice was encouraging. He'd like to know her more. "You should ask her."

"I hardly know her either." Enough to know Rachelle had a heart for teaching. Surely it would extend to adults with similar problems. She loved teaching, period. "Let's play that by ear. You know they're talking about sending the special kinner to the Englisch school."

"Dat mentioned it."

"Which means Rachelle will be out of a job. Corrine teaches the other kinner. I'm sure they'll keep her on."

"Ah." Apparently he hadn't thought of that. "She could get a job elsewhere—other districts are always looking for tietschere when theirs get married."

That was true. Which would put a ginormous kink in Mom's plan. "Let's hope it doesn't come to that. And if it does, she'd have more time to tutor."

"That's cold, Schweschder." Toby scowled. "Teaching is her first love. I've seen her with the kinner when I drop off Sadie at school. It'll break her heart not to teach them . . . Someone's coming."

The churning of wheels and *clip-clop* of a horse's hooves signaled the approach of another buggy. A horse whinnied beyond the next sweeping curve in the road. Almond responded. Toby slowed the buggy. Most likely it would be a courting couple out for a Saturday night drive. Probably a couple they knew. They would pretend they hadn't seen them so they could maintain the necessary aura of secrecy until the deacon announced their banns at church one Sunday in the future.

"I wonder who it is," Layla murmured.

"I hope it's not one of our brieder out with their special friends."

"That would be awkward."

Layla strained to see the driver against the bright headlights. He drew closer. Not one of their brothers. Or any of her friends. Thank goodness. It would be awkward if they were courting. And, if a person was willing to admit it, salt in the wound. A brother and sister out for an evening buggy ride because neither had a special friend with whom to share such a drive.

The buggy driver was a man alone. He didn't have a special friend either. Nor was he familiar. Toby pulled on the reins and stopped. "*Hallo* there."

"Hallo to you!" The man drew his buggy even with theirs. He touched his straw hat's brim with one finger. "I'm new to these parts. I think I took a wrong turn."

Toby introduced Layla and himself. "Where're you headed?"

"I'm Micah Troyer. I just moved onto my *groossdaadi*'s property—Jeremiah Troyer's farm."

Layla sucked in air. Something went down the wrong pipe. She hiccupped and coughed. She couldn't stop.

"Are you all right, Schweschder?" Toby clapped her on the back. "There's a bottle of water in the cupholder."

Still coughing, Layla grabbed the bottle and twisted off the cap. A few swallows helped. Of all the back roads in Knowles County, Virginia, how did they end up on the same one as Micah Troyer?

Was it a sign? Or just coincidence? Dad didn't believe in coincidence. God had a plan, period, he always said.

"I didn't mean to shake you up." Micah's smile broadened. "I went into town for groceries and then stopped at the bishop's house for supper. I thought I knew where I was going, but the countryside is different in the dark."

"I knew your daadi. He used to come to the produce auctions all the time." All the strain of their earlier conversation had disappeared from Toby's voice. Of all Layla's siblings, he was the most social. He never met a stranger he didn't like. "You remember him, don't you, Layla?"

She did. He was a kindly man who used to stop at the baked-goods booth to buy two dozen cookies for his grandkids or a sweet potato–praline pie for his wife. After he had a stroke, they'd moved back to Lancaster County to live with his other son—presumably Micah's father. "He's such a nice man. He had quite the sweet tooth. He always said the eppies were for his *kinnskinner*, but then he'd wink and eat one himself."

"He did love sweets. He passed away a month ago." Micah's voice turned husky. "We're all missing him. My onkel Aiden has his hands full with his chicken farm here, so I've been sent to run Daadi's hog farm."

"I'm so sorry." Micah Troyer was living exactly what Layla and Toby feared—the loss of a beloved grandfather. Her throat ached at the thought. "That must be hard."

"He lived a gut, long, and faithful life." Micah twisted the reins around his hands. His words said one thing, but his wistful tone another. "His days were done. Gott is gut."

"Even so, it's human to miss our loved ones." Toby squeezed Layla's arm. He likely knew exactly what she was thinking. "Farming his property will be a big undertaking. We'd be happy to lend a hand."

"Danki." Micah touched the brim of his hat again, this time in farewell. "I've held you two up long enough. If you'll point me in the right direction, I'll get out of your way."

While Toby explained how to get to the Troyer property, Layla took the opportunity to study the newcomer. The headlights revealed he was a medium height, wiry man. His straw hat hid most of his hair. The color of his eyes remained to be seen. His hands, with the reins wrapped around them, were huge. He had a nice voice. It had a warmth to it, like heated maple syrup.

A man who loved his grandparents. A man trusted by his family to work his grandfather's farm. A hard worker. A lot to like.

Stop it. That's what happened when Layla's mother planted an idea in her head. It was simply the power of suggestion. This must be how Toby felt.

"It was nice meeting you. I'm sure we'll be seeing a lot of each other with our farms being so close and all."

"Count on it." Toby gathered up the reins in preparation for moving on. "Like I said, if you need any help, let us know."

"I will." Micah took off down the road.

Toby snapped the reins and got the buggy moving again. "He seems like a nice guy."

"Nice enough."

Toby laughed.

"What?"

"You. Trying to be cool when you were so obviously gaping at him."

"Was not."

"Was too."

Had she been that obvious? No way. Especially with the headlights hiding expressions. "I was only curious. Mamm mentioned that he had moved onto his family's property."

"So he's the one Mamm has chosen for you? She hasn't even met him yet."

"You know Mamm."

"Indeed I do. How does the saying go? Hope springs eternal?" Toby laughed again. He had such a deep chortle it was catching.

Layla started to laugh. She couldn't stop. They both guffawed so hard she had to wipe tears from her cheeks.

"It's not that funny." She heaved a long breath. "We're a sorry lot, you and I."

"It is too funny. She hasn't even met him yet and she's sure he's the one for you." Toby hiccupped another chuckle. "We're not sorry at all. We're blessed to have a mudder who wants us to be happy. She's a gut mudder. Even if she does go overboard. She is who she is."

He was right. Layla wiped her eyes with her apron. "How'd you get so smart?"

"Haven't you heard? I'm old. Wisdom comes with age."

"That's right. I forgot." She patted his arm. "Are you sure I shouldn't drive? I wouldn't want you to tax your poor, old muscles."

"Hardy, har, har."

Layla entertained her brother with jokes about his age for the rest of the way home. That didn't keep her from thinking about Micah. For all they knew, the man had a special friend back in Bird-in-Hand. He might not think as kindly of their mother's matchmaking skills.

In fact, she shouldn't be thinking about him at all. Toby was the old guy. Ending his bachelorhood came first. Layla was young and had plenty of time to find her life mate.

At the house, Toby dropped her at the front porch. "Danki for the company."

"*Gern gschehme.*"

"Keep what we talked about under your *kapp*, sei so gut. Give me time to figure out the best way to approach it."

"I won't say a word." She could offer to approach Rachelle, but then that wouldn't bring Toby and Rachelle together in a shared purpose—the second goal of this plan. Layla mimed locking her lips and throwing away the key. "My lips are sealed. Just don't wait too long. With the store, if I don't keep up with the bookkeeping on a regular basis, it becomes that much harder to know if we're actually earning income or spending more on overhead than we're bringing in."

That was the challenge of what the experts would call a cottage industry. Their store wasn't in town where people would see it. The Millers had to rely on word of mouth and a minimal amount of advertising to encourage folks to make the trek to their store. They'd considered renting a storefront in town, but Dad nixed the idea. One business that took family members away from the farm was enough. Which brought Layla back to their dilemma with Dad and the solution: Rachelle.

"You're up to something. What is it?"

"Me? Up to something?" Layla shook her head, striving for the picture of innocence. "I'm just thinking about what I'll do tomorrow."

He frowned and squinted in the porch light. "Just remember. I'm capable of doing my own matchmaking. I know Mamm would be happy for me to get involved."

"Men don't matchmake."

Did they?

"You just keep thinking that, dear Schweschder."

He wheeled the buggy around and drove off—in the opposite direction of the barn.

Now Toby was the one who was up to something. The unsettling thought whirled around Layla. Whoever said turnabout was fair play knew what he was talking about.

Chapter 11

The new buggy's high beams came in handy as darkness descended on the dirt road lined with trees that branched out overhead, obscuring the moonlight. Toby shivered and turned up the heater against the frosty night air. He hadn't planned to keep driving after he dropped off Layla. It just happened. A barn owl hooted. Laughing at Toby, most likely. The next farm over, the only other farm in this direction, belonged to Adam Lapp, Rachelle's father.

It was late. It'd been a long day. Rachelle would be asleep. Toby should be asleep. They both had church the next morning. He should turn around. Yet he didn't. He doggedly drove on. He wasn't really driving to the Lapps' farm. He was breaking in the new buggy. He was driving past the farm.

And so went the conversation in his head for the thirty minutes it took to arrive at Adam's place. Toby turned off onto the gravel road, drove past Adam's farrier shop, and headed straight for the house. This was crazy. The product of too much sugar and too little sleep.

Something about the snap in Rachelle's eyes, the pink in her cheeks, and the fire in her words at the auction earlier in the day propelled him forward.

Rachelle sat alone on the swing, her white prayer kapp bright in the solar porch light. She had one leg tucked under her, the other down so she could push the swing with her sneaker. A woolen shawl and a quilt protected her from the chilly air. At his approach, she threw off the quilt, stood, and came to the steps. Her eyebrows rose high over her dark eyes. "Toby? What are you doing here?"

He wrapped the reins around his hands, braked the buggy, and halted a few yards from the porch. Good question. Now that he was here, he needed to come up with a reason. Soon. "The family gave me a new buggy for my birthday."

Not an answer, but it bought him time. Rachelle crossed her arms and leaned against the porch column. "That was very nice of them. What a lovely birthday present. Seelich gebortsdaag."

"Danki. I wasn't expecting such a big gift. It's more than I deserve." He stifled the urge to wiggle on the seat like a toddler at Sunday services. "I'm just breaking it in."

"I see." Her puzzled expression said she really didn't. "So you decided to drive it over here to my dat's farm?"

"It's a good drive from our farm to yours."

"It is."

An awkward pause ensued. Toby studied his hands.

"So would you like to sit with me on the porch for a few minutes before you break in the buggy some more?" Her tone had a faint teasing quality. "I could make you a cup of hot tea. The air is nippy tonight."

"That would be gut." Toby heaved a breath. Had talking to Janey been this hard? He couldn't remember past the day she scorned him and his profession. "It is cold tonight."

Rachelle slipped into the house while Toby tied the reins to the hitching post and settled into a rocker on the porch. She returned several minutes later with two large mugs. She handed one to him and took the other to the porch swing. "I hope you like apple-cinnamon-spice. I added honey."

"Danki. Sounds gut." Toby wasn't much of a tea drinker. Strong coffee was more his style, but a hot drink would hit the spot. He took a sip. "Gut, it's gut."

"Gern gschehme." She held her mug with both hands as if warming her fingers. "I'm glad you like it, but surely you didn't drive over here in the cold to do a tea taste test."

Funny. She was funny. "I wanted to tell you I'm sorry about this morning." An actual good reason for showing up at her porch steps after dark and without an invitation. "Layla says I owe you an apology."

"That's not the same as you thinking you owe me one." She frowned and gave him what could only be described as a teacher's stern stare. "Do you always do what Layla says?"

That stare. It was enough to make a man nervous. He crossed his arms. "Nee. Only when I suspect she's right."

"You only suspect? You're not sure?" Rachelle crossed her arms. "Do I need to explain to you what the Ordnung says about drawing attention to ourselves or using electricity?"

"Nee. I got caught up in the moment." Toby ducked his head like one of her students who didn't know the answer to a hard question. "Sometimes auctioneering takes me away from my Plain roots."

"Which is probably why Plain districts had so much discussion about allowing it."

"In the end, most voted in favor."

Rachelle set the swing in motion with her sneaker-clad foot. "The boys understand now why they shouldn't have done it—at least as much as a five-year-old can. As much as Jonah can understand these things. It's a lesson learned."

"For all of us."

She nodded. Her expression eased. She leaned back.

That topic had been laid to rest. What now? A cold breeze rustled through the trees. Quiet. So quiet.

"Can I ask why you're sitting out here in the cold by yourself so late?" Toby cocked his head toward the house. "It's so quiet. Sounds like everyone has gone to bed—except you."

Her expression pensive, she plucked at a loose thread on the quilt. "I'm still chewing on some news I received this evening."

"Bad news?"

"Nee. Not exactly. Good and bad, depending on who you are, I suppose. Unexpected." She studied the quilt's Lonesome Dove pattern. "We had a parents' committee meeting tonight. They've decided to send the special kinner to the Englisch school in town starting in September. Maybe you've heard about this plan."

"Jah. Your dat talked to mine about it a while back. Because of Sadie, I reckon. He wanted my dat's opinion."

"And he was in favor?"

"It's not that my *eldre* are dissatisfied with the teaching Sadie gets from you. Not at all." She looked so sad. What would it take to smooth that sadness from her heart-shaped face? "But they were pleased to hear about physical therapy and speech therapy she would get at the Englischers' school."

"They're right. It's a chance for the kinner to get all the services we can't afford." She straightened and raised her chin. "It will save the district the cost of a second teacher's salary too. It's for the best."

"But you will be out of a job."

"It's not that. Okay, it's that too. But mostly it's that I love teaching Jonah and Sadie and the other kinner—"

"And they love you. I know every other sentence out of Sadie's mouth is Tietschern says . . ."

"She's a blessing to teach. I thought I would teach her until . . ." She let the sentence trail away.

Until she married. Vague memories of grapevine stories surfaced. She'd had a special friend. Maybe it was more than one. The details escaped him. Gossip was a nasty-tasting drink. "There will be other openings in the fall, I reckon."

"Not locally. Not with special children. They're all going to town. The other districts are doing the same." She traced the quilt's pattern with her index finger. "Corinne needs the job teaching the general education children more than I do, so she'll continue at our school."

Unless she married. Everyone knew Corrine and Henry Plank had been courting for a while. Losing a job wasn't a reason to marry. Or it was a lousy reason. No one expected either woman to jump at a marriage proposal because she was no longer working.

"Would you leave Lee's Gulch then?"

"I hate the idea of being far from my family and friends. But I also love teaching so much, I can't imagine not doing it." She raised her head. Their gazes locked. "I need my salary. My eldre have many mouths to feed. Besides, a lot could happen between now and September."

Indeed it could. A person could hope. Or not. *"What woman would want to sit at home alone while you travel around the country for half the year?"*

Janey's voice shrieked in Toby's head. What woman, indeed? Especially a woman like Rachelle who had a profession she loved. So much so she was willing to pursue it in other communities far from Lee's Gulch. "It's late. I should get going. We don't want to fall asleep in church."

"Have you fallen asleep in church?" Rachelle smiled. That smile. It lit up her face. Her cheeks were red from the cold. Her eyes sparkled. "Better not let the bishop see you napping during his message."

"I sit behind my dat. He's taller. That way, if I nod off, Bart can't see me."

"Just don't snore."

"I don't snore."

"That's not what Sadie says."

Grinning, Toby took the porch steps two at a time and strode to his new buggy. Rachelle followed. She stood watching him drive away, waving the whole time.

This really had been the best birthday ever.

Chapter 12

*W*iggle. Wiggle. Finally. Rachelle knelt for the last prayer. *Gott, I'm sorry. I'm so distracted today.* Like He hadn't noticed. She was worse than the little kids who were still learning to sit still and be quiet during the three-hour church service. They ate crackers and played quietly with little toys. Rachelle, on the other hand, wiggled. The prayer ended. She stood, inhaled, and blew out a long sigh.

"I'll second that." Corrine picked up her crocheted bag. She looked as if she'd slept as badly as Rachelle had. "Do you know how hard it is to sit still and pay attention next to someone who has ants in her pants?"

"I do not have ants in my pants. I don't wear—"

"It's an expression." At her mother's frown, Corinne lowered her voice and paused until the other women moved forward a few more feet on their way out of Bart's barn. "I have as much on my mind as you do, but I managed to sit still."

"Not really. I thought maybe your foot went to sleep the way you were tapping it."

"If you'd arrived earlier, we could've talked before the service—"

"Getting sixteen people ready and out the door on Sunday

morning is no easy feat." The Lapps, like most Plain families, were experienced in the art of getting their large families up, dressed, fed, and out the door every day for school, work, church, and life. Still, some days proved especially difficult. "Darcy threw up. She was running a fever. Then Michael threw up. Whatever it is, it's probably catching, which means by tomorrow who knows how many of us will come down with it."

"I know how that is." All schoolteachers did. One student with a cold or a stomach virus—especially in the winter—and every student would have it before the week was out. "How do you feel?"

They moved out into the yard and made their way toward the house where they would join the other women preparing food in the kitchen. Rachelle sidestepped two men carrying benches from the service to the folding tables set up along the porch. Women were already bringing out trays of sandwiches and pickles and chips. Voices and laughter filled the air. After the long, cold winter, no one minded sitting outside on a cool but brilliantly sunny day. "We can't talk about it now. Not with Mamm and the other women gathered in the kitchen. And the maed. Wait until after lunch."

Corrine groaned. "I may burst by then."

Despite the warning, Corrine managed to keep her lips zipped and her thoughts corralled until after lunch had been served and the kitchen cleaned.

Rachelle grabbed an oversized plastic cup of lemonade and a sandwich made with peanut butter schmeer. Corrine did the same, and they headed out to the backyard where a noisy volleyball game that pitted the boys against the girls was already underway.

"So answer my question." Corrine stuck her paper plate on a lawn chair and carried it to the closest open spot along the sideline. "How are you feeling?"

Like she'd collided with a wall. All the air had been knocked from her lungs. "I'm trying to be okay with it. What about you?"

"Me too."

They'd both been happy teaching, letting nature take its course. No one had been rushing them to marry. Neither had ever contemplated competing with each other for the job. What was God thinking? Not that Rachelle was questioning Him. She simply wanted to know the plan.

Like God owed her an explanation. *Es dutt mer leed, Gott.*

Did the plan have something to do with Toby? His visit the previous evening had left her unsettled and restless. She'd replayed their conversation in her head over and over, all the while imagining his grin as he drove away in his new buggy. Despite a long, event-filled Saturday, sleep had been hard to come by.

"Earth to Rachelle!" Her tone exasperated, Corinne waved her hand in Rachelle's face. "You ask me how I'm doing, and then you ignore me while I'm telling you that Henry—"

"I'm not ignoring you—"

"So what did I just say?" Pouting, Corinne huffed in feigned irritation. She unbuttoned her jacket and shucked it off. "Can you believe their answer to our dilemma is for one of us to get married so the other can keep teaching?"

"It keeps them from having to make the decision. But, by the same token, that is normally what women teachers do. It's just that we can't do it on command."

"I wish."

"It's not any of my business, but do you think Henry will ask you to marry him anytime soon?" Rachelle studied the plate in her lap. Peanut butter wasn't a good choice. She had enough trouble swallowing the lump in her throat today. "Not that I think you should rush into marriage on my account."

"That's what I've been trying to tell you. There's been an outbreak of avian flu across the country. Henry's flock is infected. All fifteen thousand birds have to be put down." Corrine slumped in her chair. She put her hand to her forehead and peered at the lineup of chairs to their right, likely searching for her beau in the crowd. "It's usually like digging at a splinter to get him to talk about his feelings, but when I told him about the parents' committee, he said I needed to keep teaching. He doesn't know when or how he'll be able to start over. He tried to put on a brave face with all the right words . . . Gott has a plan . . . There will be trouble in this world . . . and so on, but he made it clear he won't ask me to marry him until he's able to make a living again."

Her expression gloomy, Corrine took a big bite of her sandwich, chewed, and swallowed. "He's such a man. He doesn't understand that I'm willing to weather that storm with him. That's what *fraas* and *menner* do. They go through trials and tribulations together. At this rate, you'll probably marry before I do. All you have to do is get yourself back to the singings. You haven't been since—"

"I know how long it's been." Since she and David Plank went their separate ways—after his proposal in what Corinne liked to call debacle number two. Debacle number one being Kyle Eash's proposal. Did Toby go to the singings? She couldn't ask Corinne. Her friend would immediately go into matchmaking mode. "David will be there."

"And Kyle, but he's already driving Miley Dotson home." Corrine raised her voice to be heard over the roar when Mandy set up the ball for Emma, who spiked it with gleeful vengeance. "Both he and David have recovered. No need to worry."

"That doesn't mean they're not reminded of an uncomfortable situation when they see me." David especially tended to dart in another direction whenever their paths were about to cross. Kyle simply nodded, his expression neutral, and kept walking. She'd liked them both. Hurting their feelings had been hard but necessary. Had she let the courting go on too long? When had she known David wasn't the one? Or Kyle? No amount of desire for like to turn into love could make it so. She'd found that out the hard way—twice. Maybe she should've said yes. Maybe love would've grown over time.

What if it didn't? Marriage was for life. What God put together, let no man—or woman—put asunder. "I'm not going to jump into courting because teaching might not be an option this fall. On the other hand, I feel selfish. I'm so disappointed and sad and at loose ends every time I think about it. We should want what's best for our kinner, shouldn't we?"

Her folding lawn chair in danger of collapsing, Corinne leaned closer. "I know you'll find this hard to believe, my friend, but you're not perfect." She employed a fake whisper loud enough to be heard five yards away. "I'm pretty sure Gott will forgive us. He's in the forgiveness business."

Corinne was right. She was always right. Unfortunately, she knew it too. She'd never courted anyone but Henry. He'd asked her to let him take her home after a singing one spring evening two years ago, and that had been it.

"How do you know Henry's the one and only for you then?"

"That's a gut question." One that pained Corrine, given the way her forehead and nose wrinkled and her lips twisted. "It's not that I get this twittery feeling in my stomach whenever he smiles at me—which I do—or that his kisses are so sweet—which they are. It's that we're always thinking the same thing at the same time. The other night we were watching the sunset, and he says to me he wants us to sit and watch sunsets every night for the rest of our lives. I was thinking the same thing, but you don't expect a chicken farmer to say something like that. My heart melted. Do you know what I mean?"

"I do." But Rachelle had never experienced it. Not with David. Not with Kyle. Toby was twenty-nine years old. Had he experienced it? He hadn't married, so it seemed unlikely. He was a man. He could have a job he loved and still have a family. Unlike Rachelle, who would have to give up the job she loved to be a wife and mother. Still, to have that unexpected yet totally right connection with that one man who made her feel like no one else in the world could—that would be a gift. "You're blessed."

"We are. You will be one day too, I just know it. You'll live happily ever after."

"No one lives happily ever after."

Showing off her best teacher frown, Corinne shook her finger at Rachelle. "Not with that attitude."

"I'm being realistic." Rachelle leaned closer and spoke as quietly as she could, given the noisy enthusiasm of the crowd cheering on the game. "Tell Henry how sorry I am about his chicks. I know it must've hurt something awful to put them down. The teaching job is yours. I know you need your salary."

Corinne's dad had suffered a series of heart attacks over the past two years. Her brothers ran the family hog farm, but money was still tight.

"You need your salary too." Corinne shook her head vehemently. "Your family has the most mouths to feed in the district, in Knowles County, for that matter. The job will be yours."

Most Plain families were large, but the Lapps did have the distinction of having the most children in the west district. Dad and Mom did their best to make the family self-sustaining when it came to raising vegetables, eggs from the chickens, milk from a handful of dairy cattle, and hunting and fishing. That didn't pay myriad other bills from a never-ending need for material to make clothes, to doctoring, shoes, coats, boots, and book learning. Rachelle's salary was needed. As her brothers and sisters got older, they would do the same, allowing her to step away from that duty one day when she married. "I'll get another job—"

A volleyball landed with a *thunk* in Rachelle's lap before she had time to raise her hands in self-defense. "Oooph!" Its force knocked the wind out of her. That didn't prevent her from wrapping her arms around it. "Whoops!"

A flock of girls descended on the sidelines and crowded her chair. "Tietschern, Tietschern, you okay?" Her pudgy face creased with worry, Sadie squeezed between two taller girls. "We no mean to hit."

"I'll live." Rachelle sucked in a big breath. That's what she got for not paying attention to the game. She handed the ball back to the girl. "Accidents happen."

"Play, Tietschern, sei so gut, sei so gut." The worry on Sadie's red, sweaty face faded, replaced with a pleading. "Play."

"Jah, we need you." Emma and Mandy joined in. "You're still the best player around."

"Hey, what am I, chopped liver?" Corrine pretended to be hurt. "I used to be a gut player too."

"You too." Sadie threw herself at Corrine in the best kind of full-body hug. "You play."

Who could resist an invitation like that? A chance to play like a child again, to throw off the yoke of responsibility. Not teacher. Not big sister. Not in charge. Not responsible for others. Rachelle shucked off her coat and dropped it on her chair. She trotted onto the field and took up her favorite position at the net. Corrine would be her setter. On the other side, the boys whooped and hollered at their new opponents. Emmett Miller, Toby's brother, shouted the loudest. "When was the last time you two played volleyball? Five years? Six? Don't hurt yourself."

Plain folks weren't big on competition, but that didn't mean the youngies were above some good-natured trash talk.

"Let them talk." Corrine hunched, knees bent, hands out, ready. "We'll let our playing do our talking for us."

Rachelle nodded, watching the other team's server. The boys were stronger servers, but the girls were better at returns. The first serve sailed overhead. Volleys back and forth drew encouraging whoops and shouts from the sidelines. Soon sweat soaked Rachelle's dress, her lungs hurt, and her legs trembled. She'd never admit it to Emmett, but she *was* out of shape.

"You're not doing so bad, even if you are old," Emmett hollered across the net. He could afford to be brash. Corrine might not have lost a step or two, but Rachelle had. Emmett mimicked laying his head on a pillow. "Are you sure you don't need to rest for a bit?"

"You're just trying to get rid of me because you know you can't win." Rachelle bent low, arms ready for the next serve. "You'd better hush up and pay attention."

The next serve went to Mandy on the back row. She bumped it perfectly to Corrine who set it up right where Rachelle needed it. She leaped high and spiked the ball hard—right into Emmett's face.

"Ach." Both hands over his nose, Emmett staggered back. Blood spurted from both nostrils. "That's what I get for taking my eye off the ball."

His hands muffled his words.

"Ach, Emmett, Es dutt mer leed." Rachelle dashed around the net, followed by Corrine. The other players crowded close. "I'm so sorry. I didn't mean for that to happen."

The yoke of responsibility settled on Rachelle's shoulders. Now it weighed twice as much. That's what she got for abdicating—even for a few minutes. Her job entailed taking care of others—especially those younger than her. Responsibilities never truly went away. *That's what happens when you let go. You're having fun and this happens.* "Let me take you to the house. We need to get some ice on it."

"That's what he gets." The unmistakable bass belonging to Toby sounded behind Rachelle. Emmett's brother worked his way through the crush of players who immediately parted for him. "It's his fault. He was too busy showing off for the maed."

"Was not." Emmett's words sounded like *shwas snot*. "Hard spike." *Shard shike.*

Toby peeled his brother's fingers from his nose. "I don't think it's busted, but you'll have a black and blue nose as big as your head."

"I really am sorry—"

"Don't worry about it. He has a hard head. He'll be fine." Toby put his arm around his brother's shoulders and nodded toward the house. "I'll walk with you around to the kitchen. Mamm's in there. She'll give you some ice and ibuprofen."

Had he been watching the whole time? Heat that had nothing to do with the afternoon sun shining in a sky unblotted by even one cloud radiated through Rachelle. She'd let down her guard and Toby had seen the results. What kind of teacher bloodied the nose of a former student?

An elbow poked Rachelle in the side. She glanced at Corrine. Her friend jerked her head toward the house. Her eyebrows waggled comically. *Go, go,* they said. Rachelle scowled at her friend, then turned to Toby. "I can take him. It really was my fault."

"We'll tag-team him. How about that?"

There was that grin again, as blinding as a drift of snow on a sunny day.

"Okay." Rachelle managed to say without stuttering. "Teamwork is gut."

Except when it resulted in a bloody, possibly broken nose.

The crowd parted again. "I come too." Sadie grabbed Toby's hand. "I want Emmett okay."

"He'll be fine." Toby patted Sadie's cheek. "Don't worry, little schweschder. You stay here and win the game. It'll serve him right."

"Okay, Bruder." Sadie frowned at Emmett, her expression the spitting image of Toby's. "Serves you right."

Rachelle led the way, with Emmett in tow, Toby one step behind, to the back porch where Emmett tromped up the steps and into the kitchen without another word. Rachelle turned to leave.

"Wait."

She paused and turned back. Toby nudged a stick in the grass with his Sunday-go-to-church boot. She waited. Finally he left the stick alone. "I was searching for you, and then I saw you playing volleyball."

"You were looking for me?" Nice response. She sounded like a parrot. "Why?"

He glanced at the house, then at the barn, and finally back to Rachelle. "I just wanted to know if you heard any snoring during the service."

The knotted muscles in Rachelle's shoulders relaxed. "As a matter of fact, I didn't. I guess that means you managed to stay awake."

"It was touch and go there for a bit, but jah, I heard every word of Bart's message." He studied his black Sunday boots for a second, then looked up at her. "What about you? I thought I might have heard a snore or two from the women's side."

"Nee, nee, if you did, it wasn't me."

"So you slept well?"

"Well, indeed. You?"

"Very well."

"Gut."

"Gut."

She couldn't move. Just like she couldn't move the previous evening, watching Toby drive away in that fancy buggy.

Movement at the kitchen's back door caught her gaze. Elizabeth Miller had stuck her head out the door. Eavesdropping? The spell was broken. "I'd better get back out front. I imagine my mamm is ready to head home."

Elizabeth disappeared inside.

"Jah, you'd better go." Toby pushed his hat back on his head. "Before you break someone else's nose."

"It was an accident—"

"I'm just teasing."

"Of course you are." Rachelle heaved a breath. What was it about this man that kept her off-balance? "You'd better go before you nod off. Old men like you need plenty of sleep."

"Old men? Who are you—?"

"Just teasing."

With a soft chuckle, he tipped his hat. "See you around, Tietschern."

"See you around." *Hopefully. Soon.*

Chapter 13

A few drops of rain were one thing. A deluge another. Toby sipped his coffee and watched the tree branches dip and sway in the wind outside the kitchen window. Showers on this first day of April meant their enormous spread of spring vegetables would flourish. That was good. His family might earn its keep auctioneering, but his parents still insisted on planting their 180-acre farm in a variety of crops. Some were sold in their family store next to the auctioneer office. Both buildings were conveniently located on the farm on the road that intersected with Highway 95. The rest was sold at produce auctions—mostly to area restaurants and wholesale grocers. Even though it added to the multitude of tasks they dealt with throughout the year, it gave them a second source of income, and his mother enjoyed overseeing its operation with help from Layla.

So why did unease keep poking its way into Toby's business? Not even the heavenly aroma of coffee mingled with bacon frying and bread toasting dispelled the sense that everything was off-kilter.

March had passed in a blur. Dad worked with Grandpa to learn his routine for two weeks, but when he left for Bird-in-Hand, everyone had pitched in to try to fill the gaps. Dad insisted he had a handle on his new duties. The state of the office suggested he didn't. Toby's offers to assist had been repeatedly rebuffed.

Take this morning, for example. According to Mom, Dad had taken his breakfast with him and gone to the office before dawn. Worried about something? Catching up? Toby needed to double-check that website updates had been done, the schedule updated, and supplies ordered—carefully without stepping on his father's toes.

"Why so glum?" Mom set a plate of two eggs over easy, bacon, buttery grits, and toast in front of him. "You are Gloomy Gus today."

"Jah, Gloomy Gus, you." Sadie deposited Matilda, whom she'd been carrying around like an oversized baby, into her bed in the corner. She brushed orange cat hair from her pale lilac dress. Apparently satisfied that nothing more clung to it, she climbed into the chair next to Toby and sat up on her knees. She clasped his face in her hands and stared into his eyes. "Glum."

"Do you even know what glum means, little maedel?" Her touch and the concern in her baby-blue eyes were enough to lift Toby's spirit. "Don't worry about it. Having you around always makes me happy."

"Gut." She reached past him and stole a piece of bacon. "Want toast."

"That's bacon, not toast." Toby grabbed a knife and slathered strawberry jam on the toast. He handed it to Sadie. "Now you can have it."

"You nice." She took a big bite. Jam decorated her upper lip. "Gut."

"Don't talk with food in your mouth." Mom added more toast to Toby's plate. "You already had breakfast, *kind*, stop eating your bruder's."

"She's a growing maedel." Toby slid his plate over so he could share it with Sadie. "I'm growing in all the wrong places."

"So. Have you talked to Rachelle lately?"

Subtlety was not Mom's specialty. He'd been on the auction circuit most of the previous two weeks. The more time that passed, the more awkward approaching Rachelle seemed. He shouldn't have gone to her house that night on his birthday. He shouldn't have flirted with her after church either. Doing so only endangered his heart and hers. Somehow he couldn't stop himself. Her quick wit, ready smile, and big heart kept him off-balance. *Stop thinking about her.* Mom didn't need to know any of these thoughts. They would only fan the flames.

"You and Layla are in cahoots, aren't you?"

"Cahoots? I have no idea what you're talking about."

"Cahoots? What cahoots?" Sadie waved Toby's toast—now her toast—in the air. "Eat cahoots?"

"Nee, you cannot, Sadie-maedel." Toby slid another napkin her way. "Wipe your face. Cahoots are your mamm and schweschder minding my business instead of theirs."

"Fine." Mom reached for his plate. "I guess you're done then."

"Hey, hey." Toby tugged the plate from her hand. "Don't be taking my eggs."

"Make a bacon-and-egg sandwich and take it with you."

"Where am I going?" Toby gobbled down his eggs just in case she decided to take another swipe at his plate. "I have to go talk to Dat at the office."

"First you can take the maed to school. The rain isn't going to let up anytime. They'll get soaked if they walk. Josie could take them in the buggy, but then it'll be at the school all day. I need to go into town for groceries this afternoon."

"I no like wet dress. Matilda no like wet coat." Sadie's woebegone tone was all Toby needed to get him moving. She had him wrapped around her proverbial finger. "We get cold."

"Matilda isn't going to school with you, Sadie." Mom's voice held a note of exasperation. This wasn't a new conversation. "She'll be nice and dry here in the house with me."

"She my *bopli*. She miss me."

"She'll have me for company."

Mom had the patience of a librarian with a building full of kindergartners. She also had a one-track mind. A drive to the school meant seeing Rachelle again. Toby's mother could've had Emmett take the girls. Or even Declan or Elijah. But no. She had a method to her madness. "Mamm!"

"What?"

"Don't pretend to be so innocent."

"I have no idea what you're talking about."

Mom conspired with the world to throw Toby and Rachelle together. Maybe for a good reason. Or maybe because he hadn't learned his lesson the first time. *"What woman wants to be stuck at home raising kids while her husband traipses around the country auctioneering?"* Janey's voice played on repeat in his head. Would her sarcastic voice ever fade? This wasn't a late-night visit. It was simply dropping his sisters off at school. Nothing more.

Toby wiped the jam from Sadie's face and handed her the last piece of bacon. "Get your lunch box. Tell Josie and Sherri to hurry up. I'll have the buggy at the back porch in ten minutes."

He stood and took his plate to the kitchen sink. His mother slid it into a tub of soapy water. "It's just that I see you with Sadie and know what a gut daed you would make."

Toby scooped up suds and blew them at her. Bubbles floated in the air. One landed on his mother's prayer covering. "Aren't I a gut bruder, a gut onkel, a gut suh? Isn't that enough?"

"You are." With a soft chuckle, she blew a bubble back at him. "But I'm afraid one day it won't be enough for you."

"Don't worry about me." Goose bumps puckered on Toby's arms. His mother was a wise woman, but she could no more see the future than he could. "Gott's will be done."

A standard response that should give them both comfort. From the frown on her face, it didn't soothe his mother's thoughts much more than it did Toby's. She plunged her hands into the water. "Go. The kinner will be late. Corinne and Rachelle don't like that."

Still intent on her plan. "If Dat comes back here, tell him I'll head to the office as soon as I return from the school."

Forty minutes later Toby pulled the buggy up to the school. Some other kids had used umbrellas to make their way to the log cabin–style building constructed by the district's men. The wind buffeted the umbrellas, making their protection meager. Even so, they were a cheerful bunch. Toby wasn't so old he'd forgotten why. Stomping in puddles and playing in mud on the way to school was like an extra recess. It worked to the teacher's benefit too. Her scholars burned off excess energy on the walk so they were ready to sit down and learn. Umbrellas, rain slickers, and rubber boots would dry by the wood-burning stove, ready for the walk home.

Rachelle stood on the small porch under the awning, welcoming the scholars. Corinne must've already gone inside. Despite the gusty winds and steady rain, Rachelle didn't have a hair out of place. Her dress and apron were neat and wrinkle free. She handed out back pats and quick hugs liberally, and the children returned the favor.

Enos King had his buggy directly in front of the ramp to the right of the porch so he could unload wheelchairs for his younger brothers Robbie and Judah. Smiling and calling out her hellos,

Rachelle grabbed an umbrella and rushed down the ramp to cover Enos and the boys as he settled them into their chairs. The brothers had muscular dystrophy, but that didn't keep them from being front and center in the classroom every day. Would they go to the English school as well?

How could the parents' committee even consider sending scholars to an English school when they'd had such strong teachers in their own small school? Rachelle did a good job of hiding her pain at their decision. Her calm demeanor never wavered. If she was bothered by the fact that he hadn't stopped by the farm to see her again, that didn't show either.

Another aspect of Rachelle Lapp to like. Shaking off the unruly thought, Toby waited for Enos to move his buggy, waved at him, and then pulled up closer. He hopped from the buggy and landed in a puddle. "*Guder mariye.* Wet enough for you?"

"I like a good shower. It means we'll have lovely spring flowers and a green countryside." Rachelle waved at Josie, who'd leaned out of the buggy to holler hello. "It was nice of you to bring the girls, though. There's still enough winter in the air to make for a cold walk."

She worked so hard to see the positive in everything. Another good quality. She had so many. Surely she would see his face and know his thoughts. Toby turned to the buggy. "Who remembered to wear their rain boots?"

"Me." Josie jumped from her perch and landed in the same puddle as Toby. Her splash soaked his already-wet pants. "Always prepared."

"Danki, Schweschder."

Giggling, she dashed to the porch, gave Rachelle a high five, and disappeared inside. Sherri followed in a repeat performance. Which left Sadie. "I forgot my boots." Her puppy dog eyes filled with sadness behind her rain-spotted glasses. Her lips turned down in a pout. "They were Josie's. They're too big. They fall off."

"So did you forget to put on the boots, or did you just not want to wear them?"

She nibbled at her thumbnail and cocked her head as if in deep thought. "Maybe both."

Josie should've been on top of that. Sherri as well. "It's okay." Toby slipped an arm around her waist, hoisted her from the buggy, and lugged her to the porch. "I'll just ferry you across the lake to the captain of your ship, your tietschern."

Sadie giggled so hard she could barely stand when he deposited her next to her teacher. The sound was infectious. Rachelle laughed, which only made Sadie giggle harder. They both sounded and looked beautiful. Toby joined in. "You two better get inside before the lake rises any more."

"Maybe we should build an ark." Rachelle leaned down and hugged Sadie. "Do you remember the story about Noah and the ark?"

"And the animals came two by two." Sadie sang off-key but with great gusto. Singing songs helped with her speech. *"Two by two they came."*

"Very gut. Go on." Rachelle high-fived Sadie. "I'm right behind you." She turned to Toby. "Danki again for bringing them."

"I didn't mind." Toby lifted his hat and shook the water from its brim. "It's hard to believe Sadie won't be coming here in the fall. She will miss you so much. She doesn't handle change well." The thought of his young sister's anguish when she learned of this particular change plucked at Toby's heartstrings. "I can't imagine it will be any different for Jonah."

"That's what I told my dat." Rachelle's voice quivered. She took a breath and let it out. "He says Jonah needs the exposure to

Englisch folks, but I know how shy he is, how scared he'll be when he has to get on that school bus and go into town on his own . . ." Her voice trailed off.

"My dat says Sadie will love it because she loves riding in cars and she loves people." Toby sought words to comfort this soft-hearted woman. "I'm praying he's right."

"Jah. That's what we have to do. We have to pray that it's the right thing. If it's not Gott's will, He'll show us."

So much uncertainty. It had to be eating at Rachelle. Yet she still put Corrine first. Her selflessness made her even more attractive. Toby couldn't stop staring. "You're right. A lot can happen. You never know what Gott can do with a situation like yours."

"That's what Corrine says too."

"There's a reason she's a teacher." Toby clomped down the steps and outside. Maybe the rain would wash away the unsettling feeling that he would lose Rachelle if she had to take a job in another district. "Work calls. I'd better get moving."

"Me too." Rachelle raised her hand in a brief wave, then turned and went inside.

Despite his claim of work to do, Toby sat in the buggy for several minutes, listening to the rain beat on its roof. That feeling of restlessness had returned, and with it, Gloomy Gus who wanted something he couldn't have.

Could he?

Chapter 14

*O*ne minute the nursery smelled of mulch, mud, and so many flowers it was impossible to identify one sweet scent of spring and April. The next the stench of something much earthier reached Layla's nose. Surveying the rows for the offending source, she slowed the squeaky-wheeled cart filled with a mixture of potted flowers and vegetable plants. The odor of manure was part of daily life on the farm, but a person didn't expect it amid such a beautiful bouquet for the nose.

"Excuse me, can I get by?"

The warm and sweet-as-maple-syrup voice. It was him. Layla tried to dust dirt from her apron. It smudged. She tugged a smile into place and turned. "Micah?"

"Ah, you're the girl from the buggy ride last month, aren't you?" His forehead wrinkled, he cocked his head. "It's been a while and I didn't get a gut look, but it's Layla, isn't it?"

Layla was never at a loss for words. Why did none come to her at this moment? "It is. You smell." *Nice.* Layla winced and gave herself a mental slap on the head. "I mean—"

"I do. I know." Micah stomped his muddy boots on the cement path. "I bought some hogs to supplement the ones Daadi left with my onkel. They are smelly creatures. The rainstorm this morning wet the dirt that mixed with their manure. The odor isn't exactly cologne."

"You'll raise hogs then?"

What was wrong with her? She sounded like a silly parrot.

"Mainly. The market's decent right now. I'll raise produce as well." He leaned to her left and peered at her cart. "You too? Nice selection of vegetables. Broccoli, cabbage, carrots, leaf lettuce, peas, radishes, spinach, potatoes, turnips. Very similar to what I chose."

Micah had dark coppery-brown hair and fair skin. His eyes were somewhere between green and gray. She'd been right about his size. He wasn't tall for a man, but he had big hands and broad shoulders. A pleasing package—that's what Grandma Joanna would call him. Layla tore her gaze from his face to study his cart. He'd selected a similar array of plants. "Are you planting all those yourself?"

"Nee, my bruder's fraa Naomi and their *dechder* will pitch in. I said I would buy the plants if they'd do the planting." He pointed at the second cart parked next to Layla's. "Is that yours too?"

"Jah. My mudder is around here somewhere. She's gabbing with one of the other women from the district we ran into earlier."

"I don't recognize some of your plants."

He probably hadn't planted many flower gardens. Those usually fell in the Plain women's domain. Tending the flowers was one of Layla's favorite pastimes. "Mamm wants to plant native flowers. She read that some of the flowers native to Virginia are going extinct. The native plants don't have to be watered as much, and they feed the hummingbirds and butterflies."

Micah's eyebrows rose. It turned out his eyes were hazel. "Interesting. My daadi liked sitting on the porch watching the butterflies and birds too. I found guides to both on his desk."

"We have milkweed, butterfly weed, golden asters, and

sundrops." Layla pointed out each plant as she named them. "These are ragwort, black-eyed Susans, and sweet alyssum."

"I'll have to come by later in the spring to see how they do."

"I hope you will." Heat curled around Layla's cheeks and neck. That sounded altogether too forward. She squeezed the cart handle and forced it from the middle of the aisle. "You were trying to get through."

"I didn't mean to rush you." He grasped his cart handle with both hands and studied her with somber eyes. "Have you always planted native plants?"

"Nee. It's something new. Mamm likes to try new things."

"What about you?"

Was there an undercurrent in his question? "I like new things."

"I used to. Now I'm more of a tried-and-true kind of person." His light tone didn't match the way his eyes darkened and his gaze bounced away from Layla. "I guess that's why my parents thought I was the best person to pick up where Daadi left off."

"I'm here, I'm here." Mamm trotted down the aisle that held small trees on one side and shrubs on the other. "Sorry, I got held up. You know how Darlene loves to talk."

Darlene. *Ha*. No one loved to talk more than Layla's mother. "Mamm, this is Micah Troyer. Micah, this is my mother, Elizabeth Miller."

Mom's face lit up like a kid at a Fourth of July fireworks display. "*Bewillkumm, bewillkumm* to Lee's Gulch." She grabbed the glasses she kept on a chain around her neck and stuck them on her nose. "Naomi told me you were here. Gut to meet you. Layla, you invited him for supper, didn't you?"

"Nee—"

"Dochder, what are you thinking? He's alone in that big house, no one to cook for him. You'll come to supper, won't you?"

"I'm sure my family won't mind if I don't tag along to their house again tonight. They have plenty of mouths to feed as it is." Micah glanced back toward the nursery building as if seeking an escape route. "In the meantime, I'd better find Naomi. She'll want to approve the plants I picked out."

Layla explained that Naomi and her daughters had agreed to plant the garden for Micah. "I imagine they'll do the picking and canning too."

"Jah. By then school will be out and the maed can help me around the house." He swatted away a bee buzzing precariously close to his slightly sunburned nose. "They're itching to paint the kitchen and bedrooms too."

"You're blessed to have them." Mom tapped her cheek with her fingers, her lips forming an exaggerated O as if a thought had just struck her. "Layla has experience painting. She can bring along Josie and Sherri. They've painted every room in our house."

"That's very kind of you. My nieces would like that. I'd better skedaddle now, but we can talk more about it tonight. See you then."

"See you then." Mom's face nearly split, such was the smile she shot him in return. "Layla can make her sausage lasagna and garlic bread."

Layla closed her eyes for a second. "Maybe Micah doesn't like sausage."

"Who doesn't like sausage?" Micah patted his stomach. "I'm happy for any home cooking that doesn't involve my own poor kitchen skills. See you then."

As soon as he was out of earshot, Layla turned to her mother. "Seriously, Mamm, could you be more obvious? Paint his house? Cook for him?"

"I don't know what you mean." Mom employed an airy tone

full of innocence. "We'll pick up what we need for the lasagna at the store before we head home. He's nice, isn't he? From the sounds of it, he's a hard worker too."

"Why are *you* working so hard on me when Elijah isn't married yet? He's older than I am."

"It's harder for girls. Boys hold the upper hand. They get to do the asking." Mom pushed the cart filled with flowering plants ahead of Layla's. She puffed as she guided it around the corner toward the cashiers. "I'm not ignoring Elijah—or Declan, for that matter—though. They both need to get their rears in gear. Elijah is shy, so it's always been hard to get him to singings. Declan is as wrapped up in auctioneering as Toby is. I don't want either of them waiting as long as Toby has."

"You know it's not normal for a mudder to be so involved in her kinner's love lives."

"That's not true. Other mudders are as interested. They just don't let it show."

"Matchmaking is frowned upon for a reason."

"This isn't matchmaking. It's a nudge here and wink and nod there."

"More like a shove here and one of those written-across-the-sky-with-an-airplane messages. It's embarrassing."

"I'm sorry." Mom halted in the middle of the aisle so suddenly Layla narrowly missed bumping into her backside with a cart full of plants. "I don't mean to embarrass you. It just hurt my heart when Ryan did what he did."

She shouldn't even know about Ryan's behavior. "I've forgiven him."

"Gut for you. I'm working on it."

That her mother could admit to having a hard time forgiving Ryan encouraged Layla more than she could ever know.

Understanding that a person must be forgiven wasn't the same as being able to do it. For Layla it had been a daily lesson in obedience. "How did you know Dat was the right one for you?"

"It wasn't any big, flashy bombshell of emotion like you read in those silly romance novels." Mom gently touched the black-eyed Susan's petals. "When he held my hand the first time, I never wanted him to let go of it. Or me."

Imagining her parents young and in love boggled the mind. Still, when they ribbed each other about getting old over supper or snatched a kiss when they thought none of the kids were watching gave Layla a clear picture of what she wanted someday. Something she would never have had with Ryan. "Ryan wasn't the one."

"Nee, or he wouldn't have done what he did."

"So he did me a favor."

"That's a gut way of thinking about it." Mom's laugh lines around her eyes and mouth crinkled. "Now you can look forward to having that something special with the man Gott has picked out for you at the time He has planned for you."

Sei so gut, Gott. "Let's get to the grocery store so we can go home and get these plants in the ground before we start supper."

Mom plucked a bloom from the sweet alyssum and presented it to Layla. "I love spring, don't you?"

Who didn't love a time for new beginnings? "I do."

Chapter 15

*R*achelle tacked Jonah's drawing of their family—all sixteen stick figures dwarfed by an enormous yellow sun—next to Sadie's on the schoolroom wall. Sadie's was more elaborate, with the girls having long skirts and hair in oversized buns on top of their heads. Both were precious. Every artwork completed, every song sung, every letter and number learned evoked a new bittersweet rush of feelings since Rachelle had learned of the parents' committee's plan the previous month. This first day of April meant less than four full weeks of school remained.

She stepped back and studied the drawings. The kids without special needs might have better motor skills, but all the sketches reflected the love the children had for their families. Each one revealed a scholar's particular personality, adeptness with crayons, and understanding of the assignment. All were beautiful.

Time to move on to the next assignment. While Corrine listened to the second graders read by her desk, Josie was working with the third graders on their multiplication tables on the far-right side of the room. That gave Rachelle the space to work on English vocabulary with her scholars. She grabbed her stack of flash cards as she strode past her desk and stopped so she could stand in front of the first row.

"Good morning, students."

She'd greeted them earlier, but every opportunity to practice social skills and pronunciation was good. Her tongue peeking from her mouth, Sadie shoved her glasses up her nose. "Gut morning, Teacher."

"*Good* morning, Sadie." Rachelle nodded at the little girl. "Good try. Can you try again?"

"Gooood mor-ning, Teacher." Sadie put extra emphasis on the *ing*. She giggled and clapped. "That gut?"

"Yes, it's *good*. You're doing a lovely job pronouncing *teacher* too." Rachelle high-fived the little girl. "How about you, Jonah?"

Glowering, Jonah ducked his head and smacked his hands on his desk. He'd been in a grumpy mood since Rachelle lured him down to breakfast with the promise of an extra serving of bacon with his scrambled eggs. It could be because he didn't sleep well, or he might be in a bad mood because the rain kept them inside during recess.

She slipped between the desks to where Jonah sat. His foam back support was in place, as was the small step stool under the desk, placed so his feet were firmly supported and not dangling. No problems there.

The earlier assignment she'd given them, to copy the words *cat, dog, horse,* and *pig* onto a lined piece of paper so they'd know how big to make each letter, lay untouched on Jonah's desk. His pencil with its rubber finger brace lay on the floor next to his chair. Rachelle picked it up and held it out. "You need this to do your assignment."

Jonah ignored her offering.

Rachelle laid the pencil next to the paper. Sometimes it was better to redirect a student—any student—rather than engage in a struggle of wills. "Would you like to try the flash cards instead?"

He crossed his arms. His frown deepened, but he nodded.

Rachelle returned to the chair she'd placed in front of the students. She sat down and sorted through her two piles. Sadie had progressed from reading words to phrases in English. Jonah and Minnie Hostetler, who was also eight, were still working on letters, sounds, and sight words. Rachelle held up a card with a pizza on it and the letter *p*. "What about this one?"

"I know." Sadie's hand shot up in the air. "Tietschern, I know."

"Teacher."

"Teacher, I know."

"This one's Jonah's. I'll get to you in a moment."

Jonah glanced at the card, then away. He drew circles on his desk with his index finger.

"Jonah?"

He shrugged. "I hungry."

"We'll eat lunch in a while. Can you tell me what letter this is?"

Shaking his head, he crossed his arms over his skinny chest again.

Only the day before, he'd completed more than a dozen sight words and several letters and sounds. Rachelle studied the rigid set of his shoulders. "What about this one?" She held up a card with a horse on it. *H.* Maybe his love of horses would spur him from his funk. "You know what this is."

The storm that brewed on her little brother's face didn't lighten. His gaze flitted toward the blackboard, then the windows. "I don't want to go." He sniffed. Tears trickled down his cheeks. "Don't make me."

"Go where?" Baffled, Rachelle laid the cards aside. She glanced at the other students. Sadie's earlier giggles were gone. She was

Jonah's best friend. If he cried, so would she. Minnie's fierce glare suggested she knew what was bothering Jonah. Rachelle retraced her steps to his desk. She knelt so she could speak to him at his level. "Why are you mad, Bruder?"

He still wouldn't look at her. Red spots glowed on his cheeks. His lower lip stuck out. Rachelle gently touched his shoulder. Sometimes when he was upset, he didn't like to be touched. "You can tell me."

"Minnie says we go town to school." He hiccupped a half sob. "I don't want to. I stay here."

"Don't worry, Jonah. We're not going to Englisch school." Sadie popped from her desk and scurried to Jonah's side. She put her arm around his shoulders. "Minnie wrong. Isn't she, Tietschern?"

Understanding hit Rachelle like a hammer to her thumb. They weren't supposed to have this conversation now. *"Tell them in the fall,"* that's what Dad had said. Why did Minnie's parents spill the news now? A painful lump swelled in her throat. She focused on the steady drone of the third graders' high, thin voices reading. Josie's quiet prompting, "two times two equals four, two times three equals six, two times four equals eight . . ." The sound of learning soothed her. The smell of chalk, crayons, Magic Markers, and little children's sweat steadied her. She swallowed hard and summoned a smile. The children would follow her lead. "What did your eldre tell you, Minnie?"

"I heard them talking. I ride in bus to school in town." Minnie nodded so hard her prayer covering slid to one side revealing her blonde curls caught up in a haphazard bun. Her almond-shaped blue eyes were wet with tears too. She needed a tissue for her runny nose. "My friends go too."

She punctuated the second statement with a wave toward the other children.

"Nee." Jonah pushed back his chair and stood. He stomped his feet. "School here."

"Jah, school here." Sadie mimicked her friend's movements. "Rachelle here. Corrine here."

"Eldre no lie." Minnie's lips turned down. Her chin quivered. "Tell them, Tietschern."

Rachelle eased up until she stood. She caught Corrine's concerned glance from across the room. *What's up? Need me?*

Nee, I've got this.

Corrine cocked her head and mouthed, *Here if you need me.*

Rachelle nodded and turned back to the children.

"Sit down, Jonah. You too, Sadie."

Rachelle waited for them to comply. Then she pulled her chair closer. Seven sweet faces full of trepidation stared at her, asking her to reassure them, to make their world safe from upheaval again.

Each child had his or her own way of dealing with stress and uncertainty. Sadie got fired up and choked with emotion. Jonah shut down and withdrew into himself. Minnie, who'd learned the hard lesson of what happened to a messenger bearing bad news, cried. Little Tracy, at six not sure what the fuss was about, sucked his thumb. Nan hugged her favorite stuffed rabbit. Jacob stared into space, his expression distant, unable or afraid to make eye contact. Danny softly hummed "Twinkle, Twinkle, Little Star."

Would the new teachers recognize these signs? How could they know these children the way Rachelle did? She'd been their teacher for three years. They'd grown together. They'd giggled, played, sang, and prayed together.

Give me the words, Gott, sei so gut.

"Your eldre will talk to you about this when the time is right, but I can tell you what I know." Words shuffled and reshuffled. Her job was to reassure them about this new path—no matter how she felt about it. Pennsylvania Dutch instead of English was in order so she could be sure they understood. "The eldre want you to have an even better chance to learn all kinds of fun things with other special kinner. That's why they accepted an invitation for you to go to a school in town starting in September. You'll get to ride in a bus every day and meet lots of new kinner. Some will be Englisch and some Plain. It'll be fun and you'll learn so much more. They have really gut tietschere there."

Rachelle stopped. She breathed through the tears that threatened. *Sei so gut, Gott, don't let me cry.* "Doesn't that sound wunderbarr?"

"You go too, Tietschern?" Tracy scooted from his desk and climbed into Rachelle's lap. His hands were sweaty and his breath warm. "I no go if you no go."

"You won't need me, I promise, but I'm sure I'll be able to visit." Rachelle hugged his skinny little body, inhaling his scent of mud and cinnamon oatmeal. "You'll see me at church and at all the frolics."

"I no go." His shoulders slumped, Jonah turned his back on Rachelle. He marched to the row of hooks next to the door where their jackets hung. He stopped in front of the colorful posters Rachelle had made, one with pictures showing the steps needed to get ready to study each morning and the other with the steps for preparing to leave each afternoon. He stared at them as if he'd never seen them before. "I tell Dat. He no make me go."

"Jonah, come back and sit down." Rachelle stood and deposited Tracy back at his desk. She went to Jonah. "Bruder, Dat is on the committee. He listened to all the pros and cons, he talked about it with the other eldre, he prayed about it, and then he voted to accept the invitation."

Jonah stared up at her. His mournful eyes reflected his pain at this perceived betrayal. "He not talk to me."

The children had been left out of the equation. Plain parents often didn't see a need to involve their children in decisions that affected them. They were expected to simply obey. Wishing it were different wouldn't make it so. "Sometimes adults have to make decisions they think are best for kinner, even if the kinner can't understand them."

"Not fair."

Life wasn't fair. Dad would say it was best for Jonah to learn this hard lesson earlier rather than later.

Rachelle knelt. She took Jonah's hands in hers. The storm raging on his young face, so like her own with his ocher eyes, high cheekbones, and long nose, touched a chord deep within her. The same storm raged in her when she thought of no longer coming to this school every day, writing their assignments on the board, teaching them songs for the Christmas program, or playing kickball at recess. "Life isn't always fair. I'm sorry. Change is hard. But you *will* make new friends. You *will* learn new things. More than you can learn with me."

The words left her throat raw and her stomach in turmoil. The truth hurt.

Shaking his head, Jonah pulled his hands away. "You gut tietschern. I no go."

Rachelle gathered him in her arms. He rested his forehead on her shoulder. "I no go," he whispered.

She didn't have the heart to tell him he didn't have a choice. Nor did she.

Chapter 16

*G*randpa's desk—now Dad's desk—looked as if an earthquake had rearranged it. Toby hung his raincoat on a coatrack by the door, along with his hat. The rain had finally let up. Scratching his forehead, he settled into the chair on wheels and picked up a stack of papers. The mess was a far cry from Grandpa's orderly everything-in-its-place approach to business. The ancient, scarred oak desk had been made by Toby's great-grandfather as a gift to Grandpa when he started the business. It was like a member of the family.

Unpaid bills for propane, web hosting, cleaning supplies, and the landline telephone covered the desk monthly calendar that lay flat directly in front of Toby. At least two were overdue. Underneath those bills he found invoices that should've been sent out to auction customers and a stack of phone messages left by Layla or Josie, who collected voice mail messages when the older men were out of the office at auctions. Had they been returned?

Dad had been on his way to the office before the break of day. Where was he now?

"Hey, Toby, how's it going?"

Brice Collier, their technology guru, stood in the doorway. "It's going." He dropped the phone messages on the desk. "At least I think it is. Have you seen my dad? My mom said he came here early this morning, but he was gone by the time I got here."

"I passed your dad on the road coming in. He was with one of your drivers." Brice took a long sip from his Mugs and Muffins coffee shop travel mug. The guy never went anywhere without it or the cell phone in his other hand. "They were headed in the direction of town."

Dad had served as the head fixer-upper for the aging trailers for years. Keeping them running required a deft touch and lots of luck—if a person believed in that sort of thing. Toby blew out a sigh. "One of the trucks broke down over the weekend. And a trailer blew a tire. It'll have to be replaced. They're probably going for parts and the new tire."

Not that Dad needed to go with the driver. All three of their drivers were crack mechanics. He should've stayed behind to take care of the paperwork.

Brice's phone dinged. He settled his mug on the one corner of the desk not covered with papers and peered at the phone screen. Rapid-fire typing with his thumbs ensued. Finally his gaze moved from the phone screen back to Toby. "Sorry about that. Another client asking for a meeting to totally upgrade his site."

Toby was used to Brice's telephone etiquette. The idea that a person should focus on the person directly in front of him didn't seem to cross the minds of folks with phones—especially if that was how they stayed in touch with customers. "No worries."

Brice extracted a small cloth from his navy polo shirt pocket, took off his rimless glasses, and proceeded to polish them. Without his glasses, he might have been twelve years old with his clean-shaven face and short little-boy haircut. "I hate to bring this up, but . . ." He held up the glasses, squinted at the lenses, then polished some more. "I submitted my invoice for last month's website updates, and I still haven't been paid."

"Don't be shy about bringing those oversights to our attention. A man has to eat." Especially a man with a wife expecting their first baby. Toby kept his tone light even as a flush of embarrassment ran through him. He dug through the papers in front of him in search of the invoice. "Where did you put it?"

"In Silas's inbox, like I always do." Brice slid the glasses back on his nose. He pointed to the wooden box now overflowing with unopened mail, circulars, and newspapers. "It's probably still in there."

"I'm sorry. We're in the middle of a big change here, but that's no excuse." Toby stood and sorted through the mail, dumping the majority of it in the trash can. He discovered Brice's invoice midway toward the bottom of the stack. "Got it. I'll write you a check right now. I guess you heard my grandfather retired."

"You could've knocked me over with a feather." Brice plopped into the cane-bottomed chair across the desk from Toby. He took a long sip of his coffee. Satisfaction flitted across his face. "That's so good. What was I saying? Oh yeah, I thought your gramps would work until he keeled over on the auction platform. I imagine it's an adjustment for everyone."

"Dad took over the administrative duties as the new head of the company." Toby tugged the oversized checkbook from the desk's lower drawer and opened it. He made quick work of writing the check. "In the future, you might want to hand the invoice to him directly—at least until he gets the hang of things."

"I'll keep that in mind. Just be sure someone lets me know when new auctions are added to the schedule so I can update the calendar and answer web queries wanting to know if you can take an auction."

While some Plain auctions were arranged through phone calls and face-to-face meetings, many others were scheduled through the website. Brice created the forms, answered email queries that came through the site, and updated the online calendar and pricing pages, as well as creating testimonial pages, and otherwise sprucing up the site as needed. He was worth every penny they paid him— and then some. "Will do." Toby held out the bill for the web server hosting. "This bill is overdue. I'll pay it today, but could you call them and let them know payment is coming?"

"Absolutely." Brice perused the document and handed it back. "Just don't let that happen with the domain name. There are guys out there just waiting for folks to let their domain URLs lapse. They purchase it and then charge you an exorbitant fee to buy it back."

Toby knew enough about websites to understand the importance of the IT expert's advice. He handed the check to Brice. "I'll let Dad know and help him stay on top of it."

"Have you considered hiring an office manager?"

"Grandpa tried to keep all the jobs in the family, unless it was something Plain folks don't do, like the technology stuff, taking care of the sound system equipment, or driving the trailers."

"Just a thought. The changing of the guard, so to speak, might be a good time to review and update your business practices with the goal of becoming more efficient." Brice glanced at his phone, frowned, and shook his head. "*My* office manager is after me to get back to my office. If it were me—and I know it's different for you Plain folks—I'd evaluate everyone's strengths and weaknesses, then decide who should be handling particular tasks. Sometimes basing these decisions on age, seniority, or simply tradition isn't what's best for the company."

A businesslike approach to running the company sounded good

in theory, but it didn't account for the human factor, how such an evaluation could take away a man's dignity by shining a spotlight on a hidden weakness that caused him to feel shame even when it was no fault of his own. It didn't account for hurting people's feelings. In the Plain world, family trumped business.

Toby closed the checkbook with a snap. "Changes like that have to be handled with diplomacy, I reckon."

Understanding sparked in Brice's pale-blue eyes. He folded the check and tucked it into his shirt pocket. "Family-owned businesses are tricky, no doubt about it."

His phone emitted a bluesy tune. He glanced at it. "I have to take this on the run. Never a dull moment, is there?"

"Nope, never."

His phone already to his ear, Brice strode from the office. Toby leaned back in the chair and twirled around a few times, contemplating the mess of paperwork on the desk.

"Family-owned businesses are tricky, no doubt about it."

So how should he approach it? First, get the paperwork under control. For the next hour, Toby wrote checks and got them ready to mail, prepared invoices, filed paperwork, and tossed anything that didn't need saving. Eventually the mess on the desk disappeared.

He was trying to decipher Grandpa's handwriting on a sticky note when the phone rang. The caller used Miller Family Auctioneering Company on a regular basis. He wanted to confirm that his upcoming livestock auction at the Cumberland County fairgrounds in May was on the calendar. "I spoke with Charlie about it last week. He said he'd ask your IT guy to email me the contract, but I haven't received it."

Toby eyed the computer. Brice had trained the younger Millers on how to log in, find the website, and respond to emails on the days when he worked in his own office. It'd been a while, though.

"Hang on. Let me see if he added it to the calendar." When in doubt, go the tried-and-true route. Toby laid the receiver on the desk and whipped over to a wall-hanging calendar used exclusively for keeping track of upcoming commitments. There was indeed an auction slated for the May date. But it wasn't the Cumberland County livestock auction.

He grabbed the receiver and stuck it to his ear. "You told my dad—Charlie—which weekend you needed?"

"I did. I repeated it twice. He said no problem."

"I show that we have a big estate sale in Richmond already booked that weekend."

"Seriously?"

"I'm so sorry for the confusion." Balancing the receiver between his ear and shoulder, Toby pawed through folders that held contracts for upcoming jobs. The estate sale indeed had a signed contract. "Unfortunately, the estate sale is already under contract for that weekend."

"That's so unlike you all. You're usually so dependable." Disappointment evident in his tone, the customer sighed. "It's a shame. I'll have to take my business elsewhere. Silas and I have done business together more than twenty years. This is the first time I've ever had this happen. That's why I called ahead, to make sure I got the date."

"I truly am sorry. I hope we can do business together again in the future."

"Me too, but you'll have to be more organized and reliable to keep my business." The customer's icy tone chilled Toby to the bone. "I should've known better. I always deal directly with Silas. I'll remember that next time."

Before Toby could tell him about Grandpa's retirement, the man signed off and hung up.

Toby stared at the receiver for several seconds. Finally he deposited it on the base. It was an honest oversight. It could happen to anyone.

Or it could also be classified as a rookie mistake. Even Emmett knew better than to confirm an auction without checking and double-checking the calendar. Toby's temples throbbed. He rubbed them in a circular motion. Benefit of the doubt. Everyone deserved the benefit of the doubt.

The door swung open. His dad strode into the office. His hands were grimy with grease and mud. A streak of one or the other decorated his left cheek. "Hey, Suh. Me and Ken got the truck running and replaced that blown tire." He held up a large white sack. "And I brought bear claws, maple logs, and jelly donuts from the Sweet Treats Bakery. There might be a chocolate cake donut too. Nee, I think I ate it."

He sounded as enthusiastic as a kid on a sugar rush. Toby accepted the offering. The sweet scent of fresh pastries made his mouth water. "I'll make a fresh pot of coffee."

"No time. I told your mamm I'd fix the wash machine. The wringer stopped working."

"Can't you ask Elijah to do that?"

"You're sure irritable today. What's stuck in your craw?"

"Nothing. I thought we could talk business—"

"The women see doing laundry for sixteen people as part of their business—the dirty clothes are piling up."

"I know, but the auctioneering business needs our attention."

"We're booked all the way through fall." Dad opened the sack and pulled out a bear claw. He held it out. "Eat this, cheer up, and lose the attitude. We don't have that many days when we can work on the homestead as a family. Today is one of those days."

Toby did as he was told. The glaze, the slightly crisp exterior, and soft interior melted in his mouth. Sweet like time spent with family. He laid the pastry on a napkin and licked his fingers. "Do you regret the amount of time we spend on the road, away from home, away from Mamm and the kinner?"

"Life is too short for regrets. You take the road Gott puts before you." Dad picked up the sack. "We can share these with the kinner when they get home from school. Today would be a gut day to finish the new shelves for the shop. Layla's chomping at the bit to expand the home-canned-goods section."

Likely that was the closest Dad would come to answering Toby's question. He'd never seemed like a man given to introspection. He was a man with calluses on his hands and deep sun lines on his face. Toby gobbled his bear claw and washed it down with lukewarm coffee. There would be time later to talk about the booking mix-up, the unpaid bills, and the unmailed invoices. Today Dad wanted the whole family to work together, and so did Toby.

Chapter 17

*W*hat's burning?"

Her mother's question penetrated Layla's thoughts just as her nose registered the stench. She jolted from her seat at the kitchen table. "My garlic bread!"

She snatched pot holders from the counter, jerked open the oven door, and pulled out the foil-wrapped loaf of French bread. "Ach. It's ruined."

Dark smoke rolling from the oven punctuated her wail.

"What were you doing that you didn't notice?" Mom shoved open the two floor-to-ceiling windows that lined one wall next to open shelving that held all the cooking supplies a big family needed. Despite the rainstorm earlier in the day, the breeze wafting through the kitchen was warm. "I can smell the burnt garlic all the way out to the front porch."

Arms wide, Layla flapped the pot holders like a bird taking flight. Stirring up the air only made the smell worse. Not even the mouthwatering aroma of sausage lasagna could overcome it. "I was concentrating on the store's spreadsheets. I'm trying to balance the books."

"That's what you get for trying to do two things at once." Mom held her nose between two fingers, giving her voice a funny plugged sound. "Our guest isn't interested in your accounting skills."

Shopping in the morning and gardening in the afternoon had caused Layla to fall behind in her bookkeeping duties. Balancing the books allowed them to know how much they needed to charge for their goods so their expenses could be covered and still have the necessary margin of profit to make the business worthwhile. Suppertime had rolled around all too soon. Micah would arrive any minute.

"Micah is coming to meet our whole family. He's a new neighbor." Layla schooled the annoyance from her voice. Her mother meant well. "I'm not auditioning for a spot as his future fraa."

"I know, I know." Mom bustled to the counter where she grabbed an oven mitt, put it on, and picked up the bread. "I'll take this out to the trash barrel. Leave the back door open. That'll create a breeze that'll blow the stink out the windows."

"Gut idea. We can serve the rolls we had left over from supper last night instead." Layla followed her mother to the back door. "I made a nice salad with a buttermilk dressing. I also brought up a jar of canned green beans from the basement. They just need to be heated. The peach dump cake I made earlier will work for dessert. It's not the end of the world."

"I never said it was." Mom threw her response over her shoulder as she traipsed out to the back porch. "I just like to feed visitors well. Stinky smells aren't very inviting."

Her innocent protestations notwithstanding, Mom had every intention of showing off Layla's cooking skills—which were better than the burned bread suggested. Layla sucked in a long breath of fresh air and turned back to the kitchen. Josie stood at the table gathering up the paperwork.

"Don't mix those up." Layla scurried over to her. "I had them in order."

"You worry too much." Josie hugged the sheets to her chest. "I'll put them on Dat's desk. You can take them out to the shop later. You should go wash your face and put on a clean kapp before your company gets here. While you're at it, a clean apron wouldn't hurt either."

"You too? He's not my company; he's *our* company." Layla threw her hands up. "Mamm's matchmaker-itis is catching."

"I'm just trying to help." Josie, who had Mom's blonde hair, blue eyes, and sunny disposition, feigned the same innocence. Her acting wasn't any better. "You don't want to look like something the cat dragged in. Go on. Sherri and me will take care of the food. Sadie can set the table."

"Matilda doesn't drag mice into the house. She leaves them on the porch."

Even so, she went. Layla made quick work of changing her apron and prayer covering. Not for Micah, but because they needed it. A splash of water on her face and she was good to go. She flew down the stairs to the living room, then headed back to the kitchen. A knock sounded on the front door.

Micah? Surely not. It wasn't time yet. The fluttering in Layla's stomach revved. More of Mom's power of suggestion.

Stop it. Stop it right now.

Layla took a breath, counted to ten, smoothed her wrinkle-free apron with damp hands, and went to the door.

Micah had his fist raised as if to strike the door again. "Oops. There you are." His hand dropped. "I hope I'm not early."

A little. A lot actually. The men weren't back from doing their chores yet. Did the air still smell like burnt garlic? Layla stuck her hand in front of her nose and tried to sniff unobtrusively. The room smelled. "Not at all. Come on in."

"I promise I don't smell this time. I made sure to clean all the manure off before I came over." A quizzical look on his face, Micah pointed to his boots. They'd been buffed to a nice shine. "Seeing how you objected to my smell the last time I saw you."

"I commented on it. I didn't pass judgment." Heat singed Layla's ears and cheeks. She stumbled back from the door. "Truth be told, I burned the bread, and it still smells like burned garlic in here."

"It smells gut." Micah raised his head and sniffed like a hunting hound. He had a good-sized nose, but it fit his face just fine. "Kind of like a pizza parlor."

"It's a sin to lie." His effort to ease her discomfort worked. Layla smiled. "I know it stinks. I'm not really a bad cook. I got distracted with paperwork."

"I never lie." If the jut of his jaw and his somber eyes were any indication, he wasn't joking. "I know I have a big nose, but it doesn't work all that well. I think it's all the time I spend with livestock. You learn to block noxious odors."

"Okay, I believe you. It doesn't smell—to you. Have a seat." Layla waved at the sofa and nearby oak rocking chairs. "Dat and the buwe will come in any minute. The maed are finishing up supper. Would you like a glass of water or some lemonade?"

Micah sank into the closest chair. His right leg bounced. "Nee, but danki." He scrutinized the room around with obvious curiosity. "Don't let me keep you from the kitchen. Unless you're using my arrival as a reason to escape the smell."

Despite the attempt at humor, his expression remained distant. He studied the empty fireplace.

Layla chose the rocking chair farthest from his. "Is something wrong?"

"Nee. Of course not." His smile appeared briefly, then disappeared again. "Your family runs an auction business and a shop

Kelly Irvin

filled with produce and goods you make yourselves. You're busy people."

True, but where was he going with that information? "Jah, partly because it's what's required to support our family, but also because Mamm wants work to do while Dat and Daadi and the buwe are gone so much, six months out of the year."

Why had she told him that? Something about his face said she could trust him with the underlying truth of their existence. The Miller family had one life when the menfolk were home and another when they were away. A split personality, as it were. Mom would scoff at such a description, but Layla had lived it all her life.

"That makes sense." Micah leaned forward, stuck his forearms on his thighs, and interlaced his fingers. "Is that bitterness I hear?"

"Nee. Simply truth."

"At least part of it." He shook his head. "Families are complicated. Leastways mine is."

"Does yours run two businesses too?"

"Nee, but my eldre weren't happy with something I did, so they tried to do some matchmaking that didn't work out, and now I'm here in Lee's Gulch. Alone."

Matchmaking again. "I'm sure they meant well. I know my eldre do, especially my mamm. She just wants all her kinner to be happy. Of course, she thinks she knows best. Don't all eldre? They always want their kinner to learn from their mistakes. It doesn't work that way, does it?"

A muscle twitched in Micah's jaw. He studied his interlaced fingers. "You're right. I'm sorry. I shouldn't have brought it up. It's just that you have a way of making a person feel at ease." He ducked his head. "And it's been one of those days. One of the mamma sows died for no apparent reason."

124

The death of livestock might be aggravating, even upsetting, but no way it resulted in the pain reflected in Micah's face at that moment. A wave of sympathy rolled over Layla, bringing with it the urge to comfort him. She squeezed her hands together in her lap. "I'm so sorry to hear that. What did the vet say?"

"Not much. He's as puzzled as I am." Micah took off his straw hat and ran his hand through coppery-brown hair that needed a trim. After a second or two, he replaced the hat with more force than necessary. "It's not a great start."

"You just arrived. The sow was likely sick before you got here."

Despite his forlorn expression, Micah smiled. His teeth were slightly crooked, but he had a nice smile. "You're kind."

The entreaty in his voice caught Layla and held her close. They'd barely spoken for a few minutes on two occasions, and yet he'd confided something important to her. He'd also found something in her that comforted him. The sweet sensation grew and pressed against her heart. They sat several feet apart, yet the feeling persisted that their hands—no, their hearts—touched.

She should go back to the kitchen. She should do something or say something. Nothing presented itself. Layla stood. She clutched her hands together, nodded, cleared her throat. "I try to be. Mostly. Sometimes. You seem sad . . ."

The front door flew open. Dad, Toby, Elijah, Declan, and the boys tromped into the house, bringing with them earthy, sweaty, manly smells. The noisy chatter, laughter, and stomping filled the room as if all of Lee's Gulch had suddenly descended.

Layla took a step back. Heat scalded her cheeks. Why? They were only talking. Simply talking. "Dat, this is . . ." Her mind went blank. What was his name? *Gott, help me.* "It's . . . I mean . . . Micah. Micah Troyer."

"We've met." If Dad noticed her embarrassment, he didn't let it show. He strode past Layla and shook Micah's hand. "At the hardware store the other day."

Dad hadn't mentioned it. Neither had Micah. Men were like that. The emotion in Micah's face was shuttered. The easy smile had returned. Layla backed away another step. Three generations of male members of her family jostled her. Common sense reconvened. *Danki, Gott.* "Get washed up, all of you. It's time to eat."

Layla shot into the kitchen like a starving bobcat chased her. The girls had set the table. Josie was pouring water into the glasses. "There you are. It took you forever to change."

"Micah came early. I was, I mean, he was, we were sitting in the living room." Never had Layla been so tongue-tied in her life. *Get a grip. He's just a man.* A man who somehow had managed to turn her feelings inside out and upside down with a simple, heart-heavy stare. "The horde is headed this way."

"Gut." Mom picked up one of the pans of lasagna and took it to the table. "The green beans are on the stove. I added some chopped onion and bacon. You can bring the other pan of lasagna over. Your mammi frosted the cake."

Life went on. Somehow it felt as if everything should've halted while Layla talked to Micah. She slid oven mitts on and grabbed the second pan of lasagna. "Sorry I got sidetracked."

"Don't be." Jason's wife, Caitlin, scooted past Layla with a basket of rolls. "If I understand all the prattle going on in the kitchen, you spending time with that man was the entire purpose of this meal."

"Maybe for Mamm, but not me."

With a loud tsk, tsk, Caitlin nestled the basket between the lasagna and the salad. "My mudder told me before I married your bruder to ignore the matchmakers. She said matchmaking could have unintended consequences. That's why the elders frown on it.

We might think we know people well enough to pair them up, but outward appearances and unimportant chitchat with a person does little to tell us what the heart wants or more importantly what it needs."

Did Caitlin know how Mom had tried to nudge Jason toward another woman in the district—a woman now married to a man from the east district? The satisfied glitter in her eyes said she did. "Danki, Caitlin. Did you hear that, Mamm?"

"I did." Her chin up, Mom sniffed. "I'm not matchmaking. I'm simply feeding a bachelor who's a long way from home and alone. No doubt he needs a gut meal and some company."

"Uh-huh." Caitlin pursed her lips as if trying to guard her words. No daughter-in-law wanted to get on her mother-in-law's bad side. She rearranged the butter dish next to the salt and pepper shakers. "My mamm also taught me not to gossip, but there is something I feel I should share with you. It has a bearing on your Micah."

"I keep saying he's not my Micah." Layla glanced at the doorway. The men would arrive any second. "What story? Tell us."

"Micah's aenti told me her brother-in-law sent him to Lee's Gulch because he was courting a *Mennischt maedel*. When the Troyers found out, they were rightly concerned that he would leave the faith for her. The maedel's family had left the Plain faith for their own reasons. They didn't want their dochder to return to it."

Caitlin paused for a breath.

"What happened?" Layla sank into the chair next to her sister-in-law. "Hurry before the men come in."

"The maedel's family sent her on a bus to live with her onkel and aenti in Pinecraft. The bus was in an accident in the Florida panhandle. The maedel died of her injuries."

The story's finale recounted with such soft, flat delivery caught

Layla off guard. Someone gasped. Josie? Layla rubbed her eyes as if she could erase the imagined scenes in her mind's eye. The tearful good-byes. The promises to stay in touch no matter what. The crash. The delivery of the news. The recriminations. She'd only met him once, twice with today, but her sense of him was a man who chose to laugh, to make jokes, to keep things light. "Micah seems so lighthearted. You'd never know he'd suffered such a loss."

"Like most men, he doesn't wear his heart on his sleeve." Mother added two kinds of homemade salad dressing to the feast on the table. "Hopefully Micah's recovered enough to know his life isn't over."

"How long ago did this happen—?"

"Is supper on the table?" Her father's inquiry in a louder, more jovial voice than he normally used brought Laylah to her feet. Dad's eyebrows rose. "You've got a bunch of hungry buwe chomping at the bit. What's the holdup? Did Layla burn something besides the bread?"

He'd heard the last part of their conversation. If he had, so had Micah, who walked in behind her father. Heat scalded Layla's face. Her stomach dropped and her chest tightened. "We were just . . . I was just—"

"You do know we have company." Apparently oblivious to the tension in the room, Toby squeezed by Micah and headed for the table. "I'm starved. I reckon Micah is too."

Layla fought to rearrange her expression. She picked up a pitcher of water. Her hand shook. Water spilled on the tablecloth. Mom took the pitcher. "Sit down, sit down. The food's getting cold. I hope you like lasagna, Micah."

"I do." His tone held none of the quiet amusement it had when he sat with Layla in the living room. "Danki for inviting me."

"You're always welcome at our table."

Layla sank onto the chair at the end of the table. Far from the one Micah took at the other end. She didn't dare glance at him. He must have felt excruciating pain and even some guilt at the death of the woman for whom he cared. His love for her—their love for each other—had led to the circumstances in which she died.

The woman's parents must feel terrible pain and guilt in losing their daughter permanently in their effort not to lose her to a Plain man or the Plain faith. Even Micah's parents must feel remorse for driving the two apart.

How did he feel now, knowing that she and the other women had been discussing his loss? She forced herself to take a quick peek. Her gaze connected with his. His was stony. Layla grabbed her glass and gulped down water. He'd heard. He'd seen. He knew that she knew.

He knew that his deepest hurt had been exposed and discussed.

How would she feel if Dad and her brothers had shared with Micah the story of Ryan's betrayal? Not that it was anything like his loss. It would be embarrassing, even hurtful, but not an invasion of privacy so unwarranted as to be unforgivable.

Dad bowed his head. With a sense of relief, Layla did the same. The first place she should go is to the Lord in confession. *Gott, sei so gut forgive me for gossiping. I talked about Micah behind his back. I was eager to know his past, but that's no excuse. I should've waited for him to tell me. Please guide him to forgive me. Es dutt mer leed. Aamen.*

Layla opened her eyes. Micah's were already open. Emotion ran rampant there. Bewilderment. Disgust. Even hurt. Certainly not forgiveness.

Chapter 18

*S*omewhere west of a hundred items, Toby lost track of how many pieces of furniture, dish sets, playscapes, and mowers he'd auctioned off on this unseasonably warm mid-April day. He grabbed his insulated water bottle and slugged down a long swallow of ice-cold water. It did little to ease his throat's dryness. The sweat rolling in his eyes probably had something do with that. He worked hard to stave off dehydration, but he couldn't keep up. He lifted his straw hat and waved it in front of his face for a few seconds. The hot air didn't amount to much either.

"Next item. Wringer-wash machine. Number 308," Elijah called from his spot in front of the stage as he pushed the appliance into place. No need to carry it up top. Everyone knew what to expect with a wash machine, and mostly Plain bidders would be interested. They would've examined it thoroughly prior to the auction's start.

"Fine and dandy, folks. Here we go. A solid, like-new wringer-wash machine adapted for propane use ready to do the job." Switching to Pennsylvania Dutch, Toby strode from one corner of the stage to the other. "Come on, fellas, think about how much laundry your fraas do every week. How many kinner do you have?

Four, six, eight? Ten? Time for a new washer? Newlyweds? Here we go. Who'll give me $40? Bid $40. Who'll give me $45? Bid $45. Now $50. Who'll give me $50?"

An English man who likely was in the business of buying and selling "antique" appliances started off the bidding. A neighbor of Toby's threw his card up at $45. They had eight kids. Probably wore theirs out. Or they wanted it for parts. Maytag had stopped making the washers in 1983.

"Here!" A young guy in a dark-purple shirt, black pants, and suspenders jammed his auction card in the air. "Here!"

A newlywed? Fifty dollars was the going rate on websites that specialized in old and refurbished Maytag wash machines. "Now $55, who'll give me $55?"

Same Plain man's card shot up.

"You're bidding against yourself, my friend." Toby stifled a grin and repeated the warning in both English and Pennsylvania Dutch. "Anybody else? $55, who'll give me $55?"

He let his pointed finger sweep across the crowd. The man, barely out of his teens, might be new to bidding. Some folks were so excited they got carried away and bid more than an item was worth. A man standing next to this bidder put a hand on his shoulder. The guy shrugged and ducked his head.

"No one? Going once, going twice, going three times. Sold to the eager beaver on the front row."

A smiling Plain woman in a bright-purple dress and black apron slipped up to the enthusiastic bidder. The bidder high-fived her, and the two made a quick circuit around the appliance. She smoothed her hand over the roller. Plain women liked their appliances the way some English women loved their jewelry or a roomy SUV for carting around their children—all two of them.

Something about their shared gleefulness stuck a pin in Toby's attempt to be content with his lot in life. It deflated and shriveled up. They were the picture of happiness. They had each other, whatever life threw at them. They had shared birthdays, anniversaries, and holidays ahead of them. As well as day-to-day living. The birth of their first child and every child after that. There would be pain and suffering—Scripture said so—but they would weather those trials together.

Gott forgive me for the sin of coveting a life I haven't tried very hard to attain. I'll try harder. I promise.

Toby forced his gaze away. It fell on a gaggle of young Plain women crowded together on the nearest bleachers. A blonde in a deep-purple dress giggled and leaned on the girl next to her. She brought her hand to her mouth and whispered into her ear. The other girl, a pretty redhead, laughed aloud. She waved at Toby, then covered her face with both hands. Did he know her? By sight maybe. They were two towns over from Lee's Gulch, but they'd done other auctions at this location in the past.

"Hey, Bruder, heads up!" Elijah carrying two large boxes with the words 12-PACK OF QUART BALL CANNING JARS printed on them in black Magic Marker. "Pay attention. This is the last of it. I'm starving, so don't mess around."

He glanced toward the bleachers where much of the crowd was dispersing. But not the cluster of Plain women. "Ah. I see. Maybe one of them will buy these jars, you'll personally carry them to her buggy, fall in love, and live happily ever after."

"Have you been reading those cheesy romance novels again?"

"Nee, but I think you have."

Toby took the boxes and set them on a table strategically placed to showcase smaller items. Since a certain auction in March, his heart had decided to make its own decisions. Beginning with a schoolteacher. It was ridiculous. Nine years since his heart had been injured, and now it had decided to forge ahead on its own. This wasn't good. He'd been pushed into a corner, in danger of being crushed if he didn't live happily ever after with that teacher. How was that for a cheesy romance story? "The quicker you get off the stage, the sooner we're done."

Elijah spun around and double-timed it.

Sure enough, the ginger-haired woman flashed her card as soon as Toby opened the bidding at $5. The large-mouth glass jars were inexpensive at discount stores, but Plain families liked to buy from estate sales like this one to support the couple who was retiring and downsizing to a dawdy haus. A gray-haired woman clothed in a navy-blue dress and white sneakers gave Ginger Hair a run for her money. And then a Mennonite woman in a pink floral-print dress, a white scarf covering her hair, jumped in.

Ginger Hair didn't give up. Her efforts were rewarded with a final bid of $35—far more than she would've paid at Walmart or Target. Even so, her cheeks flushed red, and she jumped and clapped. Her friends joined in as if she'd just bought a fine new buggy and a Morgan to go with it.

Toby thanked the dwindling crowd, laid the mic on the table, and wiped down his face. Ginger Hair and one of her friends skipped up the steps ahead of Elijah. They sashayed across the stage toward Toby. "Danki for selling these to me. My mamm likes to stock up on jars this time of year." Ginger Hair patted the boxes like they were puppies. "I'm Anna Schwartz, and this is my friend Mary Byler."

"Nice to meet you both." Toby didn't introduce himself. Everyone knew who he was. "I hope you plan to help her with all that canning."

"I do. I do. I love canning. Cooking too." Her face flushed a deeper scarlet. "Listen to me. What Plain woman doesn't love to cook?"

Her friend nodded vigorously.

"Some more than others, I reckon." Toby picked up his water bottle. He edged toward the steps. Rachelle probably liked to cook, but her best qualities centered around her love for children, especially children with disabilities. Her nurturing nature shone in everything she did. "Especially in the summer when it's so hot in the kitchen. Kind of like auctioneering outside in the summer."

Anna was no slouch. She got the hint. She backed away. "I guess I need to pay for these at the checkout table and pick them up there."

"Jah. One of my brieder will tote them down there. Be sure you have your card."

"You must be starved." Mary didn't give up as easily. "You should check out the food at the Wagon Wheel. The food's gut. Anna and me work there. Stop by tonight, and Anna will make sure you get an extra big piece of pie."

The restaurant had good pie, for sure, but not as good as Toby's mom's. He and the boys had eaten there many times. "I'll keep that in mind."

"Gut. We hope to see you there." Anna flashed him a smile. "Your brieder too."

Everything about her seemed nice. Yet nothing about her made him think twice about her. Her physical appearance was no match for Rachelle's. But looks were only a tiny piece of what made Rachelle attractive. Her dedication to her scholars, her hard work, her kindness, her generous nature—all those qualities combined to make her someone he couldn't stop thinking about. These women had gone the extra mile to meet him, but he didn't know them and never would. "Nice to meet you."

They trotted away, but not without backward glances and

waves. Toby waited for them to disappear from sight. He stomped down the steps and headed to the closest trailer. Jason was already there. He held out a can of root beer. "Ready for a cold one?"

Toby avoided carbonation before going on stage. No one wanted to hear an amplified belch coming from an auctioneer. He took his brother's offering. "Danki. That will hit the spot."

"Declan and Elijah want to go to the Wagon Wheel. I myself have a hankering for their chicken pot pie."

Pie. "I'd like to try something different." He took a long swig of icy-cold root beer. "You know how Dat likes enchiladas. There's a new Mexican restaurant on Third Street. I heard some English folks talking about it. Let's try it."

"Really. I thought you said on the drive over that you had a hankering for the Wagon Wheel's chicken-fried steak and mashed potatoes smothered in gravy. You were slobbering all over the back seat."

Jason was exaggerating as usual. Toby suppressed the urge to throw a pen at him. "I feel like living dangerously. We can have Plain dishes at home anytime."

"Any other time you'd be homesick for Plain food." Jason squinted and wrinkled his nose. "I saw those girls on the stage. What did they say?"

"Nothing much."

Nothing worth repeating. If Toby let him, Jason would take their interest and run with it. Toby had groupies. Toby had a fan club. Toby was a Plain rock star. If Dad heard him he would want to call the auction himself or have Jason do it. They were allowed to be onstage and use sound systems, but that didn't mean they were supposed to strut around hogging the limelight like they were something special. Adulation might go to their heads.

Toby didn't invite the attention. Did he? He did his job.

Sometimes that meant joking, smiling, and being playful with the audience—all of them, including the Plain girls. Was it his fault, or were they the ones who violated the spirit of the Ordnung by lavishing attention on the man instead of seeing him as simply an auctioneer?

Toby rolled his head from side to side and then his shoulders. His back hurt from standing all day. His feet didn't feel much better. A headache loomed in the back of his skull. He needed to eat and then sleep. He didn't have answers to these questions. If only Grandpa were here. Had he experienced similar problems? How had he dealt with them? Toby would have to figure it out on his own. "I want to go by the motel, take a shower, and change my clothes."

Jason groaned. "Can't it wait? If you shower, Declan and Elijah will think they need to. They do whatever you do. You know that. I'm starving."

"You'll live." At least Jason's focus had shifted from the Wagon Wheel. He scooped up his backpack and headed for the door. "Besides, it's a gut thing. The supper crowd will have thinned."

"I could eat a whole pan of enchiladas myself." Jason followed. His stomach rumbled as if to punctuate his statement with an exclamation point. "I'm a growing boy."

"There's a bunch of snacks in our room. Have a Snickers bar to hold you over." Toby tossed the empty soda can in the trash on his way out the door. "I want fajitas with grilled onions and green peppers, rice, borracho beans, flour tortillas, and chips and salsa. And guacamole."

No amount of food would fill the gaping hole inside him, but he could try. What was Rachelle doing right now? Four thirty on a Friday. Home. At home in the kitchen with her mom fixing supper. Ready for whatever weekend plans her family had. She was off on the weekends while Toby worked them during auction season. Which only made it harder to court.

Not impossible, though. Next week he would be home from Monday to Thursday. No excuses. Not the growing pile of papers on Dad's desk. Not unreturned phone calls or snarled schedules. A balance existed. It was up to Toby to find it.

Chapter 19

$\mathcal{T}$he *squeak, squeak* of Rachelle's sneakers on the shiny waxed floors at Eisenhower Elementary School reverberated in the silence of an unusually warm Saturday morning in April in which no students graced its halls. Gabriel Jackson, the team leader who'd met her at the school's exterior double doors, didn't seem to notice. He'd slowed his long-legged pace to match hers. Other than that concession, he didn't seem particularly aware of her presence at his side. He wore a Special Olympics T-shirt, faded denim jeans, and scuffed white sneakers. The ensemble—along with the silver hoop in one ear and his longish black hair—was more suited to a teenager than a teacher in charge of the school district's special education and inclusion program. Only his dark five-o'clock shadow made him appear older.

"Here we are." He stopped outside a door with a sign that read NONSTOP FUN AHEAD. It featured a photo of two boys with Down syndrome features and a smiling girl in a wheelchair. "This is where our kids come for assessments and tutoring. We have another room for occupational and speech therapy. Physical therapy is referred out as needed since we don't have the necessary equipment here. We also have our team meetings to discuss student progress with the classroom teachers here as well as conferences with the parents."

"This is for both children with intellectual disabilities and the ones who have physical disabilities?" Rachelle followed him into the room where a woman dressed in tan slacks and the same Special Olympics T-shirt studied a laptop screen at a round table near a row of windows that had been opened to allow in a brisk April breeze. "We have brothers who use wheelchairs who will be transferring as well as the children with developmental and intellectual delays."

"Yep. We have your kiddos with muscular dystrophy on our radar as well." Gabriel waved at a chair. "Have a seat. This is Kim Carter, our occupational therapist. Our other team leader couldn't be here this morning, but she sends her regards."

Rachelle nodded at Kim, who shut her laptop and extended her hand. They shook and Rachelle sat.

The room held numerous round tables, some adult-size and some child-size. A bank of computers took up space at the back of the room. Colorful posters and artwork hung on walls painted airy blues, yellows, and greens. The space exuded cheer. "How many children do you expect to have in the program this fall?"

"Right now we have sixteen, but we'll do an electronic mailing to our existing database of parents in July as well as some public service announcements via the local newspaper." Gabriel pulled out a chair and sat with his skinny legs sprawled alongside the table. "The parents' committees from the Amish districts have said they'll handle notifying their families."

"Word has spread quickly." Rachelle worked to keep her feelings from bleeding through in her words. "Most of the parents think it's a good idea. The children aren't as excited."

"We know this'll be hard at first for all the children new to this school, not just your Amish kiddos. Change is hard for children who prefer established routines, familiar faces, and familiar spaces." Gabriel opened the laptop in front of him. "We've collated all the information we have from the forms the parents filled out. That gives us the basics in terms of medical diagnoses, heath issues, medications, allergies, and a host of other important information.

"We invited you here today so we could start getting to know your students through your eyes as their teacher. In some ways, you know them even better than their parents and more objectively."

"I'll try to help any way I can." Rachelle's voice caught. She gritted her teeth. *You're a professional today, not a sister. Act like one.* "One of the students is my brother Jonah, so I may not be as objective as you think."

"Jonah, Jonah . . ." Kim opened her laptop and tapped its keyboard with lightning-fast strokes. "Jonah Lapp. Here he is. From what your parents wrote, he's well-adjusted and quite independent. He can dress himself, feed himself, and go to the bathroom on his own. He plays well with others. He does chores. He's able to communicate well." She shot a brilliant smile at Rachelle. "That's the kind of report I love to see."

Everything her parents said was true—to a certain extent. For the most part, they'd always treated Jonah like their other children, with the same expectations. "My parents see Jonah as a special gift from God. They rejoice in his every victory in learning to care for himself, to speak, and work alongside his brothers and sisters. They see the glass not as half full but completely full."

"Which is a testament to what great parents they are." Kim's eyes shone with understanding. Her voice held such kindness it made Rachelle's throat ache all the more. "But it sounds like you're able to offer a more accurate assessment of your brother's skills."

"We had Jonah screened at the Clinic for Special Children when it was obvious his speech and physical development were lagging. He was diagnosed with moderate intellectual disability due to a genetic abnormality. His IQ is 45."

Mom and Dad weren't surprised. With such a large number of children in a Plain family, it was to be expected. The doctors called it the founder effect. Plain families in Lancaster County came from a gene pool that began with only forty-four people. Not marrying outside their faith added to the odds that diseases rare in the mainstream world were less so in Plain families. Which made Rachelle's job as a teacher that much more critical.

"My view comes from the perspective of an educator. Some of his challenges are practical or physical, while other challenges have to do with emotional maturity. Jonah is easily frustrated and tends to give up quickly when we're working on English vocabulary and the essential building blocks for reading. He forgets what he's learned from one day to the next. He has sight and hearing impairments. He has difficulty sitting for any length of time— not just because he has a short attention span but because he's uncomfortable physically. He has trouble writing clearly because of weak wrists and the inability to hold the pencil correctly. He acts out when he gets tired. All kids do, of course, but he tires more quickly and has less impulse control."

Both Gabriel and Kim were typing now, glancing at her occasionally with encouraging nods. Rachelle swallowed hard. Talking this way about Jonah to strangers seemed like a betrayal. But how could they assist him if they didn't have a true understanding of his challenges?

"His behavior at school is different from what my parents see at home because of years of reinforcement for doing tasks he loves to do. He wants to be independent, yet he craves routine. He can count to twenty. He recognizes most of the alphabet. He knows his colors. He can follow simple instructions if I break them up into short sentences and repeat them as often as necessary. To understand him, I ask him to slow down and repeat himself. If that doesn't work, I ask him to show me what he wants. Sometimes I have to ask him to try again later. That frustrates him, but he does it."

"I'll develop a plan for strengthening his posture and exercises for his wrists. I'll make sure his chair and desk are suitable." Kim glanced up from the screen for a second, then went back to typing. "Speech therapy will be part of his IEP—his individualized education program. The aide will assist him with articulation exercises."

"What about the language barrier? Jonah and the other children are most comfortable speaking in Pennsylvania Dutch. Do you have teachers who speak our language?"

"No, we don't. We'll fully immerse them in English as their second language." Gabriel looked unperturbed by the challenge. "You've given them a basic foundation to work from. We'll take it from there."

He made it sound as if it would be easy. Understanding Jonah when he spoke Pennsylvania Dutch was hard enough. English even more difficult. Rachelle opened her mouth to protest.

"When was the last time Jonah had vision and hearing exams?" Kim spoke first. Apparently the language discussion was over.

"It's been a year."

"It would be good to have both assessed this summer, before he starts the new school year."

"My mother is diligent about that."

"It sounds as if Jonah is right where we would expect him to be without specialized assistance." Gabriel leaned back in his chair. "You've done what you can. We'll take it from here. In our program, he'll reach his full potential. Our speech therapist and learning specialists will help. An aide will be assigned to provide support to him in the classroom. He'll have all the support he needs to blossom."

Something in Gabriel's tone dismissed Rachelle's efforts.
Maybe he didn't mean to do it. Or maybe she was defensive. She'd
spent countless hours studying materials before she started teaching. She'd been mentored by an older teacher she met at a confer-
ence for Plain teachers. She went to workshops and meetings for
Plain teachers specializing in teaching students with developmental
delays, both intellectual and physical. She purchased curriculum
and supplies out of her own pocket. Progress had been slow, but
there had been progress.

Patience. Self-control, kindness, goodness . . . "I'm sure they will,
but like you said, no one knows my students like I do. Especially
Jonah."

"I don't mean to offend you." His expression earnest, Gabriel
straightened. He held up both hands palms out. "I promise, sin-
cerely. I'm in awe of what you've been able to do with so little education and training."

"I have training."

"You've done your very best and you've done well, but our
team leaders have master's degrees in education with specialties in
areas related to learning and physical disabilities. Even the aides
are required to have education and training in this arena, including associate's degrees from community colleges." Gabriel's tone
softened, but the words came faster and faster, which did nothing
to erase the feeling that he flung rocks at Rachelle, aiming for her
head, her brain, and her heart. "I'm aware of the Amish's objections
to formal education, and unfortunately that places you and your
students, especially those who have special challenges, at a huge
disadvantage."

He might dress like a teenager, but Gabriel had all the knowledge and command of the English language to employ words like
weapons. Suddenly the room was far too warm. Rachelle's stomach

roiled. It wanted to reject her breakfast of cinnamon-raisin-walnut oatmeal and coffee.

"Are you all right?" Kim leaned forward and stretched her hand across the table. "Your face is flushed. Can I get you a bottle of water?"

"I'm fine."

"It's warm in here. I'm sorry. I should've offered you something to drink immediately. Where are my manners?" Gabriel rose and strode to a minifridge sitting on top of a metal filing cabinet. He returned a few seconds later with a bottle of water. He twisted off the lid and held it out. "It's ice cold. Have a sip. It'll cool you off."

Physically, maybe. But it would do nothing for her boiling anger at his patronizing assessment of the Amish, their approach to education, and Rachelle's ability to teach as a result. She took his offering. What else could she do? She sipped. At least it helped deter that persistent lump in her throat. "Thank you." She turned back to Gabriel. "Let me clarify some things before we continue. We don't object to education. Our grandparents and their grandparents fought for the right to have our own schools and to end our formal education at eighth grade because we want to preserve our way of life. There's a difference, in our opinion, between book learning and education that teaches wisdom and values. We will allow you to teach reading, writing, and math, but our concern is that they not learn your worldly values.

"After eighth grade, we choose practical training over formal education." Like all Plain students, Rachelle had been taught the history of her people and the fight that took them all the way to the U.S. Supreme Court that ruled that the issue fell under the constitutional right to freedom of religion. "Our parents and their parents believed that too much formal education leads to arrogance and loss of humility. The teaching of evolutionary biology and sex education runs counter to our religious beliefs."

As a teacher, Rachelle had sometimes longed for more education. When she watched students excel in English, arithmetic, art, music, and history, she'd wanted more for them. But she understood. Their education was intended to help them be successful in their Plain communities, to be hard workers and good people, with the skills they would need to work with their families and thrive, but to do so in a godly way.

"Once they finished eighth grade, they had two years of practical training in whatever area they and their families chose—such as farming, carpentry, construction, managing a small shop, cleaning houses, babysitting, running a produce stand, or doing bookkeeping at a family-run store. Jobs in keeping with their Plain beliefs and values. Then they began their lives as working members of their communities while beginning their *rumspringas*—the search for spouses and deciding whether they intended to formally join the faith through baptism."

Gabriel opened his mouth. She held up her hand. "I'm not done yet. You think you know what we believe, but you obviously don't. We want trustworthy teachers we know who share our values. We want our schools just down the road so our children can walk or take a pony cart. Too much exposure to your values will lead our children away from their faith. Our ancestors fought hard—even to the death—for the freedom to preserve our faith and way of life. We're not giving it away because you have teachers with college degrees and laptops and shiny playscapes. Now I'm done."

Gabriel's face had turned red. The muscle in his jaw twitched. He cleared his throat. "Thank you for clarifying all that for me."

"I hope you'll keep these concepts in mind when you're talking with your teachers and your specialists. The more they understand our way of life, the better."

"Agreed. I might even have you meet with them."

One-on-one. Well, one-on-two wasn't so hard. A room full of teachers? Dread wrapped itself around Rachelle's throat. Anything for her children. She nodded. "Of course. I'd be happy to do it."

"You're welcome. Let's move on to the other students."

Fine. Rachelle took her time and carefully outlined her students' strengths and weaknesses for the next hour and a half.

"Your observations are spot-on. We've got a great head start toward tailoring their IEPs." Gabriel closed his laptop. He stretched his arms high over his head, yawned, and peered at his watch. "That should do it for now. If we have any questions, we know where to find you. I'll walk you to the door."

Just like that, the baton had been passed. Rachelle said goodbye to Kim and followed Gabriel from the room. In the darkened hallway, he slowed.

"I know I hurt your feelings. That wasn't my intent. I'm sorry if I sounded condescending. I respect many aspects of the Amish way of life, especially how Amish families embrace their children with special needs." Gabriel stopped at the doors. Instead of opening them, he turned to face her. "Believe me when I say I think you would be a great addition to our staff. I thought if we could sit down and talk about it, maybe you would consider taking the GED. That's—"

"I know what a GED is."

Self-control, Rachelle, self-control and patience.

He's not making it easy, Gott.

"You could take your General Educational Development test and then enroll in some online college courses. You wouldn't even have to leave Lee's Gulch to do it. You could use the computers at the public library. Then we could bring you on as an aide."

"That's kind of you, but it doesn't work that way." She'd just explained to him the why and wherefores of this reality. Apparently her words went in one ear and out the other, as her grandmother liked to say. "As I explained before, we don't take formal classes after eighth grade."

"I read that some Amish communities allow teachers to get GEDs and even get more training for the purpose of teaching—their chosen trade, so to speak."

"A loophole . . . so to speak." The part of Rachelle that loved school and loved learning still longed for such an opportunity no matter how much she sought to quell it. "Mine isn't one of them."

"Understood." Gabriel pushed open the door and held it for her. Instead of saying good-bye, he exited with Rachelle and began the trek with her across the parking lot where she'd left her buggy. "It's just such a shame. You're obviously very bright and a dedicated teacher. We need more of those, especially for our children with disabilities. I'd love it if you'd at least consider the possibility of working with us."

Gabriel's words were salve on an open wound, but they didn't change the facts. "I appreciate your kindness. What you're suggesting simply isn't possible." Rachelle tightened her grip on her canvas bag and stared at the cherry trees full of buds about to burst open. "It's not our way."

"How can you turn down the opportunity to continue to teach these students you've invested so much time, energy, and love in?" It wasn't a rhetorical question. Gabriel sounded truly perplexed. His pace slowed as if his body struggled with the question too. "It would allow you to make sure Jonah is comfortable and well-adjusted here. You could continue to contribute to his education as well as Sadie's and Jacob's and Minnie's and the others."

A powerful argument. As a fellow teacher, Gabriel knew exactly what sentiments would touch that wellspring of caring that flowed so deeply in Rachelle. How could she refute it? "The whole point of sending our children to this school is for them to receive the best possible education. The parents' committee believes the English teachers with their education and skills can do that better than I can." The truth still rankled. Her humanness was showing. She should want what was best for her students. To feel otherwise was selfish. "I'm not what's best for my students."

"This is an unusual situation, one not faced by your community before. Your parents' committee is making an exception for these particular children. Why not go a step further and make another exception—so you can continue to teach them and oversee what we're doing. Monitor us so we don't overstep our bounds and teach them something you find objectionable."

A powerful argument. But Gabriel wasn't done yet. "You have the most important skills already—the ability to love their differences, to see them as uniquely abled, to see past limitations to possibilities, the compassion and the empathy, the patience. You've got the important stuff. What if I talked with your . . . It's the bishop who makes these decisions, right?" Gabriel ran out of steam—or breath or words—just as they arrived at the buggy. His face red again, he paused in front of Rachelle's horse. "Don't you think it's worth a shot, or are you really not interested?"

Rachelle let her gaze roam the lot and the street. Cars drove by but no buggies. Gabriel had only spoken to her this one time, and he was so sure she should do this thing counter to her culture and faith. "It's not that I'm not interested. I love teaching. I love my scholars, but you talking to the bishop won't make a difference. I can't teach in an English school. I'm sorry." She hoisted herself into the buggy and grabbed the reins.

His forehead wrinkled, his dark eyes full of consternation,

Gabriel stepped back. "I'm still coming to your school to observe the students. Until then, take care."

"Until then," Rachelle called out. "You too."

Once out on the street, she heaved a breath and relaxed. To be able to continue to teach these children would've been a wonderful thing. She raised her face to the brilliantly blue cloudless sky. *Gott, You gave me the desire not only to teach these kinner, but to care for them as if they're mine. To love them like they're mine. Does that stop here? Is wanting more wrong? I need to know.*

Ginger's huff and the buggy's creaking filled the silence. Maybe it was a test. Maybe God expected her to figure it out on her own.

"Ach, Gott." Ginger's ears perked up at the sound of Rachelle's voice. The horse snorted. "I agree, Ginger. Gott thinks I know way more than I do."

Chapter 20

*H*ll the way home from the English school, Rachelle had rehearsed her argument. The English teachers didn't truly understand what Plain children needed in an education—or what they didn't need. The parents' committee had made a mistake. She parked the buggy next to her dad's shop and slipped through the door. The familiar clang of hammer against steel, the forge's heat, and the odor of horse manure and sweat greeted her. Dad was bent over, a horse's leg between his knees, his leather apron sagging around his thick waist, a hammer in one hand. Sweat soaked his faded blue shirt. A black smudge decorated his damp forehead.

He didn't look up and Rachelle didn't speak. A person didn't interrupt a man who was using a hook knife to clean out the growth down to the waxy layer that revealed spidery veins on a twenty-one-hundred-pound Percheron's hoof. Go too far or make a sudden move and the horse ended up with a sore foot. Or he kicked the farrier.

"Easy, my friend, easy," Dad murmured as he worked. "This will feel gut when I'm all done, you know it will."

Horses simply seemed to trust him. All the same, he took great care to straddle the back leg, knees and toes pointed out, back

150

arched, core tight, in a way that allowed him to dart away quickly if the horse should decide to kick.

"Hey, Schweschder. What you doing?" Jonah called to her from one of the stalls beyond Dad's work area. "Say hallo to Dusty."

Dusty was one of their Morgans, a sweet, gentle horse who'd carried all the Lapp children when they first learned to ride. She was getting up there in years, so Jonah liked to give her special attention. Better to wait until Dad finished with the horse to talk to him. Rachelle did as Jonah requested. She found her brother standing on a step stool so he could brush the massive animal's coat.

Runt kept guard near the stall door. He stood, letting Rachelle know he expected to be acknowledged first. She patted his scruffy head. "Hi, Runt, how's life treating you?" Runt's low bark said *well*. Satisfied, he settled back onto the hay. Rachelle turned to the horse so he wouldn't feel slighted. "Hi, Dusty. I reckon that brush feels gut. Jonah is a gut groomer."

"He love it." Jonah showed off his smooth, even strokes. "He no want me stop."

Her little brother loved all animals, but especially horses, just like his father. If their parents would allow it, Jonah would forgo school and spend his days here with Runt, who would've followed him to school if Dad allowed it, keeping him company. After Jonah's schooling ended, he could work here, but he would never be a farrier—something none of them would tell him.

"What brings you out here, Dochder?" Her father's voice carried over the pounding of hammer against white-hot steel in front of the forge where her brother John shaped new horseshoes. "I can't remember the last time you stopped by."

"Bye, Runt. Bye, Jonah. Bye, Dusty."

Rachelle trudged back to her father's work area. He tapped in the nails, smooth side out, so its small curve would cause the end of the nail to protrude from the hoof where he could bend it over with a hammer and then use a nipper to remove the excess. She'd watched him do it a million times—or so it seemed. "Hi, Dat."

"What's up?"

"I had a visit with the Englisch teachers in town."

"Jah. And?"

"I don't believe they have the right attitude, the right understanding of our ways, to teach our kinner."

There. She'd said it. Loud and clear. Grandma had said to speak up. She could do so without being disrespectful. Whether Dad saw it that way was another story. With a quick breath, she went on to outline the conversation she'd had with Gabriel and Kim.

"It sounds like you set them straight." Dad laid the nipper aside and picked up the rasp to smooth the hoof and shoe one last time. "It also sounds like your pride is wounded."

"It's not my pride." Rachelle examined the protest in her words. "Jah, a little. But our kinner are bound to be affected by their attitudes and values, simply by being around them so much."

"The parents' committee has made an agreement with the school district because we trust them to meet our kinner's needs better than we can." Dad shifted and gently let the Percheron's massive leg return to the ground. The horse whinnied, almost as in relief. Wincing, Dad straightened, one hand on his back. He patted the horse's rump. "You and me both, my friend."

He grabbed a faded green bandanna from his rolling tool kit and mopped his face. "That doesn't mean we won't be closely watching what our kinner are learning—in the classroom and on the playground and wherever else they go. I expect you will lead that effort. You communicate with Sadie and Jonah and the others better than any of the rest of us. We know that, Dochder, and we will rely on you to monitor them, making sure they're getting only what they need and nothing else. We trust your judgment."

His words bordered on a rare compliment. Heat toasted Rachelle's cheeks. "I will do my best." If she didn't have to take a job in another district. "How would you feel about me taking a job in another community?"

Her father stopped working. He faced Rachelle. His dark eyes held a softness she rarely saw there. "It would hurt my heart, kind. But if Gott's will and Gott's plan is for you to teach elsewhere, so be it. Your mamm and I pray for Gott's will in all of this. We pray you find a mann and become a fraa and mudder, but only Gott knows the plans He has for you." His voice grew raspy. He turned back to the horse.

The sound of a throat clearing broke the silence that had descended. Rachelle swiveled. The heat jumped from steamy to turn-wood-to-ashes in seconds. "Toby. I didn't see you there."

Toby Miller shifted from one foot to the other. He had a saddle slung over one shoulder. His handsome face was damp with perspiration. "Sorry. I didn't want to interrupt. My bruder dropped me off."

"You're not interrupting a thing." Dad turned back again. "Your horse is ready to go. He's in the last stall."

Toby shifted a saddle to his other shoulder and pulled a check from the pocket formed by the flap on his pants. "Here's your payment."

"Lay it on my tool kit. I'll get it later." Dad held up filthy hands. "You're planning to ride him home?"

"Jah. It's a nice day for a ride."

"He's raring to go. That Morgan is a mighty fine piece of horseflesh."

"My dat has a good eye for horses."

Their chitchat didn't include Rachelle. She squared her shoulders and raised her chin. Her conversation with Dad had gone about as well as expected. She, too, could use a ride, but she'd have to settle for a walk. She slipped out the door and started down the narrow dirt road that would take her past the enormous vegetable garden they'd planted in the last few weeks, past the pond, and to the end of the lane where it dead-ended at the highway.

When had life become so complicated? Only six weeks ago she'd been content, happily teaching scholars and daydreaming about one day in the future when she'd meet the man of her dreams. The warm sun beat down on her neck and cheeks, reminding her of the passage of time. A few more weeks and school would be finished for the year. Her time as one of the district's teachers would be over.

"Get over it, Rachelle." She inhaled the sweet scent of the purple and white woodland phlox that crowded the road's edge. A pair of scarlet tanagers flew from one cottonwood tree to another, tweeting a cheerful song. "No pity parties allowed."

"Talking to yourself?" Toby's amused bass carried over the *clip-clop* of his newly shod horse's hooves. "Tell me you don't answer."

Rachelle whirled and walked backward. She put her hand to her forehead and squinted to see his features haloed by the sun behind him. "It's a private conversation, if you don't mind."

He laughed a deep, hearty laugh that—despite everything—made Rachelle want to laugh too. "At least you know you're speaking with someone who understands you."

"Maybe, maybe not." She did an about-face and resumed her forward march. "I don't think I understand much of anything these days."

"I'm of the same mind." He'd slowed his horse to a walk. "Do you mind if I join you?"

"I thought you already had." Rachelle employed a tart tone that covered her sudden need for this man's company. "What's one more confused soul on the road to knowledge?"

Toby dismounted with the ease of a man with long legs and much experience. He fell into step next to her. "I overheard your conversation with your dat. I wasn't trying to eavesdrop, I promise, but there was nowhere else for me to go."

"My dat is a gut mann and a gut daed."

"I have a lot of respect for him."

"I just wish we saw eye to eye on this one thing."

"I'm sorry."

It was such a simple statement, but so kind, so full of empathy, Rachelle put her hand to her chest to keep her heart where it belonged. "Do you think it's wrong for me to oppose our kinder attending the Englisch school?"

"There's nothing wrong with how you feel. You have the heart of a teacher. You love them. That's one of the beauties of your nature." His voice softened. His tenderness enveloped Rachelle like a warm shawl. "Your dat is right too. The Englisch have much to offer, our district will benefit financially, and it will ease your family's financial burden."

"I must bow to the greater gut, I know that." Rachelle suppressed a sigh. She'd taken vows to obey the Ordnung. She was expected to be obedient and humble herself. Her wants and needs weren't important. "It still hurts, though."

"I know exactly what you mean." Toby slowed his stride to match hers, then stopped. "Would you like a drink of water? I have water bottles in my saddlebag."

"That would be nice." Rachelle stopped as well. She patted his horse's muzzle and watched while Toby pulled out water bottles for each of them and handed one to her. "Danki."

He turned toward the fields newly planted in corn and alfalfa.

"Have you considered tutoring? You could tutor the kinner in the evenings. English will be hard for them. I suspect that'll be the biggest obstacle to them learning at the new school. You've done a good job getting them started, but I know Sadie still struggles. It wouldn't pay, but it would give you that sense of purpose that you crave."

"That's a possibility, I suppose." If she stayed in Lee's Gulch, which might not be an option. If teaching jobs didn't open up in this area, she would consider positions as far away as Bird-in-Hand, where she had family who would happily allow her to stay with them. Plus six hours wasn't so far that she couldn't come home for weekends now and then. "But only if I can't find a paying job. Dat's business does well, but money is always tight with so many kinner."

"I understand that. We all pitch in at our house too." Toby seemed engrossed in the view. The setting sun shone on his face, lighting up his eyes. "I was really being selfish with this idea."

"What do you mean?"

He faced her. A bead of sweat trickled down his temple. "Not just kinner have trouble reading."

"You mean . . . you need tutoring?"

"Nee, not me." He moved to the shoulder of the road where his horse took the opportunity to graze on the fresh, tender shoots of grass. "This is just between you and me."

"Of course."

His mouth worked. He sighed. "My dat has trouble reading. It's making it hard for him to run the business now that Daadi has retired."

Such a personal revelation. Only the desire to be a good son would've prompted Toby to share it with Rachelle. Toby's good heart beat in time with Rachelle's. It was hard to imagine not being able to read well. For Rachelle it came as natural as breathing.

Reading was the key to knowledge. Knowledge made life interesting. "And you want me to tutor him?"

"Jah."

"Does he want to be tutored?"

"I haven't asked him yet. He doesn't want to admit it's a problem. But I know it is because of the mistakes that are being made in scheduling and billing and the paying of bills."

That Toby offered practical reasons for the tutoring did nothing to negate his desire for his dad to be able to do what so many adults did with no effort and little thought. He grabbed his horse's reins and returned to the road. Rachelle joined him. "Do you know if there's a reason he has trouble reading? Does he need glasses? Has he been to the doctor to check for glaucoma, cataracts, or macular degeneration?"

Charlie was old, but not that old. Still, having grandparents and even great-grandparents for a time had given Rachelle a good understanding of the ways eyesight could be affected by aging. "My groossmammi had cataract surgery and daadi on my mamm's side, glaucoma."

"His eyesight is fine, as far as I know. Daadi says Dat probably has a reading disability like dyslexia, but he was never diagnosed."

"My experience is with physical and mental disabilities. I've never taught someone with a reading disability." So often people who had trouble reading were classified as "slow" or "hard learners." Especially in Plain communities where parents were less likely to have their children tested for things like dyslexia. "At least that I know of. So often reading disabilities go undiagnosed because Plain parents don't know better. Or Plain teachers, for that matter."

One of the disadvantages of not having more education or specialized training. Rachelle kept that opinion to herself. Her community would argue that the teachers had all the training and education they needed to prepare students for their Plain lives. Most of the time she agreed, but at times like this, it was frustrating not to be able to do more.

"But you could research it and learn more like you've done for teaching special kinner." In his agitation, Toby picked up his pace, forcing Rachelle to do the same. She touched his arm. He slowed again. "Sorry. I know I'm asking a lot. You've got a full plate already—"

"Nee. Not at all. I'm honored you would ask me. I just hope I *can* help. I'll see what I can find using the computers at the library." Any excuse to go to the library, one of her most favorite places in the world. Free books. Free knowledge. Knowledge for knowledge's sake. "But you know I can't do anything until you've talked to your dat about it."

"I do know that. It's just that it's a hard thing for a grown man to admit he has trouble reading."

"Until he does no one can help him."

"I know."

They were almost to the highway. Their walk had passed too quickly. Toby stopped. He stuck his foot in the stirrup and hoisted himself into the saddle. His hands gripped the reins, but he made no move to leave her behind. "I knew you could be counted on. It's your nature, one of the many traits I surely like about you."

Rachelle hid her hands in the folds of her skirts. They wanted to cover her warm cheeks. His voice held a caress that touched her face, slid down her neck, and across her shoulders. A delicate shudder shook her body. What did a woman say to such a statement? "Danki," she whispered.

"Don't thank me for speaking the truth." Toby's horse pranced as if to say, *Let's get a move on.* "I'll keep working on this thing with my dat. I'll get back to you on the tutoring."

Again his tone spoke of something else, some other meaning. *"I'll get back to you . . ."*

"Gut. After school lets out, my calendar will be wide open." Two could speak in double meanings. *Come calling. Get back to me. I'm here.* Rachelle raised her hand to her forehead to see his face better. "I'll wait to hear from you."

"Until then."

"Until then."

He rode away at a slow canter, sitting tall in the saddle, until he stopped at the highway, glanced both ways, then took off at a gallop.

Only when she could no longer see him did she turn to walk home. A person could never anticipate the sudden turns and twists in life. That Toby was trying was obvious. That he found it difficult to express his feelings, also obvious. Either he was out of practice or he'd never learned. The fact that he was trying made everything about the day seem brighter. Her earlier disappointment and frustration still sat heavy on her shoulders, but their weight seemed more manageable. Anxious to see where this new path would lead, she picked up her pace.

Chapter 21

*O*nly two weeks left of school. Good thing too. As much as Rachelle would miss teaching, she shared in her scholars' spring fever. The students had one foot out the door all day long. The windows were open to let in the breeze, but the chirping of cardinals, chickadees, robins, and tanagers came with it. Dogs barked. Horses whinnied. Leaves rustled. A chorus of song inviting them to come out and play.

Corrine ran spelling bees. Rachelle allotted more slots for story and singing time as well as flash card contests. Anything to hold their attention so they could learn more before summer break. Activities had included an outdoor scavenger hunt to find ten signs of spring after a discussion of the seasons and helping Rachelle write *Spring Has Sprung* in different colors of chalk on the board.

At the moment, they were drawing pictures of their favorite flowers to round out the activities.

"You're as bad as the kids," Corrine whispered as she peered over Rachelle's shoulder at the open notebook in front of her. She grabbed the apple Sadie had brought for Rachelle and tossed it up and down in one hand. "Doodles. Lots of doodles, I see. I'm holding this for ransom—until you stop staring out the window and doodling."

"I'm not staring . . . Okay, I'm staring out the window. This day has gone on forever."

"It's only ninety minutes until we're done."

"Too long. I'm sleepy."

"You're sleepy because you're lying in bed at night thinking about a certain auctioneer instead of closing your eyes and drifting away."

"Not true."

"Lying is a sin."

"Okay. A little bit true." How could I not? The images replayed in Rachelle's head: Toby sitting tall on his beautiful Morgan. Toby handing her a water bottle. Toby sharing a family secret with her.

Toby. Tall. Broad-shouldered. Blond. Eyes a slate blue like the color of the lake on a cloudy day.

No wonder she couldn't sleep. He'd said he'd work on getting his dad to talk to her about tutoring. Would he do more than that? Was his overture solely about needing her teaching ability, or did he want something else from her?

That question alone would keep her awake until something gave.

The door opened at the back of the room. Gabriel Jackson stepped in. He carried a large leather portfolio and a wooden easel.

Suddenly Rachelle was wide awake. Corrine deposited the apple back on the desk. "Who's this?"

"The Englisch teacher I told you about."

"What's he doing here?"

Rachelle hopped up. "I told you he wants to observe the students." She smoothed her apron and summoned a welcoming smile. "I reckon today's that day."

The students had noticed him too. Sadie craned her head and

stared. The other children followed suit. Rachelle squeezed past Corrine. "Kinner, work on your flower drawings. I'll be back in a minute."

Jonah swiveled and frowned. "Englisch man?"

"Englisch teacher." Rachelle patted his shoulder as she walked by. "Finish your drawing."

"I wish he would've scheduled his visit in the morning when the kinner are wide awake and fresh," Corrine murmured.

It would have been better if he'd scheduled it, period. Showing up without letting the parents' committee know might not set well with some of them. Or the bishop.

Rachelle strode to meet her guest while Corrine stopped long enough to instruct her sixth graders to exchange their arithmetic papers and grade them.

Gabriel waved. "I hope I haven't come at a bad time."

"Not at all. Our school lets out for the summer sooner than yours, so it's probably good you came now."

"We've been doing a lot of evals and assessing what students need to finish out the year strong." Gabriel shoved back a Norfolk Tides baseball cap and glanced around, his gaze openly curious. His uniform was similar to the one he'd worn at their first meeting—jeans, a Special Olympics T-shirt, and sneakers. No one would peg him as a teacher outside a school setting. "This is the first time I've been in an Amish school. It's something right out of a time warp. A one-room school with a chalkboard and wood-burning stove on the inside and outhouses in the back."

Did he mean that to be complimentary? His eager expression said yes.

All smiles, Corrine joined their huddle on the welcome mat. Rachelle introduced her. Her fellow teacher and best friend pumped Gabriel's hand like she was meeting the president. Rachelle fought the urge to tug on her arm. "Corrine handles the children who are typically abled. The older students work with the younger ones. I focus on the children with special needs. With such a small number of students, we're able to give everyone what they most require. It's right sized."

She was rattling on much more than necessary, her nerves doing the fast-talking for her. What did she have to be nervous about? This was her and Corrine's territory. It had been for three years. Gabriel's program was taking that away.

"Rachelle's right. We can provide our students with so much individual attention. They learn English and German. They're basically trilingual by the time they leave school." Corrine didn't try to corral her pride in their work. No matter the tenets of their faith, it was an accomplishment to teach High German and English to students who spoke only Pennsylvania Dutch at home. "Our children with intellectual disabilities learn these languages as well—to the best of their abilities. Rachelle does a beautiful job with them. She has so much patience."

Corrine knew all about Gabriel's offer of a job if Rachelle could meet the educational requirements. She'd pooh-poohed the idea, saying they had all the education they needed to give their students the learning they needed, suited to the Plain lives they would live.

"It's true we have bigger classes, and we don't teach foreign languages at the elementary school level. But we have individual aides specifically assigned to our children with special needs. They'll assist your students in learning English. Plus teacher aides for the general education students, reading assistants, and specialists for speech and hearing impairments." Gabriel rattled off these enhancements with the ease of a man who'd made many presentations to parents, administrators, school boards, and foundations. "We have counselors and social workers as well. Music and art teachers. Librarians and a good library. A physical education teacher. They'll get the works."

"Good resources." This wasn't a competition. Amish schools could never win such a contest, but their students received what they needed. Their children without disabilities did well on state standardized tests—for what that was worth. "Would you like to meet the students now?"

"I'd like to observe your interactions first."

Rachelle glanced at the windup clock on her desk. An hour left. She went to the area where she'd created a half circle at the front of the room so she could do flash card work with her students that morning.

Gabriel traipsed to a spot close to her right where he deposited his portfolio and easel. He leaned back and relaxed against the wall. Like the students wouldn't notice this gangly English man watching them.

Except for Tracy, who still had the tip of his tongue on his upper lip while he drew his version of a tulip, the students had abandoned any pretense of working on their drawings. Rachelle visited each student to review his or her drawing and offer praise. Sadie's flowers were definitely daisies. Her ability to translate what she saw in the garden to a crayon drawing had improved. "I love daisies, Tietschern." She touched the crude brown strokes that outlined the white flower. "Happy flowers."

"Indeed they are." Rachelle handed her a flash card with the word *flower* on it. "Can you write *daisy* at the bottom of the paper for me?"

"Easy peasy." Sadie beamed and quickly demonstrated. "D-A-I-S-Y."

"Gut job."

Rachelle went to the chalkboard and wrote the sentence *I like flowers because* _____. "When you finish your drawing, you can write this sentence below it, then fill in the blank. Also tell me what color your flower is." She pointed to the poster hanging next to the chalkboard that displayed all the colors and the associated words. "I'll come around to help you."

She stopped at Tracy's desk first. Dropping to one knee, she praised his circle with lines sprouting around it that represented petals. "What's your favorite flower?"

Squinting, the little boy cocked his head and frowned. "The kind that grows in the ground."

Tracy's words were understandable, even though they were slurred. Between his lisp and delayed speech, he was often tricky to follow, but he had improved tremendously.

"I'm going to write *flower* here at the bottom. Can you try to write it after me?"

He sighed and shrugged. Not surprising given the lateness in the day. Tracy did well in the mornings, but in the afternoons his energy lagged.

"Just give it your best effort, okay?"

Tracy nodded. "O-tay."

Next came Jonah. He had his head down on his desk. His pencil lay on the floor near his feet. Rachelle picked it up. She tapped on his shoulder. "How is your flower coming?"

His expression sour, he raised his head. "Man watching us," he said in Pennsylvania Dutch. "Why?"

"English, please." Rachelle knelt next to him. She handed the pencil to him. "He's from the school you'll attend in the fall. I'll introduce you soon. How's your picture coming?"

Jonah removed his hands from the paper. He'd used a black crayon to scribble a blob with black squiggles under it. More like a squid than a flower. Rachelle studied it for a few seconds. "Do you remember the talk we had about feelings, like mad and sad and happy?"

His gaze didn't meet hers. Still he nodded.

"This picture makes me think you're mad and sad. Is that right?"

He shrugged.

"Sometimes we get mad because we're worried about something we think is going to be bad, even though we don't know for sure. Even when people tell us it will be okay."

"You no know."

"I don't know. Neither do you. Do you know who does?"

"Gott."

"God. You know what Bart would say about that?"

Jonah liked Bart. The bishop had a sweet tooth. He kept a stash of Tootsie Pops close by, and he believed in sharing. "Nee."

Jonah was nothing if not consistent. "English, Jonah. No." Rachelle turned the paper over to the clean side. "Bart would say not to worry. God has a plan. No matter what happens, He'll be there to walk through it with you."

"*Wo?*" Jonah made exaggerated, flapping motions with both arms. "I see nobody."

"Where? English. Faith means believing in something you can't see."

His face screwed up in a determined effort not to cry. Rachelle covered his hand with hers. "Why don't you think of something that would make you happy right now? Draw that."

"Man go away. Make me happy."

"He's a nice man. He just wants to share some pictures with all of you. Then he'll go."

Jonah shrugged. He scooped up a crayon—brown this time—

and bent over his desk. It would be a horse. It always was. Rachelle ran her hand over his thick dark hair and moved on.

It took another thirty minutes to cover the rest of her students. She glanced at the clock on her desk. Thirty minutes left. She approached Gabriel, who still leaned against the wall, hat shoved back on his head. "Your turn."

"You're such a patient teacher. Just the kind we need in special education." He straightened. "I'm really impressed with the progress you've made with these students."

He didn't say *in these conditions*. But the words lingered in the air, just the same.

Rachelle backed away. "We're running out of time, if you want to talk with them one-on-one."

"It's such a small group. Let's just do it as a huddle. Introduce me and I'll take it from there."

In the meantime, Corrine had sent the King brothers, Robbie and Judah, to park their wheelchairs alongside Rachelle's students. The children usually loved guests, but they didn't respond to Gabriel with the usual enthusiasm—except Sadie. She showed off her good manners with a hello and an old-fashioned curtsy that made the other kids giggle.

Gabriel responded in kind with a courtly bow, which he followed up with a handshake.

"I stopped by today to say hey and tell you how much I'm looking forward to seeing you this fall at Eisenhower Elementary School. I don't know how much Ms. Lapp has told you about me—"

Titters from the children interrupted his earnest words. "What?"

"Teacher." Sadie pointed at Rachelle. "Just Teacher. Or Rachelle."

"Gotcha. I thought I'd share with you some of the fun stuff

you'll be doing at your new school. Maybe Teacher can be my assistant."

Rachelle returned to the front while Gabriel made quick work of setting up his easel. From the portfolio, he extracted a stack of poster-size photos. "Rachelle, will you put this on the easel and then take them off when it's time for the next one?"

"I'd be happy to."

Gabriel didn't really need her assistance. He could've left them on the easel, but this allowed the children to see them working together. Getting along. Her smiling at him. Smart move. First up, an enlarged photo of a colorful playground that included a fort, swings, slides, and lots of other amenities—all accessible. Tracy slid from his seat and crept forward. Gabriel smiled and waved him closer. "Come on up. You're Tracy, right?"

The little boy, suddenly shy, scampered back to his desk.

"You can all get closer if you want." He pointed to the spot in front of the easel. "Feel free to sit right here if you can see better."

Two seconds later, Sadie, Nan, Tracy, and Jacob were up front. Rachelle's more outgoing students. Jonah still had his head bent over his drawing. Minnie leaned back in her chair, arms crossed. Danny sat half in, half out of his chair, as if posed to flee.

Gabriel handed the next photo to Rachelle. She placed it on the easel. It featured a smiling man standing next to a lowered volleyball net. He held a striped beach ball in his big hands. "This is Mr. Cartwright. He's our physical education teacher. You'll have P.E. with other students your age. He loves to play all sorts of games. That would be a fun job, right? Playing games all day long?"

"Games," Tracy repeated. "Fun."

Rachelle clapped. "Two good English words." Clearly said too. "Way to go, Tracy."

Next up was the library, with a smiling librarian who wore

purple glasses and a dress embroidered with flowers in red, blue, purple, and yellow across the shoulders and down the front. She held up a book all the children recognized: *Llama Llama Red Pajama* by Anna Dewdney. Rachelle liked to read that one aloud because the title rhymed and it emphasized a color.

"I know it. I know it," Minnie shrieked and pointed. "Llama Llama—"

"Red Pajama," Nan finished for her. "It good. I like *Llama Llama Misses Momma* too."

"I like *Llama Llama Mad at Momma*." Too many *l*'s challenged Jacob, but he pushed through. "I don't get mad."

The book had given them the chance to talk about feelings, especially being mad or sad. None of the children would admit to getting mad at someone so important as a mom.

Dads were different.

"Those are all good. It's hard to pick one favorite, isn't it?" Gabriel grinned at Rachelle. "Don't we make a great team?" his expression said. "You'll get to check out books with the other kids and go to story hour. Mrs. Jarvis is a great storyteller. She likes to dress up like the main character. Sometimes she shows up to work as a bookworm. She's been green eggs and ham. Little Red Riding Hood. You just never know who you'll see when you go into the library."

He had their full attention now. Rachelle peeked at Jonah. Despite his best intentions, he was listening but not smiling. Reading was so hard for him. He liked listening, but listening invariably led to being asked to read. He didn't much like any of the academic subjects, no matter how Rachelle framed them. If only reading wasn't so hard for him. That was like wishing life was fair.

Next stop was the cafeteria. A worker wearing a plastic cap over her hair mugged for the camera. She held a tray filled with a hamburger, fries, apple slices, green beans, an oatmeal cookie, and milk. Sadie "oohed." Nan "aahed." They loved cookies and milk. "Lookie, Jonah, lookie. Hamburger." Sadie pointed and swiveled at the same time. "You like fries."

He did indeed. Jonah laid down his crayon. "Fries. Cookies. Every day?"

Rachelle and Gabriel laughed at the same time. Maybe the way to this student's heart was through his stomach.

The school door opened. His boots a steady *thump, thump* on the vinyl floor, Toby strode inside.

He didn't look happy.

Chapter 22

*T*he alarm clock's shrill ring broke the sudden silence. Rachelle jumped. No time to ask Toby why he had come to the school. Twenty students perched on the edges of their seats, gazes fixed on Corrine and her, waiting for that moment when they had permission to shoot out the door.

Only Sadie couldn't contain herself. She popped up from her spot on the floor, raced past Rachelle, and flung herself at Toby. "Bruder, Bruder!"

Toby scooped her up and swung her around in a circle, eliciting a cry of delight. He sent Rachelle an inquiring glance. Rachelle ignored it. First things first. "Children, it's time to go. Line up by your desks."

She clapped. Everyone moved at once. The King brothers rolled themselves back to their respective spots, while the other kids skedaddled to their desks. It didn't matter who the special guest was when school ended—it ended.

"One thing that's the same everywhere." Chuckling, Gabriel tucked his posters into the portfolio case. "That last bell rings and kids are gone. There's no holding them back."

"Not exactly. Not here." Rachelle pointed to the handmade

poster on the wall. The children stood by their desks. The younger ones went first to grab their jackets and lunch boxes. Followed by the older kids who made sure their siblings didn't forget anything. An orderly retreat.

"Amazing."

Rachelle made eye contact with Corrine. She nodded and took over dismissal duties. Rachelle scurried to the back. "Toby. Is something wrong?"

"Who's the man?"

Before Rachelle could explain, Gabriel's scent of spicy aftershave made its presence known. He'd followed her. He stuck out his hand and introduced himself to Toby.

"Ah."

Toby didn't offer his own introduction. His one-syllable response told Rachelle plenty about his reaction to finding Gabriel here. "Mamm asked me to pick up the girls and take them to Jason's. It's his fraa's birthday. We're celebrating there."

"Tell Caitlin I said seelich gebortsdaag." Sweat dampened Rachelle's palms. "Don't eat too much cake, Sadie."

"There's no such thing as too much cake, is there, Sadie?" Gabriel chucked Sadie's arm with a light touch. "Or ice cream."

"No such thing," Sadie repeated. "Lots."

Toby took a step back. The door opened yet again. Another relative?

In a way. Only this time it was the bishop. Bart squeezed in next to Toby. They were amassing quite a crowd in the foyer. They were about to have a traffic jam. Rachelle glanced back. Corrine's eyebrows signaled, *Time to go*. Rachelle did what teachers do. She took charge. "If you men could step aside, the children are ready to be dismissed for the day. Some of them have long walks home. Let's not hold them up."

Their students made Corrine and Rachelle proud—no doubt acutely aware of the bishop's presence. They picked up their lunch buckets and jackets and speed-walked past their visitors with shy nods and quick good-byes. All three men waved, smiled, and generally acted grown-up. Toby sent Sadie out to the buggy with Josie and Sherri. She hung on to his hand long enough to give Gabriel her most careful pronunciation of "See you."

"See you." He tipped his baseball cap. "Can't wait."

Bart sent his three students out to his buggy as well. They were getting a rare reprieve from a two-mile walk.

As soon as the door closed, Bart turned to them. "I saw a car parked outside the school from the road. I thought I'd better check to see what was going on." He stopped, his round face expectant.

Rachelle jumped in with an explanation.

Bart shook hands with Gabriel and welcomed him to the school. "I've heard a lot about you from the superintendent. It's nice to put a face to the name."

"Likewise." Gabriel nodded. "I just wanted to get the kids excited about next year. I showed them poster-size photos of the cool stuff we'll offer them in our program. And I spoke in English to help them get used to the idea that they'll be talking a lot more in that language as well. Rachelle assisted with any translations needed."

"I see. Sounds like a good plan." Bart stroked his golden-blond beard. He pressed his thin lips together for a few seconds, then nodded. "Just know that in the future, it's best to approach the parents' committee for any plan to visit the school. We just like to have advance notice as a courtesy. The superintendent didn't mention site visits, so it caught me off guard."

"Understood. Understood." Only Gabriel didn't appear to understand at all. He picked up his portfolio and easel. He turned to Rachelle. "I'll get out of your way now, but it was great to see you again. You're doing a tremendous job with these kids. I can see why the district entrusts them to you." He nodded at Corrine, who'd joined them without saying a word. "You too, Corrine. I applaud what you're able to do with such limited resources and with nine grades in one room. It's phenomenal. You've made it easier for us to do the heavy lifting when they start in our program in the fall."

"That's kind of you." Sort of. His words would be what Mom would call a "left-handed compliment." They had done a lot, but the English folks could do so much more. Maybe they could. That was good, what was best for these little ones. "I hope you got everything you needed."

Gabriel nodded at the two men and took his leave. Rachelle breathed again.

"He shouldn't have been here." Toby crossed his arms. "Did you know he was coming?"

"He mentioned he intended to visit, but he never said when—"

"You're not on the parents' committee, Toby." Bart employed a gentle but firm tone. "Neither am I, for that matter, but I'll talk to them about Gabriel's visit. No sense in making a big mountain out of it. He meant well. I'm sure Rachelle did as well. A visit like this will pave the way for a smooth transition this fall. That's what we all want, isn't it?"

Bart's pointed question seemed to pin Toby to a wall. He nodded. "I know that's what Mamm and Dat want."

"But not you?"

"Jah, I do. If it were me, though, I might think Sadie was better off here with Rachelle and Corrine." Toby shifted his weight and tapped one boot. "His words didn't ring sincere, all that talk about limited resources and heavy lifting. Talk about a left-handed compliment."

Exactly what Rachelle's mother would've said. Rachelle opened her mouth to say so. Bart shook his head. "That sounds a bit like sour grapes to me. Rachelle and Corrine do an adequate job. That's all we ask of them. As a parent, I've never been unhappy with their work, but the committee has made its decision. We're to stand by it. Right, Rachelle?"

An adequate job. Not a glowing recommendation, but then Plain folks didn't offer many compliments. Compliments led to swelled heads and pride. Rachelle nodded. "Jah."

"Gut. My kinner will be gnawing off their arms by now. My fraa says they always come home starved, no matter how big a lunch she packs for them."

"Growing kinner." Rachelle followed the two men out onto the porch. Corrine joined them. "You can imagine the amount of food we go through at the Lapp house."

They could imagine. None of them had small families. Not as big as the Lapps but plenty large.

"Toby, you'd better get to the birthday party." Bart tugged his straw hat tighter on his head against a brisk breeze. He started down the steps. "The kinner won't want to miss out on taking their turns cranking the ice cream maker."

A hint that the other man shouldn't linger with the teachers either? "Jah, I should go." Toby rubbed his neck and cocked it side to side. "I'll be going then."

Yet he didn't move.

"I'll take out the trash and close up." Corrine's wink sent another wave of heat through Rachelle. Her friend had no finesse. What if Toby saw it? "You go on. I don't mind."

Usually the children took turns with the cleanup. Gabriel's visit had changed that as well. "I'm not in a rush. Let me do it."

"Nee. Go." Corrine waved her arms. "I'll be right behind you."

Rachelle glared. Corrine grinned and disappeared into the school.

"She's not very subtle, is she?"

"She means well." Rachelle headed for her buggy, parked alongside the building so her horse could graze in the shade of several red oak trees. "But no, she's about as subtle as the odor of burned popcorn."

Toby followed her. "I'm sorry."

"About what?" Rachelle fumbled with the rope she used to tether the horse. He pranced and nickered. "Time to go to work, Otis."

"Otis?"

"It was Sean's turn to name an animal. Who knows where he got that one." She slid the halter over Otis's muzzle and secured the bit. "Aren't you in a hurry to get to Jason's for Caitlin's birthday? I reckon your schwesdchdre are."

The younger Lapp and Miller girls had taken over the swings, while Rachelle's brothers were busy kicking a soccer ball around. Sadie's delighted laugh got louder with each time Emma pushed her swing higher. None of them seemed in any hurry to leave.

"I'm sorry I overreacted to the Englisch tietschern being here."

"The Englisch tietschern has a name. Gabriel."

"Gabriel's visit was a gut idea. It just surprised me."

"You have a right to be concerned about who teaches your schweschder." Of course, Gabriel would have daily contact with Sadie in the coming school year. They all needed to get used to the idea. "I feel the same about Jonah."

"I know you do. You would never do anything not in the best interest of the kinner." Toby finished hitching the horse up to the buggy without asking. He ran his hand along Otis's withers. He had strong but gentle hands. Rachelle tore her gaze from them. He faced her. "We seem to always get off on the wrong foot. I don't know why."

"We're not on the wrong foot." They weren't on any foot. Not yet. "We're fine."

"Gut."

He wanted to say something else. That was obvious. Whatever it was seemed stuck in his throat. The urge to coax it out of him overwhelmed Rachelle. She bit her tongue.

Toby backed away. "I'd better get going."

"You said that earlier."

"I did, didn't I?" His tone was diffident. "This time I mean it. You take care driving home."

Take care driving? Rachelle drove a pony cart for the first time when she was seven. She'd been driving buggies forever. "You too."

"I deserve that." He winced. "See you."

Rachelle waited until he was halfway across the yard. "See you . . . soon."

She said it quietly. If he heard, he didn't show it.

Chapter 23

"*Y*ou're back. How was your visit to Bird-in-Hand? How are Great-Onkel and Great-Aenti?"

Toby left the word *finally* unspoken, but it lingered in the brisk evening breeze all the same. After Grandpa's two weeks' notice were up, Grandpa and Grandma left for Pennsylvania for a two-week visit that had stretched into a month. Now Grandpa sat on Jason's front porch with an enormous bowl of ice cream in his hands undeterred by a cool evening breeze. He didn't speak. Instead he stuck another serving spoon loaded with vanilla ice cream drenched in chocolate syrup in his mouth.

Carrying his own oversized bowl, Toby squeezed past him and took a seat in the other lawn chair. The chair groaned under his weight. A bowl of ice cream might get rid of the sour taste in his mouth after his foolish performance at the school earlier in the day.

He still couldn't fathom why the sight of the English teacher standing so close to Rachelle had bothered him so much. Still bothered him. The man was a teacher doing a job. The fact that his hand brushed hers when she handed over the posters was purely accidental.

Wasn't it?

Toby had come so close to telling Rachelle he wanted to take her for a buggy ride, but the words wouldn't emerge. Why? He was as tongue-tied around her as a sixteen-year-old at his first singing.

Why? What was it about her? The way her dark eyes stood out against her fair skin? The nearly black hair that teased him, igniting the desire to remove the pins from her prayer covering so he could let her hair down and run his hands through it?

No. Yes. But it was more than that. She had a spark in those dark eyes when she spoke of "her" children. She loved them deeply. Rachelle nurtured. She protected. She encouraged. She put every ounce of her soul into teaching her scholars. That drew Toby to her no matter how hard he dug his heels in.

"Toby? I said jah, we're back." Grandpa tapped his spoon on his bowl. "Obviously. We got back yesterday."

Toby forced himself to abandon the endless loop that had been playing in his head since he left the school. "Gut. That's gut. You were missed."

The words were sincere but somehow came out sounding like a complaint.

Grandpa shrugged and took another bite of ice cream. They didn't have to explain the change in their plans to Toby—or anyone else. Still, it left Toby with an unsettled feeling in the pit of his stomach. A month wasn't so much time, yet Grandpa's frame seemed more hunched, his gait shakier, his wrinkles deeper, and the skin on his age-spotted hands thinner.

"Did you have a gut time?"

Grandpa nodded and kept eating. He had chocolate cake crumbs in his silver beard and barbecue sauce on his upper lip.

"Are you going to say anything?"

He picked up his napkin, wiped his face, and brushed away the crumbs. "About what?"

Toby studied the pale pinks, magentas, and yellows of a sunset slowly taking its leave from a blue sky fading to black. He squirmed in his chair. He rolled his shoulders, then cranked his head to one side, then the other. "The days have been long. At the office. Especially the office. On the road. The motels."

"Did you buy a pack of bubble gum?"

Grandpa had taught them to blow bubbles. When they got bored on the road, they would compete to see who could blow the biggest one without letting it pop. "Jah. Chewed every piece. We sang all the songs too. Twice."

Dad's voice was better than Grandpa's, but Grandpa knew more songs. Funny songs. Silly songs. Ridiculous songs.

"That's just the way life is." Grandpa scraped the bottom of the bowl. He slurped the last drops of ice cream that had melted into chocolate milk. "You're a full-grown man. You know that. A person has to make the best of it."

"It's not the same without you."

"I miss it too."

There it was. The admission Toby needed. "You could come back." He picked at a catsup stain on his pants. "That's the thing about owning a company. You make the rules. You make the decisions. You could un-retire."

"That's not what my fraa thinks."

His laugh was half chuckle, half snort. Toby joined him. Grandma had a right to want more of her husband's time. Who was Toby to deprive her of that? She'd spent most of her adult life waiting for Grandpa to come home from somewhere on the road. "When did she start making the rules?"

"When I decided it was her turn." Grandpa settled the empty bowl onto the wooden crates stacked into a makeshift table between their chairs. "After forty years of being an auctioneer's wife, she deserves to have a stretch of time to call her own before we die."

That last word pierced Toby's chest, sharper than any knife he'd ever used for butchering a deer or cleaning a fish. "Don't talk like that."

"Gott has the number of our days written in his Book of Life." Grandpa stretched out his legs and sighed, a sound replete with contentment. He patted his small paunch. "I've had more than my share of ice cream and cake. I've had a gut life. I'm ready to go whenever He calls me. As everyone should be. Including you."

"I know."

"If it is Gott's will, you still have time to experience all this life has to offer." Grandpa's voice, permanently hoarse from years of calling, softened. "Which is why you should stop wasting your time and marry. It's expected. You aren't an exception to the rule."

Startled, Toby sat up straight. *Easy.* He inhaled the scent of coral honeysuckle wafting from the vines Caitlin had planted over the length of the front porch. *Easy.* His grandfather had never expressed an opinion regarding what Mom and Dad considered their oldest son's major failing. His refusal to get married. Their opinions were important, but Grandpa's even more so. "You of all people know why I hesitate to marry."

"Ask your mammi. Ask your mudder. Ask them if they've been unhappy married to their auctioneer menner." Grandpa's voice took on a hard edge. "Are you judging us for the way we treat our fraas?"

"Nee, I would never criticize you or Dat." Toby leaned forward and stuck his elbows on his knees. He studied the line of ants that crept along the wooden slats, avoiding his dusty work boots. Worker ants, doing their jobs, doing what was expected of them. He couldn't tell Grandpa about Janey's judgment and how she'd hurt him. Jason was the only one Toby had confided in—and then only because Jason pestered him into it. "I try to put myself in the shoes of a woman who lives this life. I wonder if it takes a certain kind of woman to be happy in these circumstances and how I will know if I've found that woman who can."

"If she loves you, she'll be happy."

"Wise words, but what does it say about me if I'm willing to subject her to a life of loneliness?"

"What Plain woman is lonely with a brood of kinner, schwesdchdre, kossins, aentis, friends, family from hither and yon?" Grandpa infused the words with a mixture of sarcasm and tenderness only he could summon. "More likely they wish for a few minutes of peace."

"Maybe."

"A faithful Plain woman follows the same tenets as you or me. Die unto self. Obedience. She'll put the well-being of her mann and her family ahead of her own needs." He paused as if to let his words sink in. "Are you willing to do the same?"

A skinny tabby cat wandered up the porch steps, paused with one paw in the air, then ambled toward them. Without hesitation he jumped gracefully into Grandpa's lap. His purr revved loudly in the silence. Grandpa laid one hand on his knobby back. Even animals knew where comfort lay.

"Did Mamm put you up to this?"

"Nee. I have eyes to see. I also wonder if this is just an excuse."

It wasn't a decision so much as a state of mind. "What else would make me hesitate?"

"Fear."

"I'm not afraid. What would I be afraid of?"

"Sharing your world. Making a family."

Toby shook his head. He wasn't a coward. Was he afraid? Yes. Maybe a little. Afraid of failing. Afraid of making a woman unhappy. A legitimate fear. Maybe someday he would be able to leave the memories of his first love in the past. He'd been a boy then. He was a man now. He knew what he wanted. The question was whether he should inflict this life on a woman like Rachelle. And whether she would want it.

"That's not it." Toby stood. "It's getting late. Mamm wants me to take the maed home. They have school tomorrow."

Grandpa didn't move. His long legs blocked Toby's path. His sharp jaw jutting, he stared up at Toby with eyes that familiar slate-blue color seen throughout generations of the Miller family. "You said the days had been long at the office. Why?"

Another barbed-wire sharp topic. Toby sank into his chair. He studied the drops of melted ice cream that created a brown puddle in the bottom of his bowl. "You know Dat can't read, don't you?"

"He can read." This time Grandpa's sigh held regret. "Not well, but enough."

"Not well enough to run an office." Toby swiveled so he could see his grandfather's expression. "You knew that, but you put him in charge. Bills aren't getting paid on time. The schedule is a mess. He feels bad and frustrated. That didn't have to happen."

"He's next in line. It would've been wrong to do anything different."

"You could've broken up the duties differently. Had me run the office." It didn't feel good, this complaining about a decision made because Grandpa hadn't wanted to make his son feel ashamed or lacking. "Why can't he read?"

"Just talking came hard for him. We couldn't understand him until he was almost five. Then he started school. Things got worse."

"Why worse?"

"Learning Englisch? It ain't easy even for kinner who aren't hard learners." Grandpa's expression turned mournful. "He hated school from the get-go. On the first day of first grade, he came home and said he wasn't going back. Some days he begged us to let him stay home. His teacher said he was smart, just not at book learning. The day he finished eighth grade was one of the happiest of his life. For your mammi and me, it was a relief."

"Have you talked to him about it since then?"

"Nee. I tried a time or two before he got married, but he never wanted to talk about it, so I let it go."

"I did something. I'm thinking about doing something."

Grandpa's hand stilled. The cat raised its head and meowed pitifully. "Spit it out, Suh."

"I asked Rachelle Lapp if she would consider tutoring him in reading."

"Ach. It's a private thing. Your dat wouldn't want others to know about it."

"But it also must pain him to have so much trouble with something he needs in order to run the business." Toby rushed to justify his actions. Rachelle wasn't just any outsider. She was a teacher who had experience in teaching hard learners. "Isn't it possible he might consider it a gut idea?"

"You really think he'll want to sit down like a kind with a tietchern to learn something everyone else learned a long time ago? You'll shame him."

"That's not my intention."

The screen door swung open. Toby's dad ambled onto the porch. "What's going on out here? What are you talking about so seriously?"

"Retirement. Business. Why Toby hasn't gotten married yet."

Dad hooted. "Your mudder would like the answer to that question."

Toby followed his grandfather's lead. "It could still happen."

"Anything's possible." Dad guffawed. His hair was still blond, with only a few streaks of gray, and he had far fewer wrinkles, but he was still the spitting image of his father. Even his laugh sounded the same. "Just know it would make your mudder and me very happy."

"Mamm's made that clear. Everyone has."

"We'd better get a move on. Tomorrow's a long day."

Tomorrow they headed to set up for a three-day auction in Charlottesville. From there they headed to Winchester, West Virginia, for a livestock auction, and finally a big estate auction in Harrisburg, Pennsylvania. The auction season was in full swing. Toby stood and stretched. He picked up the dirty bowls. Grandpa nudged his feline companion from his lap and joined them. Dad pulled the screen door open and went in first.

Grandpa held the door for a second. "Let it go."

Toby nodded. For now. Whatever he decided to do, it would have to wait.

Until it couldn't.

Chapter 24

*W*all-to-wall students. So to speak. Rachelle hid a chuckle behind her hand. She stood at the front of the classroom with Corrine, surveying a sea of expectant, smiling faces. Students much larger—and older—than usual occupied every other row of desks. Their usual students sat in the rows behind them. The scholars loved this day. They were allowed to bring a parent or family member to school to sit in their chairs and be the "students." Helping them out with their studies tickled their funny bones to no end. The closer it came to the end of April and the school year, the more she and Corrine scrambled to keep their attention.

"Wow. Sadie brought Toby." Corrine leaned closer and whispered, "That's unexpected."

Rachelle followed her gaze to the door. Sure enough. Sadie had a firm hold on Toby's hand, tugging him down the aisle toward the first row where she normally sat. He was supposed to leave on the auction circuit in a day or two. Seeing him here now couldn't have been more surprising. Elizabeth or Layla would've had more time for this playful exercise.

Toby didn't seem to mind. He grinned at Rachelle and waved. "Guder mariye, Tietschern."

"English, please. Good morning, Toby." A tiny tremor shook Rachelle. Her hand went to her prayer cap of its own accord. Did she have a stain on her apron? Was she a mess? How ridiculous. This wasn't about her. *Focus.*

Corrine rang the bell. Rachelle jumped. *Get a grip.*

"Time to begin." First up, the Scripture reading. Her palms suddenly clammy, Rachelle picked up her notebook where she'd written today's verse. She'd chosen Ephesians 6:1–3. The parents would appreciate it. She cleared her throat. "'Children, obey your parents in the Lord, for this is right. "Honor your father and mother" (this is the first commandment with a promise), "that it may go well with you and that you may live long in the land."'"

Several parents nodded and smiled.

"Stand for the Lord's Prayer."

It had been many years since most of these scholars had been in a classroom, but they hadn't forgotten the daily routine. Next came songs. The parents traipsed to the front of the room and lined up according to the age of their children. Toby had a nice bass. Bart managed to be off-key in both Pennsylvania Dutch and English. Minnie's mother didn't know the words. Rachelle's mom made no attempt to sing. She was too busy staring at Toby. Rachelle slid closer and shot her a frown. Mom grinned and cocked her head toward Toby. Could she be more obvious?

It was going to be a long day.

One subject at a time.

Corrine joined Rachelle at the front of the room. The "students" would read the reports written by their scholars grades fifth through eighth resulting from the field trip they'd taken in a van that drove the hundred-mile length of Lee's Retreat—the route General Robert E. Lee and his Confederate troops took while being pursued by Union forces from Petersburg to the Appomattox Court

House in Farmville, where the final surrender was signed at the end of the Civil War. That the region was so filled with history—both Revolutionary War and Civil War—made teaching history a hands-on treat.

Grades three and four handed their arithmetic papers to Corrine, who graded them while the students practiced spelling words in pairs. Rachelle went to work on sight-word review and reading orally with her students. "Mamm—Leah—let's start with you—"

"Ach, nee—"

"English, Leah."

"We're not ready." Mom did a perfect imitation of Jonah's stubborn face. Jonah grinned and put his arm around his mother. "Ask Sadie. Sadie knows."

Rachelle stifled the urge to laugh. "The tietschern decides who goes first, not the *schieler*."

Mom ducked her head. Jonah giggled. The other students tittered.

"I know, I know." Toby raised his hand, calling out with Sadie's usual exuberance. "Tietschern, Tietschern."

"English, Toby."

"Teacher." He studied the flash card in Rachelle's hand. "Maybe I don't know. Maybe Sadie would do it better."

Sadie patted her big brother's arm. "It's okay, Brother." She pointed to the card. "That pig. *P* is for *pig*. P-i-g spells *pig*."

"That's correct. Good job, Sadie. Next time let's have Toby give it a try."

"Thanks, Sister." Toby high-fived Sadie. "You're the best."

His brilliant smile enveloped Rachelle, sharing the moment with her. Not just as Sadie's teacher, but as a friend. They both loved Sadie and Sadie loved them both, but it was more than that.

Rachelle forced herself to break away from his gaze. "How about this one?"

A buggy.

Toby pretended to sound it out. "B-u-g-g-y. *Buggy.*" His mischievous grin was so like Sadie's. "I can use *buggy* in a sentence. Amish couples court in a buggy."

Rachelle dropped her stack of cards. They scattered on the floor. "Oh, goodness."

"Let's help the teacher."

A second later, Toby knelt next to her. They reached for the same card. Rachelle held on. So did Toby. It was a purple flower. "*Flower.* F-l-o-w-e-r." He pointed at Rachelle. "Pretty like you."

"*Flower*, f-l-o-w-e-r," Sadie repeated. "I love flowers. I love teacher."

"Me too. I mean, I love flowers." Toby's face reddened. He let go of the card. "They make the world a beautiful place."

Heat curled up Rachelle's neck and around her cheeks. "That's correct—I mean, it's flower, not the pretty part, I mean . . ."

Finally ten o'clock rolled around. Time for recess. The children shepherded the "big" scholars through getting drinks of water and sharpening pencils. They reminded them to use the toilets. They took the reversal of roles seriously. Hoping for a breeze to cool her warm cheeks, Rachelle followed them out to the playground. She still had to get through lunch and the entire afternoon of lessons.

"How's it going?" Corrine joined Rachelle on the front steps. "Every time I peeked at you, your face was so red I thought you might have a fever."

"Nee. No fever. Not that kind, anyway." If anyone would understand, Corrine would. "Toby said I was pretty like a flower. He also used the word *buggy* in a sentence about courting."

"I see, I see." Corrine chuckled. "You don't know how to act when a man flirts with you."

"Do Plain men flirt?"

"Of course they do." Corrine groaned in mock irritation. She cocked her head toward the teeter-totter where Toby occupied one side and four children, including Jonah, were on the other. Runt, who spent every day waiting outside the school for Jonah, had joined them. Every time they laughed, he yipped like a happy puppy. "Toby's showing off for you right now."

"He is not."

"What do you think he was doing here the other day when he saw Gabriel's car here? He was staking his claim."

"You think?"

"No wonder your attempts at courting have failed." Corrine rolled her eyes. "Watch him. He's telling you he's gut with kinner. He loves kinner. He'll make a gut mann and a gut daed."

"He's saying all that by just riding on a teeter-totter?"

"He's saying that by showing up here today when he surely has important business to take care of. I reckon Elizabeth would've come instead. I reckon he volunteered."

"You don't know that."

"I can see it is in his face. He's smitten." Corrine nudged Rachelle. "Go on. Return the favor. Show some interest. Don't leave the poor man hanging."

Rachelle smoothed her apron. She took a long breath and let it out. *Here we go.*

Toby's deep laugh filled the air, mingling with the children's high-pitched giggles and Runt's barks. He threw his arm up in the air and yelled, "Ride 'em, cowboy! Hey, Tietschern, do you want a turn?"

Rachelle pretended to consider his offer. "That's okay. You have lots of customers already."

"We ride bucking broncos." Jonah mimicked Toby's arm waving. "Ride 'em, cowboy."

"That sounds very exciting. I know how much you like riding horses." Anytime Jonah offered Rachelle his sunniest smile, she counted it a good day. "How are you able to stay on such a wild horse?"

"Toby say gut grip." Jonah stumbled for the words, but his usual frustration didn't flare. "He says I strong."

"You are strong." Rachelle mouthed, *Danki*, at Toby. "Strong and smart and sweet."

"I not smart."

"You are. Very smart." Toby halted the teeter-totter with his boots on the ground. The other kids scrambled off, but Jonah didn't move. "You know what horses like to eat. You know how to brush horses. You know how to calm down a horse."

His expression serious, Jonah seemed to contemplate Toby's words. Runt jumped up, his front legs on the teeter-totter. Jonah took the dog into his arms. "Horse need me. I take care of horse."

"You do and you do a gut job." Toby hopped off the teeter-totter and straightened. "You can groom my horse anytime."

Jonah nodded. "You tell me. I come."

"But now recess is over." Rachelle waved her hand in the direction of the building. Getting her students to settle down and work after recess always presented a challenge. "Why don't you lead the way?" she said to Jonah.

"Ach. Recess short. School long."

Runt barked in agreement. No doubt hanging around the school, waiting for recess and lunchtime, got old for him too. Jonah had hit upon a universal truth that all kids had to learn to accept. The activities they loved flashed by in a split second. Those they disliked seemed to last forever.

"It's only ninety minutes until lunch." Rachelle bent to scratch between Runt's ears. His tongue hanging out, the dog smiled—really, he did—and panted. "You get to eat with Runt, and you get an extra-long recess."

Jonah's expression lightened. "Peanut butter–jelly sandwich."

"Your favorite."

"Runt like too."

Rachelle started after Jonah. Toby caught up with her. "He's a gut bu."

"The best."

"He's Sadie's favorite friend, and she's a gut judge of character."

"Don't tell anyone, but she's my favorite schieler—except for Jonah, of course."

"Your secret is safe with me."

The students, big and small, flooded into the school ahead of them. At the door, Toby paused. "I leave tomorrow for another two weeks."

"Auctions?"

"Manassas, Wheeling, and Columbia."

"Business is gut."

"I thought maybe when I come back I can show you how a b-u-g-g-y is used in a sentence." He seemed engrossed in the writing on the welcome mat. "If you're interested."

Suddenly Rachelle's tongue twisted. Words disappeared. Her heartbeat skipped like a girl at her first rumspringa singing.

Toby's expression turned quizzical. "Or not?"

"Nee, jah, I mean, I'm a tietschern." *Stop being a silly schoolgirl. It's simply a buggy ride.* "I'm always interested in how words are used in sentences."

"Gut. Gut."

Very good.

Chapter 25

ne more week. Just one more week and Rachelle's time teaching at this school would end.

She inhaled the scent of chalk dust and childish sweat. The sound of Corrine's second graders reading aloud hummed like a song in her ears. She ran her fingers across the scarred pine of the desk that had been hers for three years. Sweet memories she would treasure forever crowded her. Corrine was no closer to marriage than she had been when the parents' committee made its decision. Henry was focused on rebuilding his flock and restoring his ability to earn a living. Any plans for matrimony were on his back burner for the foreseeable future.

Toby still lived at home—when he was home. He'd left the day after the family/student day and wouldn't be home until the day before the school picnic. Did he ever think about buying a house of his own? Probably not. Why have that expense when he was away so much? Who would take care of his property while he was gone? Why was she thinking about him when she should be thinking about teaching?

Rachelle picked up a stack of numbered flash cards and a drawstring bag filled with black tokens. She plopped into a child-size chair at a round table one of the fathers had made for this purpose. The children took their seats in a rush. To them numbers were a game. Any time learning could be fun, Rachelle was all for it.

"Me first, me first." Minnie leaned across the table and snatched a pile of tokens. "I win today."

"Nuh-uh." Tracy took his thumb from his mouth and shook his head. "Me win."

"A positive attitude is important." Rachelle smiled encouragingly. The truth was, Sadie almost always won. She had the greatest capacity for learning and retaining what she learned. "But let's not be grabby, okay?"

Each child received five cards and their share of tokens. Whoever placed the right number of tokens on each card first won a sticker. The tiny circle became very quiet. His forehead wrinkled, his expression fierce, Jonah studied his cards. Rachelle touched the circles below the number. "What number is this? Do you remember?"

He growled like a grumpy grizzly.

"Don't growl at me, Brother."

He sighed. "Seven?"

"See, you know. Now count out seven tokens and put them on the circles."

It took time and patience, but he got there. Sadie clapped and cheered. "You win, you win, Danny."

Surprised, Rachelle peered across the table. Indeed, Daniel's five cards were done. Two of Sadie's were still empty. "Sadie?"

The little girl grinned and winked. An exaggerated wink that took all her coordination. Rachelle nodded. "Congratulations, Danny."

The little boy's chest puffed out when Rachelle placed the gold sticker on his shirt. "I win."

"Yes, you did."

For a second, Rachelle longed for a photo of their happy faces. A picture she could hang on her bedroom wall. A memory would have to do. She would never forget how it felt to see these seven children thrive. She would have other students in the future—God willing—but these were her first and her beloved.

"We play grocery store now, Teacher?" Minnie popped from her chair and danced around like a child who needed to visit the outhouse. "Can we?"

Another favorite game. "Yes, we may. Jacob and Tracy, why don't you get out the food? Minnie, you know where the money is."

The children rushed to the plastic tubs that lined shelves along one wall. They returned with two filled with plastic produce and grocery items from a toddler's kitchen Rachelle had bought at a yard sale. Minnie brought the toy register filled with Monopoly money and a supply of real coins.

"Me cashier?" Her expression eager, Sadie touched the cash register. She wanted to work in her family's shop. "I count the best."

"You can start, but we'll take turns."

Grinning, Sadie helped Jonah shove two desks together to serve as the checkout lane. In no time, her "customers" were lining up with their purchases, ranging from a ham to oranges to boxes of soap. The best part was listening to their pretend conversations, so obviously drawn from years of going with their mothers to the store. Sadie started it off with, "Good morning."

"Storm bad last night? We needed rain, though."

"Cooking oil cost so much. Must come from over sea."

"How Jesse's back treating him? My Liam got flu."

And more of the small talk that made up life in a small town. Rachelle leaned back in her chair and enjoyed their playacting while making sure the numbers added up. They did. Sadie improved weekly.

The clock on her desk dinged. Lunchtime had sneaked up on them. "Time to close up shop, Sadie. Your customers must be starving."

The timing for their grocery store activity had been strategic. They never wanted to stop playing. Only the thought of lunch followed by recess prompted them to give up without discussion.

"Surprise, surprise!"

The children slid to a halt in their dash to put away the toys. Sadie darted toward the foyer where her mother and Layla stood with an extra-large cooler between them. "We brought lunch." Elizabeth grinned, obviously proud of herself. "Hot pulled-pork sandwiches, potato salad, coleslaw, and apple pie."

A rousing chorus of cheers rang out along with applause. Parents took turns surprising the students with hot meals during the winter months, but it rarely happened this close to the end of the school year. The kids loved it. So did the teachers.

"That's so kind of you." Rachelle squeezed past the students who crowded their visitors. "Perfect timing too."

"Let's have the older kinner bring in the second cooler." Layla patted Sadie's head. "Everything is plated and covered with foil, so all we have to do is hand them out."

"Eat outside, Teacher?" Her tone pleading, Minnie tugged on Rachelle's sleeve. "A picnic, please?"

"Since you asked so nicely and in English, yes, you may." The thought of eating outside in the friendly April sun brightened the entire schoolroom. Rachelle sought out Corrine's gaze for corroboration. "If that's okay with Corrine."

"Absolutely. I've had a hankering for barbecue for days." Corrine pointed to the clock on their desk. "We should keep an eye on the time, though. Make quick work of visiting the toilet and washing your hands. Then you can help Elizabeth and Layla set up the coolers on the picnic tables."

Despite obvious glee over this disruption of the normal routine, the children managed an orderly exit. Two of Corrine's students took the cooler back outside while Rachelle joined Corrine and their visitors. They couldn't have asked for a nicer day for a picnic. A soft, cooling breeze wafted through the pine trees that lined the boundaries of the school property. Cotton ball clouds dotted the pale-blue sky. Rachelle drew in a deep breath of fresh air and closed her eyes for a second. Who could be gloomy on such a day as this? "Thank you for bringing lunch. It was just what we needed."

"I thought it might be." Elizabeth handed Rachelle a foil-covered plate and plastic silverware wrapped in a paper napkin. "Take a load off your feet. Josie and the other girls will serve. You teachers deserve a quiet moment."

After a few fleeting seconds of guilt, Rachelle obeyed. She took a seat at the picnic table across from Corrine. The pulled pork was tender, juicy, and topped with a nicely spiced barbecue sauce and served on a huge, fluffy homemade bun. The tangy vinegar and buttermilk coleslaw, coupled with dill pickle spears, served as a nice side. Elizabeth's potato salad was made with Dijon mustard and red-skinned potatoes—Rachelle's favorite.

"This is the life." Corrine grinned. She had a dab of barbecue sauce on her chin. "We might have to extend the lunch hour to include a nap after this feast."

"Or just call off the studies altogether." Layla placed plastic cups filled with iced tea in front of Corrine and Rachelle, then slid onto the bench next to Corrine. "It's so close to the end of the school year, it must be near impossible to keep their attention—or yours."

"You're right. Spring fever affects us just as bad as it does our scholars, but let's keep that our secret." Rachelle winked at the other woman. "Teachers are supposed to love school down to the very last minute before the very last bell. Schielers must never know we're as human as they are."

Besides, it would be the last time she taught these particular scholars. That thought hovered over Rachelle morning, noon, and night, like a bank of black clouds threatening a tornado with hail, wind, and lightning. Rachelle's sense of well-being slunk away. The bun turned to cardboard in her mouth. She laid the sandwich on her plate, her appetite gone.

"It must be breaking your heart." Empathy softened Layla's pretty face. "I'm so sorry. Do you two know what you'll do in the fall?"

"We'll be fine. We want what's best for the kinner, of course." Corrine answered with a crisp tone that belied the sadness that peeked through her indigo-blue eyes. "We're still waiting for Gott's plan to be made clear to us."

"Gut answer. Now tell me how you really feel." Layla's no-nonsense tone sounded just like her mother's. "You don't have to pretend with me. I'm not the parents' committee."

"It's hard." Rachelle took a long sip of her sweet tea. The lump in her throat receded. "I'll miss my schielers so much. I love them. But Corrine's right. We want what's best for them. Everyone seems to think the move is."

"Just about everyone—"

"Tietschern, Tietschern! I hurt my finger!"

One of Corrine's first graders interrupted Layla with a mournful whimper.

Corrine sighed. "I'll be right back."

Her reluctance obvious in the way she eyed her uneaten pie

made Rachelle chuckle. "It'll still be here when you get back. We promise not to eat it."

"Don't share any gossip without me either."

"As if we'd gossip."

"Ha."

Rachelle laughed and picked up her fork. Eating her own pie was one way of making sure she didn't say something she shouldn't. No one liked a gossip.

"It wouldn't be gossip to mention that Toby is one of those people who doesn't think this plan to immerse our kinner in an Englisch school is a gut idea." Layla used a chunk of bun to sop up barbecue sauce on her plate. "He's worried about Sadie picking up all sorts of worldly notions from the other kinner—and the tiet-schere too. He's said as much to my dat and mamm."

"Sadie's soul is innocent. It always will be." Rachelle sought out the little girl. She found her on a swing, her legs pumping, her head thrown back, laughter spilling from her lips. "She knows what is gut and right and fair. Nothing will change that."

"Do you really believe that?"

"Gott made her special. I believe His plan is for us to learn as much from her as she learns from us—more really." Rachelle moved on to Jonah. He was playing kickball with the other boys. What he lacked in coordination, he made up for with enthusiasm. The older boys did their best to be patient with him. It was good for them to learn the virtue now—even if they didn't always like it. "The emphasis on mainstreaming students is important because it benefits the regular students as much as it benefits the special ones."

"Our schielers have already learned that lesson. Our eldre teach us that from the time we're old enough to know the difference."

"We say that, but sometimes the kinner forget and need to be reminded. They're kinner too. They are young and impatient. Plus the parents' committee is right in saying we don't have the resources the Englisch do for helping our special schielers reach their full potential."

"You're the tietschern." Layla tossed a few bread crumbs into the grass for a robin who'd been inching closer to their table. "Which brings me back to my original question—what will you do in the fall?"

"It depends."

"On whether Henry asks Corrine to marry him?"

The grapevine had done its work. "Among other things. I may have to take a job somewhere else."

"You'd leave Lee's Gulch?"

"Not because I want to."

"Many of us would be sorry to see you go." Layla's smile turned sly. "Especially Toby."

"He has a funny way of showing it." The sentiment slipped out before Rachelle could corral it. His veiled attempts to suggest they would go on a buggy ride at some point hadn't resulted in a single ride. *Kindness. Gentleness.* He carried a heavy load with Silas's retirement and his father's issues. "I mean—"

"You mean he hasn't been good on the follow-through." Layla shook her head and rolled her eyes. "He's been gone more than he's been here this spring. Auctioneering makes it hard for a man to court properly."

It would be hard for both the man and the woman. The image of Toby's expressive eyes that changed colors with the sky and his fluctuating emotions danced in Rachelle's mind. The way his biceps flexed when he carried Sadie from the buggy to the schoolhouse porch. The way he high-fived Sadie over p-i-g. His concern for Emmett when Rachelle nearly broke his nose. His imposing figure on the auctioneer's stage. His physicality had always drawn her attention, but his nature was what sent her heart racing when she lay in bed at night, unable to sleep, thinking of the future.

"I suppose that's why he hasn't married yet." Rachelle swiped a glance at Toby's sister. How much would she be willing to share about his private life? "He must worry that a woman would reject his advances, knowing how much he's on the road."

"In the early years, my mamm went on the road with my dat." Layla took another road to answer the question. "But once they had boplin, she stopped. She said it was no place for boplin. Especially as we got older and started school. She wanted us to be with our own kind, not immersed in the Englisch world on the road."

"She sacrificed her time with your daed in order to do what was best for her kinner."

"Jah. Toby doesn't think it's fair to a fraa to have to raise kinner on her own and be apart from her mann so much."

"Because he has a soft, kind heart." A man as sweet as the cherry pie tasted on Rachelle's tongue. How could she be upset with such a man? "Because he bothers to walk a mile in the shoes of the woman he loves—or will love one day."

"Jah. He's a gut man. As gut as they come."

Rachelle dug deeper for the memory of how he stared down at her from the auction stage that day in March. Like something or someone had surprised him. Like he wanted to say something but couldn't find the words. "Was that why you and your mudder brought lunch today? To matchmake?"

"Nee. Jah. Nee. Not exactly." Layla wiggled. She scrubbed her hands on her napkin even though they were perfectly clean. "I'm sure you've heard about what happened to me—my getting dumped. I know how hard finding the right mate can be. I wanted to say . . . to say don't give up on Toby. He's worth the wait. He would never do to you what Ryan did to me."

"I guess you should be more worried about what I might do to Toby's heart."

"You were honest about your feelings toward David and Kyle. It might hurt at first, but a man surely would rather have truthfulness than marry a woman who doesn't truly love him."

She had heard the stories. Rachelle shooed away flies trying to make a meal of Corrine's pie. "Did you love Ryan?"

"I thought I did, but when my hurt feelings subsided, I wondered if he'd done me a favor. Do I want to be hitched to a man who could so easily change his mind about how he feels?"

"No one said it would be this hard."

"Nee, they didn't."

The sound of the children laughing and shouting filled the silence for a minute or two.

"All I'm saying is you won't find another man as honest and true and hardworking—"

"You don't have to convince me, Layla." Rachelle put her hand over Layla's. "You have to let time and nature take their courses. One thing is for sure, though. Two people can't fall in love if they don't spend time together."

"For sure and for certain." Layla drew her hand out and placed it on top of Rachelle's. "Toby will be home in time for the school picnic next week."

"I can see the gleam in your eyes." Rachelle shook her head and laughed. "Another certainty is that it has to be his idea—his and mine—not his sister's or his mother's or his best friend's."

"That doesn't mean we can't give a little nudge." Layla's eyes danced. She grinned. "Just a smidgen."

"Nee—"

"Jah." Layla stood and picked up their plates. "Gott helps those who help themselves."

"That isn't Scripture."

"Nee, but it could be."

Chapter 26

*N*o matter how old a man got, he didn't forget that feeling of sheer joy that came with waking up and realizing the last day of school had arrived. Freedom. Toby shifted from one foot to the other as he watched the kids and their dads compete in a hard-fought baseball game on the makeshift field next to the school. The rest of the families gathered in lawn chairs along the first and third base lines to cheer equally hard for both sides.

The last day of April had brought picture-perfect weather for an end-of-school picnic after sporadic rain during the week. The kids didn't care. It could've been snowing and they'd still celebrate being set free for an entire summer that would be spent almost entirely outdoors. It was good to be here. To be off the road. To sleep in his own bed and eat his mother's cooking. A man could only stomach so much diner food.

Food cooked by his dad wasn't so bad either. Toby had eaten a cheeseburger as big as his hand and a hot dog grilled by fathers of the students—an end-of-school picnic tradition. Of course that wasn't all. He'd also consumed homemade kettle chips, three dill pickles canned by his mother, cucumber salad, vanilla ice cream freshly churned that afternoon and topped with caramel syrup, and three brownies. If he ate one more bite, he would hurl. He hadn't been particularly hungry, but every trip to the serving tables was another chance to talk to Rachelle.

Normally teachers were guests of honor served by their scholars' family members, but Rachelle seemed determined to work her way through the picnic. Not used to idle hands? Or avoiding him?

"Get over there and talk to her." Layla sidled over to Toby with a brownie in one hand and a plastic cup of iced tea in the other. "What are you waiting for?"

"Talk to whom?"

"Don't be ridiculous. You've got lovelorn feelings plastered all over your face."

"Do not. That's a figment of your imagination."

"If you don't make a move soon, you'll lose your chance. She's letting Corrine take the teaching job in the fall. She could get a job in another district, hours away. Is that what you want?"

No, he didn't, but maybe that was him being selfish. Maybe she would be better off teaching at another school. He hadn't managed to spend time courting so far this spring. He hadn't dedicated time to exploring a relationship with her. Which only proved the point he'd been making for the last decade—auctioneers didn't make great husbands.

"Don't give me that look. Rachelle understands about your livelihood. Just like Mammi, Mamm, and Jason's fraa do. Give Rachelle some credit. She understands dedication to a job well done. She's a tietschern."

"How do you know she understands?"

"We talked. When you were in Ohio."

"You shouldn't have done that."

"Somebody had to." Layla slipped the last of her brownie in her mouth, set her cup in lush green grass, and clapped for their dad's third hit of the game. "Dat is on fire today."

Toby clapped too—even though he'd been so preoccupied with the conversation that he hadn't seen the hit that landed his father on second base and sent a runner—Bart, who still ran as fast as some of the teenagers—home to score a run. "Fine. How am I supposed to talk to her when she's surrounded by a bunch of women watching our every move? Her mudder. Our mudder. Corrine's mudder. Groossmammis, schwesdchdres, aentis, kossins. It's enough to give a man hives."

Layla pivoted so she faced the serving table. "Hmm, I see what you mean. Maybe I can find a way to lure her away—"

"Don't you dare—"

"She's going inside." Layla spun toward Toby so suddenly she knocked over her tea in the grass. She grabbed his arm. "Now's your chance. Move it!"

"Stop it." Toby tugged free. "I'll do this in my time, my way."

He took a deep breath and let it out. He'd as much as told Rachelle he'd be around for a buggy ride. Yet he hadn't done it. Not because he didn't want to, but because he couldn't carve out the time. Between the auctions and essentially running the office in his grandfather's absence, he'd been burning the propane lamps until late at night.

"Hurry up."

"Hush up."

Toby glanced at the spectators clustered along the sidelines. They were engrossed in the good-natured Plain version of trash talking. The women had covered the food and moved away from the serving tables to watch the game.

Now or never.

Ignoring Layla's encouraging murmurs, he slipped away as

unobtrusively as a six-foot-two, 190-pound man could. At the schoolhouse door he paused. What if she wanted to be alone with her thoughts for a few moments? This had to be a hard time for her. He put his hand on the door, then let it drop. He'd lost that facility for talking to women somewhere in the years since Janey dumped him.

Whose fault was that? The snarky chorus in his ear sounded like Jason and Layla.

Time to learn. Better late than never. That encouraging voice belonged to his mother.

"Here goes," he murmured. "I'm a grown man. I can do this."

He grabbed the doorknob and pulled. It came toward him far easier than expected and banged against his forehead. "Ouch!"

"I'm so sorry." Rachelle stared up at him with a startled expression. She still had one hand on the inside doorknob. "Are you all right?"

Toby rubbed his head. "I'm told I have a hard head—as hard as they come. No harm done."

"Gut."

She didn't move. Neither did Toby. Her eyebrows lifted, her expression inquiring. "What are you doing here?"

"Looking for you." The truth came out before Toby could stifle it. "I mean, I saw you go inside and thought maybe you could use some company. I reckon this is a hard day for you. For Corrine too. But especially you."

He was running at the mouth. Auctioneers tended to do that. He forced his mouth shut.

Rachelle peeked past him. Her eyes were red and her chin quivered. She took a few steps back but didn't say a word.

An invitation? Toby followed her inside and let the door close. "Are you all right?"

"I'm fine. I was just"—she made a sweeping motion with one arm—"making sure I or the schielers didn't forget anything. Sometimes kinner leave lunch boxes with fruit or other perishables in them. You can image how those smell after a few days."

Now she was the one talking fast about nothing. The more she talked, the redder her cheeks grew.

"I can."

"So did you come to talk to me about tutoring your daed? Is he okay with it?" She clasped her hands tightly in front of her. The flow of words didn't slow. "Now that school is out, I'll have plenty of time."

"Nee. I haven't talked to him. I spoke with my daadi. He says it will embarrass Dat too much. That I shouldn't have told you."

"I'm glad you did." The teacher in her took over. The red faded as her tone turned earnest. "There are ways to approach it without embarrassing him."

"I'm working on it." Perhaps her light touch would be needed. They could work together to help his dad. A project that would bring them closer together and ease his father's discomfort. And solve a problem that needed solving soon. "That's not why I came in here."

"Then why?"

Toby let his gaze skip around the room. All the children's artwork was gone. The walls were empty. The room already felt unused and dusty. "To make sure you're okay."

True, but not the whole truth.

Surely the slight shake of her head reflected disappointment. Disappointment in him. Her chin lifted. Her shoulders straightened. "I'm fine."

"Are you sure?" *I'm here because I care.*

"I'm trying very hard." She pulled up her apron and dabbed at her cheeks. "The committee thinks this is best. I want what's best for my schielers. That doesn't make it easy."

"I'm sorry for the pain this is causing you."

"It's not your fault."

Such a sweet-natured woman. An inner beauty shone through Rachelle. Not that her outward appearance wasn't equally pleasing. Toby touched her cheek. Her skin was soft. Silky. Warm. Her eyes widened. Her hand came up to cover his. Her touch ignited a fire that spread so quickly there was no containing it. Another step closer. "Rachelle."

Her lips parted. "I know," she whispered. "I know."

Another step closer. Now they stood so close her clean, fresh scent of soap and lilac shampoo enveloped Toby. She had a tiny scar on her nose he'd never noticed before. And the small mole near her left ear. Would she mind if he touched it? Or let his fingers trail down her cheek to her neck? "I've never felt this way before. Like I want to erase your pain. Or take it and carry it for you."

"I don't need you to carry it for me. I'm strong enough to bear it on my own." Her tone was firm but her expression encouraging. "But danki. You're kind to offer. Sweet and kind. Gott has a plan for me."

"I can't wait to see His plan unfold." And hoping that plan included Toby. He couldn't say that. He didn't deserve any part of her until he committed to spending the time to truly get to know her. He let his hand drop. "Maybe it will intersect with His plan for me."

Rachelle took a step back. Her gaze turned fierce. "Maybe? Maybe he expects a man to step out in faith, to take the first step, to do the work necessary to make that plan a reality."

"You're right." No wonder she was a good teacher. She had the proper technique needed to chastise even the most rebellious student. "Tomorrow night. Wait for me tomorrow night."

"I will."

"Gut."

His feet refused to move. Everything about her held him captive. Just a few more minutes alone. A true smile transformed her face. Like sun breaking through the clouds after a tornado spun him into the air and dropped him flat on his back to stare at the sky. "You should go first. The rumors will be flying."

"Right." Toby sucked in a breath. Then another. "I'm going."

"I think you have to move your feet in order to do that."

Now she was making fun of him.

"Tomorrow night."

"I think we agreed to that already."

He donned his straw hat, pivoted, and walked away. *Don't look back. Don't look back.*

If he did he would have to turn around, march back to her, take her in his arms, and thoroughly kiss her.

Chapter 27

*B*eing able to think straight was an important attribute in any man. Toby clucked and snapped the reins. His horse broke into a trot. The new buggy, so sleek and pretty, didn't even squeak. Being around Rachelle apparently interfered with Toby's ability to think straight. Whenever she was around, he said things and did things he wouldn't normally do. Such as seek her out at a school picnic and tell her he wanted to take her on a b-u-g-g-y ride. "Buggy. B u-g-g-y," he said aloud. Almond wouldn't think he was crazy, talking to himself. But he was crazy. Otherwise Toby—with all his reservations about marriage and family—wouldn't be on his way to pick up Rachelle for a buggy ride.

Maybe he should turn around and go home before he had a chance to hurt her.

Was it really Rachelle he was afraid of hurting? Was Grandpa right? Was fear keeping him from living life to its fullest? He'd been seventeen the first time he fell in love. At least it felt like love at the time. Not going there. No point in it. *Fraidy-cat. Fraidy-cat.* God must be so disappointed in Toby.

Oh ye of little faith . . .

The Lapp house came into view. Rachelle sat in a rocking chair on the front porch waiting for him. A series of images sauntered through his mind, each more beautiful than the last. Rachelle at the kitchen stove making breakfast. Rachelle singing and rocking a baby in her lap. Rachelle picking tomatoes in the garden. Rachelle sitting at the supper table telling him about her day.

No wonder he couldn't think straight.

Tobby snapped the reins. Almond complied. A few minutes later, he pulled into the yard and hopped from the buggy. "Hallo."

Rachelle strolled to the railing. "Hallo."

Late-night meetings with other women had always seemed so forced and awkward in the past. Not this one. Finally. Alone. Able to talk, just the two of them. "Do you want to take a ride, or would you rather sit here on the porch and talk?"

"You read my mind. I'd rather sit here so you don't have to pay attention to driving and the road. I could bring you a glass of cold tea and some lemon bars fresh from the oven."

"That sounds gut." Not because his throat was dry, although it was, but because it would give Toby a second to get his bearings. She was far too pretty. His palms were sweaty, and it seemed likely his shirt's armpits were wet as well. "I'll wait here for you."

Rachelle nodded and slipped back into the house.

Toby sank onto the cushioned swing and pushed off the porch's wooden floor with his church boots. The soft squeak had its own rhythm. He closed his eyes. *Easy. One step at a time. Gott's plan. Gott's will.*

Thy will not mine, Gott.

"Are you tired?"

He opened his eyes. Her forehead wrinkled in concern, Rachelle stood in front of him. She held a tray filled with two large glasses of tea and lemon bars nestled on paper napkins. "Nee, nee. I was just collecting my thoughts."

Rachelle set the tray on a pine table that likely had been made by one of her brothers. "I've been trying to do that all evening."

"No success?"

She handed him his tea. "Nee. I haven't had much success with courting. I'm sure you've heard the stories."

He had. No sense in rubbing it in. "The past doesn't matter. Let's make tonight a fresh start."

"That sounds wunderbarr." She held out a napkin heavy with two oversized lemon bars. "I hope you like lemon. If you don't, don't feel as if you have to eat—"

"I love lemon." He took a big bite to prove it. The tangy pudding-like topping made his taste buds sing. He chewed and swallowed. "Please sit down. Let's not waste time talking about food."

"You're direct, aren't you?" She did as he asked, but she chose to sit with him on the swing rather than the rocker she'd occupied when he drove up. Her scent of fresh, clean soap and lilac enveloped him. She smelled so good. Her closeness made it hard to think. She sipped her tea. "I like that."

"It's a gut thing. I don't think I can change that about me." He blurted the words out. "I'm too old to change, I reckon."

Smooth, Toby. You sound like an old coot past your prime. She's young, remember?

Rachelle laughed outright. She had an unrestrained, hearty laugh. "You're not that old. And besides, I'm not sure age has anything to do with it. Kimmie is fourteen, and she's more set in her ways than Mammi or Daadi."

"Gut to know."

"Tell me about your day."

She was good at this. *Danki, Gott. One of them had to be.* "Why don't you go first?"

"If you insist." She leaned back, her tea clutched in both hands, and relaxed against the pillow. "I'm still adjusting to school being out. The beginning of every summer is like that. But more so this time . . ."

"Because you don't know what comes next?"

"Exactly. I woke up this morning determined to be content with my lot." She traced lines in the condensation on her glass, her expression intent. "I baked bread with Kimmie and Emma. I weeded the vegetable garden. I sewed new pants for the buwe—they're all growing like weeds. Their pants are high waders. The whole time I kept thinking about the school year and the fun times we had . . . and wondering what I'll be doing in the fall."

"Have you put in applications?"

"Jah. Several. Word has gotten around that I'm available, but the openings aren't close to home."

She might move away. And Toby might lose his chance with her forever. Rachelle loved to teach as much as he loved to call auctions. Would she give it up for marriage? The shoe was on the other foot here. Janey didn't like his occupation. Rachelle didn't mind Toby's, but she might love hers more. His brain hurt with the mazelike dilemma, but his heart spoke up. Teaching was her passion. "Something will come up."

"I know it will, but I already miss my schielers—all the kinner, not just mine."

She pushed off the porch floor so the swing would rock and launched into the memories on her mind. She told stories well, all about the bees that invaded the girls' outhouse and sent them racing into the school during recess, the swing that broke under Amos Schrock's weight, and the lizard Matthew Plank brought for show-and-tell but decided to put in Sherri Miller's desk for safekeeping.

"I heard about that last one." Sherri had told the same story at the supper table, only she'd been irate that Robbie thought his little prank was funny. "Sherri said she thought it was a snake. She's not a big fan of snakes. Sadie thought it was funny, though. She likes all Gott's creatures, even the creepy-crawly ones."

"The closer it got to the end of the school year, the more creative the kinner got in finding ways to liven up the days." Rachelle chuckled. "I'm sure that's what they would call it. Corrine and I just wanted them to learn a little bit more before they spent the summer forgetting everything they've learned."

"That's because you're such a gut tietschern." The bittersweet nature of those last days wove its threads through each story. "That's how I know your teaching days are far from over."

Rachelle's sigh was soft, sad, the laughter gone. "I hope you're right. Your turn."

He had no funny stories to tell. "What about Jonah? How's he doing?"

"Jonah's quiet. He has been since he found out about the Englisch school." Her somber expression deepened. She set her tea aside. "He usually can't wait for school to be out so he can go fishing and swim in the pond and work with Dat in the blacksmith shop. But lately he's been clingy. That's not like him. Tonight he insisted I read story after story before he would settle down for the night. It's almost as if he knew . . ."

"Knew what?"

Her elaborate shrug didn't tell Toby much. "You think he knew I was coming by this evening?"

"It almost seemed that way."

"I thought Jonah liked me."

"He does. Jonah likes you a lot, but he likes his routine too."

"He doesn't want any changes."

215

"Exactly. How will I read him stories at night if I get married and move into a house with my mann?"

Rachelle was the oldest of the Lapp children. Jonah would have no experience with siblings getting married and leaving the fold. Still, Rachelle had courted before. He must've understood then about the possibilities. Or maybe not. "It's hard to know how much they understand, isn't it? As a tietschern you probably have a better sense of that than someone like me."

"Sean, Sam, and Michael understand more than Jonah does. That frustrates him. He doesn't always know what he doesn't know, but sometimes I see this expression on his face. It's confusion, it's a lost look that tells me he's trying to figure it out. He's seen a sliver of a glimpse of what he's missing. Or kinner say something mean without realizing it's mean. Or sometimes on purpose because they're tired of including him when he always misses the pitch and never stops the ground ball. He wants to play board games, do puzzles, and play checkers like other kinner. Including him requires patience and kindness, qualities kinner can sometimes be short of."

One of the many things she and Toby had in common—siblings with similar disabilities. It gave them a bond others wouldn't have and also an insight into each other's character. "Sadie wants to do everything Sherri and Josie do. Sometimes that's not possible. Mamm tells her it's because she's too young, but that excuse won't work forever."

Rachelle sighed. "Gott has a plan for Sadie and Jonah. I keep reminding myself of that. Anyway, stop putting it off. Tell me about your day."

He loved his job. Why didn't he want to talk about it with Rachelle? "We spent the day washing the trailers and stocking up on supplies."

"Because you're getting ready to go on the road again."

Was there a tiny bit of frustration or disappointment in her inflection? Or did his concerns color his perception of her response? "Jah. Richmond. Day after tomorrow."

"It's gut that you have a steady stream of auctions, isn't it?"

"Jah."

"Then why do you sound so hesitant to tell me about it?"

"Because it makes courting hard." There. He'd said it. "It makes family life hard. This is why I'm twenty-nine and not married. Auctioneering isn't like farming. And my family isn't like yours—always here, always close."

"You don't know my family. You don't know me. You're making assumptions about what I think and what I feel and what I want." Her tone fierce, Rachelle sat up straight. She tapped her black sneaker on the porch floor. "My future is a mystery right now. I don't know if I'll have a job in the fall. I might teach someplace far from here. I don't know. Neither do you. The question is whether we might find our answers together. To do that we need to get to know each other better."

"Wow. You've given this some thought."

"I have. Like you said, you're twenty-nine. You made a conscious choice not to marry. I have to ask myself why. I've made certain decisions in my life because I was holding out for love. Real love that will last a lifetime." Her voice quivered ever so slightly. She cleared her throat. "I don't plan to squander that love now."

"Gut to know." Mesmerized by her nearness, her scent, and her ferocity, Toby reached for her hand. His fingers dwarfed hers. "I wouldn't want to squander something so precious either. Do you think you might see your way clear to give me a chance? To get to know me better?"

"I do." The fire died as quickly as it had flared. Her response was a soft whisper. "Do you think you might want to get to know me better?"

"Jah." He tightened his grip. "Very much."

She swiveled to face him. Toby did the same. He leaned in first, but she followed a second later. He stared at her face, memorizing her huge, dark eyes, her upturned nose, and her full lips. "I want to kiss you. I've wanted to kiss you since that day at the auction."

She worried her bottom lip with her teeth. Then she smiled. "What's stopping you?"

Nothing. Nothing could stop him now. Toby kissed her softly, more of a touch, a butterfly kiss. He started to back away. Her hands came up and caught his face. This time she kissed him. He lost himself in the softness of her lips, her warmth, her eagerness.

Finally they parted. Just breathing. Why had he waited so long? Why had he let his job stand in the way of this, of her? "I think we're supposed to take buggy rides first, before we do that."

She laughed, a light, tinkling sound that cast more light over Toby than the porch light. "I think you're right, but too late." She scooted back to her side of the swing. "I'm available any evening for the next week if we need to get a buggy ride out of the way."

Toby stifled a groan. "For the first time in my life, I don't want to leave for an auction."

"We still have tomorrow night."

She didn't even hesitate. Toby drew her close. He kissed her cheek, then backed away before he could be tempted to do more. "Tomorrow night then. I'll take you for a proper buggy ride."

"It's a date." She followed him out to the buggy. "I'll be waiting for you on the porch."

It was easier for Toby to show her than try to express his feelings. He took her hands in his and pulled her closer. He kissed her long and hard. She backed away, but he didn't let go of her hands.

"To tell you the truth, I almost chickened out. I almost turned around and went home." He studied her face, her cheeks pink, her eyes shining. "Then I saw you sitting on the porch and I knew there was no way I wanted to miss out on spending this evening with you."

Or the rest of his life. "Can you imagine if I had? I would've missed out on kissing you."

And then he kissed her again for good measure.

Chapter 28

*Y*ou're not listening to me."

Something didn't seem right. Ignoring Emmett's irritation at his inattentiveness, Toby lowered his coffee travel mug and shielded his eyes from the early morning sun with his free hand. Something sparkled on the gravel around the extended-cab diesel trucks parked next to the trailers behind the Miller Family Auctioneering Company office building. He picked up his pace. "Do you see that?"

"See what?" Emmett squinted and stared ahead.

"Broken glass."

"That's weird." Emmett broke into a lope. His skinny legs were longer than Toby's, and at sixteen he likely hadn't grown to his full height. He reached the trucks first. "Someone broke the front passenger windows," he called back. "They cleaned out the glove boxes and the stuff in the back seats."

Toby didn't bother to ask why the trucks' alarms hadn't sounded. No one ever set them here on the farm. Just like they didn't lock up the house at night. Crime was almost nonexistent in their neck of the woods. People had to really know where they were going to find the Plain farms on the winding, hilly country roads lined with thick stands of loblolly and longleaf pines, red maples, and yellow poplars. The alarms were used, on the other hand, on the road at motels, restaurants, and the fairgrounds—the outside world, so to speak.

Besides, thieves would only find the flashlights, a first-aid kit, travel mugs, odds and ends in a Plain-owned vehicle. It wouldn't net them iPods, tablets, smartphones, laptops, DVD players, or any of the other electronic devices English folks might leave behind. He—or she—might not have realized that.

A thought hit Toby like an arrow between the eyes. Maybe the truck was just a start. Goose bumps rippled down his arms. His heart clanging against his rib cage, he strode around the trailers that had been backed into their parking spaces for ease of hookup for the trip to Richmond the next day. The heavy-duty padlocks had been cut. Doors stood open.

"Ach, Toby." Emmett whirled from his review of the trucks' contents and eyeballed the trailers. "The sound systems."

The trailers were empty. Thousands of dollars' worth of sound equipment gone.

Toby gritted his teeth against the urge to say something he shouldn't. He blew out air. *Count to ten. Again.* Material possessions, nothing more. A property crime. So much less than bodily harm. "It's okay. We have insurance. Go get Dat. I'll call the sheriff."

"Should we? Dat might want to ask Bart and the other elders before we involve the police." Emmett swallowed repeatedly. His breathing came fast and his face had a green tinge under his spring sunburn. "You know how they are about police and courts and such."

"Take it easy, Bruder. You look like you're going to puke." Toby put one hand on his shoulder and squeezed. "It's just stuff—"

"Very expensive stuff we can't afford to replace anytime soon. We need to work—"

"Like I said, we have insurance, and to collect from the insurance we need a police report. In this case a sheriff's report." Toby gave him a gentle shove. "Go. The sooner we start the process, the sooner we can get new equipment."

"Dat won't like that either. We had to get insurance because of the laws, but he never figured we'd actually use it."

Emmett was right. Plain people didn't have health or property insurance. They didn't collect workers' compensation for their Plain employees. But federal laws required businesses to insure their vehicles for accidental injury, disability, and liability, plus they had to pay unemployment and workers' compensation taxes for non-Amish employees. "Think about how hard it would be to fundraise thousands of dollars for three sound systems and how long it would take. We're blessed to have this option. Gott is watching out for us."

The same would be true if they had an accident in the trucks—especially if it was their driver's fault. Or someone got hurt at an auction and decided to sue them—they worked in a lawsuit-happy mainstream world. The district recognized that and made exceptions for their Plain-operated businesses. Just like they did for computer equipment, business phones, and websites. The members of their district examined each exception carefully for how it would affect their families and their efforts to remain immune to worldly values.

After one last, anguished glance at the trailers, Emmett raced toward the house. Toby let himself into the office and made the call on their business phone. It would take the sheriff's deputy a good thirty to forty-five minutes to arrive, the dispatcher said. "Don't touch anything. He'll want to check for fingerprints."

That much Toby knew. In the meantime, he could get the wheels turned on the insurance. He found their agent's card on the

Rolodex and punched in the number for their offices in Richmond. Randall Emerson picked up on the first ring with a cheery hello that reminded Toby that not everyone was having a bad day. He explained the situation as succinctly as possible.

Randall didn't respond. The pause stretched.

"Randall?"

"I'm surprised you don't know this. I'm sorry that I'm the one to break it to you." Randall did sound truly contrite. He cleared his throat. "We haven't received a premium payment from you since February. Your insurance policies lapsed at the end of March. I tried calling, but the voice-mail box was full. So I sent a letter—no response. I sent a letter last week notifying you that both the property and auto insurance have lapsed. I'm so sorry."

Toby's legs gave out under him. He plopped into the chair so hard it lurched back on its wheels. "That can't be right."

"I really am sorry. As soon as you send me a premium payment, I can reinstate your coverage, but it won't cover losses that occur during the lapsed period." Randall sounded truly devastated by this dismal fact. "I'm just thankful you didn't have an injury accident during the lapsed period. Insurance companies love to take uninsured motorists to court. Plus you could be charged for not carrying liability in the case of a car crash."

All facts Toby knew by heart. How would they work if they couldn't legally be on the road? "If I go to the bank and have them send you a check electronically this afternoon, will we have coverage tomorrow?"

"I can make that happen." Randall's voice perked up. "You do your part and I'll do mine."

"We have an auction in Richmond starting tomorrow. We'll swing by to pick up a copy of the insurance card."

"I'll be here."

Toby said his good-byes and replaced the receiver in its cradle. He rubbed his temples. How had this happened? Dad insisted he had the bill payments up to date.

Like Randall said, this could've been so much worse. Toby repeated that mantra in his head as he pushed through the double door and walked around the building. Declan, Elijah, Emmett, Jason, Dad, and Grandpa stood in a cluster near the trailers. Toby gritted his teeth. *Easy, calm.* He breathed and forced his hands to relax. Dad was his elder. No one worked harder than he did.

One, two, three, four . . .

"Emmett said you were calling the sheriff." Dad lifted his straw hat and ran his hand through still-thick blond hair streaked with silver. "Are you sure that's necessary?"

One, two, three, four, five, six . . . "Did Emmett explain that we need a sheriff's report to file an insurance claim?" If they had insurance they would. Toby raised his face to the sun and let its rays bathe his face. Would this matter a year from now? Five years from now? They would figure something out. That's what Plain folks did. They took care of themselves and each other. "But that turns out to be moot."

"What do you mean moot?" Grandpa tugged on his beard. "We've had insurance since the district approved us getting the trucks and using the sound systems. There's a reason for that."

Toby forced his clenched fists to loosen. He repeated what he'd learned from the insurance agent.

Grandpa's face darkened. The muscle in his jaw twitched. His eyebrows rose and stayed at attention. "How did this happen?"

"I've been trying to make sure all the bills are paid—"

"It's my fault." His tone curt, Dad interrupted Toby. "I'm the one responsible for paying the bills. No excuses. I don't know how it happened."

"You don't know how?" Grandpa's chin came up. He crossed his arms. "I showed you my system for keeping track of when bills had to be paid. It's a simple system."

Dad crossed his arms. His face was as red as Grandpa's. "Simple for someone who's been doing it for years."

Neither had raised their voices, which made the tension that much thicker. Toby eased into the space between them. "It doesn't matter how it happened. What's important is figuring out what to do next."

The rumble of an engine signaled the arrival of a Knowles County sheriff's SUV. He'd been closer than the dispatcher thought. For once it was good to see one pull onto Miller property. The deputy took his time scratching notes while Toby recited what little he knew about the theft.

The deputy spent another fifteen minutes taking pictures with his phone with an occasional murmur to himself that sounded like disgust. "You can pick up a copy of the report at the station." He tossed the words over his shoulder as he trotted toward his car. "It should be ready tomorrow."

"Wait." Toby strode after him. "Do you think you'll be able to find who did this? Did you get fingerprints? Have you had any other break-ins like this?"

The deputy removed a toothpick from his teeth and grimaced. "Lots of fingerprints, but I don't expect they'll be in the system— unless one of y'all has a rap sheet, which seems mighty unlikely. As far as the thief goes, only a stupid thief steals stuff without wearing gloves. 'Course there are plenty of those around." He tugged his door open, settled his large carcass into the seat, and stared up at Toby. "What I'm saying, I guess, is that anything is possible. We'll do our best."

Hope gave one last whimper and subsided. Toby thanked the man and let him go.

"Well. What did he say?" Dad mopped his face with the back of his sleeve. "Are we up a creek without a paddle?"

"That about sums it up." Toby dredged up a semblance of good cheer. "They'll do their best. In the meantime, we should clean up the mess. Declan, could you run into town and buy some new padlocks? I'll get to work picking up the glass."

"Your dat and I will go talk to the bishop." Grandpa headed toward the barn. "I'll hitch up the buggy."

Dad hadn't moved. Deep grooves lined his mouth and eyes. His earlier red flush had been replaced with a gaunt gray. "I let you all down—the whole family. I was sure I had everything under control."

Grandpa did an about-face and returned. "None of us has everything under control, Suh." His sharp blue-gray eyes had gone soft. "That's obvious or I wouldn't have gotten so angry earlier. We've never had a crime committed on our property in all the years we've lived here. No one expected this, but we're still blessed. Only material goods were lost. They can be replaced. No one was hurt, praise Gott."

Dad's shoulders slumped. "Be prepared. That's what you taught me and the buwe. Pay attention to every detail and the big picture will take care of itself. The first rule of planning special events."

"After we talk to Bart, we'll come back and go through every piece of paper in that office." Grandpa clapped Dad on the shoulder. "We'll get those details lined up. Then we'll start planning how we'll pay to replace our equipment."

Dad nodded. Shoulder to shoulder, the two men walked away. The same height, the same erect posture, the same loose-legged walk. From the back they could be twins. If Toby joined them, triplets. His past and future in the flesh. Their humble admission of deficiencies and the desire to do better at their ages set a high standard.

In other ways, they were very different. Grandpa with his keen mind and Dad with his skilled hands. If Grandpa had a blind spot, it was there. Dad wasn't him. Couldn't be him. Whether he admitted it or not, Grandpa knew it. The new division of duties wasn't working.

Now it was up to Toby to lead the way to a new era at Miller Family Auctioneering Company.

Chapter 29

Layla's stomach did that thing it did when she swung high over the lake and let go of the rope the boys had strung from the enormous oak on the rocky shoreline. It plummeted. Toby's skin had a green-gray tinge. His lips thinned in a grim line. He kept shaking his head. He probably didn't even know he was doing it. He had that awful grimace a person got when someone had died. It wasn't Grandpa or Dad. They'd hitched up a buggy an hour earlier and left without saying where they were going.

Layla followed Toby through the kitchen and up the stairs. His long strides ate up ground. "Toby? Toby! What's going on? Where did Dat and Daadi go? Dat looked like he'd just lost his best friend."

Toby stopped so suddenly Layla ran into his solid frame. The impact knocked her back a step. He whirled and grabbed her arm to keep her from hurtling backward down the stairs. "Sorry. I'm distracted."

"What happened?" Layla tugged free. Toby resumed his march toward his bedroom. She followed. "Why is everyone so upset?"

"We had a break-in overnight. Someone stole our sound equipment. All of it."

Layla plowed to a stop at Toby's bedroom door. "Ach, nee. Did you file a report with the insurance company?"

"There is no insurance." Toby took a clean shirt from the rows of pegs on the wall. "Dat let it lapse."

"Ach, nee." The inadequacy of her response wasn't lost on Layla. "What can I do to help?"

Toby stopped unbuttoning his sweat-stained shirt. "There is something you can do."

"You mean besides talking to Dat about tutoring? Besides talking to Rachelle?"

Toby whipped off his shirt and slid his arm into the clean one. "I did talk to Rachelle. She's willing to tutor him."

One step forward. Step two now had even greater urgency. "So why haven't you talked to Dat?"

"Do you want to do it?"

Which would be easier for their father? Hearing it come from his oldest son or his oldest daughter? Dad would see Toby as his equal, his partner in business, as well as his son. Man to man. Layla would always be his daughter. "I think it would be better if you do it, but if you can't bear it, I will."

"As a business partner, not just as his suh, it's my place to do it." Toby's mouth twisted. "But it's not just the reading. He needs to let me take over the administrative duties. They aren't his strength."

"Nor yours. Not really." Layla's stomach wouldn't behave itself. Another crazy drop. The solution stood before her in a singular moment of clarity. "I'm the one with the administrative skills."

Toby's fingers stilled halfway down the row of buttons. A look of deep concentration filtered over his face. It was a familiar expression. Toby liked to run the numbers, weighing the pros and cons, assessing the obstacles, and determining their solutions. Then and only then did he make a decision. "What about the store?"

A good question. A sign he was seriously considering her suggestion. A female family member taking a pivotal role in the auctioneering business. Grandpa had avoided that for years. Dad had followed his example. The chances of them agreeing seemed to be slim to none. "I split my time between the two businesses while I train Josie. Eventually she can take over managing the store. She's good with numbers. She can handle it."

Toby finished buttoning his shirt. He picked up his straw hat and stuck it on his head. "You know Mamm won't be thrilled."

She would agree with the men, not because she didn't believe Layla could do the job, but because her view of the world encompassed marriage and motherhood for her daughter as soon as possible. "Present it as a temporary measure. Just like women can teach until they marry. It's the same thing."

"I have to go. A company in Virginia Beach is willing to loan us their backup systems until we can get our own." Toby moved past Layla, heading for the door. "We'll continue this conversation when I get back."

"You said there was something I could do. I assume you meant right now." Layla raced down the stairs after him. "You never said what."

"Go through the papers on Dat's desk. Organize everything. Make piles of bills due or past due, important letters, magazines. Throw out the junk mail."

"He's not going to like it."

"Tell him I asked you to do it as a favor. Just don't say it might turn into a regular thing."

"When do you leave for the next auction?"

"Tomorrow early. We have to be in Richmond by nine."

No wonder he was practically running. They couldn't do an auction without a sound system. He needed to pack too. "I could take care of the office while you're gone. Answer the phone. Take care of web inquiries."

"That's a gut idea." Toby pushed through the kitchen screen door and held it so Layla could follow. "I'll talk to Dat tonight."

"When? You won't be back from Virginia Beach until late." Matilda the cat stretched and rose from her spot on the porch and ambled toward them. Layla picked her up. The cat's instant purr calmed her pounding heart. "You'll be tired. He'll be tired."

"We can't go behind his back."

"Nee, we can't. One step at a time. Just be careful in Virginia Beach and come back safe." Layla repeated their mother's words every time her menfolk left home during auction season. "We'll figure it out."

For a brief moment, the dark clouds lifted from Toby's face. "Danki, Schweschder."

He hauled his big body into a cargo van that spewed diesel fumes into the air. A minute later it took off.

Layla didn't wait for the van to disappear from sight. She settled Matilda on the gravel road and made a beeline for the office. Matilda kept her company. They'd both been in it a thousand times. Matilda on official mousing duties and Layla as a messenger when lunch was ready or Mom needed Dad to take care of something for her. Today was different. Seeing it through the eyes of someone with a job to do. Stuff covered every inch of Dad's desk. It overflowed with papers thrown about in haphazard fashion and office supplies that hadn't been put away. An ancient, clunky desktop monitor took up more real estate than necessary. An old-fashioned black push-button phone squeezed in between the keyboard and a stack of handbills advertising an upcoming auction.

"What a mess!" Layla shared her opinion with Matilda. The cat hopped into a chair in the corner, yawned widely, and proceeded to groom herself. "I guess that means you aren't going to clean up for me."

Layla sank into the desk chair. She smoothed her hand over the computer's keyboard. It represented all the technology Layla didn't have available to her at the store. She kept its books in ledgers, handwriting the numbers, using a battery-operated calculator.

That didn't mean she didn't know how to use a computer. She'd crept around the office, dusting and sweeping on the days the website guru taught Toby and Grandpa the basics of accessing email, reviewing the website, preparing tax documents, and using a program to keep track of bills. If they could do it, so could she. Maybe this experience would lead to Dad and Mom relenting the next time Layla suggested they use similar tools for the store.

But that was a discussion for another time. First up, organizing the paperwork. That took longer than Layla expected. Overdue bills in one pile, due bills in another, official correspondence from the IRS, the state of Virginia, and other governmental entities in another, and newsletters, magazines, and correspondence related to auctioneering in a fourth. The temptation to stop and read the materials prolonged the task. English women became auctioneers. How would a Plain woman attending auctioneering school go over with the district? Layla chuckled into a silence broken only by the *tick-tick* of the clock hanging at a crooked angle on the wall. Junk mail went in the trash. After about thirty minutes, the desk's stained oak became visible.

Next up, accessing the computer. She jiggled the mouse. The screen lit up. A password was required. No problem. Someone— probably her father—had written it on a sticky note and stuck it to the bottom of the monitor. Layla inputed the numbers and voilà— the desktop appeared. She squinted as if that would help her figure out the icons that lined the left side of the screen.

The phone rang. Layla jumped. Her heart lurched. She laughed, a hysterical snort. Matilda rose and leaped from the chair to the desk. Apparently she was as startled as Layla. "We can do this," Layla told her. Matilda didn't seem convinced. With a shaking hand, Layla picked up the receiver. "Miller Family Auctioneering. This is Layla. What can I do for you?"

Her voice didn't shake. It sounded businesslike. Professional. She grinned to herself. A gentleman inquired about a possible auction date in September. Layla drew a desk calendar closer. Scribbles, some legible, some not, covered many of the boxes representing the spring, summer, and fall months. More than a few were scratched out. Who knew if it was up to date?

"I'm going to take down your information and get back to you as soon as I can to confirm our availability. Will that work for you?"

Indeed, it would. Layla asked all the pertinent questions and took detailed notes. A farm retirement auction. A couple moving into their son's dawdy haus. Farm equipment, tools, wagons, furniture, a gun collection, the usual. "I've got all the particulars here. As soon as I can confirm, I'll let you know."

Still smiling, she hung up the phone. "I told you we could do this."

Matilda yawned so widely her sharp incisors showed. Layla laughed again. "Nothing fazes you, does it?"

"What are you doing?"

Layla jumped all over again. At this rate her heart would give out and she would never see her twenty-first birthday. Dad stood in the doorway. His face was even more haggard than Toby's had been earlier. Layla took a breath. "I heard what happened and came out to see what I could do." She waved her hand at the desk. "So I tidied up. I still need to dust and mop."

She was babbling. Dad's frown deepened. "I heard you talking to that customer. Whose idea was that? Toby's?"

"We talked before he left for Virginia Beach. We agreed—"

"I'm still in charge of the office." Her father stalked behind the desk and loomed over Layla. "Toby doesn't have the right to tell you to do anything for this business."

His anger billowed over her, surprising in its ferocity. This wasn't her dad. Not the man who set her on his shoulders to watch fireworks on the Fourth of July or let her tag along with the boys to a Tides game in Norfolk for Toby's fourteenth birthday. The man who brought home an ice cream treat on Saturdays for no reason at all.

"I meant no harm. Neither did Toby."

Dad heaved a sigh. His stare softened. The anger dissipated like air hissing from a deflating balloon. "I know."

Layla rose and squeezed past him. "Sorry, I'm sitting in your chair."

"It's not my chair. At least it shouldn't be." He backed away from the desk. "If the business goes under, it'll be all my fault."

"It's not going under." Layla told him about the sound system loan. "Toby will be back from Virginia Beach tonight in time to get loaded up and go to Richmond tomorrow. He'll be able to pick up proof of insurance from the agent once you get there."

"Saving my hind end once again." Dad sank into a chair intended for visitors so hard it squeaked. "It shouldn't be this way."

Layla settled into the second guest chair. Matilda joined her. Layla stroked the cat's soft fur. The motion steadied her. The conversation was coming now whether Toby thought it was a good idea. It couldn't be stopped. "It doesn't have to be."

"You don't know the half of it." He pointed at the stacks of paper on the desk, then threw his hands up in the air. "Why is it necessary for people to send us so much junk in the mail? It's such a waste."

"I can take care of that." Toby's admonition that she not say anything to Dad about the tutoring rang in her ears. The opportunity was right here, right now, in front of her. "Toby and I have some ideas, some ways we think we'll help you and the business."

"Maybe I should've been the one who retired."

"Nee. You're needed to deal with the vans, the trucks, the trailers, the sound systems." Layla let her excitement color the words. Maybe it was contagious. "That's where you do your best work. Toby, Jason, and Declan call auctions. Eventually you'll convince Elijah to come out of his shell and take the stage. Emmett's already chomping at the bit. In the meantime, they'll continue to keep the auction items moving onto the stage and work as spotters."

"How do you know so much about the business?"

"I pay attention when you menfolk talk at the table." In this moment, she and her dad were closer than they'd ever been. *Now or never.* "I pay attention because I'm interested in business. And I'm gut at the details. You know I am. I could take some of these administrative duties off your plate. Just until things slow down."

Dad sat up straighter. His glower returned. "You already have work to do at the store."

"I could split my time between the two businesses." She offered up the same plan she'd described to Toby. "At least until Josie is old enough to manage the store."

Or she would take over those duties when Layla married, whichever came first.

"Your daadi never wanted women involved in this business." Dad tapped his fingers on the desk for emphasis. "It's enough that the men are consumed by it."

"It's not as if I would go on the road with you. Besides, times have changed. Isn't that why we're allowed to use computers, have a website, and have a phone in the office instead of in a phone shack?" Layla dug deep for words to convince him, words that had been building in her since she was old enough to realize she had a gift for numbers that could be valuable to her family's businesses. "Because the members of the church met and discussed the need and weighed all the pros and cons and decided using them for business wouldn't hurt our efforts to keep us apart from the world as long as we didn't take them into our homes. Isn't that the test we use for each decision?"

"You've given this a lot of thought." Dad took off his hat and set it on his lap. His hair was flat and sweaty. Frowning, he scratched his neck. "All your mudder and I want is for you to marry, to be a fraa and a mudder."

"Gott willing, I will. But in the meantime I could do this. Just until you have time to . . ."

"Time to what?" He picked at bits of dry grass on the hat's bill. "Go on, you've come this far, say your piece before you burst."

Toby would not be happy. "Until you learn to read better."

Dad's face darkened to a deep scarlet. He opened his mouth. A hoarse stutter came out. He shook his head and his index finger simultaneously. "I read."

"I know. I've seen you read, but—"

"Who told you I couldn't read?"

"Toby said—"

"Toby spoke out of turn." Dad snatched a tissue from the box on the desk. He dabbed sweat from his face. The lines around his mouth deepened. "I get by just fine."

"But wouldn't it make you feel gut to be able to whip through all this stuff easy as one-two-three?" Layla deposited Matilda on the floor. The cat yowled once in protest, then resumed her earlier post on the chair in the corner. Layla stood and moved closer to the desk where she picked up the stack of newsletters and magazines. "You could read all these articles about changes in auctioneering, rules, regulations, latest and greatest equipment, and tips for saving your voice. You could send and receive emails with other auctioneers. You have so much experience. You could even write articles."

Dad slumped in his chair. He shrugged and shook his head again. "That's never going to happen."

"Jah, it will. Rachelle Lapp is willing to tutor you—"

"You told Adam's girl I can't read?"

"Toby—"

"He had no right."

Dad bolted from his chair. He stomped from the office. The door slammed behind him.

Quiet reigned once again. Nausea sat like a boulder in the pit of Layla's stomach. She swallowed back tears. "I meant well," she whispered.

Matilda didn't answer. She likely knew what everyone else did. The road to hell was paved with good intentions.

Chapter 30

*I*n an ideal world, Toby would be driving a buggy with Rachelle Lapp at his side. They'd be talking about anything and everything. They'd stop to admire the moon. She'd let him hold her hand. They'd kiss again.

Instead she'd sat on the porch waiting for him, not knowing he had to go to Virginia Beach. She waited and wondered. Finally, disappointed and hurt, she went to bed thinking she'd squandered her feelings and her time on him.

How could she trust a man who didn't show up when he said he would?

Toby had been right about not courting. The first time he seriously considered it, this happened. Right out of the gate he'd hurt Rachelle. A business that supported his large family had to come first in this instance. They had made commitments, taken deposits. They had to come through for their customers or lose their reputation as a first-class reliable auctioneering company. Rachelle didn't deserve to be disappointed like this, but he'd had no choice. And so early in their courtship. He needed to tell her what had happened. Tonight. Now.

Toby made quick work of hitching the horse to the buggy

despite exhaustion that made his legs feel like fifty-pound weights. As soon as he checked to make sure everything was ready for tomorrow's trip to Richmond, he would go talk to her. Would she even be awake at this hour? He had to find out. At the very least, she had to know that he hadn't simply changed his mind about the buggy ride. Work had intervened, as it often did in his world.

He hopped from the buggy, tied the reins to the hitching post, and let himself into the house. The doorknob's click sounded like a gunshot in the quiet. Every floorboard squeaked under his boots. A man his size had to work at being quiet. He'd run upstairs, make sure Emmett had packed everything, and run back out.

"You made it."

Startled, Toby turned at the sound of his dad's voice. He sprawled in the recliner, head back, legs stretched out, as if half asleep. Wearily Toby wiped his boots on the rug, then moved toward the chairs grouped around an empty stone fireplace. "What are you doing sitting in the dark? Not waiting up for me, I hope."

Dad turned on the propane lamp. The flame jumped. It illuminated his face. Dark circles ringed his eyes. "The sound system will work?"

"They're older but in good shape. The Yoders have gradually been updating and keeping the old systems for backup. They're ours as long as their new systems keep working." The minutes ticked by, making it more and more likely that Rachelle would be asleep by the time he drove to the Lapp house, but Toby trudged into the living room. His dad obviously had something to say, and Toby needed to hear him out. "We moved everything into the office. I was afraid to load anything into the trailers tonight. It'll add to our prep time in the morning, but I'll sleep better tonight."

"You told Rachelle Lapp I can't read."

The three cups of bitter convenience store coffee Toby had

consumed on the road sloshed in his belly. The acid burned. What had Layla told him? How much had she told him? "Rachelle's a teacher. She works with schielers who have disabilities." Toby kept his words matter-of-fact. His father didn't want sympathy. He didn't want pity. He didn't even want to talk about this. "It's likely you have a reading disability. She knows about such things and how to overcome them."

"You had no right to tell anyone my business."

"I want to help."

"Spreading the word about my . . . my . . ." Dad couldn't even say the word. "That's not helping."

"There's no shame in having a disability. You of all people should know that. Think of Sadie. You don't love her less or think less of her, do you?"

"Don't lecture me, Suh." Dad sat forward in the rocker, his big hands on his thighs. His cheeks were stained red, his eyes bloodshot. "I'm not ashamed. It's never been an issue until now. What I lacked in book learning, I made up for by working harder and longer with my hands. By talking to people about it behind my back, you make me feel belittled."

"That wasn't my intent. Es dutt mer leed."

"You meant well." Wincing, Dad rubbed his left knee with both hands. "You did the right thing. The lapsed insurance is my fault. We're in a terrible pickle because I was too proud to admit I couldn't do the job. Because of my pride, we have to find a way to buy new equipment. That saying, 'Pride goes before a fall,' was never truer than it is right now." His voice cracked. His Adam's apple bobbed. "You shouldn't let my feelings stand in the way of what's best for the auctioneering business. It's our livelihood. The family depends on its income. You must always put the welfare of the many over that of just one."

Even if it was his dad. A hard word. "Let Rachelle tutor you. In the meantime, Layla can take over the administrative duties in the office."

"Tell Rachelle I'm willing if she has the time and the patience. It won't be easy. My tietschern did her best. She was gut and patient, and still nothing stuck." He swiped at his face with his sleeve. "I'll talk to your mudder about Layla. I'm leaning toward letting her work in the office. She has experience with the store. She's shown she has a head for business. I was surprised, though, that you asked her to do it. All along it seemed you were angling to take those duties for yourself."

"I may have thought that at first, but I was wrong. That doesn't work either. I can't do it all. Have it all."

"I'm glad to know you've come around to understanding that." His father's frown eased. He leaned back. "What do you mean, you can't have it all?"

"Nothing. I'm just tired."

"Don't let the business stand in the way of a fraa and family, Suh."

"I've tried to keep it from interfering. But it has. It's likely to always interfere."

"Nee. Not with the right woman. It didn't with your mudder and groossmammi."

"I know they can do it. The question is should we ask that of them."

"A question the woman should be allowed to answer for herself, I reckon." Dad stood and stretched. Joints cracked. "Time to get to bed. You look like a horse that's been rode hard and put up wet."

"I have another stop to make before I hit the hay."

Dad's busy eyebrows tented. "Where are you going at this

hour?" He stuck up his hand palm out. "Don't answer that." He shuffled toward the stairs. "Tell Rachelle I said danki."

"I will." He would tell her he was sorry. Sorry he'd misled her. Sorry about standing her up. Sorry he started something he shouldn't have. And hope she'd forgive him. Hope she would still be willing to tutor Dad. She would do it because she was a good person. Better than Toby could ever be.

He'd tell her all of that, if she gave him a chance. If she was still awake and if she was still talking to him. Lots of big ifs.

Chapter 31

*T*he battery-operated clock's red numbers ticked past 11:00 p.m. Rachelle pushed it around so she couldn't see its face on the tiny table next to her bed. She rolled over and pummeled her pillow. Toby wasn't coming. She'd huddled on that porch swing, swathed in a fuzzy blanket, for almost two hours, waiting, reading a book, drinking apple-spice tea until she was in danger of floating away. No *clip-clop* of hooves. No buggy. No Toby. Finally she conceded defeat and went inside.

He had a good reason, no doubt. He didn't simply change his mind. Rachelle rolled to her back. The images kept replaying in her head. The intensity, the endless well of emotion in his eyes when he leaned down to kiss her. The feel of his soft lips on hers. His scent of soap. The strength in his big hands when they gripped hers. Her stomach dropped and her heart pounded even in the simple remembering.

She grabbed a pillow and embraced it. A poor substitute for Toby's solid frame.

Why? Where are you? Was it something she said? Something she did?

Why tell her he'd come and then bail out? How could he kiss

her like that and then decide to be a no-show? No answers sallied forth from the night.

Go to sleep.

If I could I would.

His will be done. God could make good things happen from every trial, no matter how difficult. In the world there would be trials, but she wasn't to worry. Jesus had overcome the world.

Patience. Her least favorite fruit of the Spirit. Followed by self-control. Were these trials God's way of instilling these virtues in her? It didn't seem to be working. If she believed Jesus was her Savior—and she fervently did—shouldn't she be filled with the Holy Spirit? And therefore the fruit of the Spirit?

What would Bart say if she asked that question?

The night pressed hard on her, dank, jeering her half-hearted attempts to use Scripture to ward off its bullying. God had a plan for her. So what was it? Dare she ask for a clearer picture? No teaching job. No courting. Then what? If she wasn't meant to marry, surely she was meant to teach. One or the other, but which? The answers to her questions were there, front and center, as bright as the red numbers on her clock. They simply weren't palatable.

Rachelle threw off the sheet and sat up. She grabbed a robe and slipped it over her nightgown. Maybe a glass of milk would calm her stomach. A bowl of ice cream would be better. A whole pan of brownies. She padded barefoot down the stairs and into the kitchen.

The light of a propane lamp flickered, its shadows dancing on the walls. Someone had beat her to the refrigerator. Mom sat at the table, a glass of milk and a piece of raisin cream pie in front of her. She'd opened both kitchen windows, which explained the flames' wild dance.

"You too, huh?" Mom popped a forkful of pie into her mouth,

chewed, and swallowed. "Sometimes it seems the only quiet time I can find is in the middle of the night. Not that it's unexpected with fourteen kinner. I have no right to complain. I wanted a houseful of kinner."

Her mother never showed signs of needing or wanting time alone. In fact, she seemed to thrive on the demands of motherhood. Rachelle halted inside the doorway. "Sorry. I'll just get my milk and head back upstairs."

"Nee, nee. You're here. Tell me what's keeping you awake tonight. It'll take my mind off my aches and pains."

What aches and pains? Alarm rippled through Rachelle. "What's wrong? Are you sick? I can—"

"Whoa, nee. It's nothing but the hot flashes and cold sweats of middle age. Why do you think the windows are open?" Mom fanned her face with her fingers. "That and what having fourteen kinner does to a woman's body. I'm fine. Have some pie. Finish it off or I will."

Rachelle took the last piece of pie—even though it was big enough for two servings—and a glass of milk. She settled across from her mother, who licked her fork and looked expectant. Giving advice was one of her favorite hobbies.

"Everything is so up in the air. I hate that." Rachelle sipped her milk and sighed. "So much for trusting in Gott."

"We're blessed He has such infinite grace, mercy, and patience with us."

"I wish I had as much. I've been tossing and turning for hours, wondering why I have so little patience, self-control, kindness, and you know the rest."

Her mother's sympathetic sigh matched Rachelle's. "Been there, done that. Who needs your grace, mercy, and patience tonight?"

Courting was supposed to be private. Did kissing on a

porch swing constitute courting? What had she been thinking? Thinking had nothing to do with it. The kissing had been all about feelings.

Which brought Rachelle right back to her conundrum. How could she be so disappointed in a man who could spare so little time for her? Why did her heart insist on obsessing over someone who obviously couldn't be trusted to keep his word?

"Grrr."

"That bad, huh?" Mom pointed at Rachelle's plate. "When all else fails, eat pie and tell your mamm about it. I assume we're talking about Toby."

"What makes you say that?" Rachelle took a big bite of pie and let its sweetness drown the bitter taste in her mouth.

"Dochder." Mom laughed. Her giddy titters were enough to make the worst grinch laugh with her. "You need to work on keeping your emotions hidden. Anybody half paying attention can see it on your face whenever Toby's name comes up or he's within hailing distance."

"Cannot." Rachelle washed another bite of pie down with milk. "It can't be about Toby. If he's interested, he has a funny way of showing it. He didn't keep his word. He said he would come back tonight and he didn't."

"Not a gut sign, I agree." Mom wrinkled her nose like she smelled something foul. "On the other hand, it's never gut to jump to conclusions. Did I ever tell you about how close I came to saying nee when your daed asked me for that first buggy ride?"

Mom rarely talked about her life before marriage and children. It was as if being a fraa and mamm swallowed up all her memories, like nothing that happened before then was as important. "Why would you say nee?"

"Because he waited so long to ask me. I'd seen him leave the singings with other maed. Different ones. He seemed fickle. I didn't like being his third or fourth choice and I told him so."

"What did he say?"

Mom's smile smoothed away the laugh lines around her mouth and the sun-induced crow's feet that framed her eyes. In the lamplight, she suddenly seemed young and on the brink of something exciting. "He said he was afraid to ask me. He said he was sure a maedel like me would say nee to a bu like him."

"What made him think that?"

"We all see ourselves differently than the world does, I suppose. He saw me with all my friends, enjoying my rumspringa, maybe a little too much at times. I never lacked for company or places to go. He figured I would find him boring."

It was hard to imagine her mudder as a young maedel exploring the world outside her small Plain district. "Why did he ask out those other maed? That doesn't seem like something a quiet, boring man would do."

"According to your dat, he was trying to find someone who would make him forget how he felt about me."

So romantic. Her dad was a romantic. Rachelle chuckled. Thinking about her parents that way had never occurred to her. But, of course, there had to be a spark, romance, chemistry, or whatever the romance novelists wanted to call it. The couple had fourteen children.

"Your cheeks are all red. What are you thinking?" Mom chuckled too. "You can't image your dat and me in love, can you? Or you don't want to. I can understand that. But my point is how you see a person and his motives can be way off base. You don't know what's going through his head. You don't know what obstacles he's overcome just to show up—when he finally shows up."

She cocked her head and put up her hand as if to ward off Rachelle's response. "Listen."

The sound of buggy wheels on the dirt road and a horse neighing floated through the windows. Her glass halfway to her mouth, Rachelle froze. It was almost midnight. Who showed up in the middle of the night? Only a man bent on courting. She lowered the glass to the table and scurried to the window.

The charcoal-gray-topped buggy drawn by a Morgan came around the corner to the back side of the house. Toby.

Anger warred with hope. Jitters won. "Now he shows up?"

"Better late than never." Mom deposited her glass and plate in the sink. "I'm going to bed. I reckon you better get dressed. A proper young woman doesn't court in her nightgown. Even if she is wearing a robe."

Rachelle managed to close her mouth and nod. Truth be told, attire was the least of her worries.

Relief surged through Toby. Followed by an equal wave of nerves. Rachelle wasn't asleep. He'd almost turned around and gone home at least twice. Only the knowledge that Rachelle would think he'd intentionally stood her up had kept him going. That and the need to tell her his father had agreed to her tutoring. The rest of the time he'd contemplated the probability that she would be asleep and never wanted to see him again. And how could he wake her up? He had no idea which room was hers. Throwing rocks at windows seemed way too juvenile for a man of his age. When she stuck her head out the kitchen window and announced she would be "right back," he'd been so surprised he dropped the reins.

He hopped from the buggy and tied the reins to the hitching

post. Then he paced. All the jumbled words in his head disappeared, leaving behind a blank chalkboard. *Rachelle, my life's a mess. Rachelle, my dat didn't renew our insurance. Rachelle, I had to go to Virginia Beach, but it wasn't my fault. Nee. Nee.* He couldn't blame anyone else. *Rachelle, this was a mistake.* How would she take that? Kissing her was a mistake? How could it be?

"You're going to wear out your boots, pacing like that." Rachelle pushed through the back porch screen door and came to the railing. Her tone was as stiff as her posture. Despite the late hour, her hair was neatly pinned under her prayer covering. Her teal dress and apron didn't have a single wrinkle. Her smile from the previous evening was nowhere in sight. "Come inside before you kill the grass."

Not exactly a rousing welcome, but at least she was still talking to him. And letting him into her family's house.

Toby followed her inside. She said nothing in the time it took to pull a pitcher of water from the refrigerator, fill a glass, and bring it to him.

He accepted it with his thanks. "You're not having any?"

"Nee."

"I'm sorry."

She fingered the green-and-white-checked tablecloth. Her gaze came up and met his. "Sorry isn't enough."

A simple statement delivered in an even, matter-of-fact tone. If she was angry, disappointed, or hurt, she chose not to let it show. Good for her.

Toby launched into the tale of the break-in, the stolen sound systems, the lapsed insurance, the repair work, the phone calls trying to find other auctioneers willing and able to loan them sound equipment, and the trip to Virginia Beach to pick up a system from Mennonite friends so they could keep their commitment to call an auction in Richmond the next day.

Rachelle listened without interrupting. By the time Toby finished, her expression had softened to one of concern. "Your poor dat."

"I hate that he's going through this. But there is a silver lining. He's ready for you to tutor him."

"Oh, that's wunderbarr." Rachelle's face lit up. "With school being out, I have plenty of time to do the necessary research. I'll go to the library tomorrow. We can start whenever he's ready. Whatever hours work for him. If he prefers the evening, that will work. I can meet him in your office. People will think I'm out courting."

Her enthusiasm turned her cheeks rosy. What would she say if he told her she was the prettiest girl this side of the Mason-Dixon Line? "Instead of actually courting?"

She frowned. "What do you mean?"

"All the way to Virginia Beach and back I wanted to figure out a way to be in two places at once. I couldn't stand the thought of disappointing you. I hated that I'd started something with you and it immediately got messed up." Toby groped for words that would convey just how much he cared about what she thought. "This is what I meant when I said my job and my life are different. I didn't expect it to come between us this quickly, but maybe it's better that it did."

"Why? Why is it better?"

"Before you . . . before we become too close. Before you get hurt."

"You think I wasn't hurt after sitting on the porch swing for two hours and finally admitting to myself that you weren't coming? That there would be no buggy ride? No . . . kisses?"

"I'm sorry, I truly am. The last thing I want to do is disappoint you. That's why it's best that we not do this."

The previous evening's ferocity returned in the form of a dark scowl. Her eyes were huge. "Just like that? You get to decide? You kiss me one night and tell me it's over the next?"

"I'm trying to do what's right. I've always thought this life wasn't fair to the women."

"Only because your family refuses to let the women in. Did you know English women become auctioneers—?"

"The district would never allow that."

"Maybe not, but that doesn't mean women can't work behind the scenes, taking care of the inventory items to be auctioned or the bills of sale, or making sure everything is lined up properly."

"My daadi never wanted the women traipsing around the country, the kinner following them. Especially during school. Surely, as a tietschern, you see that."

"I see that flexibility is needed. A mann and a fraa have to work together to make a life that is best for the whole family."

Why were they having this conversation? This theoretical couple, theoretical husband and wife and children? "It can't be. It just can't."

"Only because you refuse to find a way to make it work." Her voice faded away. She picked up his glass and took it to the sink. She stood with her back to him. "So you really came here tonight to make sure that I'm still willing to tutor your dat. You'd already decided not to court me after all."

"I wanted you to know I didn't stand you up for no reason. I wanted to say I'm sorry."

"Well. You've said your piece." She turned around and faced him. All emotion had fled from her face. "Next time ask Layla to let me know when your daed wants to meet for a tutoring session. No sense you taking time from your busy work schedule to come out here."

The sarcasm was faint but unmistakable.

"I'm sorry—"

"You've already said that." She strode to the back door and held it open. "You'd better get going. You have a big day tomorrow, what with your busy work schedule."

Again with the sarcasm.

He stood and walked past her, close enough to touch her rosy cheek. "I hope one day you'll forgive me."

She let the screen door shut between them. "Of course I'll forgive. We're called to forgive."

Her final words echoed in his ears as he drove away. "That doesn't mean I'll forget."

Chapter 32

*P*ainting the interior of Micah's house had turned into a frolic. Smiling at the thought, Layla exchanged her prayer cover for a scarf and wrapped an old apron over her good one. The more women who swarmed the bachelor's house, the easier the work would be. The men had shown up too. They were busy rebuilding the hog pens and repairing the farthing barn's roof. And whatever other issues came to light as the day progressed. The atmosphere on this fine May day couldn't be more festive. The women's loud chatter and raucous laughter spilled out from the kitchen, where a bunch of them were preparing an assortment of sandwiches and side dishes for lunch.

Layla used an old washrag to wipe her sweaty face. Moving all the furniture to the middle of the living room had been an undertaking. Now that everything was covered with canvas drop cloths, she could start painting. She picked up a can of pale-green paint and poured a goodly amount into a pan.

Sherri and Sadie were singing "Jesus Loves Me" at the top of their lungs to the great enjoyment of their grandma Joanna. She and her best friend, Cara Lapp, were sitting at the far end of the room in front of an open window hand-hemming new curtains for the kitchen. Josie was with a group of older girls working on the bedrooms upstairs. Some of the younger girls were cleaning the basement while others were minding the children too young to work.

This decision to invite everyone to join the fun made it hard for Layla to carry out her plan to apologize to Micah for gossiping about his life in Bird-in-Hand. Maybe the passage of time in which she'd seen neither hide nor hair of him had allowed him to forgive her loose lips.

"Can I have that paint? I used up mine." Sadie had tied an old towel around her neck. Her scarf had flecks of white paint on it. She also had a dab of green paint on the end of her nose and another blob over her right eyebrow. "I gut at painting."

"Nee, she's making a big mess." Her tone filled with mild disgust, Sherri pointed to the wall they'd been working on together. "She's getting more on the drop cloth than the wall. And herself."

Layla surveyed Sadie's handiwork. Sherri's observation was spot-on. Thank goodness for the drop cloth and the blue tape that covered the woodwork and windowsills. Sadie's swishes and swirls were nothing if not enthusiastic. And wildly artistic. "Your work is quite nice, Schweschder, but we're not painting pictures. We want to cover the walls completely."

Sadie pushed her glasses up her nose with a paint-covered index finger. "Need more paint."

"Indeed." Layla wiped a drip of paint from Sadie's frames. "Just try to get more paint on the wall and less on you."

"I gut at painting," she repeated. "Jonah say so."

"And Jonah knows what he likes." Rachelle trotted into the room. Despite dark circles around her eyes, she was smiling. She waved at Sadie. "He's a gut judge of art too."

Layla shared a smile with her over Sadie's head. "I always thought Sadie was gut at drawing. But painting too. That's great."

"Hi, Tietschern. I love you came." Sadie dropped her roller on the drop cloth. She raced to Rachelle for a hug. "You my favorite tietschern."

Rachelle's wince was plain as day. It had to hurt. She wasn't Sadie's teacher anymore. "Sadie, you'd better get back to work before the paint in your pan dries up."

Sadie broke away from the hug. "Jonah here?"

Rachelle nodded. "He's outside with our dat and the other buwe."

"I go outside." Sadie reversed directions and headed for the door. "I say hi."

"Then come back." More fancy painting. Layla stifled a chuckle. It might be better if Sadie played outdoors for a bit. "You still have work to do."

"They're such sweet friends." Rachelle straightened and stretched. "I'm so glad they have each other."

"Such a blessing," Layla agreed. "Every other word out of Sadie's mouth is Jonah this or Jonah that."

"Same with Jonah about Sadie. Teaching them was such a joy." Rachelle's smile dimmed. "I'm glad I get to see Jonah at home every day. I told Mamm not to worry, I'll take Jonah when she and Dat are gone, but John, Dillon, and Kimmie are ahead of me. We may have to draw straws."

"Mamm and Dat know I would take Sadie in a heartbeat, but Toby has already made it clear he wants her with him." Of course that meant Toby had to marry. He couldn't take Sadie on the road with him. If he and Rachelle were to marry, they would eventually have both Jonah and Sadie in their care. "Toby has such a big heart. He has room for lots of kinner in there."

A scowl chased away Rachelle's smile. She strode across the room and picked up her roller. "We'd better get busy. This room isn't going to paint itself."

"I'm sorry. That sounded like matchmaking, didn't it?" Of course it did. Would she never learn her lesson? Layla followed Rachelle's example and picked up a roller. "I didn't mean it that way."

"It's okay. Your bruder may have a big heart, but he's not going to marry. If he doesn't, Sadie will be all yours."

"He *will* marry." Sudden anger coursed through Layla. Rachelle didn't know Toby the way Layla did. Her brother was meant to be a husband and a father. He just didn't know it yet. Toby liked Rachelle. That was obvious. He'd been in a mood when she and Mom served the men breakfast before they took off for Richmond in the wee hours. "Why? Did something happen?"

"Nothing happened." Rachelle's pinched face and quivering voice made a liar of her. "That's the whole point. We were supposed to take a buggy ride last night—"

"But thieves stole our—"

"I know. He told me. When he finally showed up at midnight. He also said he couldn't court me or anyone else because the family business would always come first."

"Ach! He's such a goober." He was his own worst enemy. Men. "He's so *narrisch*. He doesn't know what's gut for him. Did he tell you Dat agreed to the tutoring?"

"That's the reason he finally showed up at my house. The only reason." Rachelle slapped paint on the wall so hard, drops flew and speckled her faded black apron. "One minute he's kissing me . . ." She dropped the roller. Her hand flew to her mouth.

"It's okay. I'm not shocked, I promise." *Danki, Gott. They were on the right track. Now to keep them there.* "If Toby went so far as to kiss you, he's hooked. Don't you worry. I'm positive that's the closest he's ever allowed a woman to get to him since he was twenty."

"So I should feel honored?" Sarcasm soaked her words.

"Nee. Hopeful. I'd say be hopeful that one day you and Toby will share a home. And that Sadie will live in that home."

"You're far more of an optimist than I am." Rachelle rubbed her temple with her free hand, leaving behind a splotch of paint. "It's a lovely picture. Toby, me, Jonah, Sadie. A ready-made family, but it's hard to see it happening with Toby being so . . . narrisch."

"You talk about me and my bruder." Sadie's high voice held indignation mixed with a pinch of pleasure. "Mamm say it not nice to talk about people behind their backs."

"You're right, but we were only saying nice things." Sort of. Calling Toby a goober probably didn't qualify, but Mom would say if the shoe fit, he should wear it. She flashed Rachelle an encouraging look. *Don't give up. Please.* Then she picked up a roller and held it out to Sadie. "Why don't you take my place next to Rachelle? I reckon she'd like singing songs with you. I need to go outside for a breath of fresh air. These paint fumes are getting to me."

"Go ahead. Sadie can help me fix my tuner." Rachelle cleared her throat and pretended to practice a few notes. "It's out of whack. Maybe you can help me get it lined up again."

"Your tuner?" Already drawn into her teacher's supposed plight, Sadie seemed to have forgotten about her earlier pique. "Do I have a tuner?"

Layla left them discussing high and low notes. After such weighty discussions, she needed a moment alone—something as rare as snow in southern Florida in her family.

Organizing a frolic and then trying to be alone was silly. She slipped out the front door and down the porch steps. Left or right? She surveyed the yard. A couple of boys were rebuilding the chicken coop. The girls were taking the toddlers for a walk—likely to wear them out so they would take good naps later. A few of the grandmas sat at the picnic table eating sandwiches. A cat had joined them. He curled up on a picnic table under a beautiful Japanese maple screaming with red leaves under the May sun.

The staccato of hammers hitting nails on the barn roof filled the air.

People everywhere. Left. She stalked through freshly cut grass to the back side of the house. No people. She breathed in the moist air scented with the red roses that climbed the back porch railing. *Danki, Gott.*

Micah's vegetable garden needed weeding. His cousins had planted it, but they weren't keeping up with it. Easy to remedy. Layla took off her sneakers and socks. The dirt between her toes tickled. She sighed in contentment, knelt, and tugged a dandelion out by its roots.

"Are you stealing my carrots?"

Layla froze. That warm maple syrup voice held its usual note of amusement. Maybe that meant he wasn't mad anymore. She took her time, first dusting off her hands, then taking a long breath. Finally she stood and turned around.

"You'd have to have carrots for me to steal them."

Arms crossed, Micah stood on the garden's edge. He shot her a look—eyebrows raised, lips turned down. She shot one back at him. "You know weeds will kill carrots. They're weak if you start them from seed."

Micah stepped into the row where Layla stood. He squatted a few feet from her. His gaze wandered over the plants. "Hmm. Aren't those carrot tops?"

Layla followed his pointed finger. Not even close. She tried not to laugh. "Those are dandelions."

"Aren't dandelions yellow?" He sounded deadly serious.

"The flowers, jah, but that's the plant part." She knelt next to him, still far enough away to be seemly. "You have a lovely collection of weeds. Thistles. Bittercress. Chickweed. And, of course, the dandelion, favorite of all kinner who love to blow on them, spreading the seeds far and wide."

"So no carrots?"

"Nary a one."

"Huh."

"Your lettuce has come and gone. And the peas. I hope you ate them and didn't let them die on the vine. I do see the tops of some beets in the next row over. Those should be ready to harvest toward the middle of the month." Layla tugged a thistle out by its roots, careful to avoid the prickly leaves. She dropped it nearby and pointed toward the garden's eastern corner. "There're some turnips in that last row. They should be fully grown about the same time. That's provided the weeds haven't choked them out."

She went back to pulling weeds. It was easier than making eye contact. What was he thinking? That Layla was a know-it-all? That he hadn't invited her to mess around in his garden? That she should keep her mouth shut and her hands off his weeds?

"I think you're getting sunburned."

"I don't get sunburned." Layla touched her forehead. Her skin felt warm, but then it would. She was embarrassed. "Even though I have blonde hair, I tan well."

"Gut to know." Why did he always sound like he was laughing at her? "Why is your face red then?"

"The least you could do is pull some weeds. They are your weeds, after all." Now she was a know-it-all and bossy. He was probably thinking no wonder she wasn't married. Or courting. Of course he wouldn't know she wasn't courting. *Stop it.* "It's red because I'm embarrassed."

"But honest. The least you could do is look at me when you're talking to me." His voice had turned soft, kind. "Sei so gut."

Layla raised her head. Forehead wrinkled, Micah shook his head. "What earthly reason would you have to be embarrassed? You're doing me a great favor by weeding my vegetable garden."

"I wasn't expecting you to be out here. I came here for a moment alone, and suddenly here you are."

"Funny. I came back here for a moment alone too. As much as I appreciate everyone showing up, I'm not used to having so many folks around. But that's not why you're embarrassed."

Now he'd caught her in a lie—another transgression to add to the list.

"You overheard Caitlin and me talking—gossiping about you." Layla stopped weeding. She locked gazes with Micah. "I'm sorry. I should've told her I didn't want to know. It was none of my business."

Micah went from a squat to kneeling. It was his turn to dig in the dirt, eyes downcast. "I knew word would spread quickly through the grapevine. I just didn't think it would move that fast." His voice turned hoarse. "I wonder if people can imagine what it feels like to have someone you love ripped away from you in such a senseless manner."

"I reckon not. Not unless a person has experienced something similar."

"What exactly did Caitlin tell you?"

Layla rushed through the story in a minimum of words.

Micah pulled a dandelion. He tossed it on the growing pile. He didn't speak. Brilliantly scarlet cardinals argued in the nearby dogwood tree. The tree might be Virginia's state tree, but its blossoms still stank like dead fish.

Maybe the smell was punishment for Layla's loose lips. "I'm sorry." The inadequacy of those words only increased with each passing second. "For your loss and for our noisiness."

"I met Astrid when her car broke down on the side of the road not far from town. I was driving by in my buggy." Sorrow tinged his hoarse laugh. "I thought it a good parable about why we should cling to our old ways, our outdated ways. Astrid just laughed. She always laughed. She had this laugh that was more of a snort. It made me laugh to hear it coming from this skinny woman.

"She wasn't pretty. Not exactly. She was too skinny. She had freckles from being in the sun all the time. Her nose was too long, and her brown hair was as thin as she was." Micah ripped a clump of chickweed from the earth and flung it on the pile. "But she had personality that went on for miles and miles. Her sweet soul shone in everything she said and did."

"She sounds nice."

"Jah, nice." Micah cleared his throat. "The gossip got it right. After I gave her a ride into town, I asked her if I could see her again. I knew I was headed down a bumpy road, but my heart refused to listen to my head. I guess she felt the same. She said jah. We kept our buggy rides to ourselves. Courting is supposed to be a secret. That's what I told myself. We went on like that for six months. The longer it went on, the harder it became. Should I leave my faith to become Mennischt? I would have to leave my church, my family, and my friends. Should she join our faith? Her eldre had left the Plain faith before she was born. They had their reasons. They wouldn't want her to return. Regardless, such decisions had to be made based on faith, not for love."

He paused. His willingness to confide in her made Layla's heart contract so hard it hurt. How could she respond? She blurted out the first question that came to mind. "How did your eldre find out?"

"Astrid's bruder was coming home from Bible study one night and saw us sitting in my buggy at the end of the road that led to their house. We weren't just sitting there. We were . . ."

Layla kept her gaze on the bittercress in her hand. No need to see his face. It would be red with embarrassment, just as hers had been earlier. Drops of sweat slid down her forehead into her eyes. They burned. She used her apron to wipe her face. "His eldre told yours?"

"Her daed came around to the house the next day. My mudder walked him out to the field where I was mending a fence. He told me Astrid wouldn't be seeing me anymore. Just like that. My dat was within earshot too. The expression on his face. Fear. My dat isn't afraid of much, but the idea that I might marry outside my faith shook him to his roots."

"I reckon my eldre would be the same." Layla hazarded a glance at Micah. Pain etched lines around his mouth and eyes. The retelling of this story aged him. "It's as if they forgot that a person can't choose who they fall in love with. Nor can you turn it on and off at will."

"I couldn't. I tried to make my case to her daed, but he walked away in the middle of a sentence. My dat looked liked a hundred scorpions had stung him." Micah's voice dropped to a whisper. "He's not one to say much about anything, but he had plenty to say about this. He reminded me of my baptismal vows. He reminded me of what would happen if I married outside my faith. As if I didn't know. None of it mattered. The thought of never seeing Astrid again . . . I couldn't breathe."

Now his voice had dropped so low Layla had to strain to hear his next words. "I went back that night. She didn't come out, but her bruder did. He told me if I didn't get off their property, he would call the sheriff and have me arrested for trespassing. He had a cell phone in his hand. I sat there for a moment. He punched in a number. I left."

"So you never saw her again?"

"Nee. A few days later, Astrid's best friend came around. She said Astrid was on her way to Pinecraft. They'd sent her there to stay with an onkel and aenti."

"They would deprive themselves of her company to keep her away from you."

"My heart was so bruised every beat hurt." He sat back on his haunches and swiped at his face with his shirtsleeve. "But nothing compared to the day her bruder showed up to tell me she'd died. He said he figured they owed me that much."

"Es dutt mer leed."

"I've come to terms with it." The quiver in his voice belied his words. "Best as I can."

"So that's why your eldre decided you should be the one to farm your daadi's land."

"Jah. Nee. First they tried to make it right by meddling."

"Meddling?"

"Meddling like your mamm did when she invited me to eat supper at your house." His effort to smile said so much about who Micah was.

Layla's mouth went dry. Her mother meant well, but she'd only added to Micah's pain. And so had Layla. "You figured that out? Of course you did. Mamm is about as subtle as using a sledgehammer to put a nail in the wall so you can hang a calendar."

"About a year after Astrid died, they decided I'd been mourning long enough. They tried to fix me up with a girl from our district. A nice girl I'd known forever. They kept pushing us together."

"What did you do?"

"I didn't want to hurt her feelings, so I took her for a ride."

"What happened?"

"Turns out she'd been hoping I'd ask her out since our first singings."

"But you never thought of her that way."

"Nee, but I hoped somehow focusing on her would help. I tried. I really tried." Anguish seeped into his words as if he was trying to convince himself as much as Layla. "I did the wrong thing, but for the right reason. At least I think I did."

"It speaks well of you that you tried."

"Nee. I finally had to tell her the truth. I couldn't feel like that about her. She was sure if I gave it enough time, I'd get over Astrid. But as time went by, I realized it wasn't about Astrid. Six months of courting and I still hadn't held this girl's hand. The hurt in her eyes still keeps me awake at night. I should've put my foot down, but I didn't. So I ended up hurting her."

"And that's why you don't like the idea of matchmaking."

"The decision to court, to find out how you really feel about a person, that belongs to you and no one else."

"My mamm is worried Toby will never marry if she doesn't nudge him along. I think matchmaking has become a habit." One Layla had happily embraced. "I'm all done with it, I promise."

"Gut." Micah tossed aside another uprooted dandelion plant. He leaned back on his haunches, then stood. He brushed off his hands and held out the right one. "No hard feelings."

"Danki." Layla shook with him. "For forgiving me."

"I hope the girl back in Bird-in-Hand has forgiven me." Micah took a step back. "We all make mistakes. It's a gut thing Gott is patient with us. I'd better get back to the barn. The other men will think I bailed out and left them to do all my work."

"And I should probably get to the kitchen."

Micah didn't move. Neither did Layla. The scent of rich earth, sweat, and dogwood blooms wafted through the air on a sultry breeze.

"Danki," Micah spoke finally.

"For what? Digging some weeds? It's the least I can do."

"For listening and not judging."

Never had a man opened up his heart like this to Layla. He'd needed someone to hear his story and he'd chosen her. "Like you said, no one is perfect. I feel honored you chose me to listen."

"Now you can feed the true story into the grapevine and let it do its thing." The sober expression lifted. "If you want."

"Nee. I've learned my lesson."

He cocked his head toward the house. "I'll go first. If we come around the house together, tongues will wag."

He went. Layla waited, her dirty hands clutched in front of her, until he was out of sight. Her heart of hearts wanted him back the second he was gone.

Chapter 33

*T*he sight of all those books coupled with the scent—perfume really—of paper and ink was enough to calm Rachelle's jittery nerves. Lee's Gulch's library wasn't large or grand, but it held the most books she'd ever seen in one place. She surveyed the area. Summer story hour was in full swing. Librarian Molly had the rapt attention of at least two dozen children who sat cross-legged on the carpet while she read a story about a little girl who befriended a baby pig.

No one would know or care that Rachelle planned to use one of the six computers arranged in a bank on the far wall of the library's adult section. Often all six were occupied. Patrons had to take a number and wait their turns. Not today. An elderly man wearing a hat with a wide brim along with a green camouflage shirt and shorts bent over the first one. Number two belonged to a mother with a sleeping baby in a sling across her chest. Rachelle's gaze traveled to number three. A Plain woman. At that moment, the Plain woman swiveled as if she'd heard the wheels turning in Rachelle's mind.

Layla.

What was she doing using a computer?

"Rachelle?"

Rachelle put her index finger to her lips. She scurried over to the next computer desk and sat. "Guder mariye."

No, what are you doing here?

"I'm trying to learn how to use a program called Excel," Layla volunteered in a whisper. "Our website guy says it's the best program for keeping accounts on the computer. It does all the math for you."

If Layla's math skills were anything like Rachelle's, such a program would come in handy. Of course, Layla was an old hand at bookkeeping. She was probably good at it. "Do you need it for the store?"

"I would love to have it for our store, but I really need it for the auctioneering business." Her face split in a wide grin bookmarked by deep dimples. She and Toby had the same dimples and the same confident air. It was almost too much to bear. "I'm handling the auctioneering business's admin duties now."

"Gut for you." Less work for their dad. And for Toby. *Not thinking about Toby.* He'd made his choice and it wasn't Rachelle. "Are we allowed to do the accounting on a computer?"

"I haven't asked yet. I want to be able to use the program before I ask about buying it. That's why I'm doing the tutorials here at the library." Layla double tapped the computer's mouse. The computer squawked. "Oops. Computers and computer programs that help business practices succeed should be allowed, don't you think? With the theft of the sound systems, we need all the support we can get."

"So you're going ahead with the idea that you'll plead for forgiveness after the fact." Rachelle could relate. "I've been known to take that route too."

"I know Toby will agree. It's Dat who'll want to discuss it with the elders." Layla winced. "Sorry. I didn't mean to bring up my bruder right off the bat."

"You don't have to act like he doesn't exist." Rachelle busied herself digging her notebook and pencils from her canvas bag. Layla didn't need to know how much Rachelle longed to hear how Toby was. Two weeks had passed since their midnight argument and parting of ways. "I'm sure I'll run into him when I'm tutoring your dat."

"Now that they're back from Pennsylvania, you can get started." Layla's usual exuberance returned. "Dat's been practicing. He doesn't know I know, but I've seen him poring over the news-paper and Mamm's birding magazines. He's been playing spelling bingo with Sadie. She loves it."

"That's gut—for both of them." The teacher in Rachelle cheered. The teacher who still had no job sighed. She missed her scholars so much. "Activities like that will support Sadie so she can be ready for school in the fall. If scholars don't practice their reading and writing skills, they lose so much learning over the summer months."

"She still asks about you."

"I miss her too."

"So, what are you doing here?" Curiosity shone in Layla's face. "Not at the library but using a computer."

"I want to learn more about teaching schielers with reading disabilities."

"Ah, that makes sense."

Layla didn't need to know Rachelle had made a promise she wasn't sure she could keep. She told Toby she had no experience with reading disabilities, but then she'd agreed to tutor his dad. What if she failed? What if the one thing Toby wanted from her was the one thing she couldn't provide?

No. If she could teach children with mental disabilities, surely she could adapt those techniques to teaching an adult who had difficulty reading. Not so she could show off to Toby or because Toby asked her to do it, but because Charlie Miller needed her assistance. He'd lived with this disability his whole life. He deserved the best tutoring she could offer.

Rachelle accessed the internet search engine and went to work. Her search *strategies for teaching adults with learning disabilities* unearthed such a wealth of information she was overwhelmed. "This is wunderbarr. Wunderbarr."

"What? What's wunderbarr?" Layla rubbed her eyes and yawned. "All these formulas, charts, and graphs are putting me to sleep. Wake me up."

"I can't wait to share some of this information with your dat." Rachelle pointed to the screen. "All these well-known, smart people had learning disabilities. People like Albert Einstein, George Washington, Pablo Picasso, Leonardo da Vinci, and Thomas Edison."

"Amazing. "

"It truly is. They found ways to work around their reading stumbling blocks before people even knew much about reading disabilities. That's what I want to help your dat do."

"How do you do that?"

"People with reading disabilities aren't dumb. Their brains are wired differently so they learn differently. Teachers are taught to use the same methods for all the kinner. They don't have time to tailor their methods to a student's ability or learning style. Kinner who are different get left behind or struggle like square pegs being shoved into round holes."

Layla scrunched up her face. "Ouch. That sounds painful."

"It is—for the kinner. It makes them feel like failures. They think they hate reading. They hate school. They feel stupid."

"That's awful. So how do you fix it?"

"In big Englisch schools, they do reading evaluations for schielers who are having difficulties. Then they design a program for that kind. Digital recorders for recording lessons. Taking tests verbally. Using phonics to assist them in decoding words—"

"Okay, you lost me there. But it's exciting to see you so excited."

"The truth is, I was afraid I might not be able to help your dat, but now I have ideas for so many activities we can do." Rachelle hit the print button and sent another article to the library printer. "There is something you can do for me."

"Anything. I'd love to be of service."

"Tell me some topics your daed is interested in. Does he have any hobbies?"

"He mostly works." Layla shrugged. "All the men in my family do."

"Surely he has some interests outside auctioneering." The elderly man in a gardener's hat and dark-rimmed glasses shot them a scowl. Rachelle lowered her voice. She leaned closer to Layla. "What would he like to know more about—so much that he'd be willing to read a book about it?"

"He reads the Bible and bedtime stories because he loves the Lord, and he knows the kinner like us to read to them. Everything else, like the newspaper, Mamm reads to him."

The gardener man took off the glasses. "Shh!"

"Sorry." Rachelle grimaced at Layla and put her index finger to her lips. "Whisper. I understand, but if he could easily read for himself, what would he want to read?"

"Ah, I see." Layla's stage whisper likely could be heard at the checkout desk. "He likes to hunt. He likes fishing. He likes birds. He builds birdhouses in his spare time, mostly in the winter months when there're no auctions."

"Anything else?"

"Sorry."

Rachelle left her stuff with Layla and went to the children's section. Finding books for Charlie to read would be tricky. They needed to be easy enough not to frustrate him, but at the same time, stories that wouldn't insult him by making him feel like a child. The library had lots of Hank the Dog and Dog Man books. Pete the Cat. Junie B. Jones. Ramona. Not much for a man with a child's reading ability. She switched to the nonfiction section where she chose two books about birds, biographies of George Washington and Thomas Edison, and a book on astronomy. Who didn't like to study the night skies?

By the time she checked out the books, Layla was packing up her stuff. "I need to go before I miss my ride."

Rachelle checked the clock on the wall. "Me too. Mudder will be done with the grocery shopping. I'm supposed to meet her back at the buggy."

"Let's walk out together."

Maybe they were becoming friends. Funny the circumstances that could bring them closer together after years of growing up nearby but disconnected. "That would be nice."

Outside the midday sun blinded Rachelle for a minute. She stuck her hand on her forehead to shield her eyes. Summer heat had arrived early. After the library's frigid air, it felt good. A horse nickered. Buggy wheels creaked. Layla's ride had arrived. Rachelle squinted to see which sister drove the buggy.

"Hallo, Rachelle."

The rich bass sent chills skipping down Rachelle's arms.

Not sister. Brother. Toby.

If scowls could start fires, Toby's eyebrows would be singed. Rachelle didn't respond to his greeting. Instead, she glowered at Layla.

"You didn't tell me he was your ride."

"You didn't ask." Layla could make her worst transgression sound like someone else's fault. "Besides, you're the one who said you can't act like he doesn't exist."

"She said that?" That Rachelle didn't want to act as if he didn't exist was good. Wasn't it? Her purple dress served as a contrast to her creamy complexion. A few freckles brought out by the sun dusted her upturned nose. Pretty. Pretty cute. Toby struggled to maintain his train of thought. "I mean I'm glad you still acknowledge my existence."

Rachelle's scowl disappeared, replaced with a politely neutral facade. "Pretending you don't exist would be immature. We're grown-ups. I'm friends with Layla. Sadie and Jonah are best friends. I'll be teaching your daed. Our paths will cross."

Frost hung from her words. Toby shivered despite the dank May air. "You're right—"

"In fact, Rachelle is coming around tonight to tutor Dat." Layla climbed into the buggy. Could she be more cheerful? "We'd better get home and let him know. He'll want to clean up after working in the fields today planting corn and potatoes."

"Then I guess we'll see you tonight." Almond chose that moment to prance, pulling on the reins as if he'd understood the conversation. The thought of seeing her wrangled with Toby's certainty that she would be better off if he stayed far, far away from her. "I'm glad you're finally getting started—"

"Finally? It's not like I could start earlier when you were out of town for the last two weeks." Rachelle shot daggers at him with her piercing frown. Maybe it would be better if she acted as if he didn't exist. "I'm ready. More than ready."

"That came out wrong." So did his words—in a stumbling stutter. He was an auctioneer. He never stuttered. "I meant to say—"

"What you think really doesn't matter. Only your daed's opinion matters." Rachelle backed away from the curb. She waved—very clearly a wave directed at Layla. "Tell him I'll come round about seven o'clock. I'll meet him at the office." Her gaze shifted to Toby with an infinitesimal pause. "If everyone leaves us alone, we should start making progress immediately." She stalked away.

"Wow. She's really peeved at you." Layla had the audacity to clap in obvious delight. "What is it they say about a woman scorned?"

"Have you been reading those cheesy romance novels again?" The question came out sounding far more disgruntled than Toby intended. "You didn't tell me you were meeting Rachelle at the library."

"I wasn't."

"You said you were checking out books for Sadie and Sherri to read this summer." No books weighed down her bag. "Where are they? Forget that. What were you really doing here?"

"Honing my skills as Miller Family Auctioneering Company's administrative assistant." Wearing a self-satisfied expression, Layla leaned back on the buggy seat and crossed her arms. "You're welcome."

"Why did you need to come to the library to hone these skills?"

Layla bent his ear for the next ten minutes about a computer program with the on-the-nose name Excel. Which was fine. Anything to take Toby's mind off Rachelle's disdain for him. Layla claimed the program would make her excel at keeping the business's books. "I need it, I really need it."

With his heart ripped to shreds by Rachelle's sharp gaze, it was hard to muster much excitement over a bookkeeping program. "You need it, or you want it?"

"I'm not six, and this isn't a Christmas present like a puppy or a pony cart." Layla snorted. "I'm trying to do what you asked me to do—get our business affairs in order and keep them that way."

"I think I've created a monster," Toby muttered, more to himself than his sister.

"I heard that." Layla waggled her finger at him. "Could you get this buggy in gear? You drive like an old man. I've got work to do."

"Did you ask Dat if he approves? I reckon you didn't because you know he'll have to talk to Bart about it."

"I want to get gut at it first so I can show Dat how it works. He'll be so impressed he'll sell the idea to the elders."

She had it all planned out. "You do know this job isn't permanent, don't you? If you're not careful, you'll end up without a mann or kinner."

"Ha! You're one to talk." She tossed her head. "Mr. My Job Comes First."

"What's that supposed to mean?"

"You're narrisch. That's what it means. You're so besotted with Rachelle you put your foot in your mouth every time you open it. Yet you refuse to let yourself believe you could have a life with her. You keep finding excuses to push her away. You're the one who is well on the way to spending your life without a fraa and kinner."

"Besotted? Now I know you've been reading those trashy novels."

"That's what you took away from my wise words just now?" Layla laughed, a big belly laugh that cut off suddenly. "Slow down."

"But you just told me to hurry up—"

"Slow down!"

Toby followed her gaze. Micah Troyer stood on the sidewalk

outside the feedstore talking with one of the employees, an Englisher who never lost an opportunity for a long-winded diatribe about anything from hot weather to presidential politics to his wife's terrible cooking. If the goofy grin on his sister's face was any indication, there was no need to worry about her becoming too invested in her job. She was far more invested elsewhere.

"Should we rescue him?"

Layla didn't answer. She had that sickly expression on her face women sometimes got. Either she was coming down with the flu or she had a crush on Micah. Toby nudged her. "Layla?"

Her lips parted, but no words came out. She shrugged.

"I'll take that for a yes."

Chapter 34

*J*ah. Nee. Jah." Layla grabbed Toby's arm. "Wait."

"I thought you'd say that." He pulled the buggy in behind Micah's. "Turnabout is fair play, wouldn't you say?"

She hadn't intentionally caused Rachelle and Toby to cross paths. How could she have known Rachelle would be at the library this morning? Of course she did make sure they'd walked out together. Did that constitute matchmaking? She'd told Micah no more matchmaking. Which brought her back to her current situation. Running into him in Lee's Gulch with Toby as an audience. "Fine. Rescue him."

"Maybe you should."

"Don't be mean."

Toby grunted, but he hopped from the buggy first. "Hallo, Micah. How's it going?"

"Gut. It's going gut." Despite his words, Micah had the shell-shocked air of a man who'd been talked to near-death in a matter of minutes. "I was just—"

"He was just telling me about his move and the sow that died, and I was telling him about the vet in Nathalie." The hardware store employee never seemed to need to breathe. He simply talked

276

until someone interrupted him. "He's way better than the one here—"

"I'll give Micah a hand loading his feed." Toby clapped the employee on the back. "I'm sure you have customers waiting in the store. Or shelves to stock."

"Sure, sure. You need anything else, just let me know. I'm here to serve." Still babbling, he trotted into the store.

"Danki." Micah's relief was almost comical. "I thought I might have to plead an emergency or just make a break for it."

"He's a gut guy. I think he's just lonely." Toby glanced up at Layla, a "jump-in-anytime" invitation on his face. "Right, Layla?"

"Right. Very nice. He's very nice." Should she get down from the buggy? Did Toby need something from the feedstore? Would he leave them alone for a few moments? Her brother's matchmaking now rivaled their mother's. "How are things at the farm?"

Lame, Layla, lame.

"Gut. They're gut."

Almost as lame. This was almost painful. Maybe their lovely talk over weeds alone in Micah's backyard during the frolic had been a fluke. If so, why couldn't she stop thinking about it, replaying their conversation, remembering how he looked? Maybe they needed more time in each other's company to know.

Maybe now was her chance.

Micah busied himself loading his purchases. Layla busied herself watching. A treat, as it turned out. What Micah lacked in height, he made up for in brawn. With his broad shoulders and thick biceps, he made lifting fifty-pound bags of feed look easy. He didn't even break a sweat. All too soon they were finished.

Toby wiped his face with his sleeve. "I don't know about you, but I've worked up a thirst. And a hunger." He nodded toward Saul's Burger Joint across the street. "Care to join us for lunch?"

Either a stroke of genius or the worst kind of matchmaking. Layla peeked at Micah's face. He seemed amenable to the suggestion. If he had any qualms, they didn't show. "I could eat."

"Are you coming?" Toby grinned up at Layla. "Last one through the door pays."

An empty challenge. Toby never allowed anyone else to pay. Generosity was one of his many attributes. Even so, Layla sprang from the buggy as if taking him at his word. Somehow Toby managed to situate himself so Layla was in the middle between Micah and him. His arm brushed hers as they stepped off the curb and into the street. Two minutes later they were seated in a booth, Micah directly across from her. For a day that started with the dry dissertation on a software program, this one had turned out nicely.

With a minimum of fuss, they placed their orders. As soon as Toby gave the waitress his choice of a double cheeseburger with bacon and jalapeños, curly fries, and a chocolate milkshake, he abandoned them to "wash up."

Micah sipped his ice water and returned the glass to the table. "So Toby has been taking lessons from your mamm?"

"I promise you, I didn't have a hand in this." Layla twisted her napkin in her lap. Toby didn't know why this was a sore point with Micah. "My bruder has good intentions, bless his heart."

"For a bachelor coming up on thirty years old, he sure seems to think he knows something about courting." Micah lined up the salt and pepper shakers, the catsup, and the mustard with studied concentration. "But I have to say I'm pretty happy with his efforts at the moment."

"You are?" A sudden rush of pleasure inundated Layla. "Why?"

"I'm sitting here in a restaurant about to eat lunch with you."

The constraints fell away. The tightness in her chest eased. "Even with Toby as a chaperone?"

"Sure. We can pretend he's not here."

"Who's not here?" Toby strode to the booth and plopped down next to Layla. "Did I miss something?"

"Not a thing," Layla and Micah answered in unison.

They passed the time waiting for their burgers and fries, talking about hog prices, fishing, and rainfall predictions. From there they moved on to upcoming frolics, vacations, and camping. Micah enjoyed fishing, he liked camping, he loved the ocean, and he'd seen both the Atlantic and the Pacific. He wasn't a big fan of hunting. He thought venison was too gamey. His favorite food was his mom's chicken-fried steak with mashed potatoes and gravy.

Layla filed it all away. Toby was good at drawing people out, better than she was. He also ate faster. He dropped his napkin onto his empty plate and eased from the booth while she and Micah were still finishing their burgers. "Andrew just came in. I've been wanting to talk to him about the horse he has for sale. Dat is thinking of buying it."

Layla waited until he walked away. "He's a gut bruder."

"Jah, he is. It's obvious he wants you to be happy."

"I want the same for him."

Micah dunked his last french fry in a mixture of mustard and catsup he claimed was delicious. "I know it's none of my business, but I wonder why he hasn't married. He's so—"

"Hardworking, smart, a gut talker, faithful, honest."

"Jah, that pretty much sums it up."

"He has his reasons, but none that should make a man spend the rest of his life alone without a fraa and family." What would his senior years be like? Eventually he would move into his house, alone. He'd tire of traveling to auctions six months out of the year. He'd have plenty of nieces and nephews to love but no kinner of his own. "We haven't given up hope. He still has time."

"Bad experience?"

Not bad like Micah's. More like Layla's, and she hadn't given up on love. "A long time ago. Do you think instead of matchmaking, we should pray Gott brings the right person into the lives of the people we love? Do you think Gott wants those prayers? Or should we be waiting for His plan to unfold? Trusting Him? Saying, 'Thy will be done'?"

Micah's forehead wrinkled. He shredded his paper napkin, balled up little pieces, and tossed them on his plate. "Scripture says we should take everything to the Lord in prayer. It doesn't say He'll give us what we ask for, but it says we should ask. He'll do what's best for us. That's what a gut daed does, isn't it? Then we have to accept His plan for us. That's where 'Thy will be done' comes in. At least that's what I think."

"I think you're right."

His smile caught and held her. His hands stilled. "I know what I'll pray for."

"Me too. Starting now."

Gott, sei so gut, show me if Micah is the one. I like him a lot. Please show me the way. Show us the way. And Gott, if Rachelle is the fraa for Toby, show them the way too. Sei so gut.

Chapter 35

The collection of notebooks, activity sheets, word games, and simple readers made a satisfying bulge in Rachelle's canvas book bag lying on the buggy seat next to her. Still, their presence left a bittersweet taste in her mouth as she pulled into the gravel parking lot in front of the Miller Family Auctioneering Company office. The opportunity to tutor Charlie Miller one-on-one couldn't come at a better time.

Only two weeks had passed since she left the district's school for the last time as a teacher, but it seemed like forever. She began each morning with an acute sense of anticipation, a sort of forced optimism. That anticipation drained away as the day passed and brought her no news of a teaching job. How long could a person hold up under the sneaking suspicion that the proverbial other sneaker had dropped? The shoelace was broken, the sole full of holes, and she had no way to buy a new one.

It couldn't be allowed to matter that tutoring Charlie almost certainly meant Rachelle would cross paths with Toby again. As if their encounter earlier in the day in front of the library hadn't been awkward enough. Charlie needed her. She needed to feel useful in a way that only teaching could offer her. As she'd informed Toby that morning, they were both grown-ups. The district was small. They would run into each other.

And every time they ran into each other, she would wonder how he could kiss her like that and walk away. Not walk, run. How could he share that part of himself with her and act as if it was nothing? It was something to her. Something that kept her awake at night and haunted her dreams. "We—I—just need to get over it."

Her horse tossed her head and nickered.

"Not you. I'm not talking to you." She hopped down, secured the reins around the hitching post, grabbed her bag, and paused to take a deep breath. "Think gut thoughts, my friend."

Whatever Caramel thought of that sentiment, she kept it to herself.

"Here we go." Rachelle shoved open the office door and stepped into the foyer. "Hallo. Anyone here?"

"Just me."

Rachelle followed Charlie's voice into the first office on the right. A propane lamp cast a yellow light on a medium-sized room made small by an old-fashioned metal desk covered by neat stacks of papers, office supplies, and a computer monitor and keyboard. Layla's work, no doubt. Toby's father rose from the chair behind the desk and came out to meet her. "I appreciate you coming."

Charlie's morose expression and rigid posture belied his words. Rachelle settled her bag on a chair and summoned her best smile. "I know this is awkward, but you can trust me to keep these tutoring sessions just between you and me. We'll work to improve your reading skills as quickly as possible. No messing around."

"I like the sound of that." He smoothed his blond beard highlighted with streaks of silver. "I sure don't want to prolong the agony."

"Reading shouldn't be agony." Rachelle pointed to the two

chairs and a simple round table grouped under a large open window. The table was empty except for business card and pamphlet holders, both stuffed with Miller Family Auctioneering Company materials. "Let's sit down and talk about why it's been so hard for you."

"I just don't get it. Not from day one." Scratching his head, Charlie did as Rachelle suggested. "The kinner called me *dumm hund* by the end of first grade."

"Shame on them."

Charlie shrugged. "They weren't wrong. I couldn't learn sight words. I sounded everything out. Englisch was hard enough for me to learn to speak, without having to read it too. There's something wrong with me."

"Nee. You simply learn differently than other people."

"The reason doesn't really matter. The end result does."

"The reason does matter. Knowing why it's hard aids us in figuring out the best way for you to learn." Rachelle tugged a third-grade-level chapter book about birds from her bag. "We don't have the option of testing you to find out what specific disability you may have, but we can use some methods employed by classroom teachers to figure it out."

Charlie's expression said brain surgery would be preferable.

"Let's start by getting a sense of where you are." Rachelle held out the book. He glanced at it, then at her, sighed, and accepted her offering. She tapped on the cover's photo of cardinals and woodpeckers. "I heard you liked birds."

"I like to see different birds. Not read about them."

"Wouldn't it be fun to see a bird and know what its name is? Know its migratory route. Know it mates for life . . ."

"Maybe." His forehead lined with fierce wrinkles, Charlie rested his reading glasses on his nose. He hunched his shoulders and opened the book. If a person didn't know better, she'd think the man was waiting for his dentist to remove his wisdom teeth.

His gaze bounced around the page, likely studying the colorful illustrations. Finally, he pointed his index finger at the first line of text next to a drawing of a robin. "T-h-e the r-o-b-i-n's ha-ha-p-e ch-earr-up s-on-g s-ee-ms to s-e-ng aw-aa-y w-in-ter and b-r-i-ng sp-r-i-ng." He paused, sucked in air, and blew it out. "At this rate we'll be here all night."

"Nee, nee. You're doing well." He was sounding out each word, even the one-syllable words children learned as sight words like *the* and *and*. When other children had learned to recognize many words immediately and decode unfamiliar words, Charlie hadn't. Rachelle handed him a small rectangle of red construction paper. "Keep going. Use this to keep your place."

A few more pages and his halting progress suggested a problem with reading fluency. Rachelle wasn't a reading specialist. She couldn't perform an evaluation. She could only do her best with her limited knowledge. The next time he paused, she jumped in. "This is what I think—and it's only based on what I've learned teaching kids for the past three years—for what it's worth. You have trouble recognizing words you already know. You sound out common words. So it takes longer for you to read sentences. It comes out choppy. You spend so much time trying to figure out the words, you can't concentrate on what the story is about. Does that sound right?"

Charlie slapped the book shut and tossed it on the table between them. "Jah."

Rachelle picked it up and opened it to the same page. "It's called reading fluency. There are lots of activities we can do to improve your fluency." She kept her voice soft, respectful. "Not reading isn't one of them."

She read the same passage aloud and then asked Charlie to read it again. The third time the two of them read it together.

"Are we going to keep reading the same thing over and over?" Charlie leaned back and crossed his arms. "Pretty soon I'll have it memorized."

"Hallo! Dat?"

Emmett charged into the office. Sweat soaked his shirt. He carried two huge, still-dripping catfish on a fishing line. "I caught some fine fish. Can you believe—?"

He plowed to a stop, mouth open. "Ach. I didn't know you had company."

His face a dull red, Charlie whipped the book under the desk. "I'm busy here. Go on. Go clean the fish. I reckon your mudder will want to fix them for lunch tomorrow."

"But what's Rachelle doing—?"

"Go."

Emmett went.

"Sorry 'bout that."

"A reading disability isn't a disease. And it isn't anything to be ashamed of." Maybe she should hang a Do Not Disturb sign on the door. "I read that about 20 percent of people have reading disabilities of some sort. That's ten million kinner."

"I'm not a kind."

"Nee, but you were never given the assistance you needed."

"You don't know what it's like. Not being able to read a map when we're on the road. Letting the boys do the navigating. Trying to figure out a menu in a restaurant. I wait until the boys order and then order that." Charlie pulled the book from his lap and laid it on the desk. He made no attempt to open it again. "Or signing forms at the doctor's office. My fraa whispers in my ear so I know what I'm signing. Insurance forms for the business. Reading to my kinner. I always read the same books because I had them memorized." His words vibrated with shame, frustration, and anger that had mushroomed day after day, year after year.

"I can't imagine." She couldn't. For Rachelle, reading was like breathing. She learned English without missing a beat. By second grade, she could read chapter books. "I'm sorry."

"Not your fault. Not anyone's fault, I suppose." He pointed upward. "Does Gott give us these crosses to bear? Is there a reason? I can't fathom it."

"I've pondered those questions too. Not for me, but for our Jonah and your Sadie and my other kinner." Rachelle hadn't spoken of these misgivings about God's plan to anyone—until now. "All I can figure is that your disability is like the thorn in Paul's side. He asked Gott three times to take it away, but He didn't—"

"'For this thing I besought the Lord thrice, that it might depart from me. And he said unto me, My grace is sufficient for thee: for my strength is made perfect in weakness. Most gladly therefore will I rather glory in my infirmities, that the power of Christ may rest upon me. Therefore I take pleasure in infirmities, in reproaches, in necessities, in persecutions, in distresses for Christ's sake: for when I am weak, then am I strong.' Second Corinthians 12:8–10. I might not read gut, but I'm gut at memorizing."

Not only did he memorize well, he delivered the verses in a vibrant, musical tone of a poem. A bass just like his son Toby's. Rachelle shook off the thought. "Do those verses speak to you?"

"I reckon there's all kinds of thorns. Some are physical. Some are thorns of the heart. Not being able to read gut isn't the worst thing that can happen to a person."

True. So true. Anger at the world, at mean children and clueless adults raced through Rachelle, like someone had tossed a lit match onto a gas-soaked pile of rags. People saw Charlie as a man who worked with his hands because he wasn't very smart. Granted, Plain people placed a far greater premium on labor than book learning. But Charlie was an intelligent man capable of introspection. He deserved respect for that too. "You can learn to read. I promise."

His raised eyebrows coupled with another shrug told her he still wasn't convinced. "Then we best get moving."

"Okay. You asked why we are reading the same passages over and over. The more you read these words, the more you'll remember them." Rachelle tugged a water bottle from her bag and took a swig. So much talk and the thought that she must not fail on this promise made her throat dry. "Repetition helps you learn the words, and then you can spend more time thinking about what they mean."

"Okay."

Still not convinced but game to try.

Rachelle brought out a book of rhymes, tongue twisters, and short, funny poems.

"A big black bug bit a big black dog on his big black nose." They took turns saying it. Charlie got through it the first two times, but by the third time, they were both tongue-tied and laughing.

"I tell Mamm reading fun. I read too." Sadie skipped into the room. She carried Matilda the cat, wrapped in a baby blanket, in her arms. "I help Dat too."

So much for uninterrupted lessons. Charlie's first genuine smile of the evening as he wrapped his arms around Sadie softened Rachelle's initial irritation. Maybe the little girl was just what the doctor ordered. "That's a lovely idea, Sadie." Rachelle slid three books toward her. "Which one do you want to read with your dat?"

"Let me see." Sadie cuddled Matilda. Then she gently laid the cat on the desk. With exquisite care, she picked up each book and examined it. "This one. Matilda love this one."

A book about a cat who befriended a lonely little boy who used a wheelchair and was homeschooled. "Gut choice."

Sadie opened the book to the first page. "Reading hard for me too, Dat." She patted his hand. "See this word? Three sounds. Ka-a-t. Cat." She pointed at the picture of a tubby gray cat with long hair and dark whiskers. "Pretty ka-a-t. Cat."

Charlie nodded. "Ka-a-t. Cat. Pretty cat, but not as pretty as Matilda."

"Nee. Matilda most pretty."

Matilda raised her head, her ears perked up as if listening to their compliments as her due.

Sadie leaned her head against her father's shoulder. He leaned into her. A silver-blond head close to her tow blonde. He moved the red square along the lines, taking turns reading with his daughter, who sounded out words the same way he did.

Rachelle leaned back in her chair and relaxed. There were many ways to teach a child. Or an adult. The trick was finding the one that worked for this particular student.

After a few minutes, Sadie straightened and clapped. "You read gut, Dat. I put Matilda bed now. Boplin go bed early."

"Gut idea." Charlie squeezed her in a tight hug. "Danki for reading with me, Dochder."

"I love read." She kissed her dad on the cheek, turned to Rachelle, and offered her a kiss as well. "I love Tietschern. You be my tietschern always, always, always."

Her heart shattering into tiny pieces, Rachelle hugged the girl. "I love you too, Sadie. I wish I could be your tietschern always, but we can't always have what we want. Sometimes we have to do what's best for us."

Her blue eyes wet with tears, Sadie shook her head. "Nee. You best."

"Matilda's yawning, Sadie. You best get her to bed right away." Charlie saved Rachelle from explaining yet again something Sadie refused to understand. "If you're going to work with your mamm in the store tomorrow, you should get some shut-eye too."

With a mournful sigh, Sadie scooped up Matilda and trudged from the office.

"I think that's enough for one night." Her throat tight with tears, Rachelle gathered up her books, all except the bird, funny poems, and joke books. Her heart couldn't take much more in one night. "How does twice a week sound?"

"I can't believe I'm saying this, but it doesn't sound bad." Charlie smiled ruefully. "As long as I'm in town and I don't have something come up with the business, twice a week is okay."

Of course. When it came to priorities, Toby was simply a case of like father like son. Rachelle stood and picked up her bag. "I hope nothing comes up. I know how easy it is for Miller men to use business as an excuse for living life."

"I reckon you're referring to my suh." Charlie stood as well. He winced and rubbed his back. "Toby and I are a lot alike."

"I shouldn't have said anything." Rachelle touched the books. "Have fun with these. Read with Sadie. She loves jokes. And poems. They're library books checked out in my name, so keep track of them, sei so gut."

She sounded like a teacher reminding a small child. "Sorry, it's a habit."

Charlie waved away her apology. "Don't give up on him."

He's the one who gave up. Rachelle managed to keep the words from tumbling out. The last person to whom she should talk about Toby was his father. "I'll see you day after tomorrow."

Charlie took off his glasses and rubbed the bridge of his nose. "Same time. Same place."

She moved into the hallway and headed toward the door. Charlie's footsteps sounded behind her. "Danki for this."

"It's my pleasure." She held open the door. "Are you coming?"

"In a few minutes. I need to review the flyers Layla created for the barbecue plate fundraiser we're doing in front of the grocery store." He scrubbed his hands over his whiskers, his expression somber. No doubt finding ways to raise enough money to replace the sound systems kept him awake at night. "The store owners donated the brisket and sausage."

"That's great news. I'm sure everyone will line up to buy plates. Our whole family is coming by."

"I appreciate that." He turned back toward the office. *"Gut nacht."*

Rachelle closed the door behind her. She breathed in the dank night air. Her nerves and uncertainty over this new undertaking drained away. It would be all right. She shouldered her bag and trotted down the three cement steps to the sidewalk that led to the parking area. No stars peeked through a thick layer of clouds that obscured the moon. Only weak rays from a solar-powered light fixture showed her the way.

A shadow stepped into her path.

"How'd it go?"

Chapter 36

*N*ot a great start. Rachelle's startled shriek and the way she dropped her book bag suggested Toby's approach hadn't been the best way to offer an apology. "I'm sorry. I didn't mean to scare you."

"What did you think would happen?" She had both hands on her chest as if to prevent her heart from jumping out. "Lurking around in the dark in a parking lot where someone recently broke into your trailers?"

"I'm so sorry. I wasn't lurking. I had decided to leave, but then I couldn't." That didn't sound good either. "I mean—"

"Were you spying on us?"

"Nee. I came to shoo Sadie out of the office." He'd gotten as far as the foyer, where he'd stopped when he heard Sadie and Dad taking turns reading lines and laughing about a cat who adopted a little boy in a wheelchair. He hadn't wanted to interrupt Rachelle's encouraging words and her soft laugh.

"Sadie already left. Why are you still hanging around? I'm sure your dat will give you a report on my performance if you ask him— once I'm gone."

"Rachelle, sei so gut." Toby's mind went blank. All the words he longed to say, the words he'd rehearsed, dried up with it. He thrashed around for a way to keep her from marching out of his life. "Can we take a walk?"

"Why would you want to take a walk with me? You've already written me off as a woman who wouldn't be willing to share her life with a man in the auctioneering business."

Hurt mixed with indignation in her voice. The last thing he'd wanted to do was hurt her. "That's what I want to talk to you about."

"We'd only just begun to court. You don't know me. Not really." She knelt and grabbed her bag. "You're so sure I won't be happy as an auctioneer's wife. You presume to know this without spending the time to really know me."

"I'm sorry. I'm truly sorry."

Rachelle's face softened—at least he thought it did. She shook her head. "I understand what it means to be self-employed and responsible for a big family. My dat has his own business. He supports sixteen people with his hard work. He doesn't turn down jobs, even when he feels poorly. My salary helped support the family too. I've always worked. That's what Plain people do. But I don't see anyone but you turning away from relationships because of their work. You, Toby. Only you."

"I agree."

She opened her mouth. She closed it. Sighed. "Okay. A short walk. Jonah will want his bedtime story."

Toby tugged the book bag from her. "We'll drop this off at your buggy."

Having accomplished that task, he led the way to a wide, hard-packed path that led to the stream that meandered through their property. His family fished and swam there, but for Toby it was a favorite thinking spot. The sound of flowing water—heavier after a rain, sluggish in the heat of summer—calmed his mind and soul.

"It's so hot and humid. I wish it would rain." Reduced to talking about the weather. Rachelle would see right through that. "Not right this minute, of course, but—"

"Have you had a change of heart about courting?"

"I still have misgivings." A man didn't change his stripes overnight. She would know and understand that. "Daadi suggested avoiding courting and marriage might be more about protecting my heart than protecting the woman I court. I realize he might be right."

"Might be right?"

"When I was sixteen, I couldn't wait to go to the singings. I was raring to court. I threw myself into my rumspringa with the purpose of finding a fraa. I wanted one just like my mudder. Devout, a gut mudder, a gut fraa, funny, comely."

"What happened?"

"Do you remember Janey Hershberger?"

"I remember the name."

"She's Janey Eash now. I was eighteen when we started courting, twenty when she broke it off. She married a man in Stuarts Draft. They have four or five kinner. That's what happened."

"Ach." She was quiet for a few minutes. "You never tried again?"

"Nee. I was done. I thought we were growing closer. My feelings for her were deepening. Then one day, without warning, she broke it off. She said she couldn't see herself with a man who was on the road six months out of the year. She said it was wrong to expect her to raise kinner by herself, to run the household, garden, and livestock by herself while I galivanted—her word—across the countryside."

"I'm sorry. That must've been terribly hurtful. I can see why

Kelly Irvin

you would be afraid to try again, but that was many years ago. Not every woman will feel as Janey did."

The trickle, trickle sound of the stream reached Toby before he could see the creek. He let it soothe the thump of his heart. Even after all these years, the disdain in Janey's eyes was an unerringly accurate arrow into the center of his heart. "I gave my heart away freely, only to have it flung back in my face. It's a hard lesson to unlearn. I weighed my life as an auctioneer traveling five states with my daadi, my dat, and my brieder against the hazards of trying to find a fraa who not only didn't mind sharing me with the road but loved me enough to embrace it."

"Your dat, daadi, Jason—they all found women willing to do that."

The stream came into sight. A cool breeze wafted over the water. Bullfrogs croaked. Mosquitoes and flies buzzed. The bright-yellow eyes of an animal flashed, then disappeared into the gathering dusk. Toby pointed to a felled tree trunk partially covered with thick, tuberous vines. "Care to have a seat?"

"For a few minutes."

"See, you have obligations that tug at you. Loved ones who depend on you."

"It's different. Short-term obligations. Not ones that keep me from a lifetime of happiness as a fraa and mudder."

She was right. So right. Toby sat next to her—close enough to inhale her sweet scent. "I'm sorry I bolted at the first sign of conflict. I didn't want you to settle for a life where you might feel like the most precious thing you have to offer isn't appreciated."

"As I said earlier, one or two kisses aren't enough to truly know me."

"You're right. I'm sorry." The flash of fireflies, descending and looping up like a *j*, pierced the night. "Look, big dippers. The

294

kinner would love to be out here. They like to catch them and put them in jars."

"I always make sure they let them go free before they go inside for the night." Rachelle's kindness, even for simple winged creatures, shone in her words. "They're never too young to learn respect for all Gott's creatures."

Toby swatted away a mosquito intent on feasting on his arm. "Does that go for mosquitoes, flies, and snakes?"

Her chuckle felt like a hard-won victory. "Apparently even bats are an important part of the ecosystem."

"Spoken like a true tietschern."

"Which brings us back to you and me and courting. I love teaching. You struggle with how your job will affect your fraa. I struggle with knowing I'll have to give up the job I love. There will be a hole in my heart if I don't find another job teaching special kinner. My heart will be glad to marry, but it will also be a little broken when I can no longer teach. So, you see, we all have our challenges. Not just you, Toby Miller."

Toby scooted closer. He slipped his hand in hers. "I never thought of it from your perspective." Was she willing to give up her vocation for him? For them? Was she willing to try after all he'd said and done to her? He rubbed his fingers across her palm. She had such soft skin. "Do you think it would be worth it? With me, I mean?"

"Two weeks ago you were positive you didn't want to court me."

"I let my discouragement over the sound systems' theft and the insurance lapsing distract me." Real problems, to be sure, but he should be able to handle them and courting this woman who deserved his undivided attention. "It won't happen again. That night on your porch, I caught a glimpse of what my life would be like with you in it. I want that. I want you."

Her expression somber, she stared at his hand over hers. "I saw it too. Despite everything, I wanted it too."

Wanted it. Past tense. "You can trust me. I promise."

She raised her gaze to meet his. "Don't make me regret kissing you again."

Again? His pulse quickened. "I won't."

This kiss was less frantic. Softer. Went deeper. Her hands moved to his chest. She paused, stared up at him, her dark eyes questioning. He nodded. She slid her hands up until her arms wrapped around his neck. He touched his forehead to hers. "We need time to really get to know each other. We need time to figure out what we mean to each other."

"I agree. We have time, especially since I don't have a job . . . yet."

"I'll have a few weeks off the auction circuit toward the end of June."

Thunder rumbled in the distance. A fiercely bright bolt of lightning carved itself across the murky clouds, gone as fast as it appeared.

"We'd better go." She nuzzled his cheek and neck. "Jonah gets worried when it storms and everyone isn't safe and sound under our roof."

"Sadie too." Even though simple common sense dictated no one in his right mind stayed outside in a storm, Toby's body didn't want to move. "She'll be pacing the floor."

The first fat drops of rain splattered on his face. Cold common sense. He stood and held out his hand. She took it. He held on to hers, on to her, on the quick walk back to the parking lot. "You can't drive the buggy home in this. You'd better come into the house."

"Nee. Jonah will worry."

"Your mudder will remind him you're safe with us."

The rain descended harder. "I'll be fine."

"And your horse? We'd better put her and the buggy in the barn."

Lightning crackled across the sky. Thunder followed. Rachelle nodded. "You're right."

"Rachelle. There you are."

Rachelle's brother Dillon sat on a horse next to her buggy. The horse tossed his head and whinnied. He sounded as irritated as Dillon.

"What are you doing here?" Rachelle stuck her hand on her prayer covering, in danger of flying away in the wind. "A storm is coming."

"It wasn't raining when I left. Mamm thought you'd want to know right away. You know how excited she gets."

"Excited about what?"

"The parents' committee from the district you applied to in Bird-in-Hand left a message in the phone shack. They offered you a teaching job this fall."

Chapter 37

*C*areful not to shut it on Matilda's tail, Layla pulled the office door closed behind her and stepped out into the hot June night. Matilda stretched and yawned. Layla did the same. Her neck and shoulders ached from hunching over the keyboard, but the invoices were in order. The bills were paid. The calendar was up to date. Flyers for another barbecue plate fundraiser were ready. Between the store and the auction office, her days were full. No time to ponder whether Micah would make the next move. It had been a month since the farm frolic. What was he waiting for? If women could orchestrate courting, would she have the courage to drive a buggy over to his house and ask him to take a ride with her?

"That must be really hard, don't you think, Matilda?"

Matilda meowed daintily. She likely had plenty of suitors among the barn tomcats who took care of the mice on the Miller property.

"Agreed. Time for bed, don't you think?"

Another plaintive meow. Tail in the air, she trotted off toward the house. The *clip-clop* of a horse's hooves joined the crickets' cheerful performance. Odd time for visitors. Layla squinted in the solar-powered spotlight cast over the trailers in the parking lot.

Micah. Layla's tiredness drained away. The breeze held anticipation. She'd prayed for God to show her the way, and Micah had shown up. *Danki, Gott.* She waited until he came to a stop to approach the buggy. "You're out and about late this evening."

He doffed his straw hat and nodded. "I thought I might find you out here."

"What made you think that?"

"I heard your sister talking to a friend in the grocery store yesterday. It seems Kimmie is quite excited to take over your duties in the combination store. Also you're quite gut at math."

"Kimmie needs to talk more quietly."

"Nee. Her excitement and her love for her sister shone through in the conversation. It was nice."

"So my acclaimed math skills made you drive over here at ten o'clock at night?"

"Something like that. I thought maybe you would be interested in taking a ride with me."

Finally. "After being cooped up all day, I think a ride would be just what the doctor ordered."

"Hop in."

In a matter of minutes, they were traveling the dirt road that traversed from the Lapp property to the Troyer farm. Stars sparkled in the cloudless sky. An owl hooted. A warm feeling that might be contentment flooded Layla. She should make conversation, but the simple act of riding in a buggy in the company of this man on a quiet country road was enough.

Apparently for Micah too. He didn't utter a word. They turned onto a second road that was more of a rutted path. The buggy jolted and swayed. Layla's body lurched against Micah's shoulder. Laughing, she straightened and grabbed the seat railing. "Are you sure you wanted to ride with me? It feels like you're trying to get rid of me."

Micah hooted. He stuck the reins in one hand and pulled her away from the seat's edge with the other. "No way. It took me a month to work up the nerve to ask you to take a ride with me. I'm not letting you get away."

He was nervous. The thought of being nervous hadn't occurred to Layla. His presence felt right. "Why would you be nervous? Didn't we have a great time talking at the restaurant? Over the weeds in your garden? At the nursery? Do I still seem unapproachable?"

"All those encounters were unplanned. I didn't have time to get nervous. The one time your mudder invited me to supper, things didn't go so well."

"That's true. But we've spent enough time now that I think we'll be okay."

"Every time I talk to you, I walk away thinking, *She's nice. I like her.*" The moonlight did little to reveal Micah's expression, but his wry tone spoke of his surprise at his own reaction. "You make me feel like life is full of possibilities. I hadn't felt that way in a long time."

"I still don't understand, though, why you'd be nervous about asking me to take a ride with you if you enjoyed those conversations so much."

"They made me want to know you more, and that scares me."

Because of what happened the last time he allowed himself to court a woman. This was different. For starters, Layla was Plain. They shared their faith, a good foundation for beginning any relationship. "I'm sorry I'm so dense. Of course it's scary for you. I should've realized that." He could trust her with his heart. Easy to say but hard to prove. "It's just a buggy ride, not a lifetime commitment."

Micah turned the buggy into a driveway half reclaimed by weeds. An abandoned barn and falling-down fence that might have been a corral loomed in front of them. "I didn't think I would want to try again—at least not for a very long time. Something about you changed that. Something told me you would be worth it. And I'm not a coward."

That he wasn't a coward was obvious in his willingness to risk it all to court a Mennonite woman. Some might call him foolish rather than brave. Not Layla. Micah cared deeply. Not like Ryan who'd dropped her for another woman with barely a backward glance. "You decided that over plants and weeds?"

"I'm a pretty good judge of character." He tugged on the reins and halted the buggy near a stand of cottonwoods that crowded what was left of the ramshackle barn. Frogs croaked. Lightning bugs flashed deep into the trees. Flies and mosquitoes buzzed. "I know what I like. That's what got me into trouble the first time. I didn't care that Astrid was Mennonite. She was gut and kind and sweet and smart and hardworking. The overwhelming obstacle was the difference in our faiths."

"She sounds wunderbarr." And a very hard act to follow. "Almost perfect."

"Nee, she had faults, just not as many as I have."

Micah was plain spoken, hardworking, kind, honest to a fault, and smart. What more could a woman ask for? "What *are* your faults?"

"I'm stubborn. Obviously I want what I want, even when I know it's wrong according to the faith for which I took vows. I should've backed off before our feelings became so entangled." He took off his hat and laid it on the seat. The hat had flattened his brown hair. It hung down to his shirt collar. "I knew it was wrong, but I threw myself headlong into a relationship. Because of my disregard for the rules by which I had agreed to abide, a woman died."

"Nee. Her eldre sent her to Pinecraft, not you. I'm sure they feel as horribly guilty as you do. Even your eldre must feel a certain amount of guilt. Even Astrid had a hand in the outcome. She made the decision to abide by her eldre's wishes and go to Pinecraft." It was a sad story, no matter what viewpoint Layla chose. "Ultimately, Gott gives us free will. We make mistakes. We repent. In His grace and mercy, He forgives."

"You're right. You find words for so much that I can't begin to express."

Of course his kind observation dried up any response Layla might have offered. The tree branches danced in the breeze, their shadows flickering against the wooden gate that lay on the ground. "What is this place?"

"It used to be my great-onkel Aaron's barn and corral. What's left of the house is beyond that curve in the road. He trained horses here when he wasn't working with my daadi raising hogs."

"What happened to him?"

"He passed away from a heart attack at a young age. His fraa moved back to Bird-in-Hand. Daadi couldn't sell a place that didn't come with any land, so it sat here empty for all these years."

"That's a bit sad."

"In some ways it's a testament to his fraa's love for my great-onkel. She couldn't stand to live here anymore. The house held too many memories."

"None of us know what we'd do in such a hard situation, I suppose, but I think I'd want to stay here to be close to those memories."

"I can see it both ways. Letting go of someone loved and lost is hard. The memories follow you around. Moving doesn't make a difference. They pack up and come with you like baggage."

He would know. "Do memories of Astrid still follow you around?"

"Time has taken the edge from them. I can cherish the good memories instead of grieving the loss." His expression held a bitter-sweetness. "I can move on."

"I'm glad." And she was. For Micah's sake but also for her own.

"Would you mind if I put my arm around you?"

Despite the warm evening air, a shiver ran through Layla. He really was moving on. With her. "That would be nice."

More than nice.

Micah slid his arm around her. The impulse to lean against his chest overwhelmed Layla. To snuggle. To nestle. This was their first real date. Did a woman cross that line? He'd blurred the line by touching her first. *Just enjoy the moment.*

"So you're gut at math."

The mood fled. Why bring up math in the middle of a romantic buggy ride? Layla straightened. "So they tell me."

"You're enjoying working in your family's office?"

"I am. I like things to be orderly." Was this a test? Had she already failed? Should she tell him about the computer program? Would he understand? "I enjoy keeping the budget balanced. It's brain work."

"I'm impressed."

"Really." Was he teasing her? Men—Plain or otherwise—didn't always appreciate women who worked with their brains. "You're not just saying that?"

"Why would I lie? I could use someone like you to run the business side of my hog farm." He rubbed the bridge of his nose and squinted. "Feed, supplies, medicine, the vet, health department inspections, equipment purchases and repairs, birthing records, it's endless. Daadi had his suhs to help him. Then everyone left and he handled it on his own. Until he couldn't. I'm young. I did okay in school. I can add and subtract."

"It's not a matter of age or how you did in school." Layla leaned back and studied the brilliant stars. They appeared close enough to touch. "It seems to be about what excites you, what interests you, where your Gott-given talents lie."

"I suppose you're right." Micah leaned back next to her. He smelled of soap and minty toothpaste, a decided improvement over past aromas. "I like working outside. I don't mind hog smells. I don't mind being dirty and sweaty. I come in at the end of the day feeling like I've done my job."

"And you have. When I leave the office after bringing the files up to date, I feel the same way. Like I've done my job."

"Do you not feel that way after you've baked bread, done laundry, and mopped the floor?"

Now they were down to the nitty-gritty. Women had jobs to do at home, as wives and mothers. "I do. But it's different. It's hard to explain. I'm happy doing housework and gardening and cooking, but it doesn't feel like real work. It's what we do. We laugh and we sing and we talk—"

"Gossip, you mean." He chuckled. He had a nice chuckle. "Tell the truth."

"It might seem like gossip, but it's really just life. Our lives." Layla laughed with him. "I'm not explaining it very well, but I have this contentment inside me when I make the numbers balance. I don't get that from baking cookies or pies. Most women can bake. Not everyone is gut with numbers."

Her words sounded so prideful. Plain people didn't strive to be better than others at anything. They didn't take joy in standing out. "I don't mean to brag. I'm just trying to explain myself and doing a terrible job. I'm no better than the next woman."

"You're not bragging. And when it comes to cooking, you've never met my schweschder. I actually understand what you're trying to say. I have that contentment when a sow births a dozen babies and they all survive. Or a foal is born and a few minutes later she's stumbling around the stall, all legs."

"The thing is, Plain men are supposed to feel that way. They come from a long line of farmers. It's true some have other jobs now, with land being so scarce, but their roots are in the land." Layla buried a sigh. "Plain women aren't supposed to prefer accounting to canning."

"Is that why you burned the garlic bread?"

"You would bring that up. Mamm was certain I didn't have a chance with you because I burned the first meal I cooked for you."

"What I like about you has nothing to do with your skills in the kitchen." Micah's voice softened. A thrill flickered through Layla. He leaned closer. "Something about a woman who understands Excel fascinates me."

"Now you are making fun!" Laughing, Layla sat up and smacked his arm. "Who told you?"

Micah grabbed her offending hand and held on. His grin widened. "I might have heard about it from Toby. Kimmie's not the only sibling who sings your praises. He said the elders agreed it's okay to use the program for business purposes."

"For what other purposes would we use it?" Layla worked to keep her voice steady. Micah hadn't let go of her hand. His fingers were calloused, his grip strong and warm. That warmth spread through her body, yet she couldn't contain a shiver. *Focus. Think.* "Are you still writing everything out by hand in ledgers?"

"Hmmm?" Micah pulled her hand closer. He ran his fingers over hers. "Ledgers? Jah. I have an old computer for emailing vendors. I know how to use the internet. I can even write letters on it, but I don't use it for keeping records."

Layla closed her eyes. His touch made it hard to concentrate on anything. Maybe if she did her multiplication tables. Four times four is sixteen. Four times five is twenty. Four times six is twenty-four.

"Layla?"

She opened her eyes. Micah had drawn closer yet. His breath tickled her cheek. His finger traced her jawline. "Would it be all right if I kiss you?"

"Jah, I think it would." She sounded as breathless as he did. "I'm sure it would."

Layla had been kissed before. Ryan had taken her first kiss and then thrown it away for another woman. This time was different. Every cell in her body responded when Micah's lips brushed hers, then nuzzled her cheek and returned to her mouth. Her heart sped up. Her pulse pounded in her ears. She struggled to breathe. He leaned back. Layla leaned forward. "More," she whispered.

Micah obliged.

When they finally drew apart, Layla blinked, surprised to find they were still parked next to a falling-down barn on a country back road in Knowles County. Her heart had flown someplace far away where a woman could count on a man to treasure it. She could count on Micah, couldn't she?

Micah's arm tightened around her shoulders. "What are you thinking?"

"I'm wondering how my heart can be so certain it's safe with you."

"You've been hurt before." He nestled his chin on her prayer covering. "But you know what I've been through. You know I wouldn't risk my heart again if I wasn't serious about it. When Astrid died, I thought I would never love again. Then I ran into you on a buggy ride with your bruder. And there was something about you. You're different."

"And that's a gut thing?"

"It is. I'm different. I can see a future with you in it, doing the books for our hog farm and me drying dishes while you wash them on a Monday night after a long day of working together."

One kiss and he'd jumped far ahead into a shared future. Somehow it didn't seem such an enormous leap. "What a nice picture."

"You like it?"

"I like it a lot. It would take time to get there."

"Lots of time. But we've made a gut start, haven't we?"

They had. "Maybe we should work on it some more."

"I like the way you think."

He turned toward her. Layla met him halfway.

Chapter 38

*E*verybody had an opinion: Mom, Dad, Corrine, Jonah. Rachelle ran her fingers over a navy-blue hand-knitted sweater. The brilliant June sun beat down on her head. Who could think about sweaters in this heat? Perspiration beaded on her face. The Farmers Market and Craft Show vendors had erected pop-up tents over their tables, but that didn't alleviate the heavy, still air. Everyone but Toby had an opinion. Since that night in May, he'd been nothing but supportive of her decision to accept the job in Bird-in-Hand. He agreed that she couldn't base her decision on their fledgling courtship. They had all summer to build their relationship—except for the weeks when he was on the road. Like now.

Living in limbo. That's what she was doing. Rachelle waited for Jonah and the twins to catch up. She'd given them enough money from her savings to buy snow cones. They needed practice handling money on their own. Mom and the girls were selling beaded jewelry, handmade dolls, and a variety of produce in a booth at the other end of the row.

"Rachelle. Rachelle! Over here." Layla waved wildly from the Millers Combination Store tent across the aisle. It had a big hand-painted sign advertising HOMEMADE PIES, BREADS, PASTRIES,

DESSERTS. The Miller women also sold canned jams, embroidered linens, crocheted sweaters, hats, and scarves, homemade hot pads, and sundry other items. The tourists loved this tent. They "oohed" and "aahed" over all things Amish-made. "Sadie wants you to try her strawberry-rhubarb pie . . . on the house."

"That wouldn't be fair." Rachelle paused to let an English mom with toddlers in a double stroller pass, followed by an older couple enjoying double scoops of ice cream in waffle cones. "I should pay."

"Nee, we're recruiting you as a taste tester."

How sweet of them. Rachelle squeezed past a cluster of teenagers taking selfies in the middle of the wide sidewalk. They didn't even notice her. At the tent, she accepted a paper plate bearing a large slice of pie with chunks of strawberry and rhubarb spilling out. "This looks scrumptious, Sadie."

The girl cast an anxious glance at her sister. "It yummy. Layla says I no say that myself, but it is."

"Gut job on the English, Sadie."

Sadie was right. A sweet and tangy mix of strawberries and rhubarb served in a flaky, melt-in-your-mouth crust made Rachelle's taste buds cheer. "Gut job, maedel. It is perfect."

Sadie squealed, clapped, and hooted. "I knowed it— "

"You knew it. It's good to have confidence in your work but not to brag about it. I think that's what Layla means."

"Exactly. It should be tasty. That's our job as family cooks and bakers." Layla put her arm around Sadie and gave her a big squeeze. "To make gut food. Not to brag about it."

"No bragging. Just saying." Sadie wiggled free. She picked up the pie server. "I give Tietschern more."

"Nee, nee. This is a big piece. Save some for the rest of Lee's Gulch."

Another customer stopped at the booth and asked for two apple pies. Layla let Sadie handle the transaction while she moved aside to talk to Rachelle.

"She's doing so well, isn't she?"

"As gut as any nine-year-old girl."

High functioning was the technical term. Whatever it was called, Rachelle thanked God for it.

"I reckon you're missing Toby these days." Layla took a washrag to a splotch of cherry filling on her apron. "This is the longest stretch he's been gone this summer."

"I'm fine."

"I know you're fine. I would never tell him differently. But it's all right to miss him. Any normal woman would."

"I don't want him to feel guilty about being on the road. That's what caused us problems to start with."

"I'd think the problem now would be your plan to teach in Bird-in-Hand in the fall. It's a six-hour drive from here. That's not exactly ideal for courting."

The sweet taste soured in Rachelle's mouth. "He encouraged me to take the job. He practically begged me to take it."

"He encouraged you because he knows how you love to teach and how gut you are at it. And he's still that hurt twenty-year-old whose heart was broken by a woman he thought loved him."

"You knew about that?"

"Jah. The walls are thin in our house. I was just a little maedel, but I heard him telling Jason about it."

Rachelle studied the pie-laden tables behind Layla. How could she tell Toby's sister about the turmoil that enveloped her every time she thought about the teaching job? Teaching was the most fulfilling of all possible jobs. The children were to be cherished. On the other hand, the idea of leaving her family, especially Jonah, who would be devastated, caused a hard knot to form in her throat. It made her stomach roil. It kept her awake at night.

"It feels like you're riding the fence." Layla picked up a lemon meringue pie and brought it to the counter. "Like you have a Plan B if this one doesn't work out. Like you don't expect it to work out."

"Or maybe Toby's the one with a Plan B." Her appetite gone, Rachelle laid her plate next to the pie. "If he wants me to stay, he should say so."

"If you want to stay, you should do it."

Easy for Layla to say. She certainly knew how to speak her mind.

The raucous, high laugh of her brothers sounded behind her. Just in time. Better to keep her mouth shut. Sam was in the lead. Despite carrying three snow cones, he skipped straight at her. "We brought you a snow cone. Your favorite. Cherry."

Cherry was her favorite—despite the fact that it turned her lips and tongue bright red. Sam's were blue—a testament to his love of blueberry flavor. Rachelle took his offering. "Danki, Bruder."

Jonah brought up the rear, Runt on his heels. The boy balanced three snow cones: one yellow, one pink, and the other yellow and green. He grinned happily. "I got pineapple for me, grape for Runt, lemon-lime for Sadie."

He was so blithely unaware of the cost to Rachelle's pocketbook spent on giving a dog a snow cone that she swallowed words meant to school him on frugality. It was hot. Runt needed a cool treat as much as his buddy Jonah.

Sadie squeezed between the tables and zipped from the tent. "Danki, Jonah. My favorite."

"I know." He handed it to her with a formal bow, as if he were presenting her with a medal. Or a crown. "I know what my maedel like."

"You like pineapple. I know what you like." She linked arms with him. "We find picnic table to sit. We feed Runt his cone there."

Layla crooked her finger at Sadie. "Whoa, hang on, Schweschder. You're supposed to be working. You can't just leave."

"And Jonah, we're headed to our tent to see if Mamm wants us to bring her lunch." Rachelle bent over to scratch Runt between his ears. "You can give Runt his snow cone there. Mamm will have a paper plate you can dump it on."

"We go together." Jonah balanced the two remaining cones while clinging to Sadie's arm. Their mutinous frowns matched. "Sadie work in our tent."

"Nee. Sadie works in *our* tent." Layla shook her finger at Jonah. "You are only eight years old. You aren't the boss of her."

"Not yet," she murmured to Rachelle.

"Not ever. Sadie more likely will be the boss of him." Rachelle winked at Layla and turned to her brother. "Let's go. Say faeriwell to Sadie."

"But—"

"Tietschern says." Sadie disentangled herself from Jonah's clutches. "You go."

"She not tietschern." Jonah glowered at Rachelle. "Not anymore."

Sadie looked momentarily confused, but then her round face brightened. "She Dat's tietschern."

"And I'm still your big schweschder." Rachelle shifted her snow cone to her left hand and stuck her other arm around Jonah. "I'll always be your schweschder, no matter what."

"You teach other schielers." He tugged from her grasp. "You go away."

Grandma Cara would say little pitchers have big ears. "Never far and I always come back."

"Why not marry Toby?" Sam did a version of hopscotch as he posed this question. "Be his fraa?"

"Jah, why not?" Sean mimicked his twin's moves, but on Jonah's other side. "Then you can stay here forever."

"Nee. She live in Toby's house." Jonah might have limitations, but he still understood some things that his younger brothers didn't. His voice quivered, not with tears but with indignation. "She not read *Noah's Ark* to us."

How could Rachelle explain the complicated dance that was her life right now to three boys under the age of nine?

"We'll get to that, but first there's something I want to explain to you, Jonah." She sipped cold, sweet juice from her snow cone before it melted and dripped down her hand and arm. "Sean and Sam, you can hear it too. Someday, a long time from now, you'll need to know these things. First of all, courting is between the bu and the maedel. You don't talk about it in public."

Jonah's frown turned into a full-fledged scowl, but he said nothing.

"Second, Plain folks who are courting don't hold hands or hug or link arms in public. We keep such shows of affection for when we take buggy rides or walks or sit on the front porch with our cold tea."

"Ewwww. I'll never hold hands with a maedel." Sean's scandalized tone matched the horror on his fair, freckled face. "Right, Sam? We'll never hug a maedel."

"Except Mamm, and she's not a maedel." Sam nodded sagely. "She's a mudder."

Rachelle hid her smile. "I'm sure you'll change your mind about that someday, but right now that's perfectly fine."

Great, in fact.

"I like Sadie. She my friend." Jonah tossed his half-eaten snow cone in a trash barrel. "She doesn't make fun of me. She like me too."

"Who makes fun of you?" It was Rachelle's turn for indignation. "Someone from school?"

"Not to my face." Jonah wiped at his mouth. Yellow syrup stained his lips and cheek. "They no want me on kickball team. Or baseball. Or basketball."

"I'm sorry. That must hurt your feelings."

"Sadie play games with me. She no care."

"Me and Sam don't care." Sean crowded Jonah on one side, Sam on the other. "We'll play kickball with you all day long."

"That's gut, buwe. Brieder and schwesdchdre have to stick up for each other." Rachelle swallowed back tears. If she went to Bird-in-Hand, she wouldn't be nearby to protect Jonah. God in his great wisdom had given her little brother many siblings to stand up for him. She cleared her throat. "I'm glad you will always have each other."

"You marry Toby, you always have him." Jonah turned around and walked backward. His somber gaze pierced Rachelle. "I marry Sadie, I always have her."

"Someday." Rachelle didn't specify who she was talking about. She really didn't know. How could she dream of a joyful, love-filled marriage for herself and not one for Jonah? "If it's Gott's plan."

"I ask Gott. The bishop say we ask Gott, He answer."

Not necessarily the way a person wanted. A person had to read the fine print. Jonah was too young to understand that—yet. "For now, you and Sadie are too young to think about courting, let alone to court. You can be friends, though."

"We friends." He swiveled front-facing and shot ahead of Rachelle and the twins. But not before she saw the fierce look on his face. Certainty coalesced with confidence and became sheer determination.

To be so sure of what she wanted.

Chapter 39

The Commonwealth of Virginia had such a rich history dating back to colonial times coupled with amazing landscapes, from beaches to rivers to mountains, that teachers never lacked for field trip destinations. Nor did families have an easy time picking vacation spots. Every July Rachelle's family chose a different one. This year they were camping at Bear Creek Lake, nestled in the Cumberland Forest State Park.

Rachelle dropped chunks of breaded catfish into a kettle of hot grease sitting on a Coleman stove. In the distance, the lake shimmered under a lofty late-afternoon sun. The mouthwatering scent of frying fish wafted through air cooled by the lake and the thick canopy of cottonwood, conifer, Douglas fir, and lodgepole pine trees overhead. The fishing had been good. The girls were jumping off a small knoll into the cold water. Their screams of laughter and excited shouts filled the air.

If only life could be like this all the time. Mom had sixteen baking potatoes wrapped in foil and buried in the firepit coals. An equal number of corn on the cob ears were ready to add to the coals when the time was right. Watermelon cooled in one ice chest, coleslaw in another. The feasting was about to begin.

"Well, look who the cat dragged in."

Where Mom got some of these phrases confounded Rachelle. She followed her mother's gaze. Toby stepped from a canoe, straightened, and picked his way across the rocky beach toward them.

"I heard the Millers were planning to come up for a few days." Rachelle plastered a nonchalant expression on her face. She busied herself moving the catfish to a paper towel–lined platter that she covered to keep it safe from flies. Preparing some of the food now would take the pressure off later when the entire family gathered around the campfire. They could reheat it as needed.

Pleased with this time-honored strategy, she added more breaded fish chunks to the grease. "I didn't realize they were nearby."

"I'm sure you didn't." Mom's smirk appeared and disappeared. She turned and strolled out to meet Toby. Her voice carried, no doubt on purpose. "Bewillkumm, bewillkumm, Toby. What a surprise!"

"Hey, Leah. We're just a ways east from here. I saw your mann and the buwe in the boat they rented. They caught a mess of fish."

"Another mess of fish," Mamm corrected. "Rachelle's already breaded and fried the first batch."

Toby lifted his head and sniffed. "Mm, mm, mm. Smells mighty fine."

"You should stay for supper." Mom laid a stack of paper plates next to napkins and plasticware on one of the picnic tables. "We have enough food to feed the entire district."

Rachelle moved so he couldn't see her face. Let him decide if he wanted to stay. *Stay. Stay.*

"I reckon I wouldn't turn down a plate of fresh fried fish. The kinner outvoted the adults at the Miller campsite. We didn't get here in time to fish today. It's hot dogs, fry pies, and s'mores on the menu."

"Oh, be sure there'll be s'mores later." Mom pointed at a half dozen bags of marshmallows, an equal number of graham cracker boxes, and a box of chocolate bars. Packing all the food into the van for this trip had been a challenge. "Fry pies are reserved for tomorrow night when my bruder and his fraa get here with their kinner."

Plain folks knew food was a key ingredient in a successful camping trip. Good food made up for mosquitoes, flies, gnats, long jaunts to the restrooms, communal showers, and sleeping on the hard ground. That and hiking, kayaking, canoeing, swimming, and archery.

"I'll be back." Mom took off at a trot, leaving Rachelle with Toby.

"Where are you going?" Could she be more obvious? Rachelle flipped the catfish over. It sizzled, the sound combining with its pleasing aroma to make her mouth water. "We have everything we need."

"Bathroom."

She'd just been there not fifteen minutes earlier.

"I've always liked your mudder." Looking pleased with himself, Toby settled on one of the picnic tables, his big boots on the bench. "How are you?"

"Gut. And you?"

"Gut."

"Now that we have that taken care of." Rachelle added the crisp fish chunks to the platter and pulled the foil over it. "What brings you over here?"

"You. But you knew that."

"I just wanted to hear you say it." Rachelle turned off the stove.

Wiping her hands on a washrag as she walked, she slipped over to the table. "I'm glad you came."

Toby grabbed her hand and pulled her closer. "Me too." He tucked his arm around her shoulders and leaned in for a kiss.

She nestled against his chest and sighed. "It seems like it's been years since we've seen each other."

The auction season had picked up steam in June and went full steam ahead in July. Time in between auctions had been spent organizing and holding fundraisers for the sound systems. Some of the families in the district had gone together and made a large cash donation. In the meantime, the loaned system continued to function well, but Charlie didn't want to keep it for too long. Their friends in Virginia Beach might need it.

"How did the buggy rides go?" Toby's brothers had come up with the idea of offering buggy rides to tourists visiting Farmville. His sisters had sold them fry pies and fresh lemonade at the beginning of each ride. "Did they make any money?"

"They did, and the tourists loved it." Toby grinned. "They wanted longer rides, but mostly they just seemed to enjoy talking to Elijah and Emmett. They asked a lot of questions. The buwe actually enjoyed it."

"Gut for them."

"I think everyone's worn out now, though. Dat agreed we all needed a breather this weekend."

"Just this weekend?" Rachelle raised her head so she could see Toby's face. Fatigue left dark circles under his eyes. "I thought you were camping for the week."

"Nee. We took on another estate sale in Holmes County this coming weekend. Plus Mamm and the maed have another farmers market in Farmville. It's prime tourist season, and what they make now holds us over during the winter months."

"I understand." Rachelle straightened. She did understand. That didn't mean she liked it. They had so little time before she traveled to Bird-in-Hand to her new job. They'd agreed to spend as much time building this relationship as possible. On the other hand, she didn't want to say anything that would push Toby away. "We'll make the most of it, then."

"So what if we start by taking a canoe ride instead of a buggy ride?"

What would her mother think when she came back and found Rachelle gone? Courting in broad daylight? Knowing Mom, she'd be thrilled. "A short ride. I'm on kitchen detail."

"I reckon you volunteered."

"I did. I enjoy cooking in the great outdoors. So does Mamm. We have fun."

"I'm not complaining. The women in my family are the same. I just think there should be time for other kinds of fun."

"Forty-five minutes."

"Not a minute longer."

Toby clasped Rachelle's hand and together they raced to the water, startling a pair of green herons fishing in the shallows. A turtle sunning on the rocks ignored them. Toby helped her step in, pushed the canoe from the edge, and hopped in himself. In a matter of minutes, they were creating lovely ripples in the otherwise smooth-as-silk blue-green waters. Toby regaled Rachelle with stories from their latest road trip to Western Virginia for a livestock sale. "By the end of the day, you don't smell the cattle or the horses. You smell just like them," he concluded.

"They're earthy smells. They're Plain people smells." Rachelle associated the smell of horses with her father. He made a good living from horses. "Which kind of sale do you like best?"

"Hmmm." Toby had a nice, almost-lazy stroke that propelled

the canoe across the waters. His powerful shoulders pressed tight against his faded blue cotton shirt. "If I had to pick one, I'd have to say the school fundraisers."

Rachelle tore her gaze from Toby's shoulders. If she didn't, she wouldn't be able to focus on the conversation. "Ach, you're just saying that to get in gut with the tietschern."

His laugh boomed. A Carolina chickadee flying nearby scolded them and zoomed off into the turquoise sky. "Maybe. But it's true. The estate sales are fun because there's so many different items representing the lives of the people who are retiring or who've passed on. The quilt auctions are fun because the quilts are so beautiful and varied. And people get very competitive in their bids. But the school fundraisers are the best because the proceeds keep our schools funded. Pure and simple."

"I'll accept that explanation."

"Gut." Toby eased up on his stroke, letting the canoe glide while two Jet Skiers whizzed by. "So what about you? What's your favorite carnival food?"

"I have to pick one?"

"Fair is fair."

In truth, she had a tie for three. "Funnel cakes, if I had to pick one. You?"

"Pretzel and mustard." Toby didn't hesitate. "For an entrée. For dessert I'd pick deep-fried Oreo ice cream."

"That's two."

"Different categories." He didn't seem the least bit sorry for breaking his own rule. "Favorite carnival ride?"

"Ferris wheel. In all honesty, Rachelle didn't like most carnival rides. They made her sick to her stomach, but she would spare Toby the details for now. "I have no need for speed, but I like being on top of the world."

Toby cocked his head and wrinkled his nose. "Boring. I like the roller coaster."

And on they went. Favorite colors, holidays, cookies, ice cream flavors, birthday cakes, and childhood memories. Amassing tidbits of information, mostly trivial, about each other. Rachelle let her hand trail through the water as she watched the clouds overtake the sun, creating shadows that hovered on the water. Contentment, coupled with a languid sleepiness, washed over her. Time was so fleeting. Which brought her, finally, back to the present. "Has your dat said anything about the tutoring lessons?"

"He doesn't say much, but I see him reading magazines at night now, and in the restaurants he orders first instead of waiting to see what we order." Toby laid his paddle across his lap. They were well away from the shore. Alone except for two beautiful sailboats in the distance. "He reads to Sadie at night. It's their time together."

"I'm so glad."

"Me too. You're a gut tietschern."

A good teacher. Was that her calling in life, or did God have other plans for her? Rachelle's drowsiness ebbed. "Do you want me to go to Bird-in-Hand?"

"The better question is, do you want to go?"

"Nee, that's not how this is supposed to work." Rachelle sat up straight. He never wanted to express his opinion. He wanted the weight of the decision to fall on her. It wasn't fair. "This should be a mutual decision."

"I disagree. I don't want to urge you to make a decision you'll regret later." He dug the paddle into the water. The canoe picked up speed. "I haven't forgot our conversation that night when you started teaching Dat. You told me how much teaching means to you. As much as auctioneering means to me. You love teaching dearly. I wonder if you still love it more than . . . what we're building between us."

His Adam's apple bobbed. He ducked his head as if concentrating on paddling.

"Why don't you ask me how I feel?"

"Maybe I'm nervous about what the answer will be."

"Maybe you're still afraid to jump into deep waters." Rachelle scooped up water and tossed it at him. "Maybe you're afraid that things are going to end badly again and your heart will be hurt."

"I'm not afraid." Toby steadied the paddle in his lap and returned fire—or in this case, flung water. "Are you running to a job or running away from me? Take that and that."

"No fair." Soaked and laughing, Rachelle threw both hands up. "I surrender!"

"Do you? Surrender totally?"

"I don't think we're talking about the same thing." She stopped laughing. "Are we?"

"I like you a lot. I want to know you better." Toby stuck the paddle back in the water. "I hope you want the same."

"I do. I like you a lot too." How far was love from like? Not far in Rachelle's case. She liked everything about Toby, from his dimples to his care for Sadie to his hard work to his love of carnival food. "Even though you sometimes make me want to throw more than water at you."

"Me? Why would you want to throw more than water at me?"

How could he possibly look so injured? So innocent? "When you insist you're right when we both know you're wrong."

Toby's laugh turned into a snort that made Rachelle laugh harder.

"I never do that. I wish we had more time." Again he wasn't talking about the canoe ride. "I know your family can use the money you'll make teaching. I know you love teaching and you're gut at it. What I don't know is Gott's plan."

"So we keep seeing each other, we keep praying, and we see what the fall brings us."

Nodding, Toby paddled harder and focused on taking them back to shore.

"Wait."

He stopped paddling. Careful not to tip the canoe, Rachelle crawled forward until she was close enough to lean in for a kiss. He returned the favor. "Now you can take us back."

"We still have four minutes. I'm not done kissing you."

They put the four minutes to good use.

Chapter 40

*A*ll the good-byes had been said. Except this one. Rachelle held out her hand to Jonah. "Time to go to the bus stop."

Jonah shook his head so hard his glasses slid down his nose. "I not go."

The belligerent scowl on his face matched the jut of his chin and the rigid set of his shoulders. He knelt next to Runt, his arms around the dog's neck. Runt panted and grinned, far happier than his best friend. Rachelle gently placed Jonah's straw hat on his head. "You have to go. School is not optional."

"I go our school. I no need Englisch school." Jonah laid his head on the dog's massive shoulders. The hat teetered, then fell off. "I do gut with you. I gut schieler. I gut?"

Time was running out on this often-rehashed discussion. The short yellow school bus rumbled in the distance. Soon it would stop at the bottom of the long dirt road that led to the Lapps' blacksmith shop. If Jonah didn't start walking now, he would miss his ride on the first day at his new school. The first week of September had come too quickly. Usually Rachelle couldn't wait for school to begin. Not this year. After lunch, her van would pick her up to take her to Bird-in-Hand.

All the more reason to get Jonah settled into his new routine now. She scooped up the hat. "Come on, Runt. You can walk Jonah to the bus with me."

The dog's tail wagged so hard his entire hind end shimmied. He nudged Jonah with his slobber-dampened snout. Jonah stumbled to his feet, but his mutinous expression didn't change. "I gut schieler."

"You are a gut schieler, but you'll get lots of assistance at the Englisch school that I can't give you." Rachelle swallowed the hard lump in her throat. Everything down to the very marrow in her bones wanted to agree with Jonah, but that would only make this harder. "Sadie will be on the bus too. You can sit with her. Minnie, Nan, Tracy, Danny, and Jacob will ride with you too. They'll all be there at the new school. You don't want to miss out."

She took her brother's hand. "Come on, Runt and I will walk with you. I want to wave at Sadie and the other kinner."

Jonah jerked his hand from hers. He grabbed the new backpack Mamm had bought him at the Walmart in Richmond and stuck it on his back. "The other kinner sad too."

"Jonah, get a move on. Now." Dad stood on the porch. Rachelle hadn't heard him come through the screen door. "We've talked about this until we're blue in the face. You do as you're told."

Jonah wrapped his fingers around the backpack straps, put his head down, and stomped away. Slowly. He might have to do it, but he didn't have to like it. Runt trotted after him.

Not trusting herself to meet her father's gaze, Rachelle joined the procession. "When you get home, Runt will be waiting for you. Mamm will have your favorite spaghetti and meatballs for supper to celebrate your first day at the new school. With garlic bread, green beans, and apple pie. Your favorite."

"But you won't. You leave."

"We've talked about that too. I won't be far away. You'll come see me on the weekends. I'll come see you. I'll send you letters. You can send me letters."

"Nee. I no read. I no write. You read to me."

"Kimmie—"

"Nee."

"She does gut voices. You know she does."

Jonah didn't answer. He kept walking. Runt huffed a low bark and ran circles around him. Rachelle stayed a few feet back out of respect for Jonah's injured feelings. Runt could offer comfort Jonah would accept. They made it to the new bus stop just as the minibus pulled up in front of the blacksmith shop. The driver, a rotund woman with a mass of bright-red hair, wearing a matching red T-shirt, opened the sliding door and waved. "You must be Jonah. Welcome! Come on up. We've got plenty of room."

No amount of angst or anger could make Jonah be rude. He waved back. "Hello."

"Hallo, Rachelle! I got new backpack." Sadie stuck her head through one of the bus's open windows. She held up the backpack. "Mamm packed me PB&J sandwich, apple, eppies. I got extra for Jonah. I save you seat, Jonah. Hurry!"

She'd stopped calling Rachelle teacher. Which was good. Rachelle wiped at her face with her sleeve. She cleared her throat. "Yum. Sounds gut. Have fun!"

Jonah didn't move to get on the bus. Shoulders heaving, he stared at the ground. Rachelle knelt in front of him, her back to the bus. "I'll come home soon, I promise." A promise she could keep. She wouldn't want to be away from her family or Toby for long. "I love you, little bruder."

He threw his arms around her neck and buried his head in her shoulder. "You no go."

"I have to go, but I'll be back." Rachelle leaned back so she could wipe tears from his face. Her voice didn't give her away. *Danki, Gott.* "You have to go now. You don't want to be late on your first day."

She stood and stepped out of his way. Shoulders still hunched, he clomped up the bus steps. He was so small. No matter what Dad said, Jonah was a little boy who didn't understand why he was being made to do something he found so scary. Every bone in Rachelle's body wanted to grab him and run back to the house.

If this was hard, how much harder would it be to go to Bird-in-Hand knowing Jonah would have to navigate life without her from this day forward? He had to grow up sometime. So did she.

It didn't feel grown-up. It felt like abandonment.

She was abandoning her family, Jonah, and Toby.

The bus driver beamed at Rachelle. "No worries, missy," she sang out. "I've been doing this for ten years. I'll get your precious son to the school and back safely. Don't you worry none."

Rachelle didn't correct her. Not her son. But close enough. She nodded and waved. The door clanged shut.

Runt plopped onto his belly and howled.

"He'll be back, Runt." Rachelle patted the dog and scratched between his ears. He howled some more. "I promise he'll be back, hund."

The bus took off. Runt dashed after it.

"Runt, come back, silly hund, come back!"

Runt ignored her.

Stinky diesel exhaust fumes carried on the breeze. The bus's engine rumbled. Tinny music from a radio carried through the open windows. Just like Grandma Cara remembered. No pony cart rides. No sweet smell of fresh-cut grass. No quick jaunts down the road to a one-room school full of friends. Rachelle gritted her teeth, forced a smile, and waved wildly until the bus was a tiny speck in the distance.

Runt finally gave up. He returned, panting, his tongue hanging out.

"Go get some water at the house, you silly hund." Rachelle patted his back and sent him on his way. "Jonah will be back before you know it."

Runt woofed his disbelief.

"You're worse than your mudder." The thud of Dad's boots coming down the road put his words to music. "You'd think a kind never went into town to school before. He'll be fine. Don't baby him. He has to learn to adjust to change."

"Jonah's not just any kind."

"Nee, but he has to learn."

"Why should life be harder for him than for other kinner?"

Dad wiggled a toothpick between his front teeth. He removed it and shrugged. "It's not our place to question Gott's plan. Maybe it's not harder. He's never known anything different. Neither has his friend Sadie, and she seems mighty happy."

"For now." Rachelle joined him in a leisurely pace toward the blacksmithing shop. A chorus of whinnies and neighing met them at the sliding barn-style doors. While Dad fired up the forge, Rachelle went down the line and petted each of the current occupants— some Lapp horses, some just visiting. "What will happen when they're older and their brieder and schwesdchdre are married and having kinner of their own? Have you thought about Jonah wanting to get married?"

His expression preoccupied, her father opened a feedbox filled with oats. "That's foolishness, Dochder. Even as a grown man, his mind will be that of a bu. The thought of marriage won't cross his mind."

Like Mom, Dad didn't want to think about these possibilities. It hurt and saddened them, even as they thanked God for their child and prayed for His will to be done in Jonah's life. "He and Sadie are already talking about courting."

Dad pursed thin lips. His forehead wrinkled. He shoveled oats into a bucket with more force than necessary. "Who put that foolishness in their minds? Not you?"

"Of course not, but they watch and listen, just like other kinner. They don't know to keep their feelings to themselves."

"I'll have a talk with him. I'll nip it in the bud."

"I've talked to him about being private about his feelings, but that's not why I told you. I wanted you to know that he has tender feelings just like any other bu or maedel."

"I know that. I don't need you to tell me that. But like any other bu, he has to learn that life can be hard and a kind doesn't always get what he wants."

Patience, self-control . . . "He knows that. He doesn't totally understand how or why he's different, but he knows he is. He's already not getting what he wants."

A grunt met her impassioned statement. A bucket in each hand, her father hustled past her. "I've got work to do. Business is gut. Are you packed and ready to go?"

A clear signal that the conversation had ended. "Nee."

"Nee, you're not packed, or nee, you're not ready to go?"

"Both."

"The district is expecting you." Dad opened the gate to the first stall. Murmuring sweet nothings, he fed a spectacular Morgan who tossed his head and responded with a happy whinny. "You wanted to keep teaching. They gave you a job. You accepted it. What's the problem?"

Dad saw the world in black and white. He worked hard, ate well, and slept deeply. Her mother understood Rachelle's dilemma so much better. "I never wanted to leave home. The parents' committee forced me into it. I haven't even finished tutoring Charlie Miller."

The minute the words were out, Rachelle wanted them back. Charlie Miller was doing much better. Layla would take over where Rachelle left off. This wasn't about the tutoring.

Dad's back stiffened. He stalked from the stall and paused in front of her. "You chose. From what I hear, you could stay in Lee's Gulch and make a certain person happy."

Everyone knew her business. Rachelle counted to ten. "Courting takes time. I won't marry simply because it lets me stay in Lee's Gulch. I want to know for sure."

"Usually people get to know each other by being in the same place at the same time." Dad towered over her, his biceps bulging with the weight of the buckets. "You've turned down two men in the past. Your mudder and I want you to pick the right person to be your mann, but sometimes there's such a thing as being too picky."

Picky? When it came to vowing to love until death do us part, surely a person couldn't be too picky. And Toby was the one on the road half the year. Still, this man was her father and deserved her respect. Rachelle spun around and headed for the doors. "I'd better do some laundry. Once that's done, I can pack."

One suitcase and a canvas bag would hold all her worldly possessions.

With Runt napping nearby, Rachelle spent the morning running clothes through the wringer-wash machine and hanging them on the line. Doing laundry was a calming task. The steady *thump* and *swish* of the machine followed by the warm sun on her face as she clothespinned dresses, shirts, and pants to the line served to center her. The clean, fresh smell of soap and bleach mingled with the sweet scent of honeysuckle and roses.

A glance at the clock on the kitchen wall told her when Corrine would be directing the older children to do their math problems or the younger ones to read to her aloud so she could assess where they needed to start the school year. Then the clock told her when they were at recess and, later, eating their lunches at picnic tables outside the school. What was Jonah and Sadie's schedule? Did they play tag at recess? What did they think of P.E. class? Did they eat lunch in a noisy cafeteria where the food smelled better than cold PB&J sandwiches?

"You're sure quiet this morning." Mom unpinned the first batch of clothes from the line. They dried quickly in the September sun. "Thinking about Jonah or your new job? Or is your face scrunched up like that because you're hungry?"

"Jah."

Mom chuckled, a tinkling sound that made Runt raise his head and stare with sleepy brown eyes. "Could Toby Miller be on your mind too?"

"I don't want to talk about it." Rachelle had hashed and rehashed her decisions with Corrine all summer long. Corrine agreed that a person didn't turn down a job and a salary in the hopes that a relationship might work out. "I'll make some ham salad for sandwiches. We have fried potatoes left over from supper last night. I can heat those up. Dat and the buwe will be hungry."

"I'll make the ham salad. You go pack. Gott has a plan. Maybe you're supposed to go to Bird-in-Hand because that's where you'll meet your beloved."

No. Toby was her beloved. Of that she was sure. The only thing not clear was whether Toby felt the same. "Shall I bring up a jar of dill pickles from the basement?"

"I'll do it. Stop procrastinating and pack."

So she did. Maybe then her mother would let the topic of God's plan go.

No such luck. Mom continued to allude to God's plan after Rachelle came downstairs and set her suitcase and backpack by the door. She talked about it throughout the meal preparations and even during lunch. It was a relief when Dat brought up the subject of a death notice he'd received from his bruder telling of their great-onkel's passing. Mom turned her attention to comforting Dad and getting all the details.

That gave Rachelle the opportunity to clear the dirty dishes. It was strange to be home with the oldest and youngest siblings while the six in the middle were at school. Her brothers shoved back their chairs and went back to the shop while the littlest ones, Michael and Darcy, trotted into the living room to play until Darcy's naptime.

Rachelle carried a stack of plates to the tub in the sink. The *clip-clop* of a horse's hooves carried through the open window. She deposited her load and took a peek.

Toby pulled up to the hitching rail on the back porch. He was getting out of his buggy.

No, no. They'd said their good-byes the night before. They'd agreed it would be easier if he wasn't there when she boarded the van.

She grabbed the dish towel and scurried through the back door to the porch. His tail wagging, Runt followed. "Did you change your mind?" Something in his slate eyes warned her. Rachelle halted at the porch steps. "What's wrong?"

"The Englisch school called our office. Sadie and Jonah apparently left the school during recess." The muscle in Toby's jaw twitched. "They can't find them."

Chapter 41

The words refused to sink in. Jonah knew better. He'd learned his lesson at the fairgrounds, hadn't he? Rachelle's stomach dropped to her knees. "I'm sure Jonah and Sadie just got turned around in the building. Did they search the other classrooms?"

"They've searched the entire school." Toby stomped up the porch steps. Scowling, he loomed over her. "They're not there."

The pickled beets burned the back of Rachelle's throat. Her hands wouldn't behave themselves. They kept fluttering all over the place. "They can't have gone far."

"Gabriel and the specialists are searching for them in the area around the school." Toby shoved his hat back on his head. He growled like an old barnyard dog. Runt woofed in response. "I told him we'd start from this end. I can't believe Jonah would do this."

Rachelle whirled and headed back inside. That didn't keep her from responding. "You think it was Jonah's idea?"

"You don't?" Toby followed her, Runt at his side. "Sadie was excited to go to school this morning. Was Jonah?"

"Nee." The image of Jonah's morose face danced in Rachelle's mind. "He wasn't happy, but he went."

Dad had his fork in a half-eaten piece of peach pie on his plate. "What's going on?"

Rachelle shared the news. Mother froze, a dirty plate in one soapy hand. Dad pushed his plate away and stood. "I'll get the buwe. They can search for the kinner while I tell the bishop—"

"My dat is already on his way to tell Bart and the others."

"Then you go back toward town." Dad was already halfway to the door. "Me and the buwe will spread out and go farm to farm."

"It doesn't make much sense to have a bunch of us in buggies driving into town," Toby objected. "They can't have gotten far on foot. They won't be out here hiding."

"If they hitched a ride, they could be anywhere." Rachelle swallowed hard against the urge to vomit. "A driver might give them a ride and drop them off nearby."

Or whisk them away to parts unknown.

If Dad had heard her, he didn't show it. "Go. There's no time to waste."

"Why would they do this?" Mother wrung a dish towel between her wet hands. "They're gut kinner."

"Jonah told me he didn't want to go." Rachelle worked to keep anger from her voice. Doubting her father's wisdom was something she should keep to herself. "He didn't understand."

She didn't need to worry about her father's feelings. He was already out the back door. Rachelle turned to Toby. "I'm going with you." Rachelle didn't wait for her mother to approve of the idea. She brushed past Toby and grabbed her canvas bag from its peg by the back door. "Are you coming? We have to find them before they take a ride from the wrong person."

"What about the van driver?" Mom followed them outside. "He'll be here any minute."

"Tell him I had an emergency. Can you call Aenti Samantha

and tell her I might not make it today? She can let the parents' committee know I might be delayed."

The regular teacher would handle Rachelle's scholars in the meantime, just as she'd done the previous year.

"Just find Jonah and Sadie."

By the time they were on the highway, the silence had grown stifling. Toby was likely right. Sadie had seemed happy this morning, while Jonah had not. But Sadie knew better. She grasped their situation better than Jonah. It didn't matter whose idea it was. They'd put themselves in danger. Rachelle cast about for the right words. "You're right about Jonah. I'm sorry I snapped."

"You're worried. You're scared for him." Toby clucked and snapped the reins, urging his horse into a canter. "Me too. I'm sorry I suggested Jonah was at fault. It doesn't matter. They both know better."

They knew better, but they had what the experts called poor impulse control. "Jonah can be as stubborn as his father."

"Sadie is as stubborn as I am."

Rachelle chuckled despite herself. "That stubborn? Goodness, you'll have your hands full when she gets older."

"We'll have our hands full, I hope."

Rachelle accepted the hand he slid over hers. Their fingers entwined. "I'm leaving, if not today, then tomorrow."

"I know."

The air hung heavy with unspoken words. *Come on, Toby, come on.*

An eighteen-wheeler passed them on the left. Air rushed as tires whapped on the warm asphalt. Almond shied onto the shoulder on the right. Toby guided her back. "Easy, girl, easy."

"Somebody could've already picked them up."

Toby snapped the reins again. "Say your prayers."

So she did. This wasn't about her or her decision. Nothing mattered but finding these two children. In the hour it took to enter Lee's Creek and find the school, they saw no sign of them. Nor did they speak again. Nothing to say.

A police car and a sheriff's car were parked nose to nose in the school's lot. Gabriel stood near the double doors talking to a man in a blue uniform and a woman in a brown one. The woman jotted notes in a skinny notebook. The man, his face drawn in a serious frown, gesticulated with both hands.

Toby pulled the buggy up to the curb that separated the lot from the closest sidewalk. Rachelle hopped out. Gabriel waved.

She ran ahead and called out, "You haven't found them?"

"No, I'm sorry." Gabriel introduced the two officers. "The police are going house to house in the closest neighborhoods. The sheriff's deputies are driving the roads leading out of town. Unfortunately, they can't put out an Amber Alert because we have no evidence that the children were kidnapped or that they're in imminent danger of bodily harm—their words, not mine."

They were even more naive than other kids their age. That made them easily preyed upon. Didn't that count?

"The men from our district are going farm to farm in case they hitchhiked and someone dropped them off close to home." Toby intervened before Rachelle could express that thought. "They'll cover all the roads off the highway."

Gabriel's fair skin blanched even whiter. "Surely they wouldn't hitchhike."

"Sadie hasn't ever met a stranger she didn't like." Toby's scowl matched the police officer's. "She thinks everyone is nice."

"Jonah's shy, but he's determined." A shudder went through Rachelle despite the warm afternoon sun. "If he thought taking a ride would get him what he wanted, he'd do it."

"What you have to ask yourself is why any thinking adult would pick up two little kids and not immediately call the authorities or their parents, or simply take them home." Gabriel mopped his damp face with his sleeve. "If I saw two little kids walking along the side of the road, I'd see all sorts of red flags."

"You're a good person, sir." The police officer's grimace held cynicism. "This world is full of people who aren't. Or they don't care. Or they figure kids who run away are being mistreated at home. There's all kinds of rationalization that go on."

"Do they speak English? Are they verbal? How special needs are they?" The sheriff's deputy glanced up from her notebook long enough to spew her questions one on top of the other. "Will they get in a car with a member of law enforcement?"

The deputy must have some passing knowledge of the Plain community and children with disabilities. She knew children didn't learn English until they went to school. She knew Plain folks didn't involve themselves with law enforcement or the courts unless absolutely necessary. "They speak. Sadie is more verbal, and she can make herself understood in English. She'll understand what's being said to her as well. She'll be thrilled to ride in a police car, and where she goes, Jonah will go."

At least they had each other. Rachelle held on to that thought as she followed Toby back to the buggy. They were on the road again before he spoke. "We're blessed that Sadie had you as a tietschern. She speaks as much English as she does because of you."

"She would've learned anyway." Still, Toby's words pleased Rachelle. She didn't need compliments, but affirmation when it came was nice. "She works really hard. She wants to learn."

"We'll find them." Toby snapped the reins. Almond picked up his pace. "For once I wish I was driving a car. It would be so much faster."

"But you can't see what's alongside the road if you're zooming by."

"True."

Maybe by some miracle they would see two little ones walking on the shoulder of the road. Or sitting cross-legged under a tree eating their peanut butter and jelly sandwiches. A person could fantasize.

Toby pulled into the first convenience store on the highway. It had a dozen gas pumps and advertised clean restrooms on its sign along with diesel, ice, and deli sandwiches. "Maybe someone here saw them."

"They don't have money. They wouldn't go inside."

"But they might ask for a ride here."

Rachelle beat Toby to the double glass doors. Inside, the frigid air dried the sweat on her face in seconds. The cashier sipped an enormous slushie and nodded as she listened to Toby's question.

"Nope, no little Amish kids have come in today." Her teeth and tongue were red from the slushie. "Sorry."

Rachelle turned to leave.

"But there was an eighteen-wheeler that pulled in a couple of hours ago carrying a couple of kids."

Rachelle turned back.

"I was out at the pumps emptying the trash barrels when I saw them." She made slurping sounds with the straw stuck in her drink. "The driver came inside. I saw the kids peeking out the window at me. The girl had some kind of bonnet on her head, like yours." She pointed at Rachelle. "The boy had a straw hat like yours, mister."

"Which direction did they go when they left?"

"The driver came out with three sodas and a bag full of snacks." The cashier cocked her head. "He took off going north on 95."

"Thank you." Rachelle's stomach lurched. They had a lead, but the thought that Jonah and Sadie had hitched a ride with a truck-driving stranger tripled her nausea. Her mouth went dry. "Can you call the sheriff's office and tell them that?"

The cashier nodded. "Absolutely."

Toby grabbed Rachelle's arm. She allowed him to propel her toward the door. Back in the buggy, he heaved a frustrated sigh. "They're headed north on I-95. They could be going anywhere. Fredericksburg, Richmond, Baltimore—"

"Nee, not anywhere." Clarity descended on Rachelle like a clear blue sky. "Turn around. We need to hire a van."

"Why—?"

"They're going to Bird-in-Hand to find me."

Chapter 42

Time tilted back and forth, slow, then faster and faster. It seemed as if days had passed since Toby watched Sadie board the bus and waved good-bye to her. It was late afternoon by the time he hired the van, shared their theory with Rachelle's mother, and Rachelle had picked up her bags. Sitting in the van and letting someone else shuttle them to Bird-in-Hand didn't sit well with him. He wanted to feel as if he was doing something. If he were driving, he would step on the gas until they were flying. Not that he'd ever driven anything other than a buggy or a pony cart.

"I hope we're right about this." Rachelle had expressed this sentiment at least ten times in the course of the six hours it had taken to drive to Bird-in-Hand. She rubbed already-red eyes. "What if I'm wrong?"

"They haven't found the kinner back in Lee's Gulch." The van driver had agreed to give his telephone number to Toby's dad so he could call with any updates. So far no calls. Toby squeezed Rachelle's hand. "They're here and so are we."

They passed a sign announcing Bird-in-Hand was five miles up ahead. The driver's GPS politely directed him to the road that led to Arlo and Samantha Lapp's farm just south of the city limits.

"Sei so gut, Gott, let them be here," Rachelle whispered. "Sei so gut."

"Gott is always gut. He's merciful and kind." Toby rubbed his thumb over the soft skin on the back of her hand. "He knows what's best for you, the kinner, and me."

"I know," she replied so softly Toby could barely hear her over the AC, the country music on the radio, and the air rushing outside the van. She sighed. "Sometimes that means suffering, though, doesn't it?"

Sometimes.

An eighteen-wheeler was parked on the shoulder of the highway a few yards from Arlo's mailbox. Toby exchanged glances with Rachelle. She heaved a breath. "That's a gut sign, don't you think?"

"Jah." *Sei so gut, Gott, let it be a good sign.*

The dirt and gravel road that led to Arlo's house needed grading. The van driver took it slowly. Toby's nerves stretched until they might snap and send him flying through the window. His heart beat in his ears in a rushing sound that made it hard to concentrate. Rachelle's hand crept across the seat. His met it halfway. Their fingers entwined.

The solar-powered porch light was on. A couple Toby surmised to be Arlo and Samantha Lapp stood talking with a tall, rotund man wearing a baseball cap and cowboy boots. Rachelle was out of the van first, but Toby hopped out right behind her. He thanked their driver, who immediately took off to visit family in town.

"They're here, don't you worry." Arlo had a deep voice and the same big body as his brother, Rachelle's father. He led the other two down the steps to meet them. "This is Tom Pittman. He's the truck driver who brought them to us."

Pittman stuck out his hand. Toby shook it. The man had a firm shake. His face was red and acne scarred. He shook his massive head like a weary mastiff. "I know you must've been awful worried, and I'm sorry about that. I was just telling these folks that the kiddos refused to tell me where they lived. They wouldn't even tell me their last names."

"I reckon that put you in a bit of a predicament." Toby wrangled unreasonable anger to the ground. The man had kept Jonah and Sadie safe. He'd brought them here. He didn't have to do that. "We're grateful they're safe."

"They're okay. They're not hurt?" Rachelle's hands went to her throat. She sagged against Toby. He slid an arm around her. "Where are they?"

"They insisted Tom come in and have a bite to eat with us. Then Sadie ate some taco casserole, drank a glass of milk, and five minutes later she was sound asleep on the couch." Samantha beamed her pleasure at this turn of events. "She couldn't even stay awake long enough to eat a piece of my carrot cake."

"And Jonah?" Rachelle's anxious gaze went to the house. "What does he have to say for himself? How did he even know how to find you?"

"Turns out he took the envelope with our return address on it from a letter I sent to your mudder. He showed it to me when I opened the door to find them standing on the porch." Samantha shook her head at the memory. "He was proud of himself for not getting lost. He's still sitting at the kitchen table, finishing his supper."

"And feeding bits of taco meat to our dog Grubby," Arlo added.

"Arlo left messages for your dat and Sadie's as soon as we got them situated. God is gut." Samantha had bright-emerald eyes, fair skin, and red hair without a single strand of gray in it. She was as short and round as her husband was tall and broad. "He gave us Tom to deliver them safely to us."

"When I saw the two of them standing on the side of the road, their thumbs stuck out, my heart liked to have jumped out of my chest. I have a granddaughter that age. My son ever caught her doing a thing like that, she'd be grounded for the rest of her life." The truck driver scratched at his five-o'clock shadow with hands as big as gallon milk jugs. "I could only imagine how frantic their parents must be. I wanted to take them home, but they weren't budging on their addresses. I grew up in these parts, so I know you Amish folks don't mix with police if you don't have to. I figured I'd bring them here and make sure this aunt and uncle they kept talking about were decent God-fearing people. I want you to know I did my best by them two sweet babies."

"You did and we're so grateful." Toby's heart finally returned to its regular rhythm. God had watched over Sadie and Jonah. He'd delivered them to this man. There was no other possible explanation. The knot between his shoulders eased. His legs no longer threatened to buckle. "Thank you for taking care of them. Believe me, they'll be learning some lessons as well."

"It was my pleasure. That Sadie could charm the socks off the grumpiest old man, I tell you what. She's a sweetheart. And Jonah knows what he wants, and he's not quitting until he gets it."

That was Sadie and Jonah summed up in a nutshell. The two had a lot to learn.

"I'd better get going. I have a load to deliver to Baltimore by tomorrow afternoon." Tom lifted his hat and resettled it on tangled brown curls without a hint of the gray that colored the stubble on his face. "Thank you for supper. A truck driver like me doesn't get many home-cooked meals. I appreciate it."

"You're more than welcome." Arlo shook the man's hand. "I wish there was more we could do to thank you."

"When I think of what could've happened to them out there on that road . . ." Rachelle's voice trailed away. She pumped the man's hand a second time. "Thank you."

"No thanks needed. I only did what any person worth the air he breathes would've done."

With a final wave, he clomped down the steps and strode away into the darkness.

"I reckon you two are starving." Arlo waved his hand toward the door. "Samantha kept supper warm in the oven."

Together they moved inside. Toby stopped off in the living room. Sure enough, Sadie was asleep, her head on a pillow embroidered with John 3:16. Her mouth was slightly open and soft snores escaped now and then. "Maedel, what are we going to do with you?" Toby gently kissed her wrinkled prayer covering and backed away before he woke her. "Mamm and Dat aren't happy with you, but that'll wait until tomorrow."

In the kitchen, Rachelle sat at the table. She had her arms around Jonah, who sobbed against her shoulder. Her eyes wet with tears, she glanced up at Toby and shrugged. "It'll be all right," she murmured. "You're fine now. Everything's all right now."

Jonah backed away from her. His eyes red, lips trembling, he faced Toby. "I sorry, Toby, I sorry."

Toby forced a stern frown. The boy had to learn a lesson so there would never be a repeat of this scene. "I know you're sorry now, but do you understand why what you did was wrong?"

"I know."

"What did you do wrong?"

"I come here to go to Rachelle's school. She my tietschern."

Toby caught Rachelle's anguished look. He shook his head. "Not anymore. You know that."

"She teach here. I go school here."

"Nee."

"Let's talk about this tomorrow." Rachelle smoothed Jonah's wild hair. "Everyone is tired."

"He has to learn." Toby squatted so he could be face-to-face with Jonah. "Where were you supposed to be today?"

"School."

"What school."

"Englisch school."

"What could happen to buwe and maed who run away?"

"Bad men hurt them." Jonah cocked his head, his expression puzzled. "But our driver gut. He give us McDonald's cheeseburger, donuts, slushies. He sing silly songs make Sadie happy."

"Was Sadie sad?"

"She missed her mamm." Jonah ducked his head. "She scared. She miss you."

Toby's heart twisted. "That's when you should've known to take her home, don't you think?"

"I told her we see Rachelle here. She happy then. She love Rachelle."

Toby tugged the boy close for a hug. "If anything ever happened to Sadie or you, we would all be very sad. Do you understand that?"

"Jah. Me sad too." Jonah raised his head. His gaze was fierce. "*I* take care Sadie."

"Someday, maybe, but now that job belongs to me and our eldre." Toby stood and took a step back. "Do you understand that?"

"Jah."

"Jonah should get some sleep. He's had a long day." Arlo stretched his arms over his head and yawned. "I could use some shut-eye myself."

"You go ahead, Mann. I'll be up in two shakes." Samantha bustled to the table carrying plates loaded with casserole and rice.

"After I show Jonah where the younger buwe's bedroom is. Sadie can stay on the couch. I don't want to wake the poor maedel. She was worn out."

"Danki, Samantha." Toby plopped in a chair across from Rachelle. "It might take us a minute or two to unwind."

"No doubt." She set a pitcher of water next to bowls of guacamole, tortilla chips, and homemade picante sauce and two gigantic slices of frosted carrot cake. A feast. "Leave the dishes in the sink. Rachelle, there's a free bunk bed in with the maed. Toby, our oldest suh's room is empty since he got married last month. The sheets are clean. It's to be Rachelle's room while she's teaching here."

She accepted their thanks and shooed Jonah from the room.

A cricket serenade through the open windows was the only noise for a few minutes. They closed their eyes and prayed. Toby picked up his fork, then laid it down. "I think I'm coming over to your side. No more roller coasters. I'm sticking to Ferris wheels."

Rachelle's half-hearted laugh matched his. "This is my fault."

"How so? The parents' committee chose to send our kinner to the Englisch school. That left you out of a job. You found another one here." Toby inhaled the scent of cumin, garlic, onion, tomatoes, and fried hamburger. His mouth watered. He hadn't eaten since breakfast. "Jonah and Sadie decided to run away. Definitely not your fault."

"Family is more important than a job."

Toby gave himself a moment to enjoy the layers of taco meat, cheddar cheese, sour cream, and black beans. Rachelle's aunt Samantha knew how to make a casserole. He chewed and swallowed. "You're doing your part to support your family with your job."

"I can do that with a job in Lee's Gulch. I'm too proud. I

thought it had to be a teaching job. It doesn't." Her voice broke. She wiped her face with her napkin and dropped it on her plate. "I'm so full of myself I think that I'm the only one who can teach these kinner what they need to know."

The level of her self-criticism was astonishing. People so often were harder on themselves than anyone else could be. She left no room for all the goodness in her that made her the teacher and the woman she was.

Toby rose and went to her. He sat as close as he could get. "You love those kinner. You wanted what's best for them."

"I gave lip service to the idea that the Englisch tietschern could do it better, but secretly I thought they needed me."

"You let them go."

"And took a job here to try to find a place where I felt the same satisfaction I received from teaching our kinner."

Toby put his arm around her. He drew her close so he could hug her tight. "You sell yourself short. You do these things because you care. That's a gut thing, not a bad thing. You have a heart for special kinner. You have the heart of a tietschern. I admire that about you."

He could say he loved her for it, but that would muddy already-murky waters. This wasn't about his feelings for her. It wasn't about him at all.

"Danki. You're kind." Rachelle eased away from him. "Too kind." She rose and took her plate to the sink. She'd barely touched her food. "I need some fresh air."

"I'm right behind you."

Toby quickly stowed the food in the refrigerator and deposited his dirty dishes in the sink. He found Rachelle sitting on the porch steps, her chin propped on her hands, her eyes closed. The inky night held no starlight. Clouds hid the moon. Only the porch light allowed him to see the way she chewed on her lower lip. He settled next to her.

"They're safe, Rachelle. By the grace of Gott, they're safe. Tomorrow they'll go home." He kissed her forehead. She fit perfectly close to his heart. She belonged there. The time to tell her that was long past due. "I'd like you to come home too."

Rachelle opened her eyes. She leaned back. "I'm due to start teaching tomorrow—today. I think it's after midnight."

"Tell them you've changed your mind. Tell them you have people who love you and need you back home."

Her dark eyes somber, she said nothing for a beat, two, three beats. Her lips quivered. "Are you one of those people who needs me back home?"

"I love you." The words came easily after all. So simple. "I love you and I don't want you to take a job six hours from home. I want you to be close to me. I'm not asking you to rush into anything. If you stay in Lee's Gulch, we can court properly. I know for a fact courting will lead to something more permanent—"

"I love you too." Her smile lit her face and the entire world. "I love you so much."

She clasped her arms around his neck and drew him down. The kiss sealed their words and served as a promise. All thought of yesterday or tomorrow washed away in the sweetness of her lips on his, the softness of her skin, and the warmth of her body against his.

Rachelle pulled away first. The desire to have her back fought with the need to breathe. Toby grabbed her hands and held on.

Smiling, she kissed his fingers, one by one, then stared up at him. "So you have a direct line to Gott then?"

"I can only hope that it was Gott who opened my eyes today. That He brought me here to your onkel's house." Toby breathed deeply, trying to manage the well of emotions that threatened to inundate his words. "I could see you eating breakfast with this family and driving a buggy to the school every morning, coming home every night. Instead of being in Lee's Gulch with me and Jonah and Sadie and all the other people who love you. As much as you love teaching, wouldn't you rather be with them, with us, than here?"

He stopped, out of breath and out of words at the same time. Could she see what he saw? Could she imagine a future different from the one laid before her only a few hours earlier?

Her smile grew. "Finally."

"Finally?"

"I've been waiting so long for you to step up and declare yourself. I'd begun to think you'd never do it." She kissed his cheek, a feathery touch gone before Toby could capture her face in his hands. "I want to stay close to home too, but I've made a commitment here and I have to honor it. I can't leave them in the lurch on such short notice. But I will let them know that I only plan to stay until the Christmas break. That will give them time to find a replacement."

"I can live with that." She was right. As much as it pained Toby, she was right. "Are you sure you can live with that? Only one more semester of teaching?"

"I will miss teaching, I truly will, but in my heart of hearts, I've always known this day would come." She stared at his hands covering hers. "This is what a Plain woman does. She dedicates herself to finding a man to share her life with—so that one day she can be a fraa and a mudder. In the meantime, I'll find a job in a bookstore or the library or anyplace close to my family and friends. I'll tutor Jonah and Sadie and your dat. I'll learn to be content."

"You have this all worked out."

"You didn't seem to care if I stayed or not—"

"I didn't want to be the reason you stayed."

"Lee's Gulch is where my heart is. My home. My family." She leaned against his shoulder and sighed softly. "It's where you are."

"You could have told me that."

"It takes two."

"Two who become one."

A delighted giggle joined the crickets chirping and frogs croaking. "You kissed."

The space between Toby and Rachelle grew by two feet. It wasn't clear who moved first or fastest. Toby twisted to see Sadie peering through the screen door. She pushed it open and joined them. Her prayer cap was missing, her apron wrinkled, and her dress spotted with cherry-red slushie stains.

"You're supposed to be asleep." Toby gathered her in his arms for a good, long hug. "You scared us, maedel. Don't ever run away again."

"I won't. I no like it." She wiggled free and launched herself at Rachelle. "I stay home. Home is gut."

"Home is very gut." Rachelle kissed the girl's cheek and pulled her into her lap. "You belong with your mamm and dat and Toby and all your brieder and schwesdchdre. Not in an eighteen-wheeler."

"Mr. Truck Driver nice. He buy us french fries and donuts. I like donuts."

"That's what Jonah said. By the grace of Gott." Toby repeated himself. If only they could see how miraculous their safe arrival at Arlo's farm truly was. The thought brought another wave of relief so strong, he rubbed his eyes to keep tears from building. "Never again."

"Never again," Rachelle agreed. She rubbed Sadie's back. "Never again will you run away from the school either. You and Jonah have to go to the school. You need to do the right thing—both you and Jonah."

Sadie ducked her head and sighed. "I try."

"That's all I ask. Running away doesn't solve a problem. It makes it worse." They'd all learned this lesson today. Toby smiled at Rachelle over Sadie, who snuggled against the woman who would always be her beloved teacher. "I will be here for you and Jonah however I can, but I need to know you'll make the best of your new school."

"I try," Sadie said again. "Jonah try too."

"Gut."

"I live with you and Toby after wedding?" Her repentance fading quickly, Sadie sported a cheeky grin. She patted Rachelle's face. "You be my new schweschder?"

Eyebrows raised, Rachelle cocked her head. "What makes you think I'm marrying Toby?"

"You kissed. Jonah says people who kiss get married."

Better not to ask. The topic of whether Jonah and Sadie had sealed their love with a kiss would wait for another day. Until then her question deserved an answer. Toby wrapped his arms around both of his girls. "I plan to marry Rachelle one day. I don't have a date yet, but you'll be the first to know after she says jah."

"You're awful sure of yourself, mister." Rachelle's laugh was infectious.

Sadie joined in. She grabbed Rachelle's hand and put it in Toby's. "Kiss her again, Bruder. Then she can't say no."

So Toby did.

Chapter 43

The Miller Family Auctioneering Company's first auction of the spring season had gone well. Toby checked his dwindling list. No rust in his voice, no hiccup in his throat, smooth all the way down to the last item—a wringer-wash machine described as in perfect working order. Good. As much as he'd enjoyed being back on the stage, his feet were tired and his back hurt.

Turning thirty a few days earlier apparently had been a sure sign his body was getting older. He cleared his throat and smiled at the crowd that had begun to dwindle after a long day filled with spirited bidding and plenty of good sales. More seats were empty than filled on the bleachers, and the area in front of the stage was wide open. Time to wrap things up with this wash machine.

"Okay, folks, everybody still awake out there? Give a hoot and holler if you're still with me."

The youngies lounging on the bleachers obliged. Micah and Layla, now newlyweds, led a round of applause from the top row. They'd bought a bed set with mattress and box springs, a set of matching dishes, and a propane-driven lawn mower. Were they hanging around for the wash machine? Only one way to find out. "Alrighty then, our final item of the day is a wringer-wash machine. Good working order. Like new. Who'll give me $40 for it?"

A card shot up on the bottom row. It didn't belong to Micah. "$40, $45, who'll give me $45 . . . ?" The face behind the card registered. Toby stumbled. He lost his place. Rachelle. Sweet Rachelle. He'd seen her at his birthday supper. She hadn't mentioned coming to the auction.

It was hard to believe it had been a year since the day he called Jonah and Michael up on the stage, incurring Rachelle's wrath. She'd been the woman in his dreams ever since. It didn't seem possible, but she was even more beautiful now than she was then. Knowing the auction season would come around all too quickly, he'd spent every free moment possible with her during the late fall and winter months, first on weekends, and then whenever possible. Sleigh rides, snowball fights, snowmen, and snow angels had occupied one particular week after the only big snowfall of the season in January.

"Toby?"

His dad's puzzled voice brought Toby back to the stage. "$45, I've got $45, $50, bid $50."

Rachelle's card went up again. "$50. Bid $55, $55, $55." Nothing. The machines went for under $60 at online stores that refurbished old ones. "Sold to the young woman on the front row."

Rachelle grinned and waved her card in victory. Toby grinned back. No matter why she was here, he never tired of seeing her beautiful face. "That's it, folks. Thanks for sticking around to the end."

The crowd was already dispersing—except for Rachelle. She stood next to her new purchase, one hand resting on the wringer. Hastily Toby laid the mic on the stand, grabbed a towel, and wiped his face. It only took two strides for him to reach the stage's edge. He hopped down and hustled over to her. "It's funny. I don't recall you telling me you planned to come to Nathalie today."

"I guess I forgot to mention it." She patted the wash machine. "I heard there were some gut bargains to be had."

"I didn't know your family was in need of a new wash machine. 'Course with that many kinner, you probably wear them out regularly."

"Mudder's machine was in perfect working order the last time I checked." Her tone was airy, her expression pleased. "This one's for me. I'll need it when I marry . . . one day."

Toby inched closer. The crowd had thinned, but plenty of people still surrounded them. Including Emmett, who was packing up equipment on the stage, and their dad, who was making sure the bid card numbers had been noted on every item. "Plain women don't usually buy appliances until they're actually married."

"I like to plan ahead. Especially when the future mann is about to get really busy . . . and be away a lot."

"That's pretty forward for a Plain woman."

"Sometimes it's necessary to be forward when a Plain man is dithering."

Toby ran his hand across the wringer until his fingertips touched hers. "What kind of word is dithering?"

"The kind you learn from reading." She glanced around, then back at Toby. Her fingers curled around his. "It means when a man takes his own sweet time, when he piddles around forever. You know that word, don't you? You piddle."

"I've never piddled in my whole life." It was Toby's turn to glance around. They were alone except for a few stragglers and Emmett, who had his back to them on the stage. Toby leaned closer.

"And I can prove it. It so happens I've put a down payment on a piece of property outside Lee's Gulch. The owners are retiring and moving to Pinecraft. We're doing their auction next month."

"Indeed? What are you planning to do with that property?"

"My fraa and I will raise our kinner there. How's that for piddling?"

"It's a fine example. I know that house. It's perfect for raising a passel of kinner."

"Gut. I'm glad you approve. No more dithering?" He swooped down and kissed her on the lips. "None whatsoever."

Her smile grew bigger. "Gut, very gut." She withdrew her hand. "Mark and Steven will haul my purchase into the van as soon as they get back from visiting with some friends who live in Nathalie. We're headed back home. And you're off to Richmond and then Intercourse and on to Berlin and Charm in Ohio—"

"You have our itinerary memorized."

"Down to the day you'll be back."

Her eyes were clear, her tone bright. No sign she regretted giving her heart to a man about to spend the next month traveling from town to town calling auctions. In the meantime, she would serve as a part-time volunteer aide at Jonah and Sadie's school in their Parent-Teacher Association's classroom volunteer program. Her presence gave all the Plain children a sense of security that smoothed the way for them to do well in the English school. It also fulfilled her need to teach when she wasn't working at the Lee's Gulch used bookstore. "I love that you are so determined to make the best of this life."

"I love you. That makes it easier."

Not easy, but easier. Toby stopped under the shade of a dogwood tree just beginning to bear buds that would one day soon be blossoms. They were alone except for the robins and the sparrows arguing over branches swaying in a crisp spring breeze. He took her hands in his. "Will you marry me?"

Rachelle didn't let go of his hands, but she laughed.

"Hey. What's so funny?"

"It wasn't my intent to guilt you into proposing."

"I planned to ask you when we get back from Ohio." Toby ran his hands up her arms. He grasped her shoulders and leaned closer. "You buying a wringer-wash machine is one of the most romantic things I've ever heard of—not that I'm an expert on romance. Obviously."

Rachelle stood on her tiptoes and planted a kiss on his lips. "Danki. It didn't seem right for me to be the one to ask, but these last six months have been so gut, so wunderbarr, I couldn't bear the thought of you leaving without things being settled between us."

"So you found a way to say it . . . without saying it."

"Exactly."

Toby cupped her face. He kissed her, softly at first, then more deeply. The memories of long buggy rides, picnics, hikes, and glances exchanged from afar at church and frolics mingled into a beautiful quilt representing the happiest times of his life. He leaned back. Her cheeks were a dusty pink, her lips red, and her eyes sparkled. She was so beautiful, inside and out. Toby's heart pounded. "You haven't answered the question."

"I didn't?"

"Maedel, don't toy with me."

"The answer's jah."

Would it be wrong to shout hallelujah? Toby settled for a murmured aamen. Rachelle threw herself into his arms. He spun her around until she gasped for air. "I can't breathe."

"Me neither." He set her gently on the ground. She leaned

against the tree and sighed. "What a beautiful day this turned out to be."

"Do you think you can wait until I get back for us to talk to Bart?"

"My lips are sealed."

"Your lips are sweet." Toby swooped in for another quick kiss. "I hope I can hold out too."

"You'll only have men around you. Think about how hard it'll be for me—my mamm, your mamm, Layla, Sadie. Especially Sadie. She keeps asking me when we're getting married."

"She informed Mamm that she saw us kissing and that we're getting married. So you can imagine how excited Mamm was."

"Not as excited as she'll be when the banns are announced."

"I'll be back in five weeks."

"Thirty-five days."

"But who's counting?"

"I am." She grabbed Toby's suspenders and tugged him close. "I've been counting the days since I was sixteen."

"I'm sorry I kept you waiting."

"Always the ditherer."

"How about I make up for it now?" Toby scooped her up in his arms. He planted kisses on her forehead, cheeks, chin, and lips. "Is that enough to make you forget?"

"I think it's going to take a lot more kisses than that."

"I'm happy to oblige."

Right then and forever.

Acknowledgments

L ife experiences so often play a role in the stories I most cherish. *The Heart's Bidding* is no exception. I grew up spending
time with my uncle Duane, who had a severe intellectual disability
but a streak of independence a mile long. He was adventuresome
and inquisitive, and he loved to take things apart to see how they
worked—even if it meant he couldn't put them back together. As
an adult, he rode his bike all over our small town, stopping at businesses where folks knew him and frequently gave him a pop or a
donut. He was safe because everyone knew him. I grew up hearing
my mother's stories about what it was like to be the younger sister
left in charge of a brother who was often bullied by other kids while
her parents worked. It might not seem like it at times, but progress
has been made in attitudes toward people who are differently abled.
I thank God for that. I'm thankful my mother taught us to have
empathy toward people who are different than we are—as much by
her actions as by her words. Now that I'm living with a disability
myself, I experience firsthand the kindness of strangers who go out
of their way to help me traverse public spaces. Much goodness still
exists in this world.

I'm also thankful for Susan Lohrer. Susan, the mother of a

sweet young woman named Nikki, who has Down syndrome, read my manuscript to help make sure I correctly drew my characters Sadie and Jonah as well as Rachelle and the others who love them so much. Her insights were invaluable. My thanks also to Elisa Stanford for her gentle guidance in word usage around disability, Down syndrome, and the stereotypes sometimes unintentionally reinforced. It's a difficult balance when Amish views about disability, family life, and theology don't coincide with those of the mainstream world. Any missteps are mine alone.

I love being able to thank my daughter Erin St. Hilaire and granddaughter Brooklyn St. Hilaire for hosting my research trip to Virginia to explore a few Amish communities. I have such sweet memories of that visit and our road trip. Love you so much!

My thanks to the usual suspects: editor Becky Monds, line editor Julee Schwarzburg, my agent Julie Gwinn, and the entire team at HarperCollins Christian Publishing. Contrary to what you may have heard, writing, when coupled with publishing, is a team sport.

None of this would be possible without my husband, Tim, who takes his vows to love and to cherish in health and in sickness very seriously.

Thank You, Jesus, for an abundance of blessings as I live out my dream.

Discussion Questions

1. Toby doesn't think he should marry because he's on the road six months out of the year. In mainstream culture, a spouse is often away traveling, particularly in the military. But English spouses have access to technology—email, phone calls, FaceTime, social media—that Plain spouses don't. Given those circumstances, do you agree with Toby? Why or why not?

2. Have you experienced being a "single" parent while your spouse traveled for work or served overseas? How did it make you feel? Did you "sign up" for it? What advice would you have for someone like Rachelle?

3. Amish families see children with developmental or intellectual disabilities as "special children," as blessings from God. How is that different from mainstream culture, with the availability of prenatal medical testing? Do you agree with the Amish viewpoint? Why or why not?

4. Micah fell in love with a Mennonite woman despite his baptismal vows. He feels he should have stepped away from her but didn't. He feels guilty. Do you think he's responsible for Astrid's death? Are the parents who intervened responsible? Why or why not?

5. John 9:1–3 says that disability is not the result of parents' sin, but rather an opportunity to reflect God's glory. If you have experience with disability—either yourself or a loved one—what does that passage mean to you? How have you seen God's glory reflected in situations with which you're familiar?

6. Do you agree with the parents' committee's decision to send their children with disabilities to the English school? Why or why not? Do you think Rachelle could do just as good a job educating these children as the more educated specialists?

7. The last several decades of research has shown that an inclusive educational model—kids with disabilities educated alongside their neurotypical peers—benefits kids with special needs as well as those who don't have a disability, both academically and socially. How do you think cultural differences, such as those Jonah and Sadie have, would make that structure more challenging? If they were your children, how would you feel about it?

8. Rachelle and Layla both have jobs they love. When Amish women marry, they give up "careers" to become full-time wives and mothers—no matter how much they love them or how good they are at them. How do you feel about that?

9. Rachelle tells the English specialists that the Amish aren't opposed to education. They simply don't think they need more than an eighth-grade education followed by "vocational training" to be well-adjusted and content as they grow into adulthood. Do you think this is "fair" to Amish children? How would you feel about receiving no more than an eighth-grade education? Can you imagine circumstances where this is a good thing?

Enjoy more stories by Kelly Irvin in the Amish Blessings series

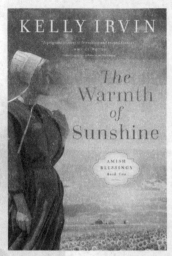
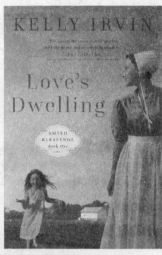

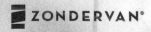

About the Author

Photo by Tim Irvin

*K*elly Irvin is a bestselling, award-winning author of thirty novels and stories. A retired public relations professional, Kelly lives with her husband, Tim, in San Antonio. They have two children, four grandchildren, and two ornery cats.

Visit her online at kellyirvin.com
Instagram: @kelly_irvin
Facebook: @Kelly.Irvin.Author
Twitter: @Kelly_S_Irvin